The Man Outside

Wolfgang Borchert

The Man Outside

Translated from the German by
David Porter

Foreword by
Kay Boyle

Introduction by
Stephen Spender

A New Directions Book

Foreword
By Kay Boyle

NINETEEN YEARS is perhaps not a remarkably long time to have
lived intimately and passionately with one particular book; but to
me it seems remarkable because Wolfgang Borchert's *The Man
Outside* is the only book that has endured for me in exactly this
way. There are days, for instance, when I have been unable to
start writing without first opening Borchert's book and reading
a page of it, or even no more than a paragraph, and then the
miracle will happen in my mind, or heart, or wherever such things
take place. At other times, I have been startled awake at night by
the terrifying conviction that the book was lost, that it was
missing from beside my bed, and I reached for the light in panic.
To understand this, one must know that the book was out of print
for years, and could not be replaced. And yet I told myself that
the fear of losing it was absurd, for even if it were to have disappeared, I carried so much of it in me for so long a time that it
could never be forgotten. The reasons for my dependence on this
book, almost as if it were an actual person, are so deep that I have
never sought to define them. I do not know if I can do so now.

To begin with, I cannot rid myself of the fantasy that I read
The Man Outside (a collection of short stories and a one-act play
which gives the book its title) long before it was actually published
in English translation by New Directions in 1952. I was living in
Marburg, Germany, in the spring of 1948, and Borchert's play
was put on by a group of young German actors in the smug little
university town, with its castle topping the hill. They had been
prisoners of war together in Colorado, these young men, and on
their return to Germany they had found that the only families
they had left to them—either physically or spiritually—were one
another. So they stayed together, and brought good (and in
Borchert's case, revolutionary) theatre to the wholly chauvinistic
people of the town. This spirited and cynical group also brought
into being in Marburg a political cabaret. Such places of outrageous political satire were flourishing in the ruins of Hamburg,
and—sharp-witted and lively as a cricket—the most famous of

them all functioned without interruption, even during the Occu-
pation, at the Théâtre de Dix Heures in Paris. But Marburg had
never seen anything like it before, and certainly never wanted to
again. For even then, with dueling forbidden to the university
students, numbers of them met clandestinely in the university
gymnasium at night and defiantly performed the ancestral ritual
of slashing one another's cheeks. Wolfgang Borchert, dead at
twenty-six, had, just the year before, written the last of his meagre
pages to say, while there was still time for him to say it, that
there was another Germany.

It was perhaps through my acquaintance with these young
actors that long before I read the facts of his life and death in print
I knew that Borchert had been born in Hamburg in 1921, and that
before entering the Wehrmacht he had been a bookseller and an
actor. I knew that he had died in a Swiss sanatorium in 1947, from
a malarialike fever contracted at the Russian front and in Nazi
prisons. (I was later to learn that Borchert wrote the play, *The
Man Outside*, in a few days in the autumn of 1946, and that it was
produced on the air, and rebroadcast innumerable times, by the
Allied-sponsored West German Radio. It was then produced in
an English version on the Third Programme of the B.B.C.—this
play that Borchert subtitled "A play which no theatre will produce
and no public will want to see," and which, ironically enough,
was given its first stage performance at the Hamburger Kammerspiele the day after the author's death.

The setting of the Prologue to the play is the banks of the river
Elbe. The time is evening, and there is a wind, and also the sound
of river water lapping against the pontoons. The Undertaker
(who is Death) stands on the quay and watches a man standing
too close to the water for his own good. God, too, is there on the
river bank: an Old Man whom no one believes in any more. The
voice that speaks the introduction to the action of the play says
in part:

A man comes to Germany.

*He's been away for a long time, this man. Perhaps too long. And he returns quite
different from what he was when he went away. Outwardly he is a near relation to
those figures which stand in fields to scare birds—and sometimes in the evening people
too. Inwardly—the same. He has waited outside in the cold for a thousand days. And
as entrance fee he's paid with his knee-cap. And after waiting outside in the cold for a
thousand nights, he actually—finally—comes home.*

The man who comes home is named Beckmann, an ordinary, limping German soldier, twenty-five years old, wearing the worn and faded uniform still, returning home from Siberia where he has been a prisoner of war. His country is in ruins, his little son has been killed in a bombing, and his wife has taken a lover. So on this particular evening, with both God and Death as witnesses, he throws himself into the waters of the Elbe. But the river, too, rejects him, making him promise "to have another go at it."

In his search for a new life (which takes place in the long dream of death), Beckmann meets with a Colonel; with a Girl, whose husband died at Stalingrad; with a Cabaret Producer, composite figure of the producers who gave Borchert himself work as an actor and director after the war; with the rejected Old Man, who is God; and with the Other One. The latter describes himself as the "one who says Yes. The one who answers" —the other self "Who drives you on when you're tired, the slave-driver, the secret, disturbing one. . . . who marches on, lame or not." In his Introduction to this collection, Stephen Spender refers to this "Otherness" as "the central point of conflict in Borchert's mind. Is it dream? Is it reality? Or is it just a name for the persistent courage which can go on creating again and again the illusion that life is worth while?"

Whenever I read Borchert's play anew, in whatever year, I say to myself: "This is taking place now. This is exactly what is taking place at this moment in our separate lives and in our history." To cite Beckmann's dialogue with the Colonel as the most relevant to this year, or to last year, or to the year that lies ahead, would be to slight his dialogue with the Girl, who has likewise thrown herself into the Elbe, or with the Cabaret Producer, or with the Old Man who is God. None of these stunning and sane (sane beyond sanity, one is tempted to add) dialogues can be belittled by comparison; but it is in the anguish of his rational appeal to the Colonel, who sits eating supper with his family, that Beckmann speaks with almost unbearable relevancy to our own national and human pain.

COLONEL: What is it you want of me?

BECKMANN: I'm bringing it back to you.

COLONEL: What?

BECKMANN: (*Almost naïve*) The responsibility. I'm bringing you back the responsibility. Have you completely forgotten, sir? The 14th February? At

Gorodok. It was 46 below zero. You came on to our post, sir, and said, "Corporal Beckmann." "Here!" I shouted. Then you said, and your breath hung as ice on your fur collar—I remember it exactly, it was a fine fur collar—then you said: "Corporal Beckmann, you will take over responsibility for these twenty men. You'll reconnoitre the wood east of Gorodok and if possible take a few prisoners. Is that clear?" "Very good, sir," I replied. And then we set off and reconnoitred. . . . all night. There was some shooting, and when we got back to our post, eleven men were missing. And it was my responsibility. That's all, sir. But now the war's over, now I want to sleep, now I'm giving you back the responsibility, sir, I don't want it any more, I'm giving it back, sir.

There are stories in this collection quite different in subject matter and in mood from the play, but in all of them is what Kafka spoke of once as "the terrifying quality of life—the heart-rending quality of art." In "Thithyphuth, or My Uncle's Waiter" there is beer-swilling gusto and humor: two strangers, each of whom has a speech impediment, meet and believe the other is mimicking him. In "God's Eye," a little boy sits in the kitchen and whizzes the eye of a codfish around the curves of his soup plate. "Eyes are not meant to be played with," says his mother as she puts the white fleshy pieces of the cod itself into the saucepan. "God made that eye exactly like yours." And the boy asks: "Is it supposed to be God's?" "Of course," says the mother, "the eye belongs to God." "Not to the cod?" the little boy persists. "To the cod as well. But chiefly to God," his mother answers. And then, left alone in the kitchen, the boy whispers urgent questions about life and death to the glaring, unanswering eye of God, pleading: "You, tell me, you're from God, tell me!" It ends with the bitter anger of the child's abandoning of faith, and his slamming the kitchen door.

There are two other stories of Borchert's that I use frequently in my short story classes: "Jesus Won't Play Any More" and "The Kitchen Clock." But what insolence it is to speak of "using" them in my classes! To "use" such stories as these in a classroom is as perilous an undertaking as cutting one man's heart out of his breast and seeking to make it function in the body of another. If the writing student has not perceived long before that every sentence he writes must be charged with the maximum of meaning, then it is doubtful that he would learn this truth even from Borchert. Ezra Pound wrote nearly half a century ago that "great literature is simply language charged with meaning to the utmost possible degree." And he added that it is "the thing that is true and stays true that keeps fresh" for the reader.

"The Dandelion" is perhaps Borchert's best-known short story, and the truth he tells in it is not a lesser truth because it is not overtly concerned with the magnitude of war and the help-lessness of God, but with a yellow dandelion growing in a prison courtyard, a "tiny, unpretending sun." Borchert was imprisoned in 1942 by the German military for speaking out too plainly in the letters he, as a soldier, wrote home. He served six months in solitary confinement. (". . . I've been locked in together with the Being I fear most of all: with my self," he writes in "The Dande-lion.") His sentence was commuted because of his youth, and he was returned to service and sent to the Russian front. In 1944, when he was twenty-three, he was again imprisoned on the same charge. "There were seventy-seven men in our circus ring and a pack of twelve uniformed, revolver-toting hounds barked around us," he writes in "The Dandelion." "Some might have been carrying out this barking job for twenty years and more, for in the course of the years, with so many thousand patients, their mouths had grown like muzzles. But this *rapprochement* with the animal world had in no way diminished their conceit. One could have used every single one of them, just as he was, as a statue for the inscription: "*L'Etat, c'est moi!*" The way Borchert described the police guards was, "*rapprochement* with the animal world." Young dissenters today are describing the police in like terms at this moment, as I write, but they give them a more specific name.

In Borchert's "This is Our Manifesto" and "Stories from a Primer," he speaks again for the young and spirited throughout the world who have sought, and are seeking now, to transmute their convictions into substance and act. And Borchert foresaw all that was to come when he wrote in "Generation without Farewell": ". . . we are the generation without limit, without restraint and without protection—thrown out of the playpen of childhood into a world made for us by those who now despise us. . . . And the winds of the world, which have made gipsies of our feet and of our hearts on roads burning hot . . . made of us a generation without farewell. . . . We are a generation without homecoming, for we have nothing to come home to, and we have no one to take care of our hearts. . . ."

Margaret Mead has described the young of today's world as like to "the first generation born in a new country." And she speaks of "all of us who grew up before the war" as "immigrants in time, immigrants from an earlier world living in an age essentially different from everything we knew before." Borchert, as if knowing this would be ultimately confessed, calls out to her in sudden hope from the page: "Perhaps we are a generation full of arrival on a new star, in a new life. . . . Perhaps we are a generation full of arrival at a new love, at a new laughter, at a new God."

The last thing Borchert wrote shortly before he died is an exhortation to all poets, all priests, to the "Mother in Normandy and the mother in the Ukraine," to the mothers in Frisco and in London, to "Girls at the counter and girls in the office," to the men in villages and cities who are being mobilized for war, and to others he calls on by name. The title of this fierce and eloquent and tender plea is "There's Only One Thing," and the lines of it might be borne on placards at this instant by our dissenting children, the words of it chanted as they demand of us, who are "immigrants in time," a new world in which mankind can survive.

"You. Judge in your robes. If tomorrow they tell you you are to go to court martial, then there's only one thing to do: Say NO!" Borchert's last summons to humanity thunders from the page. "You. Research worker in the laboratory. If tomorrow they tell you you are to invent a new death for the old life, then there's only one thing to do: Say NO!" And again: "You. Pilot on the aerodrome. If tomorrow they tell you you are to carry bombs and phosphorus over the cities, then there's only one thing to do: Say NO!"

If we do not learn to say "NO," Borchert is seeking to tell us in the final twilight of his young despair:

then the last human creature, with mangled entrails and infected lungs, will wander around unanswered and lonely under the poisonous, glowing sun and wavering constellations, lonely among the immense mass graves and the cold idols of the gigantic concrete-blocked devastated cities, the last human creature, withered, mad, cursing, accusing—and his terrible accusation: WHY? will die away unheard on the steppes, drift through the splitting ruins, seep away in the rubble of churches, lap against the great concrete shelters, fall into pools of blood, unheard, unanswered, the last animal scream of the last human animal—

KAY BOYLE—1971

Introduction
by *Stephen Spender*

WOLFGANG BORCHERT was born in 1921 in Hamburg, and he died on the 20th of November, 1947, in Basle. After his schooling, he was first a bookseller and later an actor. At the age of twenty, in 1941, he was a private in the German army invading Russia. In 1942 he was wounded and repatriated, and in the same year spent six months in solitary confinement under sentence of death for plain speaking in private letters. His sentence was commuted because of his youth. In 1944, after more service on the Russian front, he was again imprisoned. After the war he had small positions in theatres and cabarets for a few months, but his health was ruined and from the end of 1945 until his death two years later, he was in bed with some fever resembling malaria.

This appears to be the life of a perfect victim of our times, a man whose soul must bear simply the impress of the world of dictatorship and war and post-war horror into which he was born. It is in some ways like the life of a man born and bred in a prison cell.

It is therefore not surprising that his writings are like those of a man who sees hardly a day before his time or beyond it, and for whom a world outside his experiences seems completely shut off. The war which he describes is not the one for which German leaders bore, in the opinion of the rest of the world, a certain responsibility. It isn't even the one in which German youths, linked arm to arm and intoxicated with their singing, went marching over the fields of France like the embodiment of the triumphant onward-sweeping music of the first movement of Schubert's great C Major Symphony.

Borchert's soldiers are the doomed race of the Russian winter of 1941, and of Stalingrad. Nothing existed for them before they went to Russia. They are filled with the sense that if there are other soldiers, they must feel the same, and be equally passive victims of their time. The Russians are only a background to their own misery and to the German doom which is regarded as universal doom.

xi

Borchert's post-war Germany is a universal apocalypse seen in the language of symbolic horror of the ruin of German cities. For him war is simply the affirmation by mankind of a spirit of destruction in the world. If you say 'yes' to war, then

"in kitchen, larder and cellar, in cold storage and granary the last sacks of flour, the last bottles of strawberry, pumpkin and cherry juice will go bad—bread will go green under capsized tables and on splintered plates and the spread butter will stink like soft soap, in the fields beside rusted ploughs the corn will be flattened like a beaten army and the smoking chimneys, the forges and flues of the pounding factories, covered over with the ever-living grass, will crumble away—crumble—crumble

then the last human creature, with mangled entrails and infected lungs, will wander around unanswered and lonely under the poisonous, glowing sun and wavering constellations. . . ."

A sceptic might complain that this resembled a description of a cage written from the inside by a prisoner, whose only remedy for the situation is that men should abandon the manufacture of cages.

Still, we cannot read the lines without being aware that they are true—true with a remarkable exactitude, where the real seems to fuse powerfully with the poetic imagery. The limited truth which Borchert creates within his prose is not only literature; it is useful to us. Of course, the wider truth is that although if people stopped acting in a way which contributed to war, wars would cease, they will not do so. Therefore this part of Borchert's temoignage is no more useful to us than the adage that if wishes were horses then beggars would ride.

We have to look longer and further for a cause of war which, if it is grasped, may prevent further wars. That cause is guilt, with ensuing responsibility. It is this which the German mind seems to find it peculiarly hard to grasp: perhaps largely because when most people say 'guilt', they mean German guilt. Borchert does not create any picture of guilt and responsibility in his preoccupation with apocalyptic doom.

There is, though, a danger of people who talk about the causes of war, forgetting the reality itself. What Borchert does do most memorably, is create the doomed, horrible reality of the victims who are just nothing but victims; who feel no responsibility for the situation in which they are ruined; and whose widest sense of humanity is a feeling that on the other side of the barbed wire fence which surrounds them, there are other victims. One wonders whether Borchert would have felt the same about the French, if he had taken part in the campaign of June 1940, as he does about the soldiers everywhere, bound to one another in suffering, in the winter of 1941 on the Eastern Front.

But in Borchert's world there is something beside the trap itself: there is a mysterious sense of Otherness, of a World Outside. In the story *The Dandelion* there is just the little golden-yellow flower one prisoner discovers in the yard, which becomes a symbol "of sun, of sea and honey, lovely living thing! He felt its chaste coolness as the voice of the Father, never much heeded but now in its stillness so great a consolation—he felt it as the bright shoulder of a dark woman."

This Otherness is the central point of conflict in Borchert's mind. Is it dream? Is it reality? Or is it just a name for the persistent courage which can go on creating again and again the illusion that life is worth while?

Sometimes Otherness is just the point where human happiness merges into a human dream. It is the little piece of pink cloth cut from his sweetheart's petticoat, which the soldier on the Eastern Front carries in his trouser pocket. In that remarkable prose poem drama *The Man Outside*, it is The Other, the soldier who has been at Stalingrad, the one who goes on struggling while his neighbour gives in, who remains present in the consciousness of Beckmann the suicide who has thrown himself into the Elbe. It is also, of course, nature, and the beauty of the world everywhere.

But if the world is a place where everyone is involved in the murder of everyone else, the Otherness of nature and of a dream within oneself, is not an answer to the philosophic challenge which is involved in a man's determination to commit suicide. Beckmann can decide that he is not just a person who is murdered by others, because he discovers that he also is a murderer; this is the answer to his self-pity. He can listen for a time to the voice of The Other who has had as bad a time as he has, and yet decided to carry on. He can discover a girl who not only conjures into reality his erotic wish, but who also loves him. But none of these can weigh against his condemnation of life, deprive him of "the right of his suicide" if he really presses his challenge. For they are all part of life, part of the trap, and perhaps their optimism is due simply to their not having seen or experienced as much as he has. So that at the very end they all fail Beckmann:

> "Where are you, other one? You've always been here before. Where are you now, optimist? Now answer me! Now I need you, Answerer! Where are you? You're suddenly not there! Where are you, Answerer, where are you, you who grudged me death? Where is the old man who calls himself God?
> Why doesn't he speak?
> Answer!
> Why are you silent? Why?
> Will none of you answer?
> Will no one answer?
> Will no one, nobody answer me?"

The Old Man of the Prologue to *The Man Outside* is 'the God no one believes in now'. He is not so much the dead God of Nietzsche as the forgotten God, not so much dead as unborn, or waiting to be reborn. All he can do is grieve over his children: "I can do nothing about it, my children, I can do nothing about it. Grim, grim!"

There is no sense in conjecturing how Borchert would have developed had he lived. In the manifesto which is printed among his posthumous works, he has reached a stage of accepted nihilism on which he proposed to rebuild a world—or at least, a Germany —of love. "For we are no-men," he declared. "But we do not say No in despair. Our No is a protest. And there is no peace for us in kisses, for us Nihilists. For into nothingness we must again build a Yes. Houses we must build in the free air of our No, over the abysses, the craters and the slit-trenches and over the open mouths of the dead."

This is not very far from the position of Engagement of the French existentialists, who, poised on an abyss of unbelief, yet made an arbitrary moral resolve to construct a good society.

It is doubtful whether such a position provides the philosophic answer to suicide.

Since Borchert did in fact die, his work stands completely enclosed within the world in which he grew and which he saw destroyed. To read him is—to change the metaphor from that of the trap or prison—to study the sensibility of a man who is the victim of a machine which is itself destroyed, tearing his life down with it. His vision is entirely confined by this machine, and except once for the vague mention of 'Hindenburg' he does not seem to see the men who were the makers of the machine or the faces of those who destroyed it.

The world of Borchert is not very far from that of George Orwell's *1984*. And although it is possible for the reader to look at Borchert as from the outside, perhaps we are all more inside his machine than we know. At present his world, not only of the Russian Front, but also of an apocalyptic post-war Germany, seems to have disappeared for ever. He only had to live a day more to witness the success of his own play, and only a few months more a remarkable German recovery. But are the success and the recovery real, so long as the man who was immersed to the highest possible degree in the mechanical destructive forces, tells us from the grave, that those forces will destroy us —unless we unite to prevent them—or unless—and this is the "realer" challenge—we can believe in something which answers the right of the suicide to his death in a world like ours?

He leaves us with a problem, which he did not solve, but he stated that problem, and it is still with us.

As description of a moment of European history, it is difficult to think that anyone has excelled Borchert's invocations of Hamburg and the Elbe. For a young writer he has an astonishing discipline in his use of many details of observation; and a poet's gift in making the inanimate significant and personal. *Billbrook*, the story of the Canadian sergeant pilot who enters into a relationship with the suburb of Hamburg which has his own name, is an excellent example of how Borchert could use his cataclysmic vision of animated things for an ironic effect. In *Radi* his gift for breathing life into inanimate things achieves the miracle of making the dead really seem to live. And what else is literature but this? To make the dead live, and to provide a space where if there was a believed-in God, He might fit in a framework of experienced life. There is a place for the God struggling to be born in the work of the young writer which is prefaced with the words "And who will support us? God?" He achieved the task of constructing a framework with an empty space for God, even if he thought there was no God to be found in the world as he lived in it.

STEPHEN SPENDER—1952

CONTENTS

And Nobody Knows Whither

POSTHUMOUS STORIES

THE DANDELION

Tales of our Day

The stories in this collection were written in 1946. The title-story, "The Dandelion" is Borchert's first prose work of any length. He wrote it in the Elisabeth Hospital in Hamburg in winter 1945-46. The stories appeared in book form in Germany in the early summer of 1947.

And who will support us?

God?

The Surrendered

THE DANDELION

THE door shut behind me. It happens often enough that a door's shut behind one—one can even imagine its being locked. The doors of houses, for example, are locked, and then one's either inside or out. The doors of houses, too, have about them something so final, so seclusive, so abandoning. And now the door has been shoved to behind me, yes, shoved, for it's an uncommonly thick door which can't be slammed. An ugly door with the number 432. That's the peculiarity of this door, that it has a number and is covered with sheet-iron—that's what makes it so proud and unapproachable: it never unbends, and the fervour of prayer will not touch it.

And now I've been left alone with that Being, no, not just left alone, I've been locked in together with the Being I fear most of all: with my self.

Do you know what it's like to be left to yourself, when you're left alone with you, given up to yourself? I can't say it's necessarily so terrible, but it's one of the most fantastic adventures that one can have in this world: To meet one's self. To meet like this in Cell 432: naked, helpless, concentrated on nothing but one's self, without attribute or diversion and without the power to act. That's the most degrading thing: to be quite without the power to act. To have no bottle to drink from or smash, no towel to hang up, no knife to break out or cut veins with, no pen for writing—to have nothing—other than one's self.

That's damned little in an empty room with four bare walls. That's less than the spider has, which squeezes a scaffolding out of its backside and can risk its life on it, can gamble between the fall and the check. What thread catches us up if we fall?

Our own power? Does a God support us? God—is that the power that makes a tree grow and a bird fly—is God life? Then he *does* sometimes support us—if we wish it.

As the sun took its fingers from the window-bars and night crept from the corners, something came towards me out of the

7

darkness—and I thought it was God. Had someone opened the door? Was I no longer alone? I felt, there's something there, and it's breathing and growing. The cell became too small—I felt that the walls must yield before that which was there, that which I called God.

You, Number 432, little creature—don't let the night make you drunk! It's your fear that's with you in the cell, nothing else! Fear and the night. But fear is a monster, and the night can become as frightful as a ghost, when we're alone with it.

Then the moon trundled over the roofs and lit up the walls. You ape! The walls are as close as ever, and the cell is as empty as orange-peel. God, whom they call the Good, is not there. And what *was* there, what spoke, was within you. Perhaps it was a God in yourself—it was you! For you are God, too, everything, even the spider and the mackerel are God. God is life—that's all. But that is so much that He cannot be more. There is nothing else. Yet often that nothing overwhelms us.

The cell-door was as closed as a nut—as though it were never open and one knew that it didn't open of itself but must be broken open. So closed was the door. And left alone with myself, I hurtled into the bottomless pit. But then the spider yelled at me like a sergeant: Weakling! The wind had torn its web and with antlike energy it squeezed out a new one and caught me, the one hundred and twenty-three pounder, in its zephyr-fine cords. I thanked it, but it took absolutely no notice.

So I slowly grew used to myself. One imposes oneself so lightly on others and yet can scarcely endure one's own company. Gradually, however, I found me quite pleasant and amusing—day and night I made the oddest discoveries about me.

But in that long time I lost contact with everything, with life, with the world. The days dropped away from me rapidly and regularly. I felt how I was slowly emptied of the real world and filled with my own self. I felt how I went ever further away from this world, the world I had only just entered.

The walls were so cold and dead that I fell sick with despair and hopelessness. You scream out your misery for a few days—but when there's no answer you soon get tired. You beat for a few hours on door and wall—but when they don't open, fists are soon sore, and in this desert that tiny pain is the only pleasure.

But there is nothing completely final on this earth. For the proud door had opened and a lot of others as well, and each one pushed out a shy, ill-shaven man into a long row and into a yard with green grass in the middle and grey walls round it.

Then barking exploded round us and at us—a hoarse barking from blue dogs with leathern straps about their bellies. They kept us moving and were themselves always moving and barked us full of fear. But when you had enough fear inside you and grew calmer, you realized that these were men in pale blue uniforms.

We moved in a circle. When the eye had overcome the first shattering reunion with the sky and grown used to the sun again, you could see between blinks that there were many trotting as disconnectedly and breathing as deeply as yourself—seventy, eighty men, perhaps.

On and on in a circle, to the rhythm of their wooden clogs, men clumsy, intimidated and yet for half an hour happier than at other times. But for the blue uniforms with the barking faces, you could have trotted thus into eternity—without past, without future: wholly joyous present: breathing, seeing, moving!

So it was at first. Almost a holiday, a tiny happiness. But in the long run, if you have months of effortless satisfaction you begin to think of other things. The tiny happiness suffices no longer—you've had enough of it, and the sad essence of the world that holds us in thrall drips into our glass. And then the day arrives when the round becomes torture and the high sky a mockery, when you regard the man in front and the man behind no longer as brothers and fellow-sufferers, but as wandering corpses, there only to disgust us—corpses between which you are bound like a featureless lath in an endless lath fence—and more than anything else they turn us sick to our stomachs. That's what happens when for months you circle round between the grey walls, barked into exhaustion by the pale blue uniforms.

The man in front of me is long since dead. Or he sprang from a puppet show, driven by some comic demon to act as though he were a normal human being—and at the same time, was certainly long since dead. Yes! Even his bald head, surrounded by a frayed crown of dirty grey tufts of hair, lacks the greasy shine of living baldness, in which sun and rain can still dimly be reflected—no, this baldness is not shiny, it's dull and matt like cloth. If this entity, which I cannot call a man, if this imitation human being did not move, one could believe this bald head was a lifeless wig. And not even the wig of a learned man or a great tippler—no, at best that of a paperseller or a circus clown. But it's tough, this wig—out of sheer spite it won't fall out because it feels that I, the man behind it, hate it. Yes, I hate it. Why must the wig—that's what I'll call the whole man now, it's easier— why must it walk in front of me and live, when young sparrows who as yet know nothing of flying hurtle to death from the guttering? And I hate the wig, because it's cowardly—and how cowardly! It feels my hatred as it trots stupidly in front of me, always in the circle, the tiny little circle between grey walls that have no heart for us either, for otherwise they would wander away secretly at night and set themselves round the palace where our ministers live.

I've been wondering now for quite a time why they've locked the wig up in a prison—what deed can it have done— this wig, that's too cowardly to turn round at me when I'm continually tormenting it. For I do torment it: I step on its heels all the time—on purpose, of course—and make a foul noise with my mouth as though I were spitting hashed lungs at its back by the quarter pound. It winces each time, aggrievedly. Nevertheless, it daren't quite look round at its tormentor—no, it's too cowardly for that. With a stiff neck it turns only a few degrees back in my direction, but will not risk the half turn so that our eyes could meet.

What can it have done wrong? Perhaps it has embezzled or stolen? Or did it excite a public scandal in some sexual frenzy? Yes, perhaps that was it. Once in a drunken moment it was whisked by a hunchbacked Eros out of its cowardice into some stupid obscenity—well, and now it trots along in front of me, quietly enjoying itself, and astounded that it once dared to *do* something.

But I think it's secretly trembling now, because it knows that I'm behind it. I, its murderer! Oh, it would be easy for me to murder it, and it could happen quite unnoticed. I need only trip it up; then with its matchsticks of legs it would stumble over forwards and probably knock a hole in its head in doing so— and then the air would escape from it with a phlegmy pfff . . . as though from a bicycle tube. Its head would burst apart in the middle like whitish-yellow wax, and the few drops of red ink from it would look as ludicrously false as raspberry juice on the blue silk blouse of a stabbed actor.

Thus I hated the wig, a fellow whose face I had never seen, whose voice I had never heard, of whom I knew only a musty, mothbally smell. I'm certain he had a soft, tired voice lacking all emotion, as powerless as his milky fingers. I'm certain he had the protruding eyes of a calf and a thick pendulous lower lip that hankered after chocolates. It was the mask of a roué, without stature and with the courage of a paperseller whose midwife-hands had often done nothing all day but stroke seventeen pfennigs for an exercise book off the counter.

No, not another word about the wig! I really hate it so much that I could easily work myself up into an outburst of rage which would expose me unduly. Enough. Finish. I will never speak of it again, never!

But if someone you would like to keep quiet about constantly walks in front of you with sagging knees to the tune of a melodrama, then you cannot get rid of him. Like an itch on your back that you can't get at with your hands, he keeps on goading you to think of him, to *feel* him, to hate him.

I think I shall really have to murder the wig. But I'm so afraid the dead man might play a ghastly trick on me. With a vulgar laugh he would suddenly remember having been a circus clown and heave himself up out of his blood. Perhaps a little embarrassed, as though he hadn't been able to hold his blood as other people their water. He'd dance through the prison circus ring on his hands and pretend the warders were bucking donkeys to be baited to the point of madness, only to jump in simulated terror on to the wall. From there he'd loll out his tongue at us like a dishcloth and vanish for ever.

There's no knowing all that would happen if everybody suddenly realized what he actually is.

Don't think that my hatred of the man in front of me, of the wig, is hollow and without foundation—oh, you can get into situations where you overflow with hatred and are swept so far beyond your own bounds that afterwards you can scarcely find the way back to yourself—hatred has so devastated you.

I know it's hard to listen to me and feel with me. Nor should you listen as though someone were reading you Gottfried Keller or Dickens. You must come with me, accompany me in the little circle between the pitiless walls. Not beside me in thought—no, behind me physically, as the man behind. And then you'll see how quickly you learn to hate me. For if you stagger round our loin-weary circle with us (I say "us" now, for we all have this one thing in common) then you will be so empty of love that hate will froth up in you like champagne. You'll let it froth, too, in order to feel the ghastly emptiness no longer. And above all don't imagine that on an empty stomach and an empty heart you'll be disposed to outstanding acts of brotherly love!

Thus you will totter along behind me as one emptied of all kindness, concentrated only on me, on my narrow back, my over-flabby neck and empty trousers, where, anatomically, there ought really to be something more. But for the most part you will have to look at my legs. All men behind watch the legs of the man in front, and the rhythm of his step is forced on them and taken over, however strange or awkward. Yes, and then hatred will fall upon you like a jealous woman when you perceive that I have no gait. No, I have no gait. There really are people who have no gait—they have several styles which cannot be attuned. I'm one of that sort. For that you will hate me, just as pointlessly and with as much reason as I have to hate the wig because I'm the man behind. Just as you have adjusted yourself to my rather uncertain, lackadaisical step, you will be startled to find that I suddenly stride with firmness and vigour. And hardly have you registered this new style of walking than, a few steps further on, I begin to dawdle along, spiritless and absent-minded. No, you will be unable to feel any joy or friendliness for me. You will have to hate me. All men behind hate the men in front.

Perhaps everything would be different if the men in front would occasionally look round at the men behind and come to an understanding with them. But *every* man behind is the same—he sees only the man in front and hates him. But he scorns the man behind him—there he feels himself the man in front. That's how it is in our circle behind the grey walls—and that's no doubt how it is elsewhere, too. Everywhere, perhaps.

I ought to have killed the wig after all. Once it made

me so heated that my blood began to boil. That was when I made the discovery. Nothing very much. Just a tiny little discovery.

Have I already said that every morning we circled for half an hour round a small dirty green patch of grass? In the centre of this extraordinary circus ring was a pallid collection of blades of grass, pale, each blade as featureless as we in this unbearable lath fence. Seeking something living, something vivid, my eye ran casually and without any great hope over the few paltry blades, which, as they felt my gaze upon them, involuntarily collected themselves and nodded to me—and suddenly I espied among them an insignificant yellow dot, a miniature geisha in a huge meadow. I was so startled by my discovery that I thought everyone must have seen it, that my eyes remained glued to the yellow Thing and I looked quickly and with great interest at the shoes of the man in front. But just as when you're talking to someone you must always stare at the spot he has on his nose and thoroughly unsettle him, so my eyes longed for the yellow speck. Now, as I passed it more closely, I pretended as much unconcern as possible. I recognized a flower, a yellow flower. It was a dandelion—a tiny yellow dandelion.

It stood about half a yard to the left of our path, half a yard from the orbit in which every morning we paid tribute to the open air. I endured real panic, imagining that one of the blue men was following with popping eyes the direction of my glance. Yet accustomed as our watchdogs were to reacting with a furious barking to every individual movement of the lath fence, no one had shared my discovery. The little dandelion was still wholly my property.

But I had real joy of it only for a few days. It must belong to me completely. Every time our rounds came to an end I had to tear myself away from it by main force, and I would have given my daily bread ration (and that's saying something) to possess it. The longing to have something living in the cell grew so powerful within me that the flower, the shy little dandelion, soon acquired for me the worth of a human being, of a secret beloved: I could no longer live without it—up there between the dead walls!

And then came the affair with the wig. I began very cunningly.

Each time I came past my flower, I stepped as unobtrusively as possible a foot's breadth off the path on to the grass plot. We all have a hearty share of herd instinct and I banked on that. I wasn't deceived. The man behind me, the man behind him, the man behind him again—and so on—all shuffled, phlegmatic and docile, in my tracks. Thus in four days I succeeded in shifting our path so close to my dandelion that had I stooped I could have reached it with my hand. True, through my undertaking some twenty pale blades of grass died a dusty death beneath our wooden clogs—but who gives thought to a little crushed grass when he wants to pick a flower?

I was nearing fulfilment of my desire. As a test, I let my left sock slip down several times and innocently and crossly stooped and hitched it up. Nobody worried about it. Right then, tomorrow!

You mustn't laugh at me if I say that the next day I entered the yard with beating heart and damp, agitated hands. It was too improbable, the prospect, after months of loneliness and loveless-ness, of having an unexpected beloved in my cell.

We had almost ended our daily ration of rounds to the monotonous clopping of clogs—it was to happen on the last lap but one. Then the wig went into action, and in the craftiest and meanest way.

We had just turned into the last lap but one, the blue boys were importantly rattling their giant keyrings and I was approach-ing the scene of action, whence my flower looked anxiously towards me. I doubt if I was ever so agitated as in those seconds. Twenty paces more. Fifteen paces more, ten more, five. . . .

Then the monstrous thing happened! As though beginning a tarantella, the wig suddenly flung its thin arms into the air, raised its right leg gracefully to its navel and on its left foot made a turn backwards. I shall never know where it found the courage —it glared at me triumphantly, as though it knew everything, rolled its calf's-eyes till the whites gleamed, and then collapsed like a marionette. Oh, now it was certain: he must once have been a circus clown, for everyone roared with laughter!

But then the blue uniforms broke out into barking, and the laughter was wiped out as though it had never been. And one of them kicked the prostrate man and said in as matter of fact a way as one says: it's raining—he said: he's dead!

There's still something I have to confess—in fairness to myself. At the moment in which I was eye to eye with the man I called the wig, and realized that he succumbed—not to me, no, that he succumbed to life—in that second my hatred flowed out like a wave from the shore, and nothing remained save a feeling of emptiness. A lath had been broken from the fence—death had whistled past me by a hair's breadth—at such a time, one quickly tries to be good. And I have never since grudged the wig his presumed victory over me.

Next morning I had in front of me another man who immediately made me forget the wig. He looked as false as a divinity student, but I'm convinced he was expressly seconded from hell to make it absolutely impossible for me to pick my flower.

He had an impertinent way of being conspicuous. Everyone laughed at him. Even the pale blue dogs could not suppress a human grin, which looked horribly peculiar. Every inch the state official—but the primitive dignity of their dull professional soldiers' faces was twisted into a grimace. They weren't going to laugh, by God, they weren't! But they had to. Do you know that feeling, that condescending feeling, when you're angry with someone and you are both masks of implacability, and then something funny happens which compels you both to laugh—you will not laugh, by God, you won't! But then your faces do stretch wide, and take on that well-known expression best described as a 'sour grin'. This now happened to the blue boys, and it was the only human emotion that we ever remarked in them. Yes, that divinity student, he was a card! He was cunning enough to be crazy—but not so crazy as to impair his cunning.

There were seventy-seven men in our circus ring and a pack of twelve uniformed revolver-toting hounds barked round us. Some might have been carrying on this barking job for twenty years and more, for in the course of years, with so many thousands of patients, their mouths had grown more like muzzles. But this *rapprochement* with the animal world had in no way diminished their conceit. One could have used every single one of them, just as he was, as a statue for the inscription: *L'État c'est moi.*

The divinity student (later I discovered that he was really a

locksmith and had been injured while working on a church—
God took him into His care!) was crazy enough or cunning
enough to defer completely to their dignity. What am I saying—
defer? He inflated the dignity of the blue uniforms to a balloon
of unimagined dimensions, of which even the wearers had no
conception. For all they had to laugh at his foolishness, a certain
pride secretly inflated their stomachs and caused the leathern
belts to tighten.

Every time the divinity student passed one of the watchdogs,
who, standing straddle-legged, gave expression to their power
and as often as possible went for us, snarling—every time he made
an utterly genuine-looking obeisance and said: The compliments
of the season, Sergeant! in a manner so innately courteous and
well-meaning that no God could have spurned him—much less
the vain balloons in uniform. And at that he set about his bow
so diffidently that it always looked as though he were dodging
a box on the ear.

And now the devil had made this divinity student comedian
the man in front of me, and his madness radiated so strongly and
made such claim upon me that my tiny new beloved, my dandelion, was almost forgotten. I was scarcely able to cast a tender
glance at it, for I had to fight an insane battle with my nerves that
drove the sweat of fear out of every pore. Every time the divinity
student made his bow and let drop his "Compliments of the
season, Sergeant!" as honey from the tongue—each time I had
to brace every muscle not to do it, too. The temptation was so
strong that several times I nodded affably to the state monuments
and only in the last second desisted from bowing and contrived
to keep silent.

We circled the yard daily for roughly half an hour, that was
twenty laps a day, and twelve uniforms surrounded our circle.
Thus the divinity student certainly made two hundred and forty
bows a day, and two hundred and forty times I had to summon
up all my concentration not to go mad. I knew that if I did that
for three days I should get "extenuating circumstances"—I wasn't
up to that.

I got back to my cell utterly exhausted. But the whole night
I dreamed I was walking along an endless row of blue uniforms
which all looked like Bismarck—all night, with a deep bow, I

was wishing these millions of Bismarcks: "The compliments of the season, Sergeant!"

The next day I managed to arrange for the parade to go past me and to get another man in front. I lost a clog, elaborately retrieved it, and hobbled back into the lath fence. Thank God! My sun came out. Or rather—it was eclipsed. The new man in front of me was so outrageously tall that my six feet were simply swallowed up in his shadow. So there *was* such a thing as providence—it had only to be helped along with a clog. His inhumanly long limbs waved in meaningless confusion, and the strange thing about it was that with it he actually moved forward, although he certainly had no control over his arms and legs. I almost loved him—yes, I prayed that he might not suddenly sink down dead like the wig, nor go crazy and start making cowardly obeisances. I prayed for his long life and mental health. I felt so safe in his shadow that my glance embraced the little dandelion for longer than before without fear of betrayal. I even forgave this heavenly man his hideously snuffling nasal organ, oh, generously I refrained from giving him all kinds of nicknames like oboe, octopus or praying mantis. I saw only my flower now—let the man in front of me be as tall and silly as he liked!

That day was like all the others. It differed from them only in that towards the end of the half hour the prisoner from Cell 432 developed a racing pulse and his eyes assumed an expression of simulated guilelessness and ill-concealed uncertainty.

We turned into the last lap but one—again the keyrings came to life, and the lath fence drowsed through the miserly sunbeams as though behind eternal bars.

But what was that? One lath was not drowsing at all! It was wide awake and changing step every few yards in its excitement. Did no one notice? No. And suddenly Lath 432 bent over, fumbled with a sock that had slipped down—and at the same time, lightning-like, one hand pounced on a terrified little flower, nipped it off—and already seventy-seven laths were clopping in their usual dawdle into the last round.

Here's what's so funny: a blasé, chastened youth of the age of gramophone records and national planning stands under the

high-walled window in prison cell 432 and in his cloistered hands
holds up to the narrow beam of light a tiny yellow flower—a
perfectly ordinary dandelion. And then this creature, accustomed
to smelling T.N.T., perfume and petrol, gin and lipstick, raises
the dandelion to his hungry nose which for months now has
smelled only dust, the sweat of fear and the wood of his
prison bed—and so avidly does he suck into himself the essence
of that tiny yellow disc that there is nothing left of him but
nose.

Then something opens within him and pours like light into
the narrow space: something hitherto unknown to him: a tenderness, a sympathy and a warmth beyond compare unite him with
the flower and fill him utterly.

He could endure the cell no longer and closed his eyes and
marvelled: But you smell of earth. Of sun, of sea and honey,
lovely living thing! He felt its chaste coolness as the voice of the
Father, never much heeded but now in its stillness so great a
consolation—he felt it as the bright shoulder of a dark woman.

He bore it carefully as a loved one to his drinking-bowl, put
the exhausted little being into it—and then he took several
minutes, so slowly did he sit down, face to face with his flower.

He was so unbound and happy that he put off and cast away
all that burdened him: captivity, solitude, the hunger for love,
the helplessness of his twenty-two years, the present and the
future, the world and Christianity—yes, even that!

He was a brown Balinese, a savage of a savage people who
feared and worshipped sea and lightning and tree. Who venerated
coconut, codfish and humming-bird, marvelled at them, ate them
and did not comprehend them. So free was he, and never had he
been so ready to do good as when he whispered to the flower . . .
to be like you!

All night long his happy hands encompassed the familiar
tin of his drinking-bowl, and in his sleep he felt how they heaped
soil on him, good dark soil, and how he grew used to the earth
and became one with it—and how flowers burst forth from him:
anemone, columbine and dandelion—tiny, unpretending suns.

THE CROWS FLY HOME AT NIGHT

THEY crouch on the stone-cold bridge parapets and on the frost-hard metal railings along the violet-stinking canal. They crouch on the hollowed, gossip-worn area steps. Among the silver paper and autumn leaves at the side of the street, and on the sinful benches in the parks. They crouch, leaning, lolling against the doorless walls of houses, and on the nostalgic walls and moles of the docks.

They crouch in a lost world, crowfaced, shrouded grey-black and croaked hoarse. They crouch and all abandonment hangs down from them like limp, loose, crumpled feathers. Abandoned by the heart, abandoned by women, abandoned by the stars.

They crouch in the dusk and damp of the shadows of houses, shunning the gateways, black as tar and tired of the pavement. They crouch in the early haze of the world's afternoon, thin-soled and coated grey with dust, belated, daydreamed into monotony. They crouch over the bottomless pit, held by the abyss, sleep-swaying with hunger and homesickness.

Crowfaced (and how else?) they crouch, crouch, crouch and crouch. Who? The crows? The crows perhaps. But above all human beings, human beings.

At six o'clock the sun turns the city mist and smoke red-gold. And the houses are velvet-blue and soft-edged in the tender light of early evening.

But the crowfaced men crouch pallid-skinned and white-frozen in their hopelessness, in their inescapable humanity, crept deep into their patchwork jackets.

Since the day before one man had been crouching on the dock, smelling himself full of harbour smell and rolling crumbled masonry into the water. His eyebrows hung on his forehead like the fringe of a sofa, despondent but with incomprehensible humour.

And then a young man came along, his arms elbow-deep in his trouser-pockets, the collar of his jacket turned up round his bony neck. The older man didn't look up, he saw beside him the comfortless mouths of a pair of shoes and up from the water there quivered at him the tossing caricature of a melancholy male figure. Then he knew that Timm was back again.

Well, Timm, he said, there you are again. Through already?

Timm said nothing. He crouched on the quay wall beside the other man and put his long hands round his neck. He was cold.

So her bed wasn't wide enough, eh? the other began softly after many minutes.

Bed! Bed! said Timm angrily, I love the girl.

Of course you love her. But tonight she showed you the door again. So the billet was no go. It's because you're not clean enough, Timm. A night visitor like that has to be clean. Love alone isn't always enough. Oh well, anyway, you're not used to a bed now. Better stay here, then. Or do you still love her, eh?

Timm rubbed his long hands on his neck and slid deep into his coat collar. She wants money, he said much later, or silk stockings. Then I could have stayed.

Oh, so you do still love her, said the old man, hell, but if you've no money!

Timm didn't say that he still loved her, but after a while he said rather more quietly: I gave her the scarf, the red one, you know. I hadn't anything else. But after an hour she suddenly had no more time.

The red scarf? asked the other. Oh, he loves her, he thought to himself, how he loves her! And once more he repeated: Aha, your beautiful red scarf! And now you're back here again and soon it'll be dark.

Yes, said Timm, it'll be dark again. And my neck's miserably cold, now that I haven't got the scarf. Miserably cold, I can tell you.

Then they both looked at the water in front of them and their legs hung sadly from the quay wall. A launch shrieked, white-steaming, past them and the waves followed, fat and chattering. Then it was still again, only the city hummed monotonously between heaven and earth, and crowfaced, shrouded blue-black, the two men crouched there in the afternoon. When after an hour a scrap of red paper tossed by on the waves, a gay, red piece of paper on the lead-grey waves, then Timm said to the other: But I had nothing else. Only the scarf.

And the other answered: And it was such a wonderful red, d'you remember, eh, Timm? Boy, was it red!

Yes, yes, Timm mumbled dejectedly, it was that. And now my neck's damn well freezing, my friend.

How's this, thought the other, he still loves her and was with her for a whole hour. Now he won't even be cold for her. Then, yawning, he said: And the billet's a goner, too.

Lilo's her name, said Timm, and she likes wearing silk stockings. But I haven't got any.

Lilo? exclaimed the other, don't tell me that, man, she's never called Lilo.

Of course she's called Lilo, replied Timm indignantly. D'you suppose I can't know one called Lilo? I even love her, I tell you.

Timm slid angrily away from his friend and drew his knee up to his chin. And he held his long hands round his skinny neck. A web of early darkness laid itself on the day and the last rays of the sun stood lost on the sky like a lattice. Lonely, the men crouched over the uncertainties of the coming night and the city hummed, big and full of seduction. The city wanted money or silk stockings. And the beds wanted clean visitors at night.

I say, Timm, began the other and was silent again.

What is it? asked Timm.

Is she really called Lilo, eh?

Of course she's called Lilo, Timm shouted at his friend, she's called Lilo, and she said when I have anything, I'm to go back.

I say, Timm, his friend managed after a while, if she's really called Lilo, then you certainly had to give her the red scarf. If she's called Lilo, in my view, then she can have the red scarf. Even if the billet's no go. No, Timm, forget the scarf, if she's really called Lilo.

The two men looked across the misty water away to the mounting twilight, fearless, but without courage, reconciled. Reconciled to quay walls and gateways, reconciled to homelessness, to thin soles and empty pockets, reconciled. Inescapably idled away into indifference.

Thrown high, startlingly, on the horizon, blown hither from who knows where, crows came tumbling, their song and their dark feathers filled with the presentiment of night, reeling like inkspots across the chaste tissue paper of the evening sky, tired

with living, croaked hoarse, and then, unexpectedly, a little
further off, swallowed by the twilight.

They gazed after the crows, Timm and the other man, crowfaced, shrouded blueblack. And the water smelt full and mighty.
The city, a wild towering of cubes, window-eyed, began to
twinkle with a thousand lamps. They gazed after the crows, the
crows, long since swallowed, gazed after them with poor, old
faces, and Timm, who loved Lilo, Timm, who was twenty, said:
The crows, man, they're all right.

The other man looked away from the sky straight into Timm's
wide face, floating pale-frozen in the half-dark. And Timm's
thin lips were sad lines in his wide face, lonely lines, twenty-year-
old, hungry and thin from too much bitterness too soon.

The crows, said Timm's wide face softly, this face made up
of twenty bright-dark years, the crows, said Timm's face, they're
all right. They fly home at night. Just home.

The two men crouched there, lost in the world, small and
dejected in face of the new night, but fearlessly familiar with
its frightful blackness. The city, million-eyed and sleepy, glowed
through soft, warm curtains at the night streets emptied of noise,
their pavements deserted. They crouched there hard by the
depths, leaning over like tired rotten poles, and Timm, the
twenty-year-old, had said: The crows are all right. The crows fly
home at night. And the other babbled stupidly to himself: The
crows, Timm, hell, Timm, the crows.

There they crouched. Dumped there by life, the alluring, the
lousy. Dumped on the quay and the corner. On pier and pontoon.
On mole and hollowed cellar-steps. Dumped by life on the dust-
grey streets between silver paper and fallen leaf. Crows? No,
human beings! Do you hear? Human beings! And one of them
was called Timm and he'd loved Lilo for a red scarf. And now,
now he can't forget her again. The crows, the crows croak their
way home. And their croaking hung comfortless on the evening.

But then a launch stuttered, foam-mouthed, past them, and its
scattered red light crumbled quivering in the harbour haze. And
the haze was red for seconds. Red as my scarf, thought Timm.
Infinitely far off, the launch chugged away. And Timm said
softly: Lilo. Again and again: Lilo Lilo Lilo Lilo Lilo.

THERE ARE VOICES IN THE AIR—AT NIGHT

THE tram-car drove through the mist-wet afternoon. The afternoon was grey, and the tram was yellow and lost in it. For it was November and the streets were empty, noiseless and apathetic. Only the yellow of the tram-car floated, lonely, in the misty afternoon.

But inside the tram people were sitting, warm, breathing, excited. Five or six sat there, human beings, lost, lonely in the November afternoon. But in escape from the mist. Sitting beneath comforting, dim little lamps, sitting there quite isolated, in escape from the damp mist. It was empty in the tram. Only the five were there, quite isolated, and they were breathing. And the conductor was the sixth on this late, lonely, misty afternoon, there with his bland brass buttons, drawing great crooked faces on the damp breath-covered windows. The tram-car rocked and rumbled its yellow way through November.

Inside sat the five in escape and the conductor stood there and the elderly man with the huge bags under his eyes began again—began it again in an undertone:

"They're in the air. In the night. Oh, they're in the night. That's why you can't sleep. That's all it is. It's simply and solely the voices, believe me, it's only the voices."

The elderly man bent far forward. Gently the bags under his eyes trembled and his oddly bright index finger poked at the flat breast of the old woman sitting opposite him. She drew the air noisily through her nose and stared excitedly at the bright index finger. Again and again she loudly drew in air. She had to, for she had a fine abysmal November cold, which seemed to reach deep into her lungs. But despite that the finger excited her. The two girls in the other corner were giggling. But they didn't look at each other when the talk was of nocturnal voices. They knew long since that there were voices at night. They were the very ones who knew it best. But they giggled, for they were ashamed in each other's presence. And the conductor drew himself great crooked faces on the mist-lined windowpane. And then there was a young man sitting there who had his eyes shut and was pale. He sat there very pale under the little dim lamps. His eyes were shut as though he were sleeping. And the tram-car thrust its floating yellow way through the lonely, misty afternoon. The conductor drew a crooked face on the window and said to the elderly gentleman with the gently trembling bags under his eyes:

"Yes, that's obvious: there are voices. All kinds of voices. And especially, of course, at night."

The two girls were secretly ashamed and gave a fretful giggle and one thought: At night, specially at night.

The man with the trembling bags under his eyes removed his bright finger from the snuffling old woman's breast and started to poke at the conductor:

"Listen to what I say," he whispered, "to what I'm telling you! There are voices. In the air. In the night. And, ladies and gentlemen—" he took his index finger away from the conductor and stabbed with it steeply upwards: "do you know who it is? In the air? The voices? The voices at night? Do you know that too then, eh?"

The bags under his eyes trembled gently. The young man at the other end of the car was very pale and had his eyes shut, as though he were sleeping.

"They're the dead, the many, many dead." The man with the bags under his eyes whispered: "The dead, ladies and gentlemen. There are too many. They jostle each other in the air at night. There are far too many dead. They've no room. For every heart is full. Full up to the brim. And only in hearts can they live, that's certain. But there are too many dead who don't know where to go!"

The other people in the tram on this afternoon held their breath. Only the pale young man with his eyes closed breathed deeply and heavily, as though he were sleeping.

The elderly gentleman started poking at his listeners one after another with his bright index finger. At the girls, at the conductor and at the old woman. And then he whispered again: "And that's why you can't sleep. That's all it is. There are too many dead in the air. They have no room. Then at night they talk and look for a heart. That's why you don't sleep, because at night the dead don't sleep. There are too many. Especially at night. At night they talk, when it's quite quiet. At night they're there, when everything else is gone. At night, then they have voices. That's why you sleep so badly." The old woman with the cold drew a squeaky breath and stared excitedly at the wrinkled, trembling bags under the eyes of the whispering elderly gentleman. But the girls giggled. They knew other voices in the night, living ones, which lay on their naked skin like warm, masculine hands, which moved under the bed-clothes tenderly, violently, especially at night. They giggled and were ashamed in each other's presence. And neither knew that the other also heard the voices, at night, in her dreams.

The conductor drew great crooked faces on the mist-wet windows and said:

"Yes, the dead are there. They talk in the air. In the night: yes. It's obvious. Those are the voices. They hang in the air at night, over the bed. And then one can't sleep. It's obvious."

The old woman drew her cold through her nose and nodded:

"The dead, yes, the dead: those are the voices. Over the bed. Oh yes, always over the bed."

And the girls felt strange masculine hands on their skin, secretly, and their faces were red on this grey afternoon in the tram-car. But the young man, he was pale and very lonely in his corner and his eyes were shut, as though he were sleeping. Then the man with the bags under the eyes stabbed his bright finger into the dark corner, where the pale man was sitting, and whispered:

"Yes, the youngsters! They can sleep. In the afternoons. At night. In November. Always. They don't hear the dead. The youngsters, they sleep through the secret voices. Only we old people have ears inside. The young have no ears for the voices at night. They can sleep."

From a distance his index finger poked scornfully at the young man and the others breathed excitedly. Then he opened his eyes, the pale one, and stood up suddenly and swayed towards the elderly gentlemen. Startled, the index finger crept into its palm and for a moment the bags under the eyes stood still. The pale man, the young one, clutched at the face of the elderly gentleman and said:

"Oh please. Don't throw the cigarette away. Please give it to me. I feel bad. I'm rather hungry, you see. Give it to me. It'll do me good. You see, I feel bad."

Then the bags under the eyes grew damp and their wrinkles began to tremble, sadly, gently, and startled. And the elderly gentleman said:

"Yes, you're very pale. You look very ill. Have you no coat? We're in November."

"I know that, I know that," said the pale man, "every morning my mother says I should put on my coat, it's November. Yes, I know. But she's been dead for three years. So she doesn't know that I haven't a coat now. Each morning my mother says: It's November, she says. But of course she can't know about the coat, for she's dead."

The young man took the glowing cigarette and swayed out of the car. Outside were the mist, afternoon, and November. And away into the lonely late afternoon went a young, very pale man with a cigarette. He was hungry. He had no coat. His mother was dead, and it was November. And the others were sitting inside and they were not breathing. The bags under the eyes trembled gently, sadly. And the conductor drew great crooked faces on the window. Great crooked faces.

CONVERSATION OVER THE ROOFS

OUTSIDE stands the city. In the streets the lamps stand and keep watch. To see that nothing happens. Limes stand in the street and garbage cans and girls, and their smell is the smell of the night: heavy, bitter, sweet. Narrow smoke stands steep over the bright roofs. The rain has stopped drumming and has made off. But the roofs are still bright with it and the stars lie white on the dark wet tiles. Sometimes the wail of a cat rises, lustful, to the moon. Or human weeping. In the parks and gardens of the suburbs the anaemic mist rises and spirals through the streets. The cry of a locomotive, homesick for faraway, sobs deep into the dreams of the sleeping thousands. Endless windows are there. At night there are these endless windows. And the roofs are shining since the rain ran away.

Outside stands the city. A house stands in the city. Silent, stony, grey like the others. And there's a room in the house. A room, narrow, chalky, falling in, like the others, too. And in the room are two men. One is fair, and his breath moves softly and life moves, like his breath, softly, into him, out of him. His legs lie heavy as trees on the carpet, and the joints of the chair, on which he sits, creak surreptitiously. That's the one deep in the room. And one stands at the window. Long, tall, bent, slope-shouldered. The bones at his temples, the rim of his ear, float in the room mealy and grey-white. In his eye the light from the lamp in the yard twinkles shyly. But the yard, it's outside and the lamp's glow is miserly. Breathing goes up and down at the window like a saw. Sometimes the windowpane's dimmed with a woolly warm puff from this breathing. A voice is there at the window, like that of one running amok, panic-stricken, breathless, hunted, overdone, agitated:

"Don't you see? Don't you see that we're abandoned. Abandoned to the faraway, to the inexpressible, to the uncertain, to the darkness? Don't you realize that we're abandoned to laughter, to sobbing and sorrow, to bellowing. Man, it's terrible when the laughter rises up and swells in us, laughter at ourselves. When we stand at the graves of our fathers and friends and our women and the laughter rises. The laughter in the world, that's on watch for pain. The laughter that attacks sorrow, that's in us when we weep. And we've been abandoned to it.

"It's terrible, oh terrible, when sorrow grips us and tears squeeze through the cracks when we stand by our children's cradles. Terrible, when we stand by the bridal beds, and sorrow, the evil black-shrouded spirit, creeps up in us, icy, lonely. Rises up in us when we laugh, and we're abandoned to it.

"Don't you know that? Don't you know how frightful the bellowing is, growing in the world, full of fear, growing in the world, that comes up in you and bellows. Bellows in the stillness of night, bellows in the stillness of love, bellows in the silent solitude. And the bellowing means: Scorn! Means: God! Means: Life! Means: Fear! And we're abandoned to it with all the blood in us.

"We laugh. And our death has been planned from the start.

"We laugh. And our decay cannot be avoided.

"We laugh. And our ruin's at hand.

"This evening. The day after tomorrow.

"In nine thousand years. Always.

"We laugh, but our life's been surrendered to accident, abandoned, unavoidably. To the accidental, do you understand? Whatever happens in the world can happen to you and crush you or leave you standing. Just as accidents happen accidentally. And we: abandoned to it, thrown out to be devoured.

"And we laugh. Stand there and laugh. And our life, our love and our precious, personal pain—they're as uncertain and accidental as the wind and the wave. Arbitrary. Do you understand? Understand?"

But the other is silent. And the one at the window croaks on:

"And then we here in the city, deep within this loneliest of forests, deep under this crushing mountain of stone, in this city, where no voice speaks to us, no ear hears us and no eye meets ours. In this city where the featureless faces float over and past us, nameless, countless, thoughtless. Without sympathy, heartless. With no resting-place, no beginning, no haven. Weeds. Weeds in the stream of time. Weeds, green, grey, yellow, rising up dark white out of the depths, sinking back without trace into the waters of the world: weeds, faces, people.

"In this city, we here, homeless, without tree, without bird without fish: grown lonely, lost, annihilated. Abandoned, lost to a sea of walls, to a sea of mortar, dust and cement. Thrown to the doors, the carpets, stairways and steeples. We here in the city, sold to her with our fatal incurable love. Astray in the lonely forest city, in the forest of walls, façades, iron, concrete and lamps. Astray in this world, without home, without origin. Given away to the lonely, unanswering night in the streets. Abandoned to the million-faced day with its million-voiced roar, abandoned with our weak, defenceless bit of heart. Abandoned with our impetuous courage and our tiny understanding. With every heartbeat, with our noses, eyes and ears, chained to the plaster, the stones, to the tar and the sewers. With no goal to escape to. Crushed under roofs, abandoned, to parlours, to cellars, to ceilings. Do you hear? Man, that's what we are and that's how it is with us. And you think you'll bear it till tomorrow, till Christmas, till March?"

The tinny voice of the runner-amok jangles into the now dark room. But the fair man breathes softly and surely and his lips are not parted in answer. And the one at the window again stabs with his voice into the late evening silence, pitiless, tortured, driven:

"We bear it. How do you like that, eh? We bear it. We laugh. Abandoned to the beasts in us and round us, we laugh. Oh, and how we have fallen to women, our women. Fallen to their painted lips, eyelashes, throat, to the scent of their flesh. Forgotten in the play of their desires, lost in the spell of their tenderness, we smile. And parting squats freezing and grinning on the door-handles, ticks in the works of the clock. We smile, as though sure of eternities, and yet the farewell, all farewells are already waiting within us. All deaths we carry within us. In the spine. In the lung. In the heart. In the liver. In the blood. We carry our death around with us everywhere and forget ourselves and it in the thrill of a caress. Or because a hand is so slender or a skin so fair. And death, and death, and death laughs at our moaning and muttering!"

With his panic-breath the one at the window had swallowed

all the air in the room, gulped it down, and as hot hoarse words thrust it out again. There is no more air in the room and he throws the window open. The hard shells of the night insects crisp and crackle excitedly against the glass. Something rustles past, faintly. It squeaks furtively, as when a woman turns a loud laugh into a little giggle.

"Ducks," says the one in the room, softly and roundly. And he holds on to his word for a moment, as the one at the window again pours out over him:

"Did you hear how they giggle, the ducks? Everything laughs at us. Ducks, women, unoiled doors. The laughter lurks everywhere. Oh, that this laughter exists in the world! And sorrow exists and the great god Accident. And the bellowing exists, the giant-mouthed bellowing! And we have the courage: and live. And we have the courage: and plan. And laugh. And love. We live, live without death, and our death was decided from the very beginning. Settled. From right at the start. But we're brave, we death-carriers: we make children, we drive, we sleep. Each minute that was is irretrievable. Unforeseeable each that's to come. But we brave ones, marked for destruction: we swim, we fly, we walk across streets and bridges. And we sway across the boards of ships—and our destruction, do you hear, our destruction leers from behind the rail, lurks under cars, crackles in the piers of the bridges. Our destruction, inevitable.

"And we, bipeds, people, human animals, with our bit of red sap, with our bit of warmth and bone and flesh and muscle—we bear it. Our decay is decided, incorruptibly, yet: we plant. Our downfall proclaims itself irrevocably, yet: we build. Our disappearance, our dissolution, our not-being is certain, noted down, ineffaceably—our not-being-here-any-more is directly at hand, yet: we are. We still are. We have the incomprehensible courage: to be.

"And accident, the unpredictable played-out God above us accident, terrible, towering accident balances drunkenly on the roofs of the world. And under the roofs are we, the reckless, with our incomprehensible faith.

"A few grams of brain fail, a couple of grams of spinal marrow mutiny: and we are lame. We are imbecile. Stiff. In misery. But we laugh.

"A few heartbeats miss out: and we're left with no awakening, no tomorrow. But we sleep—undoubting. In deep, animal confidence.

"A muscle, a nerve, a sinew stops work: and we fall: into the depths, endlessly. But we drive, we fly and sway straddle-legged on board ship.

"That we're like that—why is it, you? That we can be like that, that we must be like that—no lips will explain. There's no solution, no reason, no shape to it. Obscure. And we? We are. For all that, always. Oh, man—we still are. Still, still."

The two men in the room are breathing. The one gently and calmly, the other at the window hurriedly, raspingly. Outside stands the city. The moon floats like a dirty egg-yolk in the bilberry-blue soup of the night sky. It looks rotten, and one feels it must smell. The moon looks so ill. But the stench comes from the canals. From the lumpy, clumsy mass of cubes, from the sea of houses with its millions of glassy eyes in the darkness. But the moon looks unhealthy, so one can believe the smell comes from it. Of course it's too far away for that and it must be the canals. Yes, it's the canals, the grey-black blocks of houses, the blue-black shining cars, the yellow tinny trams, the dark soot-red freight trains, the mauve manholes of the sewers, the wet-green graves, love, fear—those are the things that make the night so full of smell. No, it certainly can't be the moon, although it's floating so rotten and sickly, so pulpy and inflamed in the aster-coloured sky. Much too yellow in the aster-coloured violet sky.

The one at the window, the hoarse, the haggard, the hasty, he looks at this moon and he looks at the city under the moon and he stretches his arm out of the window and seizes this city. And his voice scrapes through the night like a file:

"And then this city!" scrapes the voice from the window, "and then this city. We are it, motor-tyres, apple-peel, paper, glass, powder, stone, dust, street, houses, harbour: we are it all. We are everywhere. We ourselves: stifling, burning, cold, inspiring city. We, we alone are this city. We, quite alone, without God, without grace, we are the city. And we can bear it, to be in the city and in us and around us. We can bear being a harbour. We can bear the goings and comings, we harbour cities. We can bear the inconceivable: to exist in the nights! In these harbour nights when the deathdark and dazzling go arm in arm. In these city nights, full of torn silky linen and full of the warm skin of girls. We endure these alone-nights, the storm-nights, the fever-nights and the carnival schnaps-nights, the yelled, undermining. We endure these nights of intoxication over full-written paper and beneath bleeding mouths. We can bear them. Do you hear, we come through. we survive it.

"And love, blood-coloured love's in the nights. And it hurts, sometimes. And it lies, always, love: but we love with everything we have.

"And horror, fear, despair, no escape, are in these nights full of pain—at our gin-wet tables, by our burgeoning beds, beside our song-sodden streets. But we laugh. We live with all that we can. And with all that we are.

"And we, the sceptics, we, the deceived, the trampled, confused and abandoned, we, disappointed by God and the good and by love, we with the bitter knowledge: we, we wait each night for the sun. With every lie we still wait for the truth. We believe in every new vow in the night, we nightly ones. We believe in March, believe in it in the middle of November. We believe in our body, in this machine, in its Still-being-tomorrow, in its Still-working-tomorrow. We believe in the hot, heating sun in a snowstorm. We believe in life, we: in the middle of death. That's how we are, we, with no illusions, we with the grand impossible ideas.

"We live without God, without sojourn in space, without promises, without certainty—abandoned, cast out, lost. Pathless we stand in the fog, faceless in the stream of noses, ears and eyes. Without echo we stand in the night, without mast or deck in the wind, with no window, no door for us. Moonless, starless in the dark, deceived by wretched consumptive lamps. We are unanswered. There's no 'yes'. Without home, without hand, heartless, in gloom. Abandoned to darkness, to fog, to the pitiless day and to windowless, doorless obscurity. Abandoned, we are, to the In-us and Round-us. Inescapably, with no way out. And we laugh. We believe in the morning. But the morning's unknown to us. We trust in, we build on the morning. But no one has promised it to us. We shout, we plead, we roar for tomorrow. And nobody answers us."

The high haggard crooked chimera at the window drums on the glass:

"There! There! There! There! The city. The lamps. The women. The moon. The harbour. The cats. The night. Tear open the window, scream out of it, scream, swear, sob out of it, roar out of it, everything that tortures and burns you: there's no answer. Pray!—there's no answer. Curse!—there's no answer. Scream your pain out of your window out into the world: there's no answer. Oh no, no, there's no answer!"

Outside stands the city. Outside the night stands in the streets with its smell of girls and garbage cans. And the house stands in the streets of the city, the house with the room and the men. The room with the two men. And one stands at the window, and he has screamed into the dusk of the room at his friend. Tall and narrow, hoarse as a ghost, he has flared up from faraway, crook-shouldered, consuming, ravaging, possessed. And his temples are blue-pale and wet-bright like the roofs under the moon outside. And the other is deep in the safety of the room. Broad, blond, pale and bear-voiced. He is leaning against the wall, drenched, overwhelmed by the chimera. But then his soft frank voice clutches at his friend by the window:

"Why in the name of all that's holy don't you hang yourself, you hopeless, insane, withered, glowing lath, you! You rat! Surly, snotty-nosed rat! You worm, you, milling everything into dust! You moaning, ticking, death-watch beetle! You should be plunged into petrol, you stinking rag. Hang yourself, you dithering, drunken bundle of humanity. Why aren't you hanging yet, you lost, forsaken, abandoned piece of life, eh?"

His voice is filled with concern, and kind and warm in all his curses.

But from the window the tall one sets on the speaker by the wall with his wooden noise, with his crude cracked voice. The crude, the cracked, cracks against the man at the wall, laughs at him, startles him:

"Hanging? Me? Me and hanging! My God! Don't you understand, have you never understood that I *love* this life? My God, me on a lamp-post! I want to ladle, lick, drink, taste, squeeze everything out of this wonderful, hot, senseless, fantastic, incomprehensible life! You want me to miss that? Me? Hang myself? Me? You, you say I should be strung from a lamp-post? Me? You say that?"

The pale, fair man leaning peacefully against the wall, rolls his round voice back to the window:

"But my dear boy, my dear man: why do you live then?"

And haggard, he hoarsely hiccoughs back: "Why? Why I live? Out of spite perhaps! Out of pure spite. It's spite that makes me laugh and eat and sleep and wake up again. Just spite. Out of spite I put children in this world, *in this world*! I lie love into girls' hearts and into their hips and let them realize the truth, the frightening, terrifying truth. That horrible, bloodless, slop-bosomed flat-thighed played-out whore! Building ships, using shovels, binding books, stoking engines, burning schnaps. To spite! Out of spite! Yes: living! Out of spite! Give up, be hanged: me? And tomorrow perhaps it'll happen, tomorrow it can happen, it can happen at any moment."

The dark one croaks quite softly now, the one by the window-bars, not all-knowing, but all-suspecting. And the fair one in the room, the frank, assured, sober one asks:

"What? What will happen? What's supposed to happen? Who? Where? Nothing's ever happened yet, man, not yet!"

And the other answers:

"No, nothing's happened. Nothing. We still gnaw bones, still live in caves of wood and stone. Nothing's happened. Nothing's come. I know. But: can't it come any day? This evening? The day after tomorrow? It can even be round the next corner. In the next bed. On the other side. For some time it *must* come, the unexpected, the foreseen, the great, the new. The adventure, the mystery, the solution. At last perhaps there'll come the answer. And that, I should miss that? No, man, no, never! Never and never! Don't you feel that something can happen? Don't ask what! Don't you feel that, eh? Don't you suspect it, inside and outside you? For it's coming, man, perhaps it's there already. Somewhere. Unrecognized. Secret. Perhaps we shall understand it tonight, tomorrow at noon, next week, on the death-bed. Or are we senseless? Abandoned to the laughter in us and round us? To sorrow, to tears and to the bellowing of night and terror? Abandoned? Perhaps? Perhaps surrendered? Perhaps lost? Is there no answer? Are we, we ourselves, that answer? Or not, man, answer. Tell me. Are we, in the last analysis, ourselves that answer. Do we have it in us, like death? From the very start? Do we carry death and the answer in us, you? Is it up to us, whether there'll be an answer or not? Are we, after all, abandoned only to ourselves? Only to ourselves? Tell me, man: Are we ourselves the answer? Are we ourselves abandoned to ourselves? Are we? Tell me!"

With two thin, crooked, gigantic arms, he holds on to the window-bars, the tall one, the burning ghost, the dark, the hoarse, the whispering one. But the fair one puts back his full round voice deep into his belly. The questioner at the window has answered himself with his own question. The breath of two men mixes together. Their great, good smell, the smell of horse, tobacco, leather and sweat fills the room.

High up on the ceiling the chalk grows slowly brighter, spot by spot.

Outside the moon, the lamps and the stars have grown poor and pale. Lustreless, pointless, blind.

And outside, there stands the city. Dull, dark, threatening. The city: big, cruel, kind. The city: dumb, dignified, defiant, undying.

And outside, on the edge of the city, frost-sweet and transparent, stands the new morning.

On the Move

GENERATION WITHOUT FAREWELL

We are the generation without ties and without depth. Our depth is the abyss. We are the generation without happiness, without home and without farewell. Our sun is narrow, our love cruel and our youth is without youth. And we are the generation without limit, without restraint and without protection—thrown out of the playpen of childhood into a world made for us by those who now despise us because of it.

But they gave us no God, who could have held our hearts when the winds of this world surged round it. So we are the generation without God, for we are the generation without ties, without past and unacknowledged.

And the winds of the world, which have made gipsies of our feet and our hearts on roads burning hot, on roads man-high with snow, made of us a generation without farewell.

We are the generation without farewell. We may live no farewell, we must not, for on the stray paths trodden by our feet our wandering hearts find endless farewells. Or should our heart bind itself for one night, where the morning already means farewell? Could we bear that farewell? And if we wanted to live our farewells, like you, who are other than we and savoured the farewell in its every second, then it could be that our tears would mount in a flood, which no dam, though our forefathers had built it, could ever withstand.

We shall never have the strength to live, as you have lived it, the farewell that stands on the roads by every milestone.

Do not say to us, because our heart is silent, that our heart has no voice, for it speaks no bond and no farewell. If our heart did bleed through each farewell that befalls us, ardently, sorrowing, comforting, then it could be, for our farewells are legion against yours, that the cry of our sore hearts would be so loud that you would sit in your beds at night and beg for a God for us.

Therefore we are a generation without farewell. We deny the farewell, leave it sleeping in the morning when we go, prevent it, spare it—spare ourselves and those from whom we have parted. We steal away like thieves, ungratefully grateful and take our love with us and leave the farewell behind.

We have many encounters, encounters without duration and without farewell, like the stars. They approach, stand for light-seconds beside one another, move away again: without trace, without ties, without farewell.

We meet under the cathedral of Smolensk, a man and a woman—and then we steal away.

We meet in Normandy and are as parents and child—and then we steal away.

We meet one night by a Finnish lake and are lovers—and then we steal away.

We meet on a farm in Westphalia in convalescence and contentment—and then we steal away.

We meet in a cellar in the city and are hungry and tired, and for nothing we get a good full sleep—and then we steal away.

We meet in the world as man and man—and then we steal away, for we are without ties, without resting-place and without farewell. We are a generation without farewell, stealing away like thieves, because we are afraid of our heart's cry. We are a generation without homecoming, for we have nothing we could come home to, and we have no one to take care of our hearts—so we have become a generation without farewell and without homecoming.

But we are a generation of arrival. Perhaps we are a generation full of arrival on a new star, in a new life. Full of arrival under a new sun, in new hearts. Perhaps we are a generation full of arrival at a new love, at a new laughter, at a new God.

We are a generation without farewell, but we know that all arrival belongs to us.

RAILWAYS, BY DAY AND BY NIGHT

RIVER and road are too slow for us. Too crooked for us. For we want to go home. We don't know where it is: home. But we want to go there. And river and road are too crooked for us.

But on bridge and embankment the trains are pounding. Through black-green breathing forests and silky star-spangled velvet nights the freight trains tear up and away with the ceaseless follow-my-leader of wheels. Rumbling on over a million sleepers. Irresistible. Uninterrupted: the trains. Pounding along embankments, roaring over bridges, thundering out of mists, fading into darkness: humming, thrumming trains. Freight trains, murmuring, hurrying, somehow lazy and restless, they are like us.

They are like us. They announce themselves, pompously, grandly and already in the far distant distance, with a cry. Then they're there like thunder and as though they had rolled around heaven knows what worlds. And they all resemble each other and yet are always surprising and thrilling. But in a flash, before one knows what they are really after, they are gone. And everything is as though they had never been. At best soot and burnt grass alongside proclaim their path. Then, somewhat sadly and already in the far distant distance, they take their leave with a cry. Like us.

Some of them sing. Hum and thrum through our happy nights and we love their monotonous chant, their eager meaningful rhythm: Going home—going home—going home. Or they surge on full of promise through sleeping country, howl hollowly past lonely village stations with intimidated, sleepy lights: tomorrow in Brussels—tomorrow in Brussels. Or they know so much more, *piano*, for you alone, and those sitting near you don't hear it, *piano*: Ulla's waiting—Ulla's waiting—Ulla's waiting—

But there are also placid ones among them, unending and wise and with the broad rhythm of old beasts of burden. They murmur and mumble all sorts of things to themselves and lie like never-seen chains across the moonlit landscape, chains, unbounded in their splendour and magic and colour in the pale moon: brown-red, black or grey, bright blue and white: freight cars— twenty men, forty horses—coal cars, smelling miraculously of tar and perfume—timber cars, that breathe like the forest— circus cars, bright blue, with snoring athletes and helpless animals in their insides—refrigerator cars, Greenland cool and Greenland white, fish-scented. Unbounded in their richness, they lie like costly chains on the steely tracks and glide like splendid rare snakes in the moonlight. And they tell those who at night live with their ears and travel with their ears, the sick and the imprisoned, of the inconceivable breadth of the world, of its treasures, its sweetness, its ends and its endlessness. And they murmur those who are without sleep into good dreams.

But there are also cruel ones, pitiless, brutal ones, pounding through the night without melody, and you cannot rid your ears of their beat, for it's hard and ugly, like the breath of an evil, asthmatic dog, rasping behind you: On and on—no return— forever—forever. Or grimmer, with growling wheels: All over— all over. And its song grants us no sleep and to right and left scares the peaceful villages cruelly out of their dreams, so that dogs grow hoarse with fury. And they roll crying and sobbing, the cruel, the incorruptible, under the dull stars, and even the rain does not make them tender. In their cry is the cry of home-sickness, of the lost, the abandoned—the sob of the remorseless, the parted, the known and the uncertain. And they thunder a dull rhythm, unblessed and uncomforting, on the moonlit permanent way. And you never forget them.

They are like us. No one ensures that they'll die in their homeland. They have no peace and no night rest, and they rest only when they are ill. And they have no goal. They may be at home in Stettin or in Sofia or in Florence. But they break up between Copenhagen and Altona or in a suburb of Paris. Or they break down in Dresden. Or they fumble away a few more years as pensioners—as shelters for line-workers or as weekend cottages for city-folk.

They are like us. They endure far more than anyone believed possible. But one day they run off the rails, stop dead or lose a vital member. They are always wanting to go somewhere. Nowhere do they stay. And when it's over, what is their life?

A life under way. But sublime, brutal and boundless.

Railways, by day and by night. The flowers in the cuttings with their sooty blossoms, the birds on the wires with their sooty voices, they are their friends and long remember them.

And we also stand still, with astonished eyes, when—already from the far distant distance—there's the cry of promise. And we stand, with hair streaming, when it's there like thunder and as though it had rolled round heaven knows what worlds. And we're still standing, with sooty cheeks, when—already from the far distant distance—it cries. Cries, far, far away. Cries.

Really it was nothing. Or everything. Like us.

And they beat, beyond the windows of prisons, sweet, dangerous, promising rhythms. You are all ears then, poor prisoner, all hearing, for the clattering, oncoming trains in the night and their cry and their whistle shiver the soft dark of your cell with pain and desire.

Or they crash bellowing over the bed, when at night you're harbouring fever. And your veins, the moon-blue, vibrate and take up the song, the song of the freight trains: Under way— under way—under way— And your ear's an abyss, that swallows the world.

Under way. But ever and again you are spat out at stations, abandoned to farewell and departure.

And the stations raise up their pale signboards like brows beside your dark road. And they have names, those furrowed-brow signs, names, which are the world: bed, they mean, hunger and women. Ulla or Carola. And frozen feet and tears. And they mean tobacco, the stations, or lipstick or schnaps. Or God or bread. And the pale brows of the stations, the signboards, have names, that mean: women.

You are yourself a railway track, rusty, stained, silver, shiny, beautiful and uncertain. And you are divided into sections and bound between stations. And they have signboards whereon is written women, or murder, or moon. And then that is the world.

You are a railway—rumbled over, cried over—you are the track—on you everything happens and makes you rustblind and silverbright.

You are human, your brain giraffe-lonely somewhere above on your endless neck. And no one quite knows your heart.

DO STAY, GIRAFFE

HE stood on the wind-howling night-empty platform in the great greysooted moon-lonely hall. Empty stations at night are the end of the world, extinct, grown meaningless. And void. Void, void, void. But if you go further, you are lost.

Then you are lost. For the darkness has a terrible voice. You cannot escape it and in a flash it has overwhelmed you. It assails you with memory—of the murder you committed yesterday. And it attacks you with foreknowledge—of the murder you'll commit tomorrow. And it presses up a cry in you: unheard fish-cry of the solitary animal, overwhelmed by its own sea. And the cry tears up your face and makes hollows in it full of fear and past danger, that terrify others. So silent is the dreadful darkness—cry of the solitary animal in its own sea.

And it mounts like a flood and rushes on, dark-winged, threatening, like breakers. And hisses wickedly, like foam.

He stood at the end of the world. The cold white arc-lamps were merciless and made everything naked and doleful. But behind them grew a terrible darkness. No black was as black as the darkness round the white lamps of the night-empty platforms.

I see you've got cigarettes, said the girl with the too red mouth in the pale face.

Yes, he said, I have some.

Why don't you come with me then? she whispered, close.

No, he said, what for?

You don't know what I'm like, she sniffed round about him.

I do, he answered, like them all.

You're a giraffe, big boy, a stubborn giraffe! D'you even know what I look like, eh?

Hungry, he said, naked and painted. Like them all.

You're long and dumb, you giraffe, she giggled close, but you look sweet. And you've cigarettes. Come on, boy, it's dark.

Then he looked at her. All right, he laughed, you get the cigarettes and I kiss you. But if I take hold of your dress, what then?

Then I'll blush, she said, and he thought her grin vulgar.

44

A freight train yowled through the station. And suddenly tore off. Its miserly, shimmering tail-light oozed away in embarrassment into the darkness. Banging, squeaking, crashing, rumbling—gone. Then he went with her.

Then there were hands, faces and lips. But all the faces are bleeding, he thought, bleeding from the mouth, and the hands hold hand-grenades. But then he tasted the make-up and her hand grasped his bony arm. Then there was a groan and a steel helmet fell and an eye broke.

You're dying, he screamed.

Dying, she gloated. That'd be something!

Then she pushed the helmet back on to the forehead. Her dark hair shone softly.

Ah, your hair, he whispered.

Will you stay? she asked softly.

Yes.

For long?

Yes.

For always?

Your hair smells like wet twigs, he said.

For always? she asked again.

And then from the distance: near, fat, great cry. Fish-cry, bat's cry, dungbeetle's cry. The never-heard animal cry of the locomotive. Did the train sway on its tracks, full of fear from that cry? New, never-known yellow-green cry beneath faded constellations. Did that cry make the stars shiver?

Then he tore open the window, so that the night clutched with cold hands at his naked breast, and said: I must go.

Do stay, giraffe! Her mouth shimmered sick-red in her pale face.

But the giraffe stalked away across the pavement with hollow, echoing steps. And behind him the moon-grey street, falling silent again, returned to its petrified loneliness. The reptile-eyed windows looked dead, as though glazed with a milky film. The curtains, sleep-heavy secretly breathing eyelids, billowed gently. Dangled. Dangled, white, soft, and waved sorrowfully after him.

The shutter miaowed. And her breast was cold, When he looked round, behind the pane was a too red mouth. Giraffe, it wept.

DONE WITH, DONE WITH

SOMETIMES he met himself. With loose gait and crooked shoulders, he came up to himself, his hair so excessively long that it hung over one ear, he shook hands with himself, not very firmly, and said: 'Morning.

'Morning. Who are you?

You.

Me?

Yes.

And then he said to himself: Why do you scream sometimes?

That's the beast.

The beast?

The beast hunger.

And then he asked himself: Why do you cry so often?

The beast! The beast!

The beast?

The beast homesickness. It cries. The beast hunger, it screams.

And the beast Me—it runs away.

Where to?

To nothingness. There's no valley of escape. I meet myself everywhere. Most of all in the night. But one always runs further. The beast love clutches at one, but the beast fear barks at the windows, behind which lie the girl and her bed. And then the door-handle titters and one runs away. And one's always after oneself. With the beast hunger in the belly and the beast homesickness in the heart. But there's no valley of escape. One's always meeting oneself. Everywhere. One cannot get away from oneself.

Sometimes he met himself. And then he'd run away again. Whistling under windows and coughing past doors. And sometimes for a night a heart held him, a hand. Or a blouse, that had slipped from a shoulder, from a breast, from a woman. Sometimes then, a girl held him for one night. And if she was all for him then among the kisses he forgot that other man, who was himself. And laughed. And suffered. It was fine, when one had a girl with one, one with long hair and shiny linen. Or linen, that was sometimes shiny and had flowers on it. And then if she had a bit of lipstick, that was good, too. Then there was something gay. And in the dark it was better if you had a girl with you, then the darkness wasn't so big. And then the darkness wasn't so cold, either. And the bit of lipstick made a little stove out of her mouth. And it burned. That was fine in the darkness. And the linen, one just didn't see it. But at least one had someone with one.

He'd known one, whose skin looked in summer like haws. Bronze. And her hair came from gipsies, more blue than black. And it was wild as the woods. There were bright little hairs on her arm, like chicken-down, and her voice was as alluring as a harbour girl's. But she understood nothing. And was called Karin.

And the other was called Ali and her buttercup hair was as bright as sand. She wrinkled her nose when she laughed, and she bit. But along came a man, who was her husband.

And in front at a door, growing smaller and smaller stood a man, grey and bony, and said: All right, my boy. Later he realized: That was my father.

And the one with the legs that were restless as drumsticks was called Carola, deer-legged, nervy. And her eyes drove you mad. And in front her teeth stood slightly apart. He'd known her.

And at night sometimes the old man said: All right, my boy.

One was broad at the hips, he'd been with her. She smelt of milk. Her name was a fine one—but he had forgotten it. All over.

Sometimes in the morning the yellow-hammer sang in astonishment—but his mother was far away and the thin grey man said nothing. For no one came past.

And his legs moved under him, quite on their own: done with, done with.

And the yellow-hammers knew it already in the morning: done with, done with.

And the telegraph wires hummed: done with, done with. And the old man said nothing more: done with, done with.

And in the evenings the girls held their hands against their yearning skins: done with, done with.

And his legs moved of their own accord: done with, done with.

He had once had a brother. They were friends. But then a

piece of metal buzzed through the air at him, humming like a hateful insect. It was war. And the piece of metal splashed like a raindrop on human skin: Then the blood blossomed like poppies in the snow. The sky was of lapis lazuli, but it would not accept his scream. And the last scream that he screamed was not "Fatherland". It was not "Mother" and not "God". His last screamed scream was sour and sharp and was: Knackered. And was cursed very softly: Knackered. And it pulled his mouth shut. For ever. Done with.

And the thin grey man, who was his father, never again said: All right, my boy. Never again. That was all, now, all, all done with.

THE CITY

A MAN of the night was walking on the railway lines. They lay in the moonlight and shone bright as silver. But cold, thought the man of the night, they are cold. Far off to the left an isolated glow, a farm. And by it, a harsh-barking dog. The glow and the dog made the night into night. Then the man of the night was alone again. Only the wind made its long-breathed ooh-notes past his ears. And the track was dotted with stains: clouds over the moon.

Then came the man with the lamp. It shook, as it was raised between the two faces.

The man with the lamp said: Well, lad, where are you off to?

And the man of the night pointed with his arm towards the brightness beyond in the sky.

Hamburg? Asked the one with the lamp.

Yes, Hamburg, answered the man of the night.

Then the stones rattled softly beneath their feet. Clicked against one another. And the wire on the lamp squeaked to and fro, to and fro. In front of them lay the rails in the moonlight. And silver the rails ran on towards the brightness. And the brightness in the sky on this night, the brightness was Hamburg.

It's not really like that, said the one with the lamp, the city's not really like that. It's bright there, sure enough, but under the bright lamps there's nothing but people who are hungry too. I'm telling you, man.

Hamburg! laughed the man of the night, then nothing else matters. You always have to go back there, always have to go back, if you've come from there. You have to go back. But then, and he said it, as though he thought much of it, that's life! The only life!

The lamp squeaked to and fro, to and fro. And the wind ooh-ed in a minor key past his ears. The rails lay moon-glazed and cold.

Then said the one with the dangling lamp: Life! My God,

49

what is it: Remembering scents, grasping at door-handles. You walk past faces and at night feel the rain in your hair. And that's doing quite well.

Then behind them a locomotive cried out like a giant child utterly homesick. And it made the night into night. Then a freight train rattled harshly past the men. And it snarled like danger through the silken, star-studded night. The men breathed sturdily against it. And the roundly revolving wheels rolled rattling under rust-red red wagons. Raced restlessly rumbling away—away—away.

And much further, still softly: away—away.

Then the man of the night said: No, life is more than running in the rain and clutching at door-knobs. It's more than walking past faces and remembering smells. Life is: Being afraid. And being happy. Afraid you'll fall under the train. And happy you haven't fallen under the train. Happy that you can go on.

Then there was a small house lying beside the track. The man turned down the lamp and shook the youngster by the hand: Well, then, Hamburg!

Yes, Hamburg, he said and went.

The rails shone bright in the moon.

And beyond on the sky was a brighter patch: The city.

City, City:
Mother between Heaven and Earth

HAMBURG

HAMBURG!
That's more than a heap of stones, roofs, windows, carpets, beds, streets, bridges and lamps. It's more than factory chimneys and the hooting of traffic—more than gulls' laughter, trams screaming and the thunder of railways—it's more than ships' sirens, crashing cranes, curses and dance music—oh, it's infinitely more.

It's our will to be. Not to be anywhere and anyhow, but to be here and only here between Alster stream and Elbe river— and only to be, as we are, we in Hamburg!

We admit it without shame: that the sea wind and the river mist have crazed and bewitched us to stay—to stay here, to *stay here*! That the Alster lake has seduced us into building our houses all richly around it—and that the river, the broad grey river has seduced us into sailing the seas in the wake of our yearning— travelling, wandering, drifting away—sailing, in order to return, to return sick and small with the longing for home, for our little blue lake among grey red roofs and green-helmeted towers.

Hamburg, city: stone-forest of towers, lamps and six-storeyed houses: stone-forest whose paving stones, with the rhythm of a song, conjure up the floor of a forest where you still hear the steps of the dead, at night sometimes.

City: primitive animal, scuffling and snuffling, animal of courtyards, glass and sighs, tears, parks and shouts of joy— animal with blinking eyes in the sunlight: silvery, oily canals! Animal with shimmering eyes in the moonlight: quivering, glimmering lamps!

City: home, heaven, homecoming—beloved between heaven and hell, between ocean and ocean: mother between meadow and mud, between river and lake: angel between waking and sleeping, between mist and wind: Hamburg!

And that's why we're related to the others, to those in Harlem, Marseilles, Frisco and Bombay, Liverpool and Cape Town—and who love Harlem, Marseilles, Frisco and Cape Town as we love our streets, our river and harbour, our gulls, the mist, the nights and our women.

Ah, our women, with their locks blown about by gulls' wings—or was it the wind? No, it's the wind, which gives our women no peace—neither their skirts nor their tresses. This wind which watches the sailors' adventures at sea and in port and then seduces our women with its singsong of faraway, homesickness, travel and tears—homecoming and soft, sweet, stormy embraces.

Our women in Hamburg, in Harlem, Marseilles, Frisco, and Bombay, in Liverpool and Cape Town—and in Hamburg, in Hamburg! We know them so and love them so, when the wind with an impudent gust, for two seconds, gives us their knee; when it bestows an unexpected tenderness on us and blows a soft curl against our nose: dear, wonderful wind of Hamburg!

Hamburg!

That's more than a heap of stones, inexpressibly more! It's the strawberry-laden, apple-blossoming meadows on the banks of the Elbe—it's the flower-laden, schoolgirl-blossoming gardens of the villas on the banks of the Alster.

It's white, yellow, sand-coloured and bright green low pilots' houses and captains' cabins on the hills of Blankenese. But it's also the dirty, slovenly, bustling quarters of factories and wharves with their stink of grease, scent of tar and smell of fish and sweaty breath. Oh—it's the mighty sweetness of the parks on the Alster and in the suburbs, where the Hamburgers, the genuine Hamburgers, who never go to the dogs and always steer a straight course, are made in the blissful passionate nights of love. And these truly lucky children are tossed into this immortal life on a cushion-scented boat, croaked at by frogs, on the moonlit Alster.

Hamburg!

It's the fantastic tropical trees, bushes and flowers of the mammoth graveyard, of that bird-gladdened, best-tended jungle in the world, where the dead dream away their death, and throughout their whole death murmur of gulls, of girls, of masts and walls, of May evenings and sea winds. That's no sterile, military cemetery, where the dead (forced into rows among privet hedges, decorated with primulas and rose-trees, as though with medals), keep watch on the living and have to share in the sweat and shouting of the working and procreating—ah, they cannot enjoy their death! But in Ohlsdorf—there the dead, the undying dead, gossip about undying life! For the dead don't forget life—and they cannot forget the city, their city!

Hamburg!

It's these grey, vital, inevitable infinities of disconsolate streets, in which we were all born, and in which one day we all must die—and that is so very much more than a heap of stones!

Walk through it and distend your nose like a horse's nostrils: That's the smell of life! Swaddling-clothes, cabbage, plush sofa, onions, petrol, young girls' dreams, carpenter's glue, cats, geraniums, schnaps, motor-car tyres, lipstick—blood and sweat—smell of the city, breath of life: more, more than a heap of stones! It's death and life, work, sleep, wind and love, tears and mist!

It's our will to be, Hamburg!

BILLBROOK

THE Canadian sergeant-pilot, who arrived in Hamburg in the late evening, put his heavy suitcase down on the stone flags of the station hall. He blew out his cheeks and puffed. He blew a long puff in front of him, but one could not decide whether he did it because the air was so bad or because he was sweating. His left and right hands disappeared into his trouser-pockets and emerged from their depths into the daylight with a lighter and packet of cigarettes. No, not into the daylight. Into the lamplight. Into the dismal, misty, blind, damp lamplight of the nocturnal railway station. Then with his teeth he nibbled a cigarette out of the paper wrapper and made his lighter click. The lighter made its practised little click and the thin, weak, yellow tongue of flame burned the sergeant's narrow dark-red moustache. It did not burn the moustache badly. But the unmistakable smell of burning assailed his nose. As though of burning rubber. Rubber? he thought. It didn't occur to him that singed hair smells much the same. And even the thought of rubber was only incidental. The cigarette remained unsmoked. It lay white, oddly new and clean on the dark ground. It had fallen out of his mouth. His lips were a little open. And he forgot to click his lighter shut again. The little flame crept, forgotten and forsaken, back into the wick. He even forgot to investigate, with the help of his pocket mirror, the ravages to his moustache. He actually forgot his singed, ravaged, narrow red moustache and that would have seemed to him extremely astonishing, if he had been observing himself. For of this moustache, so rusty red and at the same time so respectable in its narrowness, of this respectable rusty moustache he thought a lot. Everything, really. And now it had undoubtedly been ruined and he didn't even take the mirror out of his pocket, to have a look at it. Instead he left his lips and lighter standing wide open and a new, white cigarette lying on the ground. Instead, he forgot lips, lighter, cigarette. Forgot suitcase, Canada, moustache and smell of burning. Forgot and opened his mouth. And looked fixedly at a large

56

enamel sign with a lot of unintelligible black-lettered words on it. Looked fixedly at the one word with the nine black-lacquered letters. For this word, these nine letters, this nine-lettered black-lacquered word, was his name. He closed his eyes tight and suddenly tore them wide open again. His name was still there. Nine black letters, lacquer-bright, on a big white enamel sign with a lot of other unintelligible black-lettered words. He looked at the sign. My name, he thought. Quite clearly, quite obviously. And in enamel and lacquer. Crazy, he thought, crazy. In enamel and lacquer. Silly! Mad! Idiotic! He was in Hamburg for the first time in his twenty-six years of life. For the first time he was in this station, in this station hall, under these blind station lamps, on these damp station flagstones. And there was standing, right here, where he'd come for the first time, his name. In enamel and lacquer. Yes, suddenly his name was written there. That's to say, not suddenly, for it must surely have been standing there some time. Only for him, very suddenly. For him, very suddenly, in black and on white, in enamel and lacquer. Black-lettered it was standing there on a white sign, the name that was his name, quite simply: Billbrook. Standing there. Written there as large as life. And after all it was his own name. In the middle of a foreign country, lacquered and enamelled: Billbrook. One could see it well and read it quite clearly.

When he went to nibble a fresh cigarette out of the packet with his teeth, he saw that his hand was shaking. He grinned. Yes, he was grinning now. He had just had a fright.

When he reached his hotel room he was still excited. After he had greeted his two room mates with a loud "hallo" and got to know them, he immediately told them about his adventure. He called it an adventure. He had experienced it so vividly that for him it was an adventure. He told them his name, extra slowly and extra clearly, and then they had to "listen very carefully". This name that was his name, his name, which he had brought with him from America, from Canada, from Chester, this, his own name stood big and very easy to read in enamel at the station. At the station here in Hamburg. And then several times he swore to his two listeners that on no account could it be a case of a memorial tablet. No, no. Not that. He had never yet rhymed two lines together, nor had he invented a cure for corns or a cheap kind of oil. Nor had he won a boxing championship. Nor was there a warrant out for his arrest, really there wasn't. And he was in Hamburg this evening for the first time. Really, the first time.

When he had got so far with his excited explanation, his two comrades burst out laughing. Mightily they roared. Spitefully, maliciously, tinnily the small dark one at the window laughed. And vitally, vulgarly, humorously the dunghill-blond athlete roared and beat on the table with his fists. And between roaring and nudging they informed him that Billbrook was a part of the city, a part of the city of Hamburg. Yes, indeed: a part of Hamburg was called Billbrook. After all they had already been in Hamburg a year. And as such age-old Hamburgers, who now almost belonged to the original native clan, they must, in the end, know that. And Bill Brook, the sergeant-pilot from Chester, had to believe them. He had to believe them, believe them in spite of their laughter, because they now shoved a map of the city across the table and under his nose, on which with thick, coarse strokes of a blue pencil they encircled and marked with a cross that part of the city called Billbrook. Yes, and when he saw it and understood, he was almost a little proud. Without justification, of course. But he didn't think of that. He allowed himself a tiny secret pride in his name. And he could hardly blame himself for that. After all, it wasn't every day of the week that one sailed the wide waters from Chester to find one's name here in Hamburg magnificent and shiny-black on white enamel. Yes, he allowed himself just a little pride in the fact and a generous good temper. It came quite unexpectedly, when he realized that in his pride he had completely forgotten his fright. He saw himself standing in the kitchen in Chester mussing his mother's hair for sheer joy and laughter. He would hear laughter all over the house in Chester and right down to the harbour in Chester, when he told them this story about the part of the city called Billbrook. What laughter and fun and astonishment. He'd hit his cows in the ribs with his fist and challenge them to be a little prouder. Oh, he'd do that all right. And because of it, because he would do that, it was a long time on this night before he fell asleep.

His pride and his good humour lasted till the next day. In the morning the sergeant marvelled at it all. Then in the afternoon he secretly tried to put the map of the city in his pocket. But the one with the tinny laugh caught him at it. And, like a tin can in the wind, he jangled: "You're going to have a little outing, eh? Bill Brook has a picnic in Billbrook. Go on, pal, perhaps they'll give you the freedom of the borough. Or don't you want to go? Not to your own borough, eh? You'll see they'll make you mayor. Mr. Bill Brook of Billbrook. Enjoy yourself, pal, seriously, enjoy yourself!" His malicious tin-can laugh clattered so outrageously loud through the room that the flat droning laughter of his blond comrade gurgled shyly away into nothing. Bill Brook grinned at them both. With his second finger he stroked his narrow rusty moustache, then wiped the tears of laughter from his short, bristling eyebrows and said: "Well, see you this evening. Going to take a little walk in my borough. See you later." Then, with his great good humour and his pride, he stepped through the door.

For a moment he enjoyed the lake, which lay in the middle of this crazy city, where there were boroughs with the same names as those of respectable people from Chester in Canada. Which had the same name as he had. It was certainly some city, with so fine a lake in the middle of its stomach, that could manage a thing like that. He sniffed. Oh, it smelt of water. Salt water, he tasted. Terrific, this city, he thought and turned round. He looked towards the cloudy sun, the grey Hamburg sun. Then he set off. That's my direction, he said, east-south-east. And his step was firm and free.

The afternoon was warm and golden grey. Grey Hamburg clouds were hanging in the sky. With the golden grey sun at his back and in great good humour Bill Brook marched towards the south-east. After an hour he took the map out of his pocket. He compared the distance he'd already covered with that which lay before him. He would have to walk for another two hours. He'd made a mistake. One didn't get along as fast as one wished in a strange city. The map disappeared into his pocket and he looked again towards the south-east. He breathed the friendly golden grey of a summer's day in Hamburg.

But then he noticed that his pride was spinning like a shot-down aeroplane. Nothing sudden. Slowly spinning down. In great curves. And his wonderful mood began to crumble away like a dried-up cake. He blinked back into the sun. It was as golden grey as before. He considered. I'm tired, he thought. He took a cigarette. Of course, he thought, I'm tired. That's all. And besides I'm not used to walking so far. When was the last time I walked for an hour? At home perhaps. Yes, possibly at home. A few years ago. With the toe of his shoe he kicked the rest of his cigarette across the pavement like a little glowing football.

But it wasn't because he was tired. No, it wasn't that. It was this: Until a while ago he had been coming through streets in which people were living. Now and then the corner of a house had been lacking, a block had collapsed or been burnt out, a garden ploughed up, a balcony displaced, a roof uncovered. But the streets in that part of the city still looked like streets, a bit damaged, a little wobbly and clattery, but they were streets in which, to right and left, lived people. Dogs barked in the streets between the trees. Children screamed in the doorways and stair-wells, in the forecourts and backyards, children, cheering and sobbing. Women beat carpets in the streets, shouted from the windows, drivers cursed and dustbins stank in those streets. Girls giggled and boys whistled in those streets, through which Bill Brook, the Canadian sergeant-pilot from Chester on the Atlantic Ocean, had already come. To left and right in those streets lived people, girls sang as they cleaned the windows, canaries trilled long rolling trills, bicycle bells and milk bottles jingled in those streets, cars braked, coughed, hooted and in one house somebody hacked at Mozart on the piano, and even in the street one heard a sharp old woman's voice counting and beating time with some hard object. Till now people had been living in the streets to left and right and the streets had still been proper streets. Proper streets, just as there were in Chester, too. Or in Ottawa. Or in Quebec. But for half an hour it had been getting quieter and quieter. Fewer and fewer people lived in the houses to left and right and fewer and fewer houses were standing to left and right of the street. Children, dogs and cars grew rarer, ever rarer. Only the hacked-up Mozart still drifted in scorn ᵗhrough the sudden stillness. Life grew ever smaller, rarer, quieter.

Then it disappeared altogether, returned, scarcely hinted at, for a few hundred yards, then disappeared for twice as long, for a step or two, trickled a few houses beside the street again, rarer, fewer. Quieter, ever quieter. Life grew quieter ever quieter.

He was standing at a big cross-roads. He looked back: No child? No dog? No car? He looked to the left: No child. No dog. No car. He looked to the right and in front: no child and no dog and no car. He looked along the four endless roadways: No house. No house? Not even a cottage. Not even a hut. Not even an isolated, still standing, trembling, tottering wall. Only the chimneys, like the fingers of corpses, stabbed the late afternoon sky. Like the bones of a giant skeleton. Like tombstones. The fingers of corpses, clutching at God, threatening heaven. The bare, bony, burnt, bent fingers of corpses. In whichever direction he looked, and he had the feeling that from the cross-roads he could see for miles in each direction: No living thing. Nothing. Nothing living. Bits of stone by the billion, scraps of stone by the billion, crumbs of stone by the billion. City thoughtlessly crumbled by merciless war. Billions of crumbs and a few hundred corpses' fingers. But otherwise, not a house, not a woman, not a tree. Only deadness. Destroyed, decayed, disintegrated, crooked and crumbled. Only deadness. Deadness. Miles wide, miles long, deadness. He stood in a dead city and it tasted stale and sickly on his tongue. He was proud no longer. His wonderful mood had been left behind, oh far behind, with the last children, the last dog and the last cars. Even the air here has died, he thought. He felt the corpses' fingers clamping his breast. It was so quiet and he did not dare to breathe.

He took his map, held it firmly in his hand, and it was as though he were holding on to it for safety. He looked at the sun, already lying quite low and dusty gold in the haze of the distant city. He saw the towers of the churches, quite thin. They're not true, they're an illusion, he thought. So near were the corpses' fingers, so close they stood around him. Only the corpses' fingers are true, and the crumbs. They are no illusion.

He decided to walk twice as fast for the hour he still had to go. He walked in the middle of the street. That's to say, he now had to walk in the middle of the street, for the houses, collapsed, torn apart, had often fallen far forward, leaving of the broad street only a little track, narrow and irregular as a rabbit run, for a footpath. He looked stubbornly before him at the ground. But he did not recover his lost, premature pride, nor his high-spirited humour. Lost, crumbled, dead.

Suddenly he saw that there actually was something living in this dead, houseless, noiseless, corpse-fingered city: grass. Green grass. Grass as in Chester. Ordinary grass. Billion-bladed. Insignificant. Poor. But green. But alive. Alive like the hair of the dead. Uncannily alive. Grass, as everywhere in the world. Sometimes a bit greying, fraying, crumbled over, dusty. But still green and living. Living grass everywhere. He grinned. But the grin froze, because his brain thought of a word, a single word. The grin became grey and dusty as, in some places, the grass. But icily dew-sodden. Graveyard-grass, thought his brain. Grass? Sure. Grass, yes. But graveyard-grass. Grass on graves. Ruin-grass. Gruesome, ghostly, gracious, grey grass. Graveyard-grass, unforgettable, everlasting grass on graves, full of the past, sated with memory. Unforgettable, shabby, sickly: Unforgettable gigantic grass carpet over the graves of the world.

Grass. But apart from that he met no one. Or rather, he did. A lamp-post met him, a telephone kiosk and an advertisement pillar. These he met. And the sorrowful, crooked, bent lamp-post came up to him and tittered, tear-choked: I can't light any more. I'm kaputt. I'm liquidated. Ruined. Utterly ruined. I don't light any more. I don't shine any more. My life's lost its point: I don't light any more.

And at a corner a sorrowful telephone kiosk awaited him full of holes as a sieve, and whispered, tear-choked: They've torn out my entrails and pinched my brain. And my beautiful new red book with all the numbers and names. All finished. Now not a beggar telephones in me any more. Only this common grass makes itself at home in me. And then a crooked gossipy advertisement pillar waved to him and whispered in a thick stupid voice, tear-choked: It's scandalous, isn't it? One hasn't a single poster. Eh? No appeals, no cinema advertisements, no bye-laws. Not a poster. Nix. Scandalous, isn't it? Not to mention standing here all heeling over and naked. By the way, it all comes from the bombs, you know, this heeling over. And the other, too. All from the bombs. Those bombs really had a terrific effect. Disgustingly, fantastically terrific.

And all of them, lamp-post, telephone kiosk and advertisement pillar, all were equally sorrowful and choked with their own tears. And Bill Brook, Canadian, pilot, farmer from Nova Scotia, too: sorrowful. And he felt as they: crooked, full of holes, heeling over. And he made his steps a few inches longer. Behind him the sun was growing tired and only half of it still looked out across the silhouette of the city. Bill Brook, the sergeant, who had set off so proudly and so good-humouredly, was now taking giant strides. And they drifted away without echo in the flat, dead, comfortless city, which was no longer a city, now only a waste, plain, desert, field of stone: a graveyard without peace, with several hundred chimneys, still standing, astonished, as bony, gloomy, threatening corpses' fingers.

He felt uneasy, Bill Brook, and he was glad when he was standing on a slightly cracked, parapet-less bridge before a bright little green-silver mud-black canal. He gladly forgot the wasteland, encircling him with a circle miles wide. All at once he was quite happy and he almost clapped his hands as though at a birthday party, this twenty-six year old man, when he saw on the canal bank a few tiny colourful living gardens, clothes-lines and pennants of smoke. Boy, oh boy! he ground between his broad white teeth. For children were shouting there, a woman was singing, a few men were cursing as they played cards, a watering-can was hissing, a dachshund was coughing. Boy, oh boy, and the pants, the stockings, the bright blue, pale pink brassieres on the clothes-line wagged and waved and beckoned excitedly: Hey, sergeant, don't worry, come nearer. You can safely come over. Really, sergeant, don't be embarrassed. Just come.

And, in relief, Bill Brook, the man from Nova Scotia, beat with both fists on the bit of parapet, which by an oversight had been left standing. And he thought happily: Just look! These sweet little wooden huts! Like dainty little palaces! And out of the windows and roofs come these wonderful, cute, twisted bent stove-pipes. And out of these splendid pitch-black snouts of stove-pipes comes such fine blue dancing curling smoke. Wood smoke, cardboard smoke, the smoke of stolen planks and fences. Real living life-giving innocent sky-blue curly smoke! One moment, you bold old smoke, a moment, you old, coughing dachshund, a moment you beautiful brassieres, one moment: I'm coming! I'm just coming down to you now, if that's all right by you.

The Canadian let go of the parapet, crossed over a low wall of rubble and slid down the slope to a little yellow sand path. This little yellow sand path twisted toward the few cottages and two women were standing there wiping their hands on their aprons and looking greedily at the stranger, greedy for news, greedy for people, greedy for diversion. And then a watering-can stopped right in the midst of its hissing, and a girl expectantly licked the tip of her nose with her tongue. But the two women, the watering-can and the girl were disappointed. The stranger, this novelty, this event, did not come quite so far. They craned their necks, women, watering-can and girl, but he came no nearer.

The stranger stopped before that. He stopped, because in front of him, beside the little yellow sand path on the quay wall, two men and a cat were sitting and fishing. The men were fishing with sticks and string and worms. The cat with its eyes. And there the stranger stopped. And the women and the watering-can and girl started their work again, when they saw it.

The two men sat on the quay wall and let three legs hang over the water. Three legs? Three legs. One was old and grey and worn out and sly and cheerful. The other was quite young, just started, ruined, plucked to pieces, destroyed and quite young. And he only had one leg, which he could hang over the quay wall. And then there was the cat, too, and she acted all disinterested and turned-away-from-the-world. But Bill Brook saw that she had a thoroughly fish-greedy face. The cats in Chester made faces like that, too, exactly the same. Bill Brook laughed and then he greeted the two men (and the cat, actually, as well), as he stopped beside them. They looked up. And they looked at him, as though he and his greeting were ten miles away. Then the elder one nodded, and one could see that once, formerly, he could certainly have been cheerful. He nodded. The young man, who had only kept the one leg for hanging down, he didn't nod. But he looked at him again and put him another hundred miles further away. With this one look he put him back in Canada and in this Canada there was no sun, no love, no understanding. He put him in a land without watering-cans, without dogs, without girls' glances. And he left him standing there and wasted his eyes on him no longer. He continued carefully crumbling a few butt ends into a piece of paper, which he had spread out on his stump and smoothed with the ball of his thumb. The Canadian felt the hundred miles and he felt the banishment into a land without understanding, and in order not to stay so far away, he sat down on the wall beside the old man. Now there were five legs hanging over the water. He took his packet of cigarettes and gave it to the old man. He made it clear to him that he should keep it and share it with the young one. The old man suddenly looked at him from very close and said: Thank you. And said it like: There you are, you're a fine chap. Knew it at once. Even without cigarettes. And with that he gave the young man beside him the rest of the packet. He, however, slowly and with almost exaggerated deliberation, took the cigarettes out of the wrapper and with two fingers flicked them, as though unconcerned and bored, into the water. Far out into the canal water. One by one. Sensually he did it. One by one with his fingertips he flicked eight cigarettes far out into the green-black canal, and the cat watched them excitedly.

Bill Brook rumpled his forehead. Then he thought of the one leg hanging from the quay wall.

The old man pulled his snowy eyebrow-bushes up to the start of his hair and growled at the young man: "Angry, eh? You can't read faces." The young man licked a cigarette together, spat a shred of tobacco into the canal and said, without moving his mouth: "I'd sooner have a light."

Then they all three looked at the black-green silver mud. Bill Brook froze in the land without sun and without watering-can and he took his map and held tight to it. He asked the old man if this was the way to Billbrook. The borough of Billbrook, he repeated importantly. And as though there might be something else for the fishermen with the three legs that could be called Bill Brook. The old man nodded, raised six times his short fingers covered with black earth from searching for worms and then said: "Minutes." Again he showed sixty short black fingers: sixty minutes. Bill Brook looked for the golden-grey sun, and as he saw that it was no longer there, he thought: Now it's too late to go to Billbrook, to the borough of Billbrook, to my borough. Otherwise it'll be midnight before I get home. And he was almost glad that he had to turn back. He thought of the poor crooked lamp-post, of the sorrowful telephone kiosk and he thought of the unhappy advertisement pillar. He stood up. The old man looked up at his long blue-uniformed legs. He licked his thumb and first finger clean, cautiously, took the blue material between them, rubbed it respectfully and on his lower lip pushed out his expert opinion. "Good, good," he said. Bill Brook looked down at himself. He was slightly ashamed. "Good, yes, good," he said then, at last. Then he pointed in all four directions and asked: " Everything kaputt?" The old man answered. He did it quite quietly, "Everything," he nodded. "Three hours to the left. Three hours to the right. Forwards and backwards, too: Everything." And he said: "Barmbeck, Eilbeck and Wandsbek" and "Hamm and Horn," he said. And "Hasselbrook." And "St. George and Borgfelde." He said "Rothenburgsort and Billwarder." And "Hamburg" and said "Harbour" and again "Hamburg." And he said it in such a way that Bill Brook thought he'd said Canada and Chester. "Harbour" he said, and "Hamburg"! And then he wanted to raise his short earthy fingers again and count out figures to the stranger—but then he dismissed it all with both arms and only said: "Ach! In two nights. In two nights everything kaputt. Everything." And his arm made a circle in which there was room for a world.

Bill Brook raised two fingers: "Two nights? No! Two? Two nights?" He laughed loud and frightened. He laughed, and it was like little screams, loud and frightened. The whole great mighty city—in two nights? He didn't know what he should do, other than laugh. He thought of Chester and he thought: Two nights. Chester would be like a lie. In two nights Chester would no longer be true. An illusion. Blotted out. He thought that perhaps there were ten thousand people left lying under the flattened city. He laughed: Ten thousand dead. Squashed, flat and dead. Ten thousand in two nights. A whole city! In two nights. Squashed, flat, dead.

The Canadian could not stop laughing. He laughed and laughed. But it was not for joy that he laughed nor for pleasure.

He laughed. Laughed in disbelief, in surprise, in amazement, in doubt. He laughed because he could not conceive it. He laughed because it seemed to him impossible. Laughed, because it was monstrous. Laughed, because it froze him, because he was numbed by it, because it horrified him. It horrified him and he laughed. The Canadian stood in his clean blue uniform in an immeasurable, unforgettable wasteland of stones and death and laughed. Stood with his smooth clean face in the evening by the canal beside two fishermen, and they had dusty wrinkled faces and only had three legs. The Canadian stood thus by the canal in the evening and laughed. Then the one-legged man let one word fall from his motionless mouth on to the green-black mud. And the word cracked like a smack in the face. And as he said it he looked at the laughing soldier, so that the laughter stuck in his throat like a scream for help.

But the old man had felt that the stranger could do nothing other than laugh. And he had felt that it was a laugh of horror. That it was full of horror, horrible. Horrible not only for the two of them, horrible for the laugher, too. And the old one said to the one-legged man: "You can't read faces, I just told you." The young man shivered. And once more the old man said: "You can't read faces, I tell you. That's all."

Bill Brook did not understand what the two men were saying. But he felt the hatred in the eyes of the one-legged man. And he saw that the eyes of the old man begged him to go. He stroked the cat's fur tenderly with his foot. "Yes," he said, "good night." " 'Night," hurried the old man, " 'night." Bill Brook turned and went, and he thought: It's a good thing I'm going.

When he was on the street again, a few red stains in the sky disturbed him. They still came from the sun. Bloodstains, he thought, and made long energetic strides towards the blood-drenched sun. Regular rusty bloodstains—unpleasant, he thought. But then suddenly came the night wind. And it came towards him cool and kind, and was full of tenderness as it blew softly hither from the city. Tender it was and soft, kind and comforting, it breathed in the man's face. Cool and comradely like an old acquaintance from Canada. Wind. Wind of Hamburg. Wind of Chester. Night wind. World wind. Cool, soft and out of the city. Night wind of the world. The Canadian opened his shirt wide. Wind, night wind, lamenting, wind of the levelled city, of the flat city, wind of the dead city. Breath, night breath of ten thousand flat-pressed sleepers. The Canadian walked quickly, quickly and he sang loudly to himself. And meanwhile it had grown so dark that every few steps he stubbed his foot against bricks, charred beams and crumbled masonry. But he didn't swear. Not once. He sang loud into the darkness. He sang loud and he sang lustily. He sang perhaps because he didn't want to curse when he stubbed his toe. He sang perhaps because he didn't want to think of the dead. Of the ten thousand laid flat, with their night breath, the soft sorrowing wind. Or because it was so dark. Yes, perhaps that was why he sang so loud, because it was so dark. And he walked quickly and sang. Before him, in its darkly shining haze, lay the city. This crazy city, of which part was called Billbrook. Which had a grey-green lake with white sails in its middle. And just as an example, ten thousand dead in their own dead city. Crazy city, he thought. Crazy, living, dead city. And he walked quickly and singing and was happy that it lay there before him, visible, audible, smellable, in the darkly shining haze of its night life, dark and full of promise, with the lake in its middle. And he walked quickly and singing loud into the darkness in front of him. And beside him walked his shadow. When he saw his shadow beside him, he thought: My God, is he by any chance *running*? And then he compelled himself to walk ten steps quite slowly, and he didn't sing. And when he wanted to look for a star from Chester and stopped and looked up at the ink-coloured sky, he heard a shout, otherworldly, unreal, inescapable, ghostly. And the shout was: "Hey, Mr. Bill Brook, won't you just look this way a minute? Just read my latest poster?" And what was shouting there, bass-voiced, droning, was the leaning advertisement pillar, which in its eagerness to serve bowed still nearer the ground. It was bald and naked and spectral and shimmered bright grey and pale-bellied through the dirt-stained velvet of the early night. And the Canadian walked quickly. "Yoo-hoo! Bill Brook! What about a little phone call? Little trunk call to Canada at your service? Eh? Something like: Seen dead city! Smelt ten thousand corpses! And seen crumbs, crumbs of a city, crumbs of the world. But don't run away, Bill Brook, hi there, yoo-hoo!" The fat dark red glassless skeleton of a telephone kiosk flapped its door hysterically and its torn wires dangled in the wind like serpents. The Canadian walked quickly. And he sang. And then he saw that it looked as though his shadow was running. He intended to walk slowly. But he walked quickly, the Canadian. Then the crazed, crooked, bent, blinded lamp-post stumbled tittering towards him and stuttered excitedly: "Hop-la. Hallo, Billy, boy! Shall I light your way? Light your way home? I'm a wonderful light, my friend. But, Billy, stay here, Billy!" The Canadian walked quickly. And he sang loud. He had his shirt wide open. He saw Hamburg before him and thought: Chester. And he walked quickly. He took giant steps and his shadow ran behind. It looked as though he was running. The night wind came cool and Bill Brook walked towards it with naked breast and burning forehead. And the dark was a mouth that spat. And suddenly spat out two yellow glimmering gliding eyes. And the eyes came towards him. And the eyes grew bigger. And were yellow and glowed at him malignantly. That must be a car, he said to himself. Of course, what else? And then if it isn't a car? But certainly it's a car. Just as he thought perhaps it isn't a car, the two yellow glimmering eyes unexpectedly stood still. He heard squeaking. That must be the brakes. Then the monster was blinded and the eyes put out. The Canadian came up to it. It was a car. Goddam, he said then and laughed. And he found that he didn't really need to walk so fast at all. He walked more slowly. He noticed that he was quite wet. I've been running so. Much too quickly. Like a madman. I think this dead city with its ten thousand flattened inhabitants was too much for me. I think I was frightened. Perhaps I was frightened. Of course: frightened. He confessed to himself he'd been frightened. Not very, but—frightened. And why shouldn't I be frightened? It's a good thing if you can be frightened. Sometimes it's a good thing. Those who aren't frightened become boxers, and their noses and souls are shapeless and flattened and hideous. And they daren't be frightened. Poor boxers. All the worse for them if ten thousand corpses don't frighten them. There are lots of boxers like that.

All right then, I was afraid of the flat-headed, flat-chested ten thousand. But now houses are coming towards me. With bright, warm windows and round-headed, living people. Bill

Brook stopped and breathed deeply and thirstily, as though for hours he'd been holding his breath. And the night wind, that had breathed on him as the breath of the dead, grew warm and familiar as the breath of a great, grey beast. And the beast that breathed it out was called Hamburg. And its breath smelt of potted flowers, freshly watered gardens, supper, open windows, people. Smelt living and warm like cows' breath, like horses' breath at night in the stables.

There was even a dog sitting at the corner of a house, dachshund in front, terrier behind, brushing the hard flagstones with his tail, enthusiastically from left to right. When the Canadian reached the corner, he saw the reason for the enthusiasm of the dog's tail. The reason was a thirteen-year-old girl playing with a ball. She threw it round behind her at the wall and caught it again on her breast, when it bounced back from the wall. In the dark of evening the dog perhaps took the ball for some exciting, mysterious animal. And the ball sprang lightly and sharpsounding to and fro between the wall and the breast of the thirteen-year-old girl. And the dog's tail accompanied: wall—breast. Wall—breast. Wall—breast.

Sweet, thought the man, who came from the dead city. Sweet. But in five years' time she won't do that any more. Because of her breast. By then she'll be eighteen, perhaps. Or twenty.

He laughed loud at his thoughts. Then he walked on. And walked with long confident stride into the living city.

When an hour later Bill Brook was standing in the bath at his hotel, letting the icy water ripple down his back, the little dark man came from next door with his tin-can laugh, spread his arms against the doorway and shouted tin-throated: "Well old boy, are you so filthy, you old dung-beetle, that you have to get straight under the shower? Had a nasty little affair, eh, old boy? Or did they throw dirt at you in your own borough, eh?" He bent double with laughter, as though bad schnaps burned in his stomach. Bill Brook threw the soap at him and grinned: "No, just took a little trip into the dead city. Had a little boxing match with ten thousand corpses. And all with amputated legs. Just imagine, all of them one-legged."

The black-haired man with the tinny laugh made huge round

eyes and a stupid great open mouth. "Aha," then clattered out of his throat, "so that's it, you've been drinking!" And with that he vanished, reassured and yawning, into the next room. Shortly afterwards Bill Brook heard the snores of his two comrades, mighty and manly.

Then he sat down at the table, pulled the table-cloth off and laid it over the lamp, so that the two snorers shouldn't wake up. He took a piece of paper. And then he sat in front of the empty paper and looked at the lamp. He wanted to write about Bill-brook, the borough of Billbrook, about the telephone kiosk, the advertisement pillar, the lamp-post. He wanted to write about the two fishermen with the three legs, about the cigarettes in the water and about the grass, the great green grey grass of the great city. He wanted to write about the corpses' fingers, about the dead city and its ten thousand levelled flattened inhabitants. He wanted to write about the dead city and about the girl with the ball. That was what he wanted to write about. He wanted to write it to those at home, to those in Canada, to those in Labrador. But he wrote not a word of it. He wrote not a word about the dead city. He wrote only of Chester, of the wind in Chester, of the harbour in Chester and of the water in Chester. He looked at the lamp.

And then at the end of his letter he added a sentence: "I don't think it's so bad that the two cows are dead." He wrote that. And then added: "No, it's definitely not all that bad." He licked the envelope shut and said: "It's really not all that important about the two cows."

He stood up and turned the light out. Then he went to the window and looked out into the night. Over there the stars twinkled in the Alster. And the Alster lay there black, in its middle. And suddenly the window clattered. Outside a column of fat heavy lorries drove past, their great yellow eyes twinkling through the night mist. Their motors snorted like a herd of raging elephants. The windows rattled in secret agitation.

"Lovely. Lovely!" whispered the Canadian and pressed his hot forehead against the cold glass.

"Lovely that everything's so alive here. Here. And in Chester." And he went quietly back into the room. In secret agitation the windows rattled.

THE ELBE

View from Blankenese

To the left lies Hamburg. Where all the haze is. And it comes from all the noise, from the people and the work that are there, in Hamburg.

Over there lies Finkenwerder. But Finkenwerder is small, for it lies right over there, and the river lies between. And over there, that's pretty far.

To the right there are a few more houses and occasionally a road or a ditch. And then soon after comes the North Sea. And a lot of haze. From all the water that's there.

That's how it is to the left, over there, to the right. Hamburg and Finkenwerder and the North Sea. And behind?

Behind lie a few fields and a few woods. In the fields and the woods there are cows, cowpats, mist and night. Rabbits, sun, heather and mushrooms. Now and then there are thatched roofs among them, dunghills, foxholes, rain-puddles and crooked lanes. But otherwise not much. And soon afterwards, too, comes Denmark.

Above is the sky and the stars lie in it.

Below lies the Elbe. And the stars lie there too.

The same stars that lie in the sky lie in the Elbe, too. Perhaps after all we're not so far away from heaven. We in Blankenese. We in Barmbeck, in Bremen, in Bristol, Boston and Brooklyn. And we here in Blankenese. But of course the stars floating down here in the Elbe must be seen in the Dnieper, in the Seine, in the Hwangho and in the Mississippi.

And the Elbe? It stinks. Stinks, just as the washing-up water of a great city should stink: of potato peel, soap, flower-water, swedes, chamber pots, chlorine, beer and of fish and of rats' dirt. That's what it stinks of, the Elbe. As only the slops of a few million people can stink. And how it stinks. And not a single stench that exists in the world is left out of it.

But those who love it, who are far away and yearning, they say: It smells. It smells of life. Of home here on this lost globe. Of Germany. Ah, and it smells of Hamburg and the whole great world. And they say: Elbe. They say it softly and sadly and sensually, as one says the name of a girl. Like this: Elbe!

There used to be gigantic ships. Steamers, boxes, palaces, risking an exuberant tearless farewell. Which lay in the river at evening like vast blocks of flats, like boldly constructed, narrow-cut, inspired, gigantic apartment houses, and pressed sluggishly, world-weary, sea-sated against the nightly excitement of the quays. These used to be, these Cyclopean floating ant-hills, lit by a million glow-worms, glimmering cheerfully, generously and securely, green or red and glowing hectically white. With the bluster of brass bands they could risk a turbulent, tearless, terrific arrival. Arrival and departure: to the brave brass bands. That's how it used to be. Yesterday.

Whether they sailed away to the wide waters of the world full of longing and power and courage—or whether they came home from the lakes between continents full of the breath of the world and the wares of the world and wisdom: they always lay full of courage in the Elbe river. Titans behind the coughing tugs, towering, shimmering out of the smother of launches, fortresses, inviolate, mountainous, haughty.

An abundance of courage always sparkled from the thousand window-mouthed port-holes. An excess of gladness always quivered from the brass mouths of their bands. It was always an exuberance of strength that screamed and steamed, panted and ranted from the proud mouths of their funnels. Strength, that hissed airy-white from the carp-mouthed sirens. Laughing, lusty, living Elbe!

So it was. Once. Yesterday.

But occasionally there are times, and they lie, greyer than the grey haze of Hamburg, across the age-old, ever-young Elbe, when courage and gladness and strength have stayed at sea, when they are lost on strange, cold, deserted coasts. Then they are overdue, gladness, and courage, and strength.

Those are the mist-grey, the fog-grey, the world-grey times,

in which it can happen that small, white washed-up human
wrecks are thrown on the dirty, yellow-grey sand at Blankenese
or Teufelsbrücke. Then again it happens that distended, fishy-
smelling, inhuman dead bodies rustle and whisper against the
reeds at Finkenwerder or Moorburg. Then it happens that on
these grey days the loving, the unloved, the desperate, the tired,
the sad unto death, the suicidal, whom the courage for life has
deserted—the joyless and friendless, the powerless, to whom the
River Elbe was the only remaining friend, whose only remaining
power was to die—that these (and in the grey nights then it
happens), that these, tipsy with Elbe water, that these, who have
drunk themselves to death in the waters of the Elbe, bump
heavily, threatening, thudding, against the pontoons at Altona
and the landing stages. Rhythmically they thud against them,
monotonous, regular as breath. The wash of Elbe waves, the
breath of the river, is now their rhythm—the water of the Elbe
is now their blood. And then in the grey nights the cold, chalky
human corpses slap lamenting against the quay walls of Köhlbrand
and Athabaskahöft. And their only brass bands are the brassy
screams of gulls, whirring, lewd and full of greed, over the
human fish. That's how it is in the grey times.

Sea-hungry giants' boxes, ocean-crazed apartment houses,
wind-weathered palaces, all departure and arrival to the blustering
music of fat-bellied brass bands—

Dropsical human wrecks, death-yearning living creatures,
wave-knowing, wave-loving water corpses, all farewell and
finality to the lonely brass scream of the narrow-winged sea-gulls:

Happy, heartbreaking Elbe! Happy heartbroken humanity!

But then come the inextinguishable, ineffaceable, unforgettable
hours, when at evening young people, brimful of desire for
adventure, stand on the mysterious wooden crates that have the
mysterious name "pontoon", a name that betrays all the magical
lapping and slapping, the rise and fall of the breath of the river.
Filled with courage for the adventure of life, ever and again we
shall stand on the pontoons and feel the world breathing under
our feet.

Above us blinks the Great Bear—before us blubbers the river.
We stand in between: In the laughing light, in the grey night
mist. And we are filled with hunger and hope. We are filled with
hunger for love and hope for life. And we are filled with hunger

for food and with hope for friendship. And we are filled with hunger for travel and with hope for homecoming.

Ever and again in the grey times we shall stand on the ripe-smelling, sleep-swaying, life-breathing pontoons with our burning hunger and blessed hope.

And in the grey times, the times without the floating palaces, we wish ourselves full of courage, in the little motor boats, in the fishing-boats, in the tramp steamers, we wish ourselves hard liquor in the belly and soft warm wool round the breast and an adventure in the heart. We wish ourselves full of courage for departure, full of courage for farewell, full of courage for the storm and the sea.

And we wish ourselves (in these grey times, when there are no giants' boxes) muscle-tired on the little homecoming fishing cutter, sailing into the Elbe with asthmatic puttering in its body, in order once to be so filled with homecoming, full of cargo and experience. For once to have the city of homesickness the city of homecoming in one's blood—to shout, to sob, splendidly, achingly, Hamburg—for once to be filled with coming home. And we wish ourselves beaten and wind-tired on the little fishing cutters, gossiping, swabbing, cursing or silent—wish ourselves the joy, the inconceivable weeping joy of once being a home-comer to a harbour town.

And when at evening we are standing on the swaying pontoons—in the grey days—then we say: Elbe! And we mean: Life! We mean: You and I. We say, roar, sigh: Elbe—and mean: World! Elbe, we say, we, the hoping, hungry ones. We hear the chugging metallic hearts of the gallant abandoned poor faithful little cutters—but in secret we hear again the trombones of the mammoth boats, of the mighty, magnificent monsters. We see the shivering little cutters with one red and one green eye in the river at evening—but in secret we see again, we living, hoping, hungry ones, the port-holed, light-squandering, brass-banded colossi, the giants, the palaces.

We stand on the shaking pontoons at evening and feel the silence, we feel the graveyard and death—but deep in us we hear again the rumble, the thunder and thud of the wharves. Deep in us we feel life—and the silence on the river will burst open again, like an illusion, with the noise and the joy of loud life! That's what we feel—deep in us at evening on the whispering pontoons.

Elbe, city-stinking, quay-crashing, reed-rustling, sand-babbling, gull-capped grey-green great good Elbe!

To the left Hamburg, to the right the North Sea, in front Finkenwerder and not far behind, Denmark. Around us Blankenese. Above us the sky. Below us the Elbe. And we: In the middle of it!

THE MAN OUTSIDE

*A play which no theatre will produce
and no public will want to see*

Borchert wrote this play in a few days in the late autumn of 1946. It was first produced as a radio play by the allied-sponsored North-West German Radio on 13th February, 1947. The broadcast was repeated several times and rebroadcast by other German stations. The radio play was three times produced in English translation on the Third Programme of the B.B.C. in November–December 1948.

The stage version, in Wolfgang Liebeneiner's production, had its première at the Hamburger Kammerspiele on 21st November, 1947, one day after the author's death. Almost every German theatre of any significance has put the play into its repertoire. It appeared in Germany as a book in November 1947.

FOR HANS QUEST

The Characters are:

BECKMANN, one of the many
his WIFE, who forgot him
her BOY FRIEND, who loves her
a GIRL, whose husband came home on one leg
her HUSBAND, who dreamed of her for a thousand nights
a COLONEL, who is very jovial
his WIFE, who shivers in her warm living-room
the DAUGHTER, in the middle of supper
her smart HUSBAND
a CABARET PRODUCER, who would like to be brave, but then
    prefers to be cowardly after all
FRAU KRAMER, who is nothing more than Frau Kramer, and that
    is just what's so frightful
the OLD MAN, in whom no one believes any more
the UNDERTAKER with the hiccough
the OTHER ONE, who is no one at all,
the ELBE.

A man comes to Germany.

He's been away for a long time, this man. A very long time. Perhaps too long. And he returns quite different from what he was when he went away. Outwardly he is a near relation of those figures which stand in fields to scare birds—and sometimes in the evening, people too. Inwardly—the same. He has waited outside in the cold for a thousand days. And as entrance fee he's paid with his knee-cap. And after waiting outside in the cold for a thousand nights, he actually—finally—comes home.

A man comes to Germany.

And there he sees a quite fantastic film. He has to pinch his arm several times during the performance, for he doesn't know whether he's waking or sleeping. But then he sees to right and left of him other people all having the same experience. So he thinks that it must indeed be true. And when at the end he's standing in the street again with empty stomach and cold feet, he realizes that it was really a perfectly ordinary everyday film, a perfectly ordinary film. About a man who comes to Germany, one of the many. One of the many who comes home —and then don't come home, because there's no home there for them any more. And their home is outside the door. Their Germany is outside in the rain at night in the street.

That's their Germany.

PROLOGUE

(The wind moans. The Elbe laps against the pontoons. The undertaker. The silhouette of a man against the evening sky)

UNDERTAKER: *(Belches several times)* Hrıp! Hrrp! Like—hrrp! Like flies. Just like flies. Aha, there's one, there on the pontoon. Looks as though he had a uniform on. Yes, that's an old soldier's greatcoat. No hat—his hair's short as a brush. He's standing rather near the water. Almost too near the water, actually—hm, suspicious—people who stand near the water at night are either lovers or poets. Or he's one of the great grey number who don't feel like it any longer. Who throw in their hand and won't play any longer. He looks like one of those, that fellow. Standing dangerously near the water. And pretty much alone. Not a lover, for then there'd be two of them. Nor a poet—poets have long hair. But this fellow here on the pontoon's got a head like a brush. Interesting cove, this, very interesting.

(There's a dark, heavy splash. The silhouette has vanished)

Hrrp! There. He's gone. Jumped in. Standing too near the water. Got him down, no doubt. And now he's gone. Hrrp! A man dies. So what? Nothing. The wind goes on blowing. The Elbe still prattles. Tram bells still ring. Whores still lie soft and white in their windows. Herr Kramer turns on his side and goes on snoring. Hrrp! A man is dead. So what? Nothing. Only a few circles in the water prove that he was ever there. And even they've soon subsided. And when they've disappeared, then the man's forgotten, vanished, without trace, as though he'd never existed. And that's all.

Hullo. Here's someone crying. Strange—an old man standing there and crying. Good evening!

OLD MAN: *(Not complaining, but shattered)* Children! Children! My children!

UNDERTAKER: What are you crying for, old man?

OLD MAN: Because I can do nothing about it, because I can do nothing about it.

UNDERTAKER: Hrrp! Pardon! That's certainly hard lines, but that's no reason for breaking out like a deserted bride. Hrrp! Pardon!

OLD MAN: Oh, my children! They are all my children, don't you see?

UNDERTAKER: Oho, who are you then?

OLD MAN: The God no one believes in now.

UNDERTAKER: And why are you crying, eh? Hrrp! Pardon!

GOD: Because I can do nothing about it. They shoot themselves. They hang themselves. They drown themselves. They go on killing themselves—a hundred today, a hundred thousand tomorrow. And I, I can do nothing about it.

UNDERTAKER: Grim, grim, old man. Very grim. But as you say no one believes in you any more. That's what it is.

GOD: Very grim. The God no one believes in now. Very grim. And I can do nothing about it, my children, I can do nothing about it. Grim, grim!

UNDERTAKER: Hrrp! Pardon! Like flies! Hrrp! Damnation!

GOD: Why do you keep belching so disgustingly? It's frightful!

UNDERTAKER: Yes, yes, it's terrible! Just terrible! Occupational disease. I'm an undertaker.

GOD: What, Death? You're all right. You're the new God. They believe in you. They love you. They fear you. You can't be deposed. You can't be denied. No one can give you blasphemy. Yes, you're all right. You're the new God. No one can dodge *you*. You're the new God, Death, but you've grown fat. I remember you as quite different. Much thinner, drier, bonier, but you've grown fat and round and good tempered. Death used to look so starved.

DEATH: Why, yes, I've put on a bit of weight this century. Business has been good. One war after another. Like flies! Like flies the dead hang on the walls of the century. Like flies they lie stiff and dried up on the windowsill of the times.

GOD: But this belching? Why all this hideous belching?

DEATH: Gormandizing, gormandizing. That's all. You just can't keep from belching nowadays. Hrrp! Pardon!

GOD: Children! Children! And I can do nothing about it. Children! My children! (*Exit*)

DEATH: Ah, well, good night then, old man. Go to bed. Watch

out you don't fall in the water as well; there's one fellow only just gone in. Be very careful, old man. Dark, it's very dark. Hrrp! Go home, old man. You can do nothing about it, anyhow. Don't cry for the one who's just plopped in. The one with the soldier's greatcoat and the cropped hair. You'll cry yourself to pieces! The people who stand by the water at night, they're no longer lovers or poets. This fellow here, he's just one of those who can't and won't go on. Those who just can't go on, at night they step quietly into the water somewhere. Plop. All over. Forget him, old man, don't weep. You'll weep yourself to pieces. He was only one of those who can't go on—one of the great grey number— one—only.

THE DREAM

(*In the Elbe. Monotonous lapping of little waves*)

BECKMANN: Where am I? In God's name, where am I?

ELBE: With me.

BECKMANN: With you? And—who are you?

ELBE: Who should I be, you chicken, if you throw yourself into the water from St. Pauli landing-stage?

BECKMANN: The Elbe?

ELBE: Yes, that's who. The Elbe.

BECKMANN: (*Astonished*) The Elbe? You?

ELBE: Aha, that's opened your baby blue eyes for you, hasn't it? You thought no doubt I was a romantic young girl with a pale green complexion? The Ophelia type with water-lilies in her flowing hair, eh? You thought at the end you could spend eternity in my sweet-scented lilywhite arms, eh? Not a bit of it, my son, that's just where you're wrong. I'm neither romantic nor sweet-scented. A decent river stinks. Stinks! Of oil and fish. What do you want here?

BECKMANN: Sleep. Up above I can't stick it any longer. I'm through. I want to sleep—to be dead. Be dead for life. And to sleep—to sleep in peace at last. To sleep for ten thousand nights.

ELBE: You want to rat, you greenhorn, eh? You think you can't stick it any longer up above, is that it? You kid yourself you've been through enough, you little twit. How old are you, then, you dispirited beginner?

BECKMANN: Twenty-five. And now I want to sleep.

ELBE: Hark at that, now, twenty-five. And he wants to sleep away the rest of it. Twenty-five, and in the middle of the night he steps into the water because he can't cope any longer. What can't you cope with, you greybeard?

BECKMANN: Everything. There's nothing up above I can cope with now. I can't starve any more. I can't limp any more and stand by my bed and then limp out of the house again because the bed's occupied. My leg, my bed, my food—I can't cope with it any longer, d'you hear?

ELBE: No. You snotty-nosed little suicide. No, d'you hear? Do you really suppose that because your wife won't play with you any more, because you've a limp and your stomach rumbles, that entitles you to creep in here under my skirts? To jump into the water, just like that? Listen, if everyone who's hungry wanted to drown himself, then the good old earth would be as smooth as a bald man's pate, naked and shiny. No, no, my boy, we can't have that. You won't get past me with that sort of excuse. You'll land a raspberry. You want your little bottom smacked, my child! Even if you *were* six years a soldier. Everyone was. And they're all limping around somewhere. Find yourself another bed, if your own's occupied. I don't want your miserable little slice of life. You're small fry for me. Take an old woman's advice: live first. Take the kicks. Kick back. When you're fed up, right up to here, when you're trampled flat, when your heart comes crawling on all fours, then perhaps we can talk about it again. But no nonsense just yet, d'you understand? Now make yourself scarce, my pretty one. Your little handful of life is too damned small for me. Keep it. I don't want it, you day-old tenderfoot. Keep your mouth shut, my little manchild. I'm going to tell you something quite quietly, in your ear. Come here. I spit on your suicide! You suckling. Just you see what I'll do with you. (*Loud*) Hey, lads! Throw this baby on the sand here at Blankenese. He's just promised to have another go at it. But be gentle, he says he's got a bad leg, the louse, the greenhorn!

SCENE I

(*Evening at Blankenese. The wind and the water are heard. Beckmann. The Other One*)

BECKMANN: Who's that? In the middle of the night! Here by the water. Hallo! Who's there?

THE OTHER ONE: I am.

BECKMANN: Thank you. And who's I?

THE OTHER: I am the other one.

BECKMANN: The other one? What other one?

THE OTHER: The one from yesterday. The one from long ago.

The one from always. The one who says Yes. The one who answers.

BECKMANN: The one from long ago? From always? You are the other one from the school bench, from the ice rink? The one from the stairwell?

THE OTHER: The one from the snowstorm near Smolensk. And the one from the dug-out at Gorodok.

BECKMANN: And the one—the one from Stalingrad, that other one, are you that one too?

THE OTHER: That one too. And also the one from this evening. I'm the other one from tomorrow.

BECKMANN: Tomorrow. There is no tomorrow. Tomorrow's without you. Beat it. You've got no face.

THE OTHER: You won't get rid of me. I am the other one who's always there. Tomorrow. In the afternoons. In bed. At night.

BECKMANN: Beat it. I have no bed. I'm lying here in the dirt.

THE OTHER: I am also the one from the dirt. I am everywhere. You cannot escape me.

BECKMANN: You have no face. Go away.

THE OTHER: You cannot escape me. I have a thousand faces. I am the voice that everyone knows. I am the other one, who is always there. The other self, the answerer. Who laughs when you weep. Who drives you on when you're tired, the slave-driver, the secret, disturbing one. I am the optimist who sees good in evil and light in the deepest darkness. I am the one who believes, who laughs, who loves! I am the one who marches on, lame or not. Who says Yes, when you say No. I am the optimist. Who—

BECKMANN: Say Yes as much as you like. Go away. I don't want you. I say No. No. No. Go away. I say No. D'you hear?

THE OTHER: I hear. That's just why I'm staying. Who are you then, you pessimist?

BECKMANN: My name's Beckmann.

THE OTHER: I suppose you have no Christian name, pessimist?

BECKMANN. No. Not since yesterday. Since yesterday I've only been called Beckmann. Just Beckmann. As you call a table, table.

THE OTHER: Who calls you table?

BECKMANN: My wife. No, the woman who was my wife. You
see, I was away for three years. In Russia. And yesterday I
came home again. That was the misfortune. Three years is a
long time, you know. Beckmann, my wife called me. Simply
Beckmann. And after I'd been away for three years. Beckmann
she called me, as one calls a table, table. Beckmann. A piece
of furniture. Put it away, that Beckmann table. So you see;
that's why I've no longer a Christian name. You understand?

THE OTHER: And why are you lying here on the sand? In the
middle of the night? Here by the water?

BECKMANN: Because I can't get up. It so happens I brought a
gammy leg back with me. By way of a souvenir. Just as well
to have a souvenir, you know, or you forget the war too
quickly. And I didn't want that at any price. It was all far
too beautiful for that. Boy, oh boy, was it beautiful!

THE OTHER: And that's why you're lying here at night by the
waterside?

BECKMANN: I fell.

THE OTHER: Oh! You fell. Into the water?

BECKMANN: No, no! No! Listen, I let myself fall in. On purpose.
I couldn't bear it any longer. This limping and lumping it.
And then that business with the woman who used to be my
wife—just called me Beckmann, as you call a table, table.
And the other fellow who was with her, he grinned. And
then these ruins. This rubbish heap here at home, here in
Hamburg. And somewhere underneath lies my boy. A bit of
mud and mortar and sludge. Human mud, bone mortar.
He was just one year old and I'd never seen him. But now I
see him every night. Under ten thousand stones. Rubble,
nothing but a bit of rubble. I couldn't bear it, I decided. And
so I let myself fall. It'd be quite easy, I thought: Off the
pontoon, plop! Done for! Finished!

THE OTHER: Plop? Done for? Finished? You've been dreaming.
Here you are lying in the sand.

BECKMANN: Dreaming? Yes. Hunger-dreaming. I dreamed that
she spat me out again, the Elbe, the old . . . She didn't want
me. I ought to have another go, she said. I had no right to it.
I was too green, she said. "I spit on your wretched little life",
she said. Whispered it in my ear, "I spit on your suicide".

Spit, she said, the damned woman—and screeched like a fish-wife. Life is grand, she said, and here I am lying in my wet rags on the shore at Blankenese and I'm cold. I'm always cold. I had my fill of cold in Russia. I've had enough of this everlasting freezing. And the Elbe, the damned old woman—yes, that's what I dreamt—with hunger.
What's that?

THE OTHER: Someone's coming. A girl or something. There! There she is.

GIRL: Is anyone there? Just now someone was talking, surely. Hallo! Is there anyone there?

BECKMANN: Yes, lying here. Here. Down here by the water.

GIRL: What are you doing there? Why don't you get up?

BECKMANN: I'm lying here, can't you see? Half on land and half in the water.

GIRL: But why on earth? Get up then! I thought at first it was a dead man when I saw that dark heap by the water.

BECKMANN: Yes, indeed. Dark heap is right, I can tell you.

GIRL: You've a funny way of talking, it seems to me. Actually there are often dead bodies here by the water nowadays. At night. Sometimes they're all fat and slippery. And as white as ghosts. That's why I was so frightened. But you're still alive, thank God. You must be wet through and through, though.

BECKMANN: So I am. Wet and cold like a genuine corpse.

GIRL: Well then, get up now. Or have you hurt yourself?

BECKMANN: Yes, I have. They stole my kneecap. In Russia. And now I have to limp through life with a gammy leg. And I always seem to be going backwards instead of forwards. There's no question of getting up.

GIRL: Come along then, I'll help you, or by degrees you'll be turning into a fish.

BECKMANN: If you think I won't start going backwards again, we might as well try it. Ah. Thank you.

GIRL: You see, you've even gone upwards now! But you're wet, and cold as ice. If I hadn't come past, you really would have turned into a fish soon. And you're very nearly speechless. May I tell you something? I live just here. And I have dry things in the house. Will you come with me? Yes? Or are

you too proud to let me change you? You half fish. You
dumb, wet fish, you!

BECKMANN: You'll take me with you?

GIRL: Yes, if you like. But only because you're wet. I hope
you're very ugly and undemanding, so that I have no cause
to regret it. I'm only taking you with me because you're so
wet and cold, is that clear? And because—

BECKMANN: Because? Because what? No, no, only because I'm
wet and cold. There's no other because.

GIRL: There is. There is indeed. Because your voice is so hopelessly sad. So grey and utterly comfortless. Ah, that's nonsense,
isn't it? Come, my old dumb, wet fish.

BECKMANN: Stop! You're running away from me. My leg won't
take it. Slowly.

GIRL: I see. Right then, slowly. Like two prehistoric age-old,
wet, cold fishes.

THE OTHER: They're away. That's how they are, these bipeds.
Really strange people they are in this world! First they
fling themselves into the water, dead set on dying. Then,
quite accidentally, another biped comes along in the dark,
one with a skirt, with breasts and long hair. And then life
is suddenly splendid and sweet again. Then no one wants to
die. They want never to be dead. Because of a few locks of
hair, a white skin and the scent of a woman. They get up
from their deathbeds as right as rain, like ten thousand stags
in spring. Then even the half-drowned bodies come to life
again. Those who really and truly couldn't stand it any
longer on this wretched miserable, damned old earth. Water
corpses become mobile again—and all because of a pair of eyes,
because of a little softness and warmth and sympathy, and
little hands and a slender neck. Even the water-corpses. These
bipeds! These most extraordinary people here on earth.

SCENE II

(A room. Evening. A door creaks and slams shut. Beckmann. The Girl)

GIRL: There! Turn on the light. Now let's see what sort of a fish we've caught. Well—*(she laughs)* Well, for heaven's sake, what are those supposed to be?

BECKMANN: These? These are my glasses. Yes, you're laughing. But they're my glasses. Worse luck.

GIRL: You call those glasses? I think you're trying to be funny.

BECKMANN: Yes, my glasses. You're right: perhaps they do look a bit funny, with these grey lead rims round the lenses. And then these grey bands that you fix round your ears. And this other grey band right across the nose! You get a sort of grey standardized face. A sort of leaden robot's face. A sort of gasmask face. But then they're respirator glasses.

GIRL: Respirator glasses?

BECKMANN: Yes, for soldiers who wore glasses. So that they could see with a respirator on.

GIRL: But why do you still go about in them? Haven't you any proper ones?

BECKMANN: No. I had, but they were shot to pieces. No, they're not pretty, but I'm glad I've at least got these. They're extremely ugly, I know. And that makes me nervous when people laugh at me. But it can't be helped. I'm hopelessly lost without glasses. Really, completely helpless.

GIRL: Oh? You're completely helpless without them? *(Gaily, not unkindly)* Then give me the beastly things at once. There —now what do you say? No, you won't get them till you go. In any case it's more reassuring to me to know that you're completely helpless. Much more reassuring. Without the glasses you look quite different at once. I think you only make such a comfortless impression because you have to wear these appalling respirator glasses.

BECKMANN: Everything's just a blur to me now. Cough them up. I can't see a thing. Even you suddenly seem far away. Quite indistinct.

GIRL: Grand. That suits me perfectly. And it suits you much better too. With the glasses you look like a ghost.

BECKMANN: Perhaps I am a ghost. Yesterday's ghost that no one wants to see today. A ghost from the war, temporarily repaired for peace.

GIRL: (*Warmly and sympathetically*) And what a grumpy, grey, old ghost! I have an idea you wear a pair of these gas-mask glasses inside, too, you fish. Leave the glasses with me. It's quite a good thing for you to see everything a bit blurred for one evening. Do the trousers fit you at all? Well, they'll do. Here, take the jacket.

BECKMANN: Look at me! You pull me out of the water and then let me drown again. This jacket was made for a Hercules. Have you been robbing a giant?

GIRL: The giant's my husband—was my husband.

BECKMANN: Your husband?

GIRL: Yes. Did you think I was a men's outfitter?

BECKMANN: Where is he? Your husband?

GIRL: (*Bitterly, quietly*) Starved, frozen, killed, how should I know? He's been missing since Stalingrad. That's three years ago.

BECKMANN: (*Taken aback*) Stalingrad? In Stalingrad, yes. Yes. There's many a one was killed in Stalingrad. But some come back. And they put on the clothes of those that don't. The man who was your husband, who was the giant, who owns these clothes, he's dead. And I—I come back and put them on. Grand, isn't it? Isn't that grand? And his jacket's so big that I nearly drown in it. (*Hurriedly*) I must take it off. Yes. I must put on my own wet one. This jacket's killing me. It's throttling me. I'm a joke in this jacket. An evil, ghastly joke, made by the war. I won't wear it.

GIRL: (*Warmly, desperately*) Be quiet, fish. Keep it on, please. I like you in it, fish. In spite of your ridiculous haircut. I suppose you brought that from Russia, too? Those short little bristles? Along with the glasses and the leg. I thought as much. You mustn't think I'm laughing at you, fish. I'm not, indeed I'm not. You look so wonderfully sad, you poor grey ghost, in that huge jacket, with your hair and your stiff leg. Take it easy, fish, take it easy—I don't think it's funny. No, fish, you look wonderfully sad. I could cry when you look at me with those comfortless eyes. And you're so quiet. Say something, fish, please. Say anything. It doesn't have to make sense. Just say something. Say something, fish, the world's so terribly quiet. Say something, then I won't feel so alone. Open your mouth, please, fishman. Don't stand there all night. Come, sit down. Here, beside me. Not so far away, fish. No harm in coming closer, I'm blurred to you anyway. Come on, shut your eyes if you like. Come and say something, so that there's something there. Don't you feel how horribly quiet it is?

BECKMANN: (*Confused*) I like looking at you. You, yes. But I'm terrified with every step that it's going to be backwards. I'm afraid.

GIRL: You silly. Backwards, forwards. Up, down. We may all be lying in the water tomorrow, white and fat and quiet and cold. But today, we're still warm. Still warm, fish, d'you hear me? Fish—say something, fish. You're not going to swim away this evening. Be quiet. I don't believe a word. But I think I'd better lock the door.

BECKMANN: Don't do that. I'm no fish and you've no need to lock the door. No, God knows I'm no fish.

GIRL: (*Affectionately*) Fish! Dear fish! You grey, wet, patched-up ghost.

BECKMANN: (*Far away*) Something's stifling me. I'm drowning. It's strangling me. It's because I can't see properly. It's a complete haze. But it's strangling me.

GIRL: (*Fearfully*) What's the matter? What's the matter with you? What is it?

BECKMANN: (*With growing fear*) Now I'm slowly but surely going crazy. Give me my glasses. Quickly. It's only because everything's so misty. There! I've got a feeling there's a man standing behind you. He's been there all the time. A big man. A sort of Hercules. Like a giant, you know. But that's only because I haven't got my glasses, because the giant only has one leg. He's coming nearer, the giant's coming nearer, with one leg and two crutches. Can you hear—tick tock. Tick tock. That's the crutches. Now he's behind you. Don't you feel his breath on your neck? Give me my glasses, I don't want to see him any more. There, now he's close, quite close.

GIRL: (*Screams and rushes out. A door creaks and slams. The crutches are heard quite loudly*)

BECKMANN: (*Whispers*) The giant!

ONE LEG: (*Tonelessly*) What are you doing here? You! In my clothes? In my place? With my wife?

BECKMANN: (*Uncomprehendingly*) Your clothes? Your place? Your wife?

ONE LEG: (*Quite toneless and apathetic*) You. What are you doing here?

BECKMANN: (*Low and halting*) That's what I asked the man who was with my own wife last night. In my shirt. In my bed. What are you doing here? I said. And he raised his shoulders and dropped them again and said, "Yes, what am I doing here?" That's what he answered. Then I shut the bedroom door, no, first I put out the light again. And then I was outside.

ONE LEG: Let me see your face in the light. Come closer. (*Heavily*) Beckmann!

BECKMANN: Yes. That's me. Beckmann. I didn't think you'd know me again.

ONE LEG: (*Quietly, but with immense reproach*) Beckmann— Beckmann—Beckmann! ! !

BECKMANN: (*Agonized*) Shut up, you. Don't say that name! I won't have that name! Shut up!

ONE LEG: (*Harping*) Beckmann. Beckmann.

BECKMANN: (*Screams*) I'm not! I'm not Beckmann. I won't *be* Beckmann any more!

(*He runs out. A door creaks and slams. Then the wind is heard and a man running through the silent streets*)

THE OTHER: Stop! Beckmann!

BECKMANN: Who's there?

THE OTHER: I. The other one.

BECKMANN: Are *you* here again?

THE OTHER: Still here, Beckmann. Always here.

BECKMANN: What do you want? Let me past.

THE OTHER: No, Beckmann. That path leads to the Elbe. Come, the road's up here.

BECKMANN: Let me past. I want the Elbe.

THE OTHER: No, Beckmann. Come. You want this road.

BECKMANN: This road? I'm to live, am I? I'm to carry on? I'm to eat, sleep, all that?

THE OTHER: Come, Beckmann.

BECKMANN: (*More in apathy than agitation*) Don't say that name.
I won't *be* Beckmann any longer. I have no name now. I'm
to go on living, when there's a human being, when there's a
man with one leg, who's only got one leg because of me?
Who's got only one leg, because there was once a Corporal
Beckmann who said, "Corporal Bauer, you'll hold your
ground to the last". I'm to go on living, when there's a one-
legged man who keeps saying Beckmann! The whole time!
Beckmann! And he says it as though he said Grave. As
though he said Dog or said Murder. Who says my name as
one would say Doom; muffled and threatening and without
hope. And you say I should live? I'm outside, outside again.
Last night I was outside. Today I was outside. I'm always
outside. And the doors are shut. And yet I'm a man with
legs that are tired and heavy. With a stomach that yelps with
hunger. With blood that's freezing out here in the night.
And the one-legged man keeps saying my name. And I can't
even sleep at night any more! So where shall I go, man?
Let me past.

THE OTHER: Come, Beckmann. We'll take the road. We'll pay a
man a visit. And you'll give it back to him.

BECKMANN: What?

THE OTHER: The responsibility.

BECKMANN: Pay a man a visit? Yes, let's do that. And the
responsibility, I'll give it back to him. Yes, we'll do that.
I want a night's sleep without cripples. I'll give it back to
him. Yes, I'll take the responsibility back to him. I'll give his
dead back to him. To him! Yes, come, there's a man we want
to see who lives in a warm house. In this town, in every town.
There's a man we want to see, we want to give him something
—a dear good, honest, man, who's only done his duty all his
life, only and always his duty! But it was a cruel duty! It
was a frightful duty! A cursed—cursed—cursed duty! Come!
Come on!

SCENE III

(A room. Evening. A door creaks and shuts. The Colonel and his family. Beckmann)

BECKMANN: Good appetite, sir.

COLONEL: *(Chewing)* What's that?

BECKMANN: Good appetite, sir.

COLONEL: You're interrupting supper. Is it so important?

BECKMANN: No. I only wanted to decide whether to drown myself tonight or go on living. And if I go on living, how to set about it? And by day I'd like something to eat now and then perhaps. And at night, at night, I'd like to sleep. That's all.

COLONEL: Come, come, come! Don't talk such unmanly nonsense. You were a soldier, weren't you, after all?

BECKMANN: No, sir.

SON-IN-LAW: What d'you mean, no? You're wearing uniform.

BECKMANN: *(Tonelessly)* Yes. For six years. But I always thought if I were to wear a postman's uniform for ten years, that's still far from being a postman.

DAUGHTER: Daddy, do ask him what he really wants. He keeps staring at my plate.

BECKMANN: *(Kindly)* Your windows look so warm from outside. I just wanted to feel again what it's like to look through such windows. But from inside, from inside. Do you know what it's like to see such warm lighted windows in the evening, and be—outside?

MOTHER: *(Not nastily, but with horror)* Father, tell him to take those glasses off. It makes me shiver to look at them.

COLONEL: Those are so-called respirator glasses, my dear. Introduced into the armed forces in 1934 for personnel with bad eyesight, to be worn under the respirator. Why don't you throw the things away? The war's over.

BECKMANN: Yes, yes, it's over. They all say that. But I still need the glasses. I'm short-sighted; without the glasses everything looks blurred. With them on, I can distinguish everything. From here I can see quite clearly what you've got on the table——

COLONEL: (*Interrupting*) Tell me, where did you get that extra-ordinary haircut? Been in the glasshouse? Done time, eh? Come on, my man, out with it, broken in somewhere, what? And caught, eh?

BECKMANN: Quite right, sir. Broke in somewhere. In Stalingrad, sir. But the job went wrong and they got us. Three years we got, the whole hundred thousand of us. And our big chief put on civvies and ate caviare. Three years of caviare. And the others lay under the snow with the sand of the steppes in their mouths. And we spooned hot water into ourselves. But the chief had to eat caviare. For three years. And they shaved our heads. At the throat—or just the hair. There was no definite ruling. The ones with amputated heads were the luckiest. At least they didn't have to eat caviare all the time.

SON-IN-LAW: (*Incensed*) What do you think of that, father? Eh? What do you think of that?

COLONEL: My dear young friend, you're thoroughly distorting the whole thing, you know. We're Germans, after all. Let's please stick to good German truth. He who prizes truth makes the best trooper, says Clausewitz.

BECKMANN: Right, sir. That's fine, sir. In a question of truth I'll play. We eat till we're full, sir, really full, sir. We put on a new shirt and a suit with buttons, with no holes in it. And then we light the stove, sir: yes, we've got a stove, sir. And we put the kettle on to make a nice hot rum. Then we pull down the blinds and drop into an armchair, for we've an armchair too, you know. We can smell our wife's fine perfume, and no blood, eh, sir, no blood, and we think about the white bed we've got, the two of us, sir, the bed that's waiting for us upstairs, white, warm and welcoming. And then we prize truth, sir, our good German truth.

DAUGHTER: He's mad.

SON-IN-LAW: Nonsense, he's drunk.

MOTHER: Put a stop to it, father. The creature makes me shiver.

COLONEL: (*Without asperity*) You know I have a strong impression that you're one of those whose mind and ideas have been a bit confused by this spot of warfare. Why weren't you commissioned? You'd have had entrée into quite different circles. Had a decent wife, and you'd have had a decent house now, too. You'd have been quite a different person. Why weren't you commissioned?

BECKMANN: My voice was too quiet, sir. My voice was too quiet.

COLONEL: There you are, you see, you're too quiet. Now, honestly, one of those who're a bit tired, a bit weak, eh?

BECKMANN: That's right, sir. That's it. A bit quiet. A bit weak. And tired, sir, tired, tired, tired! I can't sleep, you know, sir, never can. That's why I'm here, why I've come to you, sir, for I know you can help me. I want to be able to sleep again at last! That's all I want. Just sleep. Deep, deep sleep.

MOTHER: Father, stay with us. I'm afraid. This man gives me the shivers.

DAUGHTER: Nonsense, mother. He's only one of those who's come home with a screw loose. They're harmless.

SON-IN-LAW: I think the gentleman's pretty uppish.

COLONEL: (*Superior*) Just leave it to me, children, I know the type from the troops.

MOTHER: My God, he's asleep on his feet.

COLONEL: (*Almost paternally*) They have to be treated a little sharply, that's all. Leave it to me, I'll settle it.

BECKMANN: (*Far away*) Sir?

COLONEL: Well now, what *do* you want?

BECKMANN: (*Far away*) Sir?

COLONEL: I can hear. I can hear.

BECKMANN: (*Drunk with sleep, dreamily*) You can hear, sir? That's all right, then. If you can hear, sir, I'd like to tell you my dream. The dream I dream every night, sir. Then somebody screams—dreadfully, and I wake up. And do you know who's screaming? I am, sir, I am. Funny, isn't it, sir? Then I can't go to sleep again. Every night, sir. Just think, sir, of lying awake every night. That's why I'm tired, sir, so terribly tired.

MOTHER: Stay with us, father. I feel cold.

COLONEL: (*Interested*) And your dream wakes you up, you say?

BECKMANN: No, the scream. Not the dream. The scream.

COLONEL: (*Interested*) But the dream is what sets you off screaming, eh?

BECKMANN: Well, well. Just so. It sets me off. You should know

that it's a most unusual dream. I'll just describe it to you.
You're listening, sir, aren't you? There's a man playing the
xylophone. He plays incredibly fast. And he sweats, this man,
because he's extraordinarily fat. And this xylophone's gigantic. And because it's so big he has to dash up and down with
every stroke. And he sweats, because he's really very fat.
But it's not sweat that he sweats, that's the odd thing. He
sweats blood, steaming dark blood. And the blood runs down
his trousers in two broad red stripes, so that from a distance
he looks like a general. Like a general! A fat, bloodstained
general! He must be a real old campaigner, this general, for
he's lost both arms. Yes, he plays with long thin artificial
arms that look like grenade throwers, wooden with metal
rings. He must be a very strange sort of musician, this general,
because the woods of his xylophone are not made of wood.
No! Believe me, sir, believe me, they're made of bones.
Believe me, sir, bones!

COLONEL: (*Softly*) Yes, I believe you. They're made of bones.

BECKMANN: (*Still in a trance, ghostlike*) That's it, not wood, bones.
Wonderful white bones. He's got skull-bones, shoulder-
blades, pelvises. And for the higher notes, arms and leg-bones.
And then ribs—thousands of ribs. And finally, right at the
end of the xylophone, where the really high notes are, come
little finger-bones, toes, teeth. Yes, right at the end come the
teeth. That's the xylophone played by the fat man with the
general's stripes. Isn't he a funny sort of musician, this general?

COLONEL: (*Uncertainly*) Yes, very funny. Very, very funny,
indeed.

BECKMANN: Yes, and now it really gets going. Now the dream
really begins. Well, the general stands in front of his giant
xylophone of human bones, and with his artificial arms beats
out a march. Prussia's glory or the Badenweiler. But mostly
he plays the 'Entry of the Gladiators' and 'The Old Comrades'.
Mostly that. You know it, sir, don't you, 'The Old Comrades'? (*Hums*)

COLONEL: Yes, yes, of course. (*Hums as well*)

BECKMANN: And then they come. Then they move in, the
Gladiators, the Old Comrades. Then they rise up out of their
mass graves and their bloody groaning stinks to the white
moon. That's what makes the nights what they are. As

piercing as cat's dirt. As red, as red as raspberry-juice on a white shirt. Then the nights are such that we can't breathe. Then we smother if we have no mouth to kiss and no spirits to drink. The bloody groaning stinks to the moon, sir, to the white moon, when the dead come, the lemonade-spotted dead.

DAUGHTER: He's crazy, don't you hear? The moon's supposed to be white, he says! White! The moon!

COLONEL: (*Soberly*) Nonsense. Of course the moon's yellow. Always has been. Like honey bread. Like an omelette. The moon was always yellow.

BECKMANN: Oh no, sir, oh no! These nights when the dead walk, she's white and sick. Like the belly of a pregnant girl drowned in a stream. So white, so sick, so round. No sir, the moon is white on these nights when the dead walk and the bloody groaning stinks to the moon, sharp as cat's dirt to the white sick moon. Blood. Blood. Then they rise up out of their mass graves with rotting bandages and bloodstained uniforms. They rise up out of the oceans, out of the steppes and the streets, they come from the forests, from the ruins and marshes, frozen black, green, mouldering. They rise up out of the steppes, one-eyed, one-armed, toothless, legless, with torn entrails, without skulls, without hands, shot through, stinking, blind. They sweep up in a fearful flood, immeasurable in numbers, immeasurable in agony! The fearful immeasurable flood of the dead overflows the banks of its graves and rolls broad, pulpy, diseased and bloody over the earth. And then the General with his stripes of blood says to me: "Corporal Beckmann, you'll take responsibility. Count off". And then I stand there before the millions of grinning skeletons, the wrecks and ruins of bone, with my responsibility, and count them off. But the fellows won't count off. Their jaws jerk terribly, but they won't count off. The General orders fifty knee-bends. The rotting bones rattle, lungs squeak, but they don't count off. Is that not mutiny, sir? Open mutiny?

COLONEL: (*Whispers*) Yes, open mutiny.

BECKMANN: They won't damn well count off. But the ghosts form up into choruses. Thundering, threatening, muffled choruses. And do you know what they roar, Colonel?

COLONEL: (*Whispers*) No.

BECKMANN: Beckmann, they roar. Corporal Beckmann. Always Corporal Beckmann. The roaring grows. And the roaring rolls up, brutal as the cry of gods, strange, cold, gigantic. And the roaring grows and rolls and grows and rolls! And the roaring grows so big, so stiflingly big, that I can't breathe. Then I scream, then I scream out in the night. Then I have to scream, scream so frightfully, so frightfully. And it always wakes me up. Every night. Every night. Every night the concert on the bone xylophone, and every night the choruses, and every night the frightful screams. And then I can't go to sleep again, because, you see, I was responsible. I had the responsibility, you see. Yes, I had the responsibility. And that's why I've come to you, sir, for I want to sleep again. I want to sleep once more. That's why I've come to you, because I want to sleep, want to sleep again.

COLONEL: What is it you want of me?

BECKMANN: I'm bringing it back to you.

COLONEL: What?

BECKMANN: (*Almost naïve*) The responsibility. I'm bringing you back the responsibility. Have you completely forgotten, sir? The 14th February? At Gorodok. It was 46 below zero. You came to our post, sir, and said, "Corporal Beckmann". "Here", I shouted. Then you said, and your breath hung as ice on your fur collar—I remember it exactly, it was a fine fur collar—then you said: "Corporal Beckmann, you will take over responsibility for these twenty men. You'll reconnoitre the wood east of Gorodok and if possible take a few prisoners, is that clear?" "Very good, sir", I replied. And then we set off and reconnoitred. And I—I had the responsibility. We reconnoitred all night. There was some shooting and when we got back to our post, eleven men were missing. And it was my responsibility. That's all, sir. But now the war's over, now I want to sleep, now I'm giving you back the responsibility, sir, I don't want it any more, I'm giving it back, sir.

COLONEL: But, my dear Beckmann. You're exciting yourself unnecessarily. It wasn't meant like that at all.

BECKMANN: (*Without excitement but intensely serious*) It was. It

was, sir. It must have been meant like that. Responsibility
is not just a word, a chemical formula for changing warm
human flesh into cold, grey earth. One can't let men die for
the sake of an empty word. We've got to take our responsibility somewhere. The dead don't answer. God—doesn't
answer. But the living ask. They ask every night, sir. When I
lie awake, they come and ask. Women, sir, sad, sorrowing
women. Old women with grey hair and coarse wrinkled
hands—young women with lonely longing eyes. Children,
sir, children, a thousand little children. And out of the darkness they whisper: Corporal Beckmann, where is my father,
Corporal Beckmann? Corporal Beckmann, what have you
done with my husband? Corporal Beckmann, where is my
son, where is my brother? Corporal Beckmann, where is my
fiancé, Corporal Beckmann? Where, Corporal Beckmann,
where? Where? Where? So they whisper, till it gets light.
There are only eleven women, sir, only eleven come to me.
How many come to you, sir? A thousand? Two thousand?
Do you sleep well, sir? Then I suppose it won't worry you if I
add to your two thousand the responsibility for my eleven.
Can you sleep, sir? With two thousand ghosts each night?
Can you even live, sir, can you live for one minute without
screaming? Sir. Sir, do you sleep well at night? Then it won't
worry you, then I can go to sleep at last—if you'll be so kind
and take it back. The responsibility. Then at last my soul can
sleep in peace. Peace in my soul, that was it, yes. Peace in my
soul, sir. And then—sleep! Oh, God!

COLONEL: (*He is staggered after all. But then he laughs off his dis-
comfort, not unpleasantly, rather jovially and roughly, with good
temper; then says, very uncertainly*) Young man! Young man!
I really don't know. I really don't know. You aren't a secret
pacifist, eh? Just a bit bolshie, eh? But—(*He laughs, at first
constrainedly, then, his good healthy Prussianism winning, he gives
a full-throated roar*) Young fellow! Young fellow! I'm half
convinced you're a young rascal, eh? Am I right? Eh? A
young rascal, eh? (*He laughs*) Exquisite, man, really exquisite!
You certainly know your stuff. Really! That basic humour!
You know (*Interrupted by laughter*) you know, with that stuff,

with that turn, you should be on the stage. On the stage!
(*The Colonel does not wish to offend Beckmann, but he is so
healthy and so naïve and so much the old soldier that he can only
grasp Beckmann's drama as a joke.*) Those absurd glasses, that
ridiculous haircut! You should do the whole thing to music!
(*Laughs*) Oh Lord, that priceless dream! The knees-bends,
the knees-bends to xylophone music! Really young man,
you must go like that on the stage! Humanity will laugh till
it cries! Oh, by Jove! (*Laughs with tears in his eyes and puffs
and blows*) I didn't realize to start with that you wanted to do
a comic turn. I honestly thought you were slightly astray in
the head. Never imagined you were such a comedian. Young
man, you've really given us a delightful evening—that's worth
something in return. I tell you what! Go down to my
chauffeur, get some warm water, wash yourself, take that
beard off. Make yourself human. Then make the chauffeur
give you one of my old suits. Yes, I'm serious! Throw those
rags of yours away and put on one of my old suits, go on,
you can quite happily accept that, and then at least you'll
become human again, my boy! Then you'll become human
again, for a start!

BECKMANN: (*Wakes up: Also wakes out of his apathy for the first
time*) Human! Become? For a start I should become human
again? (*Screams*) I'm supposed to *become* human? Well, what
are all you then? Human? What? Are you human?
Are you?

MOTHER: (*Screams shrilly. Something falls*) Oh no! He'll kill
us! No!

(*Great confusion and racket: the family is heard shouting excitedly
together*)

SON-IN-LAW: Hold on to the lamp!

DAUGHTER: Help! The light's out! Mother's knocked over the
lamp!

COLONEL: Quiet, children!

MOTHER: For heaven's sake, light!

SON-IN-LAW: Where's the lamp?

COLONEL: There. There it is.

MOTHER: Thank God we've light again.

SON-IN-LAW: And the fellow's gone. I thought straight away there
was something odd about the chap.

DAUGHTER: One, two, three—four. No, everything's there still. Only the serving-dish is broken.

COLONEL: Good heavens, yes! What on earth was he after?

SON-IN-LAW: Perhaps he was really just daft.

DAUGHTER: No, look! The rum bottle's gone.

MOTHER: Oh, father, your lovely rum.

DAUGHTER: And the half loaf—it's gone too!

COLONEL: What's that? The loaf?

MOTHER: Has he taken the loaf? What should he want with the loaf?

SON-IN-LAW: Perhaps he wants to eat it. Or pawn it. These people stop at nothing.

DAUGHTER: Yes, perhaps he wants to eat it.

MOTHER: Yes, but—*dry bread*?

(A door creaks and shuts)

BECKMANN: *(In the street again. A bottle gurgles)* Those people are right. *(He gets gradually drunker)* Cheers! That warms you up. No, those people are right. Shall we sit around and mourn death, when he's sitting right on our own heels? Cheers! Those people are right. The dead are piling up over our heads. Ten million yesterday. Up to thirty million today. Tomorrow a fellow'll come and blow up a whole continent. Next week a fellow'll invent the murder of everyone in seven seconds with ten grams of poison. Shall we mourn? Cheers! I've a dismal feeling that we should pretty soon look around for another planet. Cheers! Those people are right. I'm off to the circus. They're right, man. The Colonel laughed himself sick. He says I should go on the stage. Limping, with this coat, with this mug, with these glasses on my face and this brush on my head. The Colonel's right, humanity will laugh itself silly! Cheers! Long live the Colonel! He's saved my life. Hail, Colonel! Cheers! Long live blood! Long live laughter about the dead! I'll go to the circus, the people'll laugh themselves silly when it gets really gruesome with blood and lots of corpses. Come, bottle, gurgle again. The schnaps has saved my life, my senses are soused! Cheers! *(Splendidly and drunkenly)* Whoever has schnaps or a bed or a girl, let him dream his last! Tomorrow may be too late! Let him build a Noah's Ark of his dream and sail drinking and crying over

the horror into eternal darkness! The others drown in dread
and despair! Whoever has schnaps is saved! Cheers! Long
live the bloodstained Colonel! Long live responsibility! Hail!
I'm off to the circus! Long live the circus! The whole bloody
circus!

SCENE IV

(*A room. A Cabaret Producer. Beckmann is still slightly tipsy*)

PRODUCER: (*With great conviction*) You see, the field of Art is just
where youth's needed again, a youth that takes its stand in
all problems. A courageous, sober——

BECKMANN: (*To himself*) Sober, yes, it must be sober.

PRODUCER: . . . revolutionary youth. We need the spirit of
Schiller, who wrote *The Robbers* at twenty. We need a Grabbe,
a Heine! A spirit of aggressive genius, that's what we need!
An unromantic, realistic, sturdy youth, which steadfastly
faces up to the dark side of life, unsentimentally, objectively,
with detachment. We need young people, a generation that
sees and loves the world as it is. Which prizes truth, has plans,
ideas—they needn't be profound truths. Nothing finished,
mature and serene, for heaven's sake! It should be a cry, a
cry from their heart. A question, a hope, a hunger!

BECKMANN: (*To himself*) Hunger, yes, we have that.

PRODUCER: But this youth must be *young*, passionate, courageous.
Particularly in Art. Look at me. At seventeen I stood on the
cabaret stage and showed the bourgeois my teeth and spoiled
the taste of his cigar. What we lack is the *avant-garde* to present
the living grey suffering face of our times!

BECKMANN: (*To himself*) Yes, yes. Always presenting something.
Presenting faces. Presenting arms. Ghosts. Something's always
being presented.

PRODUCER: Face! That reminds me: why do you run around in
those grotesque glasses? Where did you get hold of such weird
things? It gives one the hiccups to look at you.

BECKMANN: (*Automatically*) They're my respirator glasses. We
got them in the Services, those of us who wore glasses, so

that in respirators we could still recognize the enemy and strike him down.

PRODUCER: But heavens, the war's long since over! Peace has been rampant for donkey's months. And you still turn out in that military get-up.

BECKMANN: You mustn't hold that against me. I only arrived from Siberia the day before yesterday. Day before yesterday? Yes, day before yesterday.

PRODUCER: Siberia? Dreadful, eh? Dreadful! Ah, that war! But the glasses—have you no others?

BECKMANN: I'm lucky to have at least these. They've been my salvation. There's no alternative salvation—no glasses, I mean.

PRODUCER: My good man, why didn't you lay in an extra pair?

BECKMANN: Where, in Siberia?

PRODUCER: Oh, of course. Silly old Siberia! Now look, I've covered myself on glasses. Yes, my boy. I am the happy owner of three pairs of high-class horn-rimmed glasses. Genuine horn-rims, my friend! A yellow pair for work, an unobtrusive pair for going out. And in the evening, for the stage, you understand, a heavy black pair. They look good, my friend: class!

BECKMANN: And I've got nothing to give you in exchange for one. I know I look thrown together and patched up. I know how absurdly stupid the thing looks, but what can I do? Couldn't you possibly——?

PRODUCER: My dear man, what are you thinking of? I can't spare a single pair of them. All my ideas, my effect, my moods depend on them.

BECKMANN: That's just it. So do mine. And one can't get schnaps every day. And when that's finished, life is like lead: tough, grey and worthless. But on the stage these fantastically hideous glasses would probably be much more effective.

PRODUCER: How do you mean?

BECKMANN: I mean, funnier. People laugh themselves sick when they see me in these glasses. And then the haircut and the coat. And my face, just think, my face! It's all tremendously funny, don't you think?

PRODUCER: (*Who begins to have the creeps*) Funny? Funny? The laughter will stick in their throats, my friend. At the sight of

you, cold horror will creep up the nape of their necks: damp
horror at a ghost from the underworld. But after all, people
want to enjoy Art, be taken out of themselves, edified—they
don't want to see cold, damp ghosts. No, we can't let you
loose like that. The approach has got to be more genial, more
self-assured, more cheerful. Positive! Positive, my friend!
Think of Goethe! Think of Mozart! The Maid of Orleans,
Richard Wagner, Schmeling, Shirley Temple!

BECKMANN: Of course, I can't come up to names like that. I'm
just Beckmann. B in front—eckmann behind.

PRODUCER: Beckmann? Beckmann? At the moment it doesn't
ring a bell with me in cabaret. Or have you used a stage
name?

BECKMANN: No, I'm quite new. I'm a beginner.

PRODUCER: (*Complete volte-face*) A beginner? Now honestly,
things aren't as easy as all that in this life. No, no, that's just
a bit too simple. You can't have a career just like that! You
underestimate the promoter's responsibility! Present a
beginner? It can mean ruin. The public wants names!

BECKMANN: Goethe, Schmeling, Shirley Temple, etc., eh?

PRODUCER: The very thing. But beginners, newcomers, unknown
artists! How old are you?

BECKMANN: Twenty-five.

PRODUCER: There, you see. Let the wind blow round your nose
a bit, young fellow. You want to smell a bit of life first.
What sort of things have you done up till now?

BECKMANN: Nothing. War: been starved, been frozen, used a
rifle. War. Nothing else.

PRODUCER: Nothing else? Well, and what's that? Let yourself
mature on the battlefield of life, my friend. Work! Make a
name for yourself, then we'll put you in at the top of the bill.
Learn to know the world, and then come back. Become
somebody!

BECKMANN: (*Who has so far been quiet and on one note, now
gradually becomes more excited*) And where shall I start? Where?
A man's got to be given a chance somewhere, some time.
Somewhere or other a beginner must begin. The wind didn't
blow round our noses in Russia, true enough, but metal did,
a lot of metal. Hot, hard, heartless metal. Where are we to

begin then? Tell me, where? We want to get cracking at last, damn it all!

PRODUCER: Save your language. After all, I didn't send anyone to Siberia. Not I.

BECKMANN: No, nobody sent us to Siberia. We went quite on our own. All of us, on our own. And some stayed there, all on their own. Under the snow, under the sand. The ones that stayed had a chance, the dead ones. But we, we can't get a start anywhere. Nowhere.

PRODUCER: (*Resigned*) As you wish! Well then, start. Please stand there and start. Don't take too long. Time's expensive. Now, please. If you would be so kind as to begin. I'm giving you a great chance. You have tremendous luck: I'm lending you my ear. You should value that, young man, you should appreciate that, I can tell you. So in God's name, start. Please. Ah. There.

(*Soft xylophone music. The tune of 'Tapfere kleine Soldatenfrau' is recognizable*)

BECKMANN: (*Sings, almost speaks, softly, apathetically and monotonously*)

> Noble little soldier's wife
> The song re-echoes through my life
> That sweet and charming song.
> But in reality: everything went wrong.

Refrain:

> The world laughs in scorn
> At the life I must mourn.
> And the mists of the night,
> Have concealed it from sight.
> Only moons grin green
> And are seen
> Through the torn curtain!

> Coming home tonight I spied
> Another with my wife
> And if I had a grain of pride
> I'd take my bleeding life.

Refrain:

> The world laughs in scorn
> At the life I must mourn.
> And the mists of the night,
> Have concealed it from sight.
> Only moons grin green
> And are seen
> Through the torn curtain!

> So midnight comes I start to woo
> Another maiden, someone new.
> Of Germany was nothing said.
> To Germany we were as good as dead.
> The night was short, the morning came
> And standing staring in the door
> I saw a one-legged man who was her husband.
> And that was in the morning at four.

Refrain:

> The world laughs ——

> I run around outside again
> Within my head the old refrain
> > The song of the life
> > The song of the life
> > The song of the life of the soldier's wife.
> (*The xylophone plays discordantly and dies away*)

PRODUCER: (*With cowardice*) Not so bad really, not so bad at all. Quite a good effort actually. For a beginner, very good. But of course, my dear young man, the whole thing still lacks spirit. It doesn't sparkle enough. It lacks a certain polish. Of course it's hardly a lyric. It still lacks timbre and the discreet but piquant erotic quality which the infidelity theme demands. The public wants to be tickled, not pinched. Otherwise, however, it's a very good effort considering your youth. The moral—and the deeper wisdom are still lacking, but as I say: not at all bad for a beginner! It's still far too declamatory, too obvious——

BECKMANN: (*Slowly, to himself*)—genial.

PRODUCER:—nonchalance, that assurance. Think of the master Goethe. Goethe took the field with his duke, and at the camp-fire wrote an operetta.

BECKMANN: (*Slowly, to himself*) Operetta.

PRODUCER: That's genius! That's the big difference!

BECKMANN: Yes, one's got to admit there's quite a big difference.

PRODUCER: My friend, let's wait a year or two.

BECKMANN: Wait? I'm hungry! I've got to work!

PRODUCER: Yes, but Art must mature. Your delivery has as yet no elegance, no experience. It's all too grey, too *naked*. You'll infuriate my public. No, we can't feed people on black bread——

BECKMANN: (*Slowly, to himself*) Black bread.

PRODUCER:—when they demand cake. Have a little patience. Work on yourself, round off the corners, let yourself mature. It's already quite a stout effort, as I say, but it's still not Art.

BECKMANN: Art! Art! But it's the truth!

PRODUCER: Truth! Truth's got nothing to do with Art!

BECKMANN: (*Slowly, to himself*) No.

PRODUCER: Truth won't get you far!

BECKMANN: (*Slowly, to himself*) No.

PRODUCER: You'll only make yourself unpopular. Where would we all be, if everyone suddenly started telling the truth? Who wants to know anything about truth nowadays? Eh? Who? Those are facts you must never forget.

BECKMANN: (*Bitterly*) Yes, yes. I understand. And thank you. Slowly I'm beginning to understand. Those are facts one must never forget. (*His voice gets harder and harder, until, as the door creaks, he is almost shouting*) One must never forget: truth won't get one far. The truth will only make one unpopular. Who wants to know anything about truth these days? (*Loud*) Yes, I'm slowly beginning to understand, those are the facts——

(*Beckmann goes out without a leave-taking. A door creaks and slams*)

PRODUCER: I say, young man. Why suddenly so touchy?

BECKMANN: (*In despair*) The schnaps was finished
> And the world grew tough
> Like the hide of a sow
> And as grey and rough.

Straight on for the Elbe.

THE OTHER: Stay here, Beckmann. This is the road! Up here!

BECKMANN: This road stinks of blood. Here they massacred truth. My road's to the Elbe! And it goes down here.

THE OTHER: Come, Beckmann. You mustn't despair! Truth lives!

BECKMANN: Truth is like a well-known whore. Everyone knows her, but it's embarrassing to meet her in the street. Therefore, one must do it at night in secret. By day, they're grey, raw and ugly, the whore and the truth. And some never stomach her, their whole lives long.

THE OTHER: Come, Beckmann. There's always a door open somewhere.

BECKMANN: Yes, for Goethe. For Shirley Temple or Schmeling. But I'm just Beckmann. Beckmann with funny glasses and a funny haircut. Beckmann with a gammy leg and a Father Christmas coat. I'm just a bad joke that the war's made, a ghost of yesterday. And because I'm only Beckmann and not Mozart, all doors are shut. Bang. And again Bang. Again and again. Bang. Outside again. Bang. And because I'm a beginner I'm not allowed to begin. And because I'm too quiet, I was never commissioned. And because I'm too loud I frighten the public. And because I've a heart that nightly weeps for the dead, therefore I must become human again. In the Colonel's old suit.

> The schnaps was finished
> And the world grew tough
> Like the hide of a sow
> And as grey and rough.

The road stinks of blood, because truth has been massacred and all doors are shut. I want to go home, but the roads are dark. Only the road to the Elbe is light. Oh, how light!

THE OTHER: Stay here, Beckmann. This is your road up here.

Here's the way home. You must go home, Beckmann. Your father sits in the parlour and waits for you. Your mother's already at the door. She has recognized your footsteps.

BECKMANN: My God! Home! Yes, I'll go home, I'll go to my mother! Yes, I'll go at last to my mother! To my——

THE OTHER: Come. This is your way. There. The place one should go to first is the last one thinks of.

BECKMANN: Home, where my mother is, my mother——

SCENE V

(A house. A door)

BECKMANN: Our house is still standing. And it has a door. And the door's there for me. My mother will be there and will open the door to me, and let me in. (*In wonder*) To think that our house is still standing! The stairs still creak, too. And that's our door. My father comes out of it at eight every morning. And in again every evening at six. Except on Sundays. He fumbles around with his bunch of keys and grunts to himself. Every day. A whole lifetime. That's where my mother goes in and out. Three, seven, ten times a day. Every day. A lifetime long. A whole life long. That's our door. Behind it the kitchen door squeaks, behind it the clock with its hoarse voice grates away the irrevocable hours. Behind it I've sat on an upturned chair and played at racing cars. And behind it my father coughs. Behind it the emptying waste-pipe belches and the tiles in the kitchen click as my mother potters about. That is our door. Behind it a life is rolled off an endless reel. A life which has been always thus, for thirty years. And will always continue thus. War has gone past this door. It hasn't broken it in, nor ripped it from its hinges. It has left our door standing, accidentally; an oversight. And now the door's there for me. It will open for me, it will shut behind me, and I shall no longer be outside. Then I shall be—home. That's our old door with the paint peeling off and the dented letterbox. With the wobbly white bell-pull and the shining brass plate, which my mother cleans every morning and which bears our name. Beckmann——

No, the brass plate isn't there now! Why isn't the brass plate there? Who's taken our name away? What's this dirty card on the door? With this strange name? No Kramer lives here! Why isn't our name still on the door? It's been there for thirty years. It can't just be taken off and replaced by another! Where's our brass plate? The other names in the house are all still on their doors. As always. So why's Beckmann not there? You can't simply nail on another name when Beckmann's been there for thirty years! Who is this Kramer?

(*He rings. The door creaks open*)

FRAU KRAMER: (*With an indifferent, ghastly, smooth amiability, more frightful than any rudeness or brutality*) What do you want?

BECKMANN: Oh, good day, I——

FRAU KRAMER: Yes?

BECKMANN: Do you know where our brass plate's gone?

FRAU KRAMER: What do you mean by "our brass plate"?

BECKMANN: That plate that's always been here. For thirty years.

FRAU KRAMER: I don't know.

BECKMANN: Don't you know then where my parents are?

FRAU KRAMER: Who are they? And who are you?

BECKMANN: My name's Beckmann; I was born here. This is our flat.

FRAU KRAMER: (*Still chatty and patronizing rather than intentionally nasty*) No, that's not right, it's our flat. For all I know you may have been born here, that's all the same to me, but it's not your flat. It belongs to us.

BECKMANN: Oh! Oh! But what's happened to my parents then? They must surely live somewhere.

FRAU KRAMER: You're the son of those people, the Beckmanns, you say? Your name's Beckmann?

BECKMANN: Yes, of course. I'm Beckmann. I was born here in this house.

FRAU KRAMER: You may have been, for all I care. It's all one to me. But the flat belongs to us.

BECKMANN: But my parents! Where have my parents got to? Can't you tell me where they are?

FRAU KRAMER: Don't you know? And you're supposed to be their son, eh? Strikes me you're a green one, not to know that, you know.

BECKMANN: For God's sake where have they gone to then, the

old people? They've lived here for thirty years, and now all
of a sudden I'm told they're not here any more! Say something! They must be somewhere!

FRAU KRAMER: They are. As far as I know in Chapel 5.

BECKMANN: Chapel 5? What does that mean?

FRAU KRAMER: (*Pitying, resigned, rather than brutal*) Chapel 5 at
Ohlsdorf. Do you know what Ohlsdorf is? It's a burial
ground. Do you know where Ohlsdorf is? It's near Fuhlsbüttel. Hamburg's three terminus stations are out there. In
Fuhlsbüttel the prison. In Alsterdorf the asylum. And in
Ohlsdorf the cemetery. You see? And there they've stayed,
your old people. They live there now. Moved out, departed,
gone. And you say you didn't know?

BECKMANN: What are they doing there? Are they dead? But they
were alive just now! Why did they die before I came home?
How should I know, I've been three years in Siberia. More
than a thousand days. They're dead? But they were here just
now! There was nothing wrong with them. Only that father
had a cough. But he'd always had it. And my mother had
cold feet with the tiled kitchen. But you don't die of that.
Why did they die? They'd no reason at all. They can't just
simply die off like that without a murmur.

FRAU KRAMER: (*Familiarly, vulgarly, uncouthly sentimental*) Well,
you are a one, I must say, you rummy son! All right, forget
it. A thousand days in Siberia is no joke at that. I can imagine
it might get you down a bit. The old Beckmanns couldn't
take it, you know. They'd carried on a bit too much in the
Third Reich—you know that. Why does an old man like
him want to wear uniform? And he was a bit hot on the Jews,
you know that, don't you, as his son? Your old man couldn't
stomach the Jews. They raised his bile. He was always shouting about wanting to chase them all to Palestine single-handed.
In the air-raid shelter, you know, every time a bomb came
down, he'd let fly about the Jews. He was just a bit too active,
your old man. He gave a bit too much of himself to the Nazis.
So when the Brown Age was over, he was for the high jump.
Because of the Jews. It was a bit thick too, that Jew business.
Why couldn't he keep his mouth shut, anyway? Just *too*
active, old Beckmann. And when it was all over with the

brown boys, they touched him on his sore spot. And a sore spot it was, I can tell you, a very sore spot—I say, you know, I can't help laughing the whole time about that comic thing you've run up on your nose for glasses. You look a proper fright. You can't call those sensible glasses. Haven't you got a proper pair, young man?

BECKMANN: (*Automatically*) No. These are the respirator glasses which soldiers got who——

FRAU KRAMER: I know. I know. Eh, but I'd never put them on. Rather stay at home. How my old man'd laugh! Do you know what he'd say to you? He'd say: Man alive, take the bridgework off your mug!

BECKMANN: Go on. What happened to my father? Tell me some more. It was getting so exciting. Come on, Frau Kramer, more, carry on!

FRAU KRAMER: There's nothing more to tell. They gave your dad the sack, no pension, of course. Then they had to get out of the house as well. All they could keep was the kettle. That was not so good, of course. And it put the lid on it for the old couple. They couldn't cope any more, I suppose. They had no wish to. Well, they denazified themselves once and for all. Now that was consistent of your old man, I'll grant him that.

BECKMANN: What's that? What did they do?

FRAU KRAMER: (*Good-natured rather than mean*) Denazified themselves. Just an expression, you know. It's a sort of private joke amongst us. Yes, those old people of yours didn't feel like it. There they were one morning lying blue and stiff in the kitchen. So stupid, my old man said, with all that gas we could have done a month's cooking.

BECKMANN: (*Softly, but with frightful menace*) I think it would be as well if you shut the door—fast. Fast! And lock it! Be quick and shut your door, I tell you!

(*The door creaks, Frau Kramer screams. The door slams*)

(*Softly*) I can't stand it! I can't stand it! I can't stand it!

THE OTHER: Yes, Beckmann, yes. One can stand it.

BECKMANN: No! I won't stand it any longer! Go away! You stupid optimist! Go away!

THE OTHER: No, Beckmann. Your road's up here. Come, stay up here, Beckmann, there's still a long way to go. Come!

BECKMANN: You're a brute! One can stand it, oh yes! You can stand it and carry on on this road. Sometimes you can lose your breath, sometimes you feel like murder. But you go on breathing and the murder doesn't happen. You scream no more and you sob no more. You stand it. Two corpses! Who bothers these days about two corpses?

THE OTHER: Quiet, Beckmann. Come.

BECKMANN: Of course it's irritating when they happen to be your parents, the two corpses. But then, two corpses, two old people? A pity about the gas! We could have done a month's cooking with it.

THE OTHER: Never mind, Beckmann. Come. The road's waiting!

BECKMANN: Yes, never mind. When one's got a heart that's screaming, a heart that'd commit murder. A poor fool of a heart that'd murder these mourners who grieve for the gas. A heart that would sleep, deep in the Elbe, d'you understand. A heart that's screamed itself hoarse: and no one has heard it. No one below. No one above. Two old people have wandered off to Ohlsdorf burial ground. Yesterday it was perhaps two thousand, the day before yesterday perhaps seventy thousand. Tomorrow it'll be four hundred thousand or six million who've wandered off into the world's mass graves. Who cares? No one. Not a man below. Not a God above. God sleeps and we go on living.

THE OTHER: Beckmann! Beckmann! Don't heed it! Beckmann! You see everything through your respirator glasses. You see everything distorted, Beckmann. Pay no attention. There *was* a time, Beckmann, when people reading the evening newspaper in the green-shaded light of Cape Town sighed for two girls frozen to death in the ice of Alaska. There was a time when they couldn't sleep in Hamburg because a child in Boston had been kidnapped. There was a time when it could happen that they mourned in San Francisco if a balloonist crashed in Paris.

BECKMANN: There *was* a time, there *was*, there *was*! *When* was it? Ten thousand years ago? It takes casualty lists with six naughts to do it now. But mankind doesn't sigh in the lamplight, it sleeps deeply and peacefully where it still has a bed. Brimful of pain, the people look dumbly past one another: hollow-cheeked, hard, bitter, warped, lonely. They're fed with numbers, which they can scarcely pronounce because they're so long. And the numbers mean——

THE OTHER: Don't heed it, Beckmann.

BECKMANN: Do heed it, heed it till you perish! The numbers are so long that one can scarcely pronounce them. And the numbers mean——

THE OTHER: Don't heed it.

BECKMANN: Heed now! They mean the dead, the half-dead, men killed by grenades, by shell splinters, starvation, bombs, ice storms, drowning, despair, the stranded, the lost, the lifeless. And these numbers have more naughts than we have fingers!

THE OTHER: Never mind. The road is waiting, Beckmann, come!

BECKMANN: For God's sake where does it lead? Where are we? Are we still here? Is this still the old earth? Have we acquired no hide, eh? Have we grown no tail, no beast's jaws, no *talons*? Do we still walk on two legs? Man! Man! What sort of a road are you? Where do you lead? Answer, you other one, you optimist! For God's sake answer, you eternal Answerer!

THE OTHER: You're losing the way, Beckmann. Come stay up here, your road is here. Don't listen. The road goes up and down. Don't yell when it goes down and when it's dark— The road goes on and there are lamps everywhere: Sun, stars, women, windows, lanterns and open doors. Don't yell, when you stand for half an hour at night in the fog alone. You'll meet others on the way. Come, boy, don't get tired! Don't listen to the sentimental tinkling of the sweet xylophone player, don't listen.

BECKMANN: Don't listen? Is that all your answer? Millions of dead, half-dead, missing—is all that of no account? And you say: don't listen, you say? I've lost my way? Yes, the road's grey, cruel, abysmal. But we're on it outside on the move, limping, weeping and starving along, poor, cold and tired! But the Elbe threw me up again like rotten meat. The Elbe

won't let me sleep. I should live, you say! Live! Live this life?
Then just tell me why? For whom? For what?

THE OTHER: For yourself! For life! Your road is waiting. And
every so often there are lamps. Are you such a coward that
you're afraid of the darkness between them? Do you want
only lamps? Come, Beckmann, on to the next one.

BECKMANN: I'm hungry, I tell you. I'm freezing, d'you hear? I
can't stand up any longer. I'm tired. Open a door, won't you?
I'm hungry. The road's dark and all the doors are shut. Keep
your mouth shut, optimist. Spare your lungs for others: I'm
homesick for my mother! I'm hungry for black bread! It
doesn't have to be biscuits, no, that's not necessary. My
mother would have had a piece of black bread for me, and
warm socks. And I would have sat myself down, full and
warm, in a soft armchair opposite the Colonel and read
Dostoievsky. Or Gorki. It's grand when one's full and warm,
to read about the misery of other people and sigh, oh! so
sympathetically. But unfortunately, my eyes keep shutting.
I'm dog, dog-tired. I want to yawn like a dog—to yawn my
whole head off. And I can't stand any longer. I'm tired, I tell
you. I won't go on. I *can't* go on, d'you understand? Not an
inch. Not a——

THE OTHER: Beckmann, don't give up. Come, Beckmann, life's
waiting. Beckmann. Come!

BECKMANN: I don't want to read Dostoievsky. I'm afraid myself.
I'm not coming. No. I'm tired. No, I tell you, I'm not
coming. I want to sleep. Here in front of my door. I'll sit
on the steps in front of my door and I'll sleep. Sleep, sleep,
till one day the walls of the house begin to crack and crumble
with age. Or till the next mobilization. I'm as tired as a whole
yawning world!

THE OTHER: Don't tire, Beckmann! Come, live!

BECKMANN: This life? No, this life is less than nothing. I won't
do it. What is it you're saying? Come on, friends. The show
must of course go on right through to the end. Who knows
in what dark corner we shall lie or on which sweet breast,
when at last the curtain falls. Five grey, rain-drenched acts!

THE OTHER: Carry on! Life is fine, Beckmann. Join in with the
living!

BECKMANN: Be quiet. Life is like this:
  Act I: Grey skies. A man is hurt.
  Act II: Grey skies: A man hurts back.
  Act III: It grows dark and rains.
  Act IV: It grows still darker. A door is seen.
  Act V: It is night, deep night, and the door is shut. The man is outside. Outside the door. He stands by the Elbe, by the Seine, by the Volga, by the Mississippi. He stands there with his thoughts, cold, hungry, and damned tired. Suddenly there's a splash, and the waves make neat little round circles and the curtain falls. Worms and fishes break into noiseless applause. That's how it goes! Is that more than nothing? I, at any rate, won't play any longer, not I. My yawns are as wide as the wide world.

THE OTHER: Don't fall asleep, Beckmann. You must go on.

BECKMANN: What do you say? You've suddenly gone so quiet.

THE OTHER: Stand up, Beckmann, the road is waiting.

BECKMANN: The road will have to do without my weary tread. Why are you so far away? I can no longer—scarcely—understand— (*He yawns*)

THE OTHER: Beckmann! Beckmann!

BECKMANN: H'm— (*He falls asleep*)

THE OTHER: Beckmann, you're asleep!

BECKMANN: (*In sleep*) Yes, I'm asleep.

THE OTHER: Wake up, Beckmann, you must live.

BECKMANN: No, I wouldn't think of waking up. I'm just dreaming. I'm dreaming a wonderful dream.

THE OTHER: Dream no longer, Beckmann, you must live.

BECKMANN: Live? Nonsense, I'm just dreaming that I'm dying.

THE OTHER: Get up, I say! Live!

BECKMANN: No. I don't want to get up again. I'm having such a wonderful dream. I'm lying in the road dying. My lungs won't work, my heart won't work and my legs won't work. The whole Beckmann won't work, d'you hear? Rank disobedience. Corporal Beckmann refuses to work. Terrific, eh?

THE OTHER: Come, Beckmann, you must go further.

BECKMANN: Further? Downwards, you mean, further downwards! *A bas*, as the French say. Dying's so wonderful, you know, I'd no idea. I believe death must be quite tolerable. So far no one's come back because he couldn't stand death. Perhaps death's quite nice, perhaps much nicer than life, perhaps— D'you know I believe I'm already in heaven. I can no longer feel, and that's as though one were in heaven, not to feel any longer. And there's an old man coming who looks like God. Yes, almost like God. Good evening, old man, are you God?

GOD: (*Tearfully*) I am God, my boy, my poor boy!

BECKMANN: Oh, so you're God. Who actually called you that, God? Mankind? Or you yourself?

GOD: Mankind calls me God.

BECKMANN: Odd, they must be very odd men who call you that. They must be the Contented, the Replete, the Happy Ones, and those who are afraid of you. Who walk in the sunshine, in love or contented or replete, or who are frightened at night. They say: Dear God! Dear God! But I *don't* say, Dear God, d'you hear, I know no dear God.

GOD: My child. My poor——

BECKMANN: When exactly are you dear, dear God? Were you dear when you let my little son, my little son, who was just a year old, be torn to pieces by a screaming bomb? Were you dear, dear God, when you had him murdered?

GOD: I didn't have him murdered.

BECKMANN: No, quite right. You only permitted it. You didn't heed when he screamed and the bombs roared. Where were you actually, when the bombs roared, dear God? And were you dear, when eleven men from my patrol were missing? Eleven men too few, dear God, and you weren't there, dear God. The eleven men must have screamed loud in the silent wood, but you weren't there, dear God, you just weren't there. Were you dear in Stalingrad, dear God, were you dear there, eh? No? When in fact were you dear then, God, when? When have you ever bothered yourself about us, God?

GOD: No one believes in me any longer. Neither you nor anyone. I am the God no one believes in. And no one cares about me any longer. None of you cares about me.

BECKMANN: Has God studied His theology? Who's supposed to care for whom? Oh, you are old, God, you're old-fashioned, you can't cope with the long lists of our dead and our agonies. We no longer really know you, you're a fairytale God. Today we need a new one, you know, one for our misery, our fear. A completely new one. Oh, we've searched for you, God, in every ruin, in every shellhole, in every night. We've called for you, God! We've roared for you, wept for you, cursed for you! Where were you then, dear God? Where are you tonight? Have you turned away from us? Have you completely walled yourself in in your fine old churches? Can't you hear our cries through the shattered windows, God? Where are you?

GOD: My children have turned away from me, not I from them. You from me, you from me. I am the God no one believes in. You have turned away from me.

BECKMANN: Go away, old man. You're spoiling my death. Go away, you're only a tearful theologist. You twist the phrases: Who cares for whom? Who's turned away from whom? You from me? We from you? You are dead, God. Live. Live with us, at night, when it's cold, and lonely, and the stomach hungers in the silence—live with us then, God. Oh, go away, you ink-blooded theologist, go away. You pitiful old man.

GOD: My boy, my poor boy. I cannot help it. I cannot, cannot help it.

BECKMANN: Yes, that's it, God. You can't help it. We fear you no longer. We love you no longer. And you're old-fashioned. The theologists have let you grow old. Your trousers are patched, your soles are worn out, and your voice has grown soft—too soft for the thunder of our time. We can no longer hear you.

GOD: No, none hears me, none hears me any more. You are too loud!

BECKMANN: Or are you too quiet, God? Have you too much ink in your blood, God, too much thin theologist's ink? Go, old man, you have walled yourself into the churches, we can no longer hear one another. Go, but before total darkness falls, make sure that you find a hole somewhere, or a new suit, or a dark forest, otherwise they'll shove everything on to your shoulders when it's gone wrong. And don't fall in the dark, old man, the road is very precipitous and strewn with skeletons. Hold your nose, God. Oh and sleep well, old man, may you sleep as well as ever. Good night!

GOD: A new suit or a dark forest? My poor, poor children! My dear boy——

BECKMANN: Yes, go! Good night!

GOD: My poor, poor children. (*Exit*)

BECKMANN: It's hardest nowadays for old people who can't adapt themselves to new conditions. We're all outside. Even God's outside, and no one opens a door to him now. Only death, at the last only death has a door for us. And I'm on the way there.

THE OTHER: You must not wait for the door that death opens to us. Life has a thousand doors. Who has promised you that behind death's door there's more than nothing?

BECKMANN: And what's behind the doors that life opens to us?

THE OTHER: Life! Life itself! Come, you must go on.

BECKMANN: I can't go on. Don't you hear my lungs wheezing? Wheeze—wheeze—wheeze. I cannot.

THE OTHER: You can! Your lungs are not wheezing.

BECKMANN: My lungs *are* wheezing. What else could it be? Listen—wheeze—wheeze—wheeze. What else?

THE OTHER: A roadsweeper's broom! Look, there's a sweeper coming. He's coming past us, and his broom is scratching on the roadway like asthmatic lungs. *Your* lungs are not wheezing. Just you listen! Wheeze—wheeze—wheeze. That's the broom!

BECKMANN: The roadsweeper's broom makes a noise like the lungs of a man in his death rattle. And the roadsweeper has red stripes down his trousers. He's a roadsweeper general. A German General of Roadsweepers. And when he sweeps, lungs in their death rattle go wheeze—wheeze—wheeze. Hey, roadsweeper!

ROADSWEEPER: I am no roadsweeper.

BECKMANN: Not a roadsweeper? What are you then?

ROADSWEEPER: I'm an employee of the Rot and Rubbish Interment Institute.

BECKMANN: You're death! And you work as a roadsweeper?

ROADSWEEPER: As a roadsweeper today. As a general yesterday. Death mustn't be choosy. The dead are everywhere. And today they actually lie in the streets. Yesterday they lay on the battlefield—then death was a general and the incidental music a xylophone. Today they lie in the streets, and the broom of death goes wheeze—wheeze.

BECKMANN: And the broom of death goes wheeze—wheeze. From general to roadsweeper. Are the dead so devalued?

ROADSWEEPER: They're going down. They're going down. No salute. No death bell. No funeral oration. No war memorial. They're going down. They're going down. The broom goes wheeze—wheeze.

BECKMANN: Must you go so soon? Stay here, won't you. Take me with you. Death, Death, you're forgetting me—Death!

ROADSWEEPER: I forget no one. My xylophone plays 'The Old Comrades', and my broom goes wheeze—wheeze—wheeze. I forget no one.

BECKMANN: Death, Death, leave the door open for me. Death, don't shut the door. Death——

ROADSWEEPER: My door is always open. Always. Morning, afternoon and at night. In light and in darkness. My door is always open. Always. Everywhere. And my broom goes wheeze—wheeze.

(The noise fades as Death moves off)

BECKMANN: Wheeze—wheeze. D'you hear my lungs wheezing? Like a roadsweeper's broom. And the roadsweeper leaves the door wide open. And the roadsweeper's name is Death. And his broom sounds like my lungs, like an old hoarse clock: Wheeze—wheeze.

THE OTHER: Stand up, Beckmann, there's still time. Come, breathe, breathe yourself well again.

BECKMANN: But my lungs sound like——

THE OTHER: That's not your lungs. That was the broom of a civil servant.

BECKMANN: A civil servant?

THE OTHER: Yes, and he's long since gone. Come, stand up again, breathe. Life waits with a thousand lamps and a thousand open doors.

BECKMANN: One door, one's enough. And he's leaving it open for me, he said, always, any time. One door.

THE OTHER: Stand up, you're dreaming a deadly dream. You'll die of your dream. Stand up.

BECKMANN: No. I'll stay here. Here in front of the door. And the door is open—he said. Here I'll stay. Stand up? No, I'm having such a wonderful dream. I'm dreaming, dreaming that it's all over. A roadsweeper came by and called himself Death. And he promised me a door, an open door. Roadsweepers can be nice people. Nice as death. Just such a sweeper came by me.

THE OTHER: You're dreaming, Beckmann, you're dreaming an evil dream. Wake up, live!

BECKMANN: Live? I'm lying in the road and it's all over, all over, I tell you. I'm certainly dead. It's all over and I'm dead, beautifully dead.

THE OTHER: Beckmann, Beckmann, you must live! Everyone's alive. Beside you. Left, right, in front of you: the others. And you? Where are you? Live, Beckmann, everyone's alive.

BECKMANN: The others? Who are they? The Colonel? The Producer? Frau Kramer? Live with them? Oh, I'm so wonderfully dead. The others are far away and I never want to see them again. The others are murderers.

THE OTHER: Beckmann, you're lying.

BECKMANN: Lying? Aren't they evil? Are they good?

THE OTHER: You don't know people. They are good.

BECKMANN: Oh, they're good. And in all goodness they've killed me. Laughed me to death. Shown me the door. Chased me away. In all human goodness. They are hard even in their deepest dreams—hard even in deepest sleep. And they pass my corpse—hard even in sleep. They laugh and chew and sing and sleep and digest their way past my body. My death is nothing.

THE OTHER: You're lying, Beckmann.

BECKMANN: Yes, optimist, these people pass my corpse by. Corpses are unpleasant and boring.

THE OTHER: Mankind does not pass your death by, Beckmann. Mankind has a heart. Mankind mourns your death, Beckmann, and lies long awake at night for your corpse. They don't pass by.

BECKMANN: Yes, they do, optimist. Corpses are ugly and unpleasant. They just go by quickly and hold their noses and shut their eyes.

THE OTHER: They do not. Their hearts contract at every corpse.

BECKMANN: Now look, here's someone coming. Do you remember him? It's the Colonel who wanted to make me human by means of his old suit. Colonel! Colonel!

COLONEL: Bless my soul, beggars again? Just like old times.

BECKMANN: Exactly, sir, exactly. Just like old times. The beggars actually come from the same social circles. But I'm no beggar, sir, no. I'm a drowned corpse. I'm a deserter, sir. I was a very tired soldier, sir. Yesterday I was Corporal Beckmann, sir, do you remember? Beckmann. I was a bit quiet, wasn't I, sir, remember? Yes, and tomorrow evening I shall drift dumb and numb and bloated on to the beach at Blankenese. Horrid, eh, sir? And you'll have me on your account, sir. Horrid, eh? Two thousand and eleven plus Beckmann makes two thousand and twelve. Two thousand and twelve nocturnal ghosts! Brr!

COLONEL: I don't know you at all, man. Never heard of a Beckmann. What was your rank?

BECKMANN: But, sir! Surely you must still remember your last murder! The one with the respirator glasses and convict's haircut and gammy leg! Corporal Beckmann, sir.

COLONEL: Of course! That fellow! Just shows, these lower ranks are all out and out unreliable. Dunderheads, army lawyers, pacifists, suicide candidates. So you drowned yourself. Yes, you're the type that got a bit wild and unmanned by the war. Utterly lacking in soldierly qualities. Deplorable sight, a thing like that.

BECKMANN: Yes, isn't it, sir, a deplorable sight, all the soft, white, water-corpses nowadays. And you are the murderer, sir, you! Can you really stand it, sir, being a murderer? How does it feel to be a murderer, sir?

COLONEL: I beg your pardon! I?

BECKMANN: Yes, sir, you laughed me to death. Your laughter was more frightful than all the deaths in the world, sir. You laughed me to death.

COLONEL: (*Completely uncomprehending*) Really? Oh, well, you were the type that would have gone to the dogs anyway. Good evening.

BECKMANN: Pleasant dreams, sir. And many thanks for the obituary. Did you hear, optimist, you friend of man? Obituary for a drowned soldier. Epilogue of a man for a man.

THE OTHER: You're dreaming, Beckmann, you're dreaming. Mankind is good.

BECKMANN: You're so hoarse, you optimistic tenor! Has it ruined your voice? Oh yes, mankind is good. But sometimes there are days when you keep on meeting the few bad ones there are. But mankind's not really that bad. I'm only dreaming, of course. I don't want to be unjust. Mankind is good. It's only that they're all so terribly different, that's it, so incredibly different. The one man's a Colonel, while the other's only a lower rank. The Colonel's content, healthy and has woollen pants. At night he has a bed and a wife.

THE OTHER: Beckmann, dream no more. Get up! Live! You're dreaming everything wrong.

BECKMANN: And the other, he starves, he limps, and hasn't even a shirt. In the evening he has an old deck chair as a bed, and the squeaking of asthmatic rats in the cellar takes the place of his wife's whispers. No, mankind is good. Only they're different, quite extraordinarily different from one another.

THE OTHER: Mankind is good. Only they are so unaware. Always so unaware. But their hearts, look into their hearts—their hearts are good. Only life won't allow them to show their hearts. Believe it, at bottom they're good.

BECKMANN: Of course. At bottom. But the bottom is usually so deep, you know. So incredibly deep. Yes, at bottom they're good—just different. One is white and the other is grey. One has pants and the other hasn't. And the grey one without pants, that's me. Had bad luck. Corpse Beckmann, Corporal (retired), fellow-creature (retired).

THE OTHER: You're dreaming, Beckmann. Stand up! Live! Come, see, mankind is good.

BECKMANN: And they pass by my corpse and chew and laugh and spit and digest. That's how they pass my death by, the good, good ones.

THE OTHER: Wake up, dreamer! You're dreaming an evil dream, Beckmann. Wake up!

BECKMANN: Oh, yes, I'm dreaming a terribly evil dream. Here, here comes the cabaret producer. Shall I interview him, Answerer?

THE OTHER: Come, Beckmann! Live! The street is full of lamps. Everyone's alive! Live too!

BECKMANN: Live too? With whom? The Colonel? No!

THE OTHER: With the others, Beckmann. Live with the others.

BECKMANN: And with the Producer?

THE OTHER: With him as well. With everyone.

BECKMANN: Good. With the Producer as well. Hallo, Mr. Producer!

PRODUCER: What's that? Yes? What's the matter?

BECKMANN: Do you know me?

PRODUCER: No—Yes, just a moment. Respirator glasses, Russian haircut, soldier's greatcoat. Yes, the beginner with the song about infidelity! What was your name again?

BECKMANN: Beckmann.

PRODUCER: Of course. Well?

BECKMANN: You murdered me, Mr. Producer.

PRODUCER: But, my dear fellow——

BECKMANN: Yes, because you were a coward. Because you betrayed truth. You drove me into the wet Elbe, because you wouldn't give the beginner a chance to begin. I wanted to work. I was starving. But your door shut behind me. You chased me into the Elbe, Mr. Producer.

PRODUCER: Must have been a sensitive fellow. Running into the Elbe, into the wet——

BECKMANN: Into the wet Elbe, Mr. Producer. And there I let Elbe water run into me till I was full. Full for once, Mr. Producer, and died of it. Tragic, eh? Wouldn't that make a number for your revue? Song of the times: Full for once and died of it!

PRODUCER: (*Only very superficially sympathetic*) But that's terrible! You were the type that's a bit too sensitive. Such a mistake nowadays, completely out of place. You were madly obsessed by truth, you little fanatic! You'd have made the entire public shy on me with that song!

BECKMANN: So you slammed the door on me, Mr. Producer. And the Elbe was down there.

PRODUCER: (*Very superior*) The Elbe, yes. Drowned. Finished. Poor beggar. Run over by life. Rolled out flat. Full for once and died of it. Well, if we were all as sensitive as that. . . .!

BECKMANN: But we're not, Mr. Producer, we're not so sensitive.

PRODUCER: God knows we're not, no. You were merely one of

those, one of the millions, who have to limp through life and are glad when they fall. Into the Elbe, into the Spree, into the Thames—it doesn't matter where. Until then they have no rest.

BECKMANN: And you tripped me, to enable me to fall.

PRODUCER: Nonsense! Who says so? You were predestined for tragic parts. But the material's terrible! A beginner's ballad! The water-corpse with the respirator glasses! It's a pity the public doesn't want that sort of thing. A pity. (*Exit*)

BECKMANN: Pleasant dreams, Mr. Producer. Did you hear? Should I go on living with the Colonel? And with the Producer?

THE OTHER: You're dreaming, Beckmann, wake up.

BECKMANN: Am I dreaming? Do I see everything distorted through these wretched respirator glasses? Are they all marionettes? Grotesque, caricatured, human marionettes? Did you hear the obituary my murderer dedicated to me? Epilogue for a beginner: Another of the many—you other one! Shall I go on living? Shall I go on limping along the road? Along with the others? They've all got the same disgustingly indifferent faces. And they all talk so much, but if one asks for a single "Yes", they're all numb and dumb like—yes, like humanity. And they're cowards. They have betrayed us. Betrayed us terribly. When we were quite small they had a war. And as we got bigger they told us stories of the war. Enthusiastically. They were always enthusiastic. And as we got bigger still they thought out a war for us too. And they packed us off to it. They were enthusiastic. They were always enthusiastic. And nobody told us where we were going. Nobody told us you're going to hell. Oh no, no one. They invented marching songs and celebrations. And courts-martial and campaigns. And heroes' songs and initiation ceremonies. They were so enthusiastic. And at last came the war. And they packed us off to it. And they said to us—Make a job of it, boys! They said. Make a job of it, boys. That's how they betrayed us. Yes, betrayed us. And now they're sitting behind their doors. The Professor, the Director, the Judge, the Doctor. No one's packed us off this time. No, no one. They're all sitting behind their doors and the doors are firmly shut. And we're outside. And from their pulpits and their armchairs they point their fingers at us. That's how they've betrayed us. Betrayed us terribly. And now they ignore their murder, simply ignore it. They ignore the murder they've committed.

THE OTHER: They do not ignore it, Beckmann. You exaggerate. You're dreaming. Look at their hearts, Beckmann. They have hearts. They're good.

BECKMANN: But Frau Kramer ignores my corpse.

THE OTHER: No! Even she has a heart.

BECKMANN: Frau Kramer!

FRAU KRAMER: Yes?

BECKMANN: Have you a heart, Frau Kramer? Where was your heart, Frau Kramer, when you murdered me? Yes, Frau Kramer, you murdered the old Beckmanns' son. Didn't you finish off his parents as well, eh? Now, honestly, Frau Kramer, you did give just a little help, didn't you? Just made their life a little sour, eh? And then chased the son into the Elbe—but your heart, Frau Kramer, what does your heart say?

FRAU KRAMER: You with the funny glasses? Threw yourself into the Elbe? Fancy me not thinking of that. And you looked so sad, too. I might have known it. Threw himself into the Elbe! Poor boy! Imagine!

BECKMANN: Yes, because you informed me so tactfully and sympathetically of the passing away of my parents. Your door was the last one. And you kept me outside. And for a thousand days and a thousand Siberian nights I'd looked forward to that door. You committed a little murder on the side, didn't you?

FRAU KRAMER: (*Robust so as not to cry*) There are people who always have hard luck. You were one of them. Siberia. Gas tap. Ohlsdorf. It was all too much for you. It goes to my heart, but where would we be if we started crying for everyone? You looked so gloomy. Such a boy! But we mustn't let it get us or we'll be done for. Simply throws himself into the water! We certainly see life! Somebody does himself in every day!

BECKMANN: Yes, yes, farewell, Frau Kramer! Did you hear, you other one? Obituary for a young man by a woman of good heart. Did you hear, you silent Answerer?

THE OTHER: Wake—up—Beckmann.

BECKMANN: You're suddenly so quiet. You're suddenly so far away.

THE OTHER: You're dreaming a deadly dream, Beckmann. Wake up! Live! Don't take yourself so seriously. There's death every day. Should eternity be full of weeping? Live! Eat your bread and margarine, live! Life has a thousand facets. Take hold of it! Stand up.

BECKMANN: Yes, I'll stand up. For there comes my wife. My wife is good. No, she's got her friend with her. But once she was good, all right. Why did I have to stay three years in Siberia? She waited three years, I know that, for she was always good to me. It's my fault. But she was good. Is she still good today?

THE OTHER: Try it! Live!

BECKMANN: Don't be afraid, my dear, it's me. Look at me! Your husband! I've taken my life. You shouldn't have done that, my dear, with the other man. I only had you. You're not listening! You! I know you had to wait too long. But don't be sad. I'm all right now. I'm dead. Without you I couldn't go on. You! Look at me! Look at me!

(*The wife goes slowly past in the arms of her lover, without hearing Beckmann*)

You! You were my wife! Look at me. You killed me, surely you can look at me! You, you're not listening! You murdered me and yet now you simply pass me by? You, why don't you listen?

(*The wife has gone past with her friend*)

She didn't hear me. She doesn't even know me any more. Have I been dead so long? She has forgotten me and I've only been dead for a day. So good, oh mankind is so good! And you? Optimist, Cheerleader, Answerer? You say nothing. You're so far away. Shall I go on living? It was for her I came back from Siberia. And you say I should go on living! Every door to left and right of the road is shut. All the lamps have gone out, all of them. And one only moves forward by falling! And you say I should live! Have you not got another fall for me? Don't go so far away, you silent one, have you still got a lamp for me in the darkness? Speak, as a rule you know so much!

THE OTHER: Here comes the girl who pulled you out of the Elbe and warmed you. The girl, Beckmann, who wanted to kiss your stupid head. She doesn't ignore your death. She has searched for you everywhere.

BECKMANN: No! She hasn't searched for me! Not a soul has searched for me! I will not go on believing it again and again. I cannot fall again, do you hear? Not a soul searches for me!

THE OTHER: The girl has searched for you everywhere.

BECKMANN: You're torturing me, optimist! Go away!

GIRL: (*Without seeing him*) Fish! Fish! Where are you? Little cold fish.

BECKMANN: I am dead.

GIRL: Oh, you are dead? And I'm searching for you all over the world.

BECKMANN: Why are you searching for me?

GIRL: Why? Because I love you, poor ghost! And now you're dead. I should have loved to kiss you, little cold fish.

BECKMANN: Do we stand up and carry on because a girl calls us? Girl?

GIRL: Yes, fish?

BECKMANN: And if I were not dead?

GIRL: Oh, then we'd go home together, to my house. Yes, be alive again, little cold fish! For me. With me. Come, let's be alive together.

BECKMANN: Should I live? Have you really searched for me?

GIRL: Always. You and only you. You all the time. Oh, why are you dead, poor grey ghost? Won't you be alive with me?

BECKMANN: Yes, yes, yes. I'm coming with you. I will be alive with you.

GIRL: Oh, my fish!

BECKMANN: I'll stand up. You are the light that burns for me. For me alone. And we'll be alive together. And we'll walk close together on the dark road. Come, let's be alive together and close, close together——

GIRL: Yes, I'm burning for you alone on the dark road.

BECKMANN: You burn, you say? But everything's getting dark! Where are you?

(*The tick-tock of the one-legged man is heard in the distance*)

GIRL: Do you hear? The death worm's knocking. I must go, fish, I must go, poor cold ghost!

BECKMANN: Why? Why? Stay here! Everything's suddenly so

dark! Light, little light! Shine! Who's knocking? Someone's knocking! Tick-tock, Tick-tock! Who knocks like that? There, tick-tock, tick-tock! Louder! Nearer! Tick-tock, tick-tock. (*Screams*) There! (*Whispers*) The giant! The one-legged giant with his two crutches. Tick-tock, he's coming nearer. Tick-tock, he's coming to me. Tick-tock-tick-tock. (*Screams*)

ONE LEGGED: (*Quite matter of fact and serene*) Beckmann?

BECKMANN: (*Softly*) Here I am.

ONE LEGGED: You're still alive, Beckmann? You've committed a murder, Beckmann. And you're still alive.

BECKMANN: I've committed no murder.

ONE LEGGED: Yes, you have, Beckmann. We are murdered each day and each day we commit murder. You murdered me, Beckmann! Have you forgotten already? I was three years in Siberia, Beckmann, and yesterday I wanted to go home. But my place was taken—you were there, Beckmann, in my place. So I went into the Elbe, Beckmann, yesterday evening. Where else should I go, Beckmann, eh? The Elbe was cold and wet. But I'm used to it now, now I'm dead. That you should have forgotten that so quickly, Beckmann! One doesn't forget murder as fast as that. It runs after you, Beckmann. Yes, I made a mistake. I should not have come home. There was no place for me at home, Beckmann, for you were there. I don't blame you, Beckmann, we all commit murder, every day, every night. But let's not forget our victims so rapidly. Let's not ignore our murders. Yes, Beckmann, you took my place from me. On my sofa, with my wife, my wife, of whom I had dreamt for three years, a thousand Siberian nights. At home there was a man with my clothes on, Beckmann. They were far too big for him, but he had them on, and he was warm and well in my clothes with my wife. And you were the man, Beckmann. So—I withdrew. Into the Elbe. It was pretty cold, Beckmann, but one soon gets used to it. I have only been dead for a day—and you murdered me and you've already forgotten the murder. You must not do that, Beckmann, you shouldn't forget murders, only bad people do that. You won't forget me, will you, Beckmann? You must promise that you won't forget your murder!

BECKMANN: I won't forget you!

ONE LEGGED: That's good of you, Beckmann. Then I can be dead in peace if one man at least is thinking of me, at least my murderer—just now and again—at night sometimes, Beckmann, when you can't sleep! Then I can at least be dead in peace— (*Exit*)

BECKMANN: (*Wakes up*) Tick—tock—tick—tock! Where am I? Have I been dreaming? Am I not dead? Am I still not dead? Tick-tock-tick-tock through life! Tick-tock right through death! Tick-tock-tick-tock! Do you hear the death worm? And I am supposed to live! And every night there'll be a guard at my bed and I shall never be free of his tread—tick-tock-tick-tock! No! This is life! There is a man, and the man comes to Germany, and the man freezes. He starves, and limps! A man comes to Germany! He comes home and his bed is occupied. A door slams and he is outside.

A man comes to Germany! He finds a girl, but the girl has a husband, who has only one leg and keeps groaning a name. And the name is Beckmann. A door slams and he is outside. A man comes to Germany! He looks for humanity, but a Colonel laughs himself sick. A door slams, and he is outside again.

A man comes to Germany! He looks for work, but a Producer is a coward and the door slams and he is again outside.

A man comes to Germany! He looks for his parents, but an old woman mourns the waste of gas, and the door slams and he is outside.

A man comes to Germany! And then comes the one-legged man—tick-tock-tick-tock, and the one-legged man says Beckmann. Always Beckmann. He breathes Beckmann; he snores Beckmann; he groans Beckmann, he cries, he curses, he prays Beckmann. And he walks through the life of his murderer—tick-tock-tick-tock! And I am the murderer. I? I, the murdered, I whom they have murdered, I am the murderer? Who protects us from becoming murderers? We are murdered each day, and each day we commit murder! And the murderer Beckmann can stand it no longer, murdering and being murdered. And he screams in the face of the world: I die! And then he lies down somewhere in the street, the man who came to Germany, and dies. In the old days, cigarette butts, orange peel and paper lay in the street, nowadays it's people. That doesn't mean a thing. And then a roadsweeper comes along, a German roadsweeper in uniform with red stripes, from the firm of Rot and Rubbish, and finds the murdered murderer Beckmann. Starved, frozen, abandoned. In the twentieth century. In the fifth decade. In the street. In Germany. And people pass his death inattentive, resigned, bored, sickened and indifferent, indifferent, so indifferent! And the dead man deep in his dream feels that his death was like his life: pointless, insignificant, grey. And you—you say I should live! Why? For whom? For what? Have I no right to my death? Have I no right to my suicide? Shall I go on murdering and being murdered? Where *shall* I go? *How* shall I live? With whom? For what? Where shall we go in this world! We are betrayed. Terribly betrayed. Where are you, other one? You've always been here before. Where are you now, optimist? Now answer me! Now I need you, Answerer! Where are you? You're suddenly not there! Where are you, Answerer, where are you, you who grudged me death? Where is the old man who calls himself God?

Why doesn't he speak?

Answer!

Why are you silent? Why?

Will none of you answer?

Will no one answer?

Will no one, nobody answer me?

ON THAT TUESDAY

Nineteen Stories

The stories contained in this collection were written in the period between autumn 1946 and summer 1947. They appeared in Germany in book form shortly after the death of the author.

TO MY FATHER

"In the Snow, in the Clean Snow"

We are the skittle-players.
And we ourselves, the ball.
But we, too, are the skittles
that fall.
And the skittle-alley, where the thunder is,
Is our heart.

THE SKITTLE-ALLEY

Two men had made a hole in the ground. It was quite roomy and almost snug. Like a grave. It was bearable.

In front of them they had a gun. Somebody had invented it, so one could shoot at people with it. Mostly people one didn't know at all. One didn't even understand their language. And they'd never done anything to one. But one had to shoot at them with the gun. Somebody had commanded it. And so that one could shoot plenty of them, somebody had invented a gun that shot more than sixty times a minute. For that he had been rewarded.

A little further on from the two men was another hole. Out of it peeped a head, that belonged to a man. It had a nose that could smell perfume. Eyes that could see a flower or a city. It had a mouth that could eat bread and say Anna or Mother. This head was seen by the two men who had been given the gun.

Shoot, said one of them.

He shot.

Then the head was kaputt. It couldn't smell perfume again, nor see a city again nor say Anna again. Never again.

The two men were in the hole for many months. They made a lot of heads kaputt. And they always belonged to people whom they didn't know at all. Who had never done anything to them and whom they didn't even understand. But somebody had invented the gun that shot more than sixty times a minute. And somebody commanded it.

By degrees the two men had made so many heads kaputt, that one could have made a great mountain out of them. And when the two men slept, the heads began to roll. As in a skittle-alley. With a soft thundering noise. Which woke the two men up.

But someone commanded it, whispered the one.

But we did it, shouted the other.

But it was terrible, groaned the first one.

But sometimes it was fun, laughed the other.

141

No, screamed the whisperer.

Yes, whispered the other, sometimes it was fun. That's just it. Real fun.

For hours they sat in the night. They didn't sleep. Then the first one said:

But God made us like that.

But God has an excuse, said the other, he doesn't exist.

He doesn't exist? asked the first one.

That's his only excuse, replied the second.

But we—we exist, whispered the first one.

Yes, we exist, whispered the other.

The two men, who had been commanded to make plenty of heads kaputt, didn't sleep at night. For the heads made a soft thundering noise.

And the first one said: And now we're stuck with it.

Yes, said the other, now we're stuck with it.

Then somebody shouted: Get ready! We're starting again.

The two men stood up and took the gun.

And every time they saw a man they shot at him. And it was always a man they didn't know at all. And who'd done nothing to them. But they shot at him. For that purpose somebody had invented the gun. And for that he had been rewarded.

And somebody—somebody had commanded it.

FOUR SOLDIERS

FOUR soldiers. And they were made of wood and hunger and earth. Of homesickness, beards and snowstorms. Four soldiers. And over them roared shells and bit, barking black venom, into the snow. The wood of their four lost faces stood out sharp-edged in the sway of the oil-light. Only when the iron screamed above and burst in terrible barking, then one of the wooden heads laughed. And afterwards the others grinned greyly. And the oil-light bowed in despair.

Four soldiers.

Then two blue-red lines curved in a beard: By heaven! This won't need to be ploughed in spring. Nor dunged either, croaked out of the corner.

One was confidently rolling a cigarette: I hope this isn't a turnip field. I can't stand a death full of turnips. But for instance, how would you like radishes? Radishes for all eternity?

The blue-red lips curved: If only there weren't any worms. One'll have to get mighty used to them.

The one in the corner said: You won't notice them any more.

Who says so? asked the cigarette roller, eh, who says so?

Then they were silent. And above them a raging death screeched through the night. Blue-black it tore up the snow. Then they grinned again. And they looked at the beams above them. But the beams promised nothing.

Then the one coughed out of his corner: Well, we'll find out. You can depend on that. And the "depend" came so hoarse, that the oil-light swayed.

Four soldiers. But one, he said nothing. He slid his thumb up and down on his rifle. Up and down. Up and down. And he pressed the rifle to him. But there was nothing he hated so much as this rifle. Only when it roared above him, then he held fast to it. The oil-light flickered failing in his eyes. Then the cigarette-roller nudged him. The little man with the hated rifle, startled, wiped the pale undergrowth of beard round his mouth. His face was made of hunger and homesickness.

143

Then the cigarette-roller said: You, give me that damned lamp.

Of course, said the little man, and put the rifle between his knees. And then his hand came out of his coat and took the oil-light and held it towards him. But then the light fell out of his hand. And went out. And went out.

Four soldiers. Their breathing was too big and too lonely in the dark. Then the little man laughed loud and raised his hand to his knee:

Boy, have I got the jitters! Did you see that? The damned lamp fell right out of my hand. Am I jittery!

The little man laughed. But in the darkness he pressed the rifle close to him, the rifle he so hated. And the one in the corner thought: There's not one among us, not one, who's not trembling.

But the cigarette-roller said: Yes, one's trembling all day. It's because of the cold. This terrible cold.

Then the iron roared over them and hacked up the night and the snow.

They'll make all the radishes kaputt, grinned the one with the blue-red lips.

And they held fast to the rifles that they hated. And laughed. Laughed themselves across the dark, dark valley.

LOTS AND LOTS OF SNOW

Snow hung in the branches. The machine-gunner sang. He stood in a Russian forest, far forward, on guard. He sang Christmas carols although it was already the beginning of February. But that was because the snow lay yards high. Snow between the black tree-trunks. Snow on the black-green twigs. Left hanging in the branches, blown on to bushes like cotton-wool and caked on to black tree-trunks. Lots and lots of snow. And the machine-gunner sang Christmas carols, although it was already February.

Now and then you must let fly a few shots. Otherwise the thing freezes up. Just hold it straight out into the darkness. So it doesn't freeze up. Take a shot at those bushes there. Yes, those, then you'll know if there's anyone sitting in them. It reassures you. Every quarter of an hour you can safely let fly a burst. It reassures you. Otherwise the thing freezes up. And then it's not so silent, if one fires now and then. The man he'd relieved had said that. And also: You must pull your balaclava back off your ears. Regimental order. On guard, you must push your balaclava back off your ears. Otherwise you hear nothing. That's an order. But you don't hear anything anyway. Everything's silent. Not a squeak. For weeks now. Not a squeak. Well, I'm off. Fire every now and then. It reassures you.

That's what he said. Then he stood there alone. He pulled the balaclava back off his ears and the cold clutched at them with sharp fingers. He stood there alone. And snow hung in the branches. Stuck on the blue-black tree-trunks. Heaped up over the bushes. Piled up high, drifting, and sinking in hollows. Lots and lots of snow.

And the snow in which he was standing made danger so quiet. So far off. And it could be standing right behind one. It silenced it. And the snow in which he was standing, standing alone in the night, standing alone for the first time, it made the nearness of the others so quiet. It made them so far away. It silenced

145

them, for it made everything so quiet that the blood grew loud in one's ears, grew so loud that one couldn't escape it. So silent the snow.

Then there was a sigh. On the left. In front. Then on the right. Then left again. And behind, suddenly. The machine-gunner held his breath. There, again. A sigh. The rushing in his ears grew enormous. Then it sighed again. He tore his coat-collar open. His fingers tugged, trembled. They tore his coat-collar open, so that it didn't cover his ear. There. A sigh. The sweat came out cold from under his helmet and froze on his forehead. Froze there. There were forty-two degrees of frost. From under his helmet the sweat came out and froze. A sigh. Behind. And on the right. Far in front. Then here. There. There, too.

The machine-gunner stood in the Russian forest. Snow hung in the branches. And the blood rushed loud in his ears. And the sweat froze on his forehead. And the sweat came out from under his helmet. For it was sighing. Something. Or someone. The snow concealed it. So the sweat froze on his forehead. For fear was big in his ears. For it was sighing.

Then he sang. He sang loud, so as not to hear the fear any more. Nor the sighs any more. And so that the sweat wouldn't freeze any more. He sang. And he no longer heard the fear. Christmas carols he sang, and he no longer heard the sighs. He sang loud Christmas carols in the Russian forest. For snow hung in the blue-black branches in the Russian forest. Lots of snow.

And then a branch broke suddenly. And the machine-gunner was silent. And whirled round. And tore out his pistol. Then with great bounds the sergeant came towards him through the snow.

Now I shall be shot, thought the machine-gunner. I've been singing on guard. And now I'll be shot. There's the sergeant already. And how he's running! I've been singing on guard and now they'll come and shoot me.

And he held the pistol firmly in his hand.

Then the sergeant was there. And held on to him. And looked round. Shaking. And then gasped:

My God! Hold me tight, man. My God! My God!

And then he laughed. His hands shook. And yet he laughed: I'm hearing Christmas carols. Christmas carols in this damned Russian forest. Christmas carols. Isn't it February? Sure it's February now. But I hear Christmas carols. It's because of this terrible silence. Christmas carols! God in heaven! Just hold me tight, man. Be quiet a minute. There! No. Now it's gone. Don't laugh, said the sergeant and gasped again and held the machine-gunner tight, don't laugh, man. But it's because of the silence. Weeks of this silence. Not a squeak! Nothing! So after a while you hear Christmas carols. Although it's long since been February. But it comes from the snow. There's so much here. Don't laugh, man. It drives you mad, I tell you. You've only been here two days. But we've been sitting in it here for weeks now. Not a squeak! Nothing. It drives you mad. Everything always silent. Not a squeak! For weeks. Then gradually you start hearing Christmas carols. Don't laugh. Only when I saw you they suddenly stopped. My God. It drives you mad. This everlasting silence. Everlasting!

The sergeant gasped again. And laughed. And held him tight. And the machine-gunner held him tight, too. Then they both laughed. In the Russian forest. In February.

Sometimes a branch bent under the snow. And then between the blue-black twigs it slid to the ground. And sighed as it did so. Quite softly. Sometimes in front. On the left. Then here. There, too.

It sighed everywhere. For snow hung in the branches. Lots and lots of snow.

MY PALEFACE BROTHER

NEVER had anything been so white as this snow. It was almost blue with it. Blue-green. So terrifyingly white. The sun scarcely dared to be yellow against this snow. No Sunday morning had ever been as clean as this one. Only at the back stood a dark-blue wood. But the snow was new and clean as a beast's eye. No snow was ever so white as this on this Sunday morning. No Sunday morning was ever so clean. The world, this snowy Sunday world, laughed.

But after all there was a stain somewhere. It was a man lying in the snow, crumpled, on his stomach, in uniform. A bundle of rags. A ragged bundle of little bits of skin and bone and leather and cloth. Drizzled over, black-red, with dried-up blood. Very dead hair, dead like a wig. Crumpled up, the last scream screamed, barked or perhaps prayed, in the snow: A soldier. Stain in the unbelievable snow-white of the cleanest of all Sunday mornings. Impressive war picture, rich in nuance, attractive theme for a water colour: blood and snow and sun. Cold cold snow with warm steaming blood in it. And over all the dear sun. Our dear sun. All the children in the world say: the dear, dear sun. And it shines on a dead man who screams the unheard scream of all dead marionettes: the dumb frightful dumb scream! Who among us, stand up, pale brother, oh, who among us can bear the dumb screams of the marionettes, when torn from their wires they lie around on the stage so stupidly out of joint? Who, oh, who among us can bear the dumb screams of the dead? Only the snow, the icy one, can bear it. And the sun. Our dear sun.

In front of the torn-off marionette stood one that was still intact. And working. In front of the dead soldier stood a live one. On this clear Sunday morning in the unbelievably white snow the one standing addressed to the one lying flat the following frightful dumb speech:

Yes. Yes, yes. Yes, yes, yes. That's the end of your good temper now, my friend. With your everlasting good temper. You aren't saying anything more now, eh? You aren't laughing any more now, eh? If your women only knew how pitiful you look now, my friend. Quite pitiful you look without your good temper. And in that silly position. Why have you pulled your legs up so fearfully into your stomach? Oh I see, you got one in the bowels. Dirtied yourself with blood. Looks unappetizing, my friend. Spattered it all over your uniform. Looks like black inkspots. Good thing your women won't see it. You were always just so with your uniform. With its wonderful cut. When you were made a corporal, then you only wore dress boots. And for hours they were polished, when you were going into town in the evening. But you won't go into town again now. Your women are going with the others now. For you won't be going anywhere at all any more, d'you understand? Never again, my friend. Never, never again. You won't be laughing any more now, either, with your everlasting good temper. You're lying there now as though you couldn't count up to three. You can't, either. Can't even count up to three any more. Bad show, my friend, thundering bad show. But it's a good thing, a very good thing. For never again will you say to me "My paleface brother Drooping Eyelid" Never again now, my friend. From now on, never again. Never again, see. And the others won't toast you for it any more. The others won't laugh at me any more, when you call me "My paleface brother Drooping Eyelid". That's worth a lot, d'you know? That's worth a whole heap to me, I can tell you. Fact is they started tormenting me at school. They set about me like lice. Because my eye has this little defect and because the lid droops down. And because my skin is so white. So cheesy. Our little pale one looks so tired again, they were always saying. And the girls always asked if I was already asleep, one of my eyes was already half shut. Sleepy, they said, man, I was supposed to be sleepy. I'd just like to know which of the pair of us is sleepy now. You or me, eh? You or me? Now who's "My paleface brother Drooping Eyelid"? Eh? Who then, my friend, you or me? Me, by any chance?

As he shut the dug-out door behind him, a dozen grey faces came towards him from the corners. One of them belonged to the sergeant. Did you find him, Herr Leutnant? asked the grey face and was terribly grey as it did so.

Yes. Near the pines. Shot in the stomach.

Shall we fetch him?

Yes. Near the pines. Yes, of course. He must be fetched. Near the pines.

The dozen grey faces disappeared. The subaltern sat by the tin stove and deloused himself. Exactly like yesterday. Yesterday he had also deloused himself. Then someone had to go to battalion H.Q. Best of all he, the subaltern, himself. While he was pulling on his shirt, he listened. There was firing. There had never been such firing. And when the runner tore open the door again, he saw the night. There had never been so dark a night, he thought. Sergeant Heller was singing. He was talking at length about his women. And then this Heller, with his everlasting good humour had said: Herr Leutnant, in your place I wouldn't go to Battalion H.Q. I'd sooner ask for double rations. You could play the xylophone on your ribs. You look terrible. That's what Heller had said. And in the darkness no doubt they had all grinned. And one of them had to go to Battalion H.Q. Then he'd said: Well, Heller, you can let your good temper cool off a bit. And Heller said: Very good. That was all. No one ever said more. Simply: Very good. And then Heller had gone. And then Heller didn't come back.

The subaltern pulled his shirt over his head. He listened to those outside coming back. The others. With Heller. Never again will he call me "My paleface brother Drooping Eyelid", whispered the subaltern. From now on he'll never say that to me again.

A louse was caught between his thumb-nails. It cracked.

The louse was dead. On his forehead—he had a tiny splash of blood.

JESUS WON'T PLAY ANY MORE

Uncomfortably he lay in the shallow grave. As always it had turned out very short, so that he had to bend his knees. He felt the icy cold in his back. He felt it like a tiny death. The sky seemed to him to be very far away. So uncannily far away that one no longer cared to say, it's fine or it's beautiful. Its distance from the earth was uncanny. All the blue that it poured out made the distance no shorter. And the earth was so unearthly cold and stubborn in its icy numbness that one lay most uncomfortably in the far too shallow grave. Ought one to lie so uncomfortably one's whole life long? Ah no, actually one's whole death long! That was so very much longer.

Two heads appeared in the sky over the edge of the grave. Well, will it do, Jesus? asked one head, letting a ball of vapour like a cotton-tuft fly out of his mouth. From his two nostrils Jesus thrust out two thin, equally white vapour columns and answered: Yep. It'll do. The heads in the sky disappeared. Like blots they were suddenly wiped away. Without trace. Only the sky was still there in its uncanny distance.

Jesus sat up and the upper part of his body projected slightly out of the grave. From afar it looked as though he had been buried up to his stomach. Then he leaned his left arm on the side of the grave and stood up. He stood in the grave and looked sadly at his left hand. In standing up he had again torn open the second finger of his freshly darned glove. The red-frozen finger-tip protruded from it. Jesus looked at his glove and grew very sad. He stood in the far too shallow grave, breathed a warm vapour against his uncovered freezing finger and said softly: I won't play any more. What's the matter, gaped at him one of the two who had been looking into the grave. I won't play any more, said Jesus again equally softly and put the cold naked finger in his mouth.

Did you hear that, Corporal, Jesus won't play any more. The other, the corporal, was counting detonators in an ammunition box and growled: How's that? He blew the wet vapour out of

his mouth at Jesus: Eh, how's that? No, said Jesus still just as
softly, I can't do it any more. He stood in the grave and had his
eyes shut. The sun made the snow so unbearably white. He had
his eyes shut and said: Blasting out graves every day. Every day
seven or eight graves. Yesterday actually eleven. And every day
people squeezed into graves that don't fit them. Because the
graves are too small. And the people are sometimes frozen so
stiff and crooked. Then it crunches so, when they're squeezed
into these narrow graves. And the earth is so hard and icy and
uncomfortable. They're supposed to put up with that their whole
death long. And I, I can't stand the crunching any more. It's
like grinding glass. Like glass.

Shut your mouth, Jesus. Quick, out of the hole. We've got
five more graves to make. Furiously the vapour fluttered away at
Jesus from the corporal's mouth. No, he said and thrust two fine
streaks of vapour out of his nose, no. He spoke very softly and
had his eyes shut: The graves are far too shallow, too. Later on
in the spring the bones'll be coming out of the earth everywhere.
When it thaws. Bones everywhere. No, I won't do it any more.
No, no. And always me. It's always me has to lie in the grave,
to see if it fits. Always me. I'm beginning to dream about it.
It's dreadful, I tell you, that it's always me has to test the graves.
Always me. Always me. You dream about it afterwards. It's
dreadful, that it's always me has to get into the graves. Always me.

Jesus looked again at his torn glove. He climbed out of the
shallow grave and took four paces towards a dark mound. The
mound consisted of dead people. They were out of joint, as
though they had been surprised in some indecent dance. Jesus laid
his pickaxe softly and carefully beside the mound of dead people.
He could just as well have thrown the pickaxe down, it wouldn't
have hurt the pickaxe. But he put it down softly and carefully,
as though not to disturb nor wake anyone up. For God's sake
wake no one up. Not only out of consideration, but out of fear.
Fear. For God's sake wake no one up. Then, paying no attention
to the other two, he walked past them through the crunching
snow towards the village.

Horrible, the snow crunches exactly the same, just exactly the
same. He lifted his feet up and stalked through the snow like a
bird, purely to avoid the crunching.

Behind him the corporal shouted: Jesus! Turn back at once! That's an order! You are to go on with the work immediately! The corporal shouted, but Jesus did not look round. He stalked like a bird through the snow, like a bird, just to avoid the crunching. The corporal shouted—but Jesus did not look round. Only his hands made a movement, as though he were saying: Softly, softly! For God's sake wake no one up! I won't do it any more. No. No. Always me. Always me. He grew smaller, ever smaller till he disappeared behind a snowdrift.

I'll have to report him. The corporal made a damp cottony vapour ball in the icy air. I'll have to report him, that's obvious. That's rank disobedience. We know he's got a screw loose, but I'll have to report him.

And then what'll they do with him? grinned the other.

Nothing much. Nothing much at all. The corporal wrote a name in his notebook. Nothing. The old man'll have him brought in. The old man always has a bit of fun with Jesus. He'll roar blue murder at him, so he won't eat or speak for two days, and let him go. Then he'll be quite normal again for a time. But first I'll have to report him. If only because the old man gets a bit of fun out of it. And the graves do have to be made. Somebody has to get in, to see if they fit. It can't be helped.

Why do they call him Jesus, grinned the other.

Oh, there's no real reason for that, either. The old man always calls him that, because he looks so meek. The old man thinks he looks so meek. Since then he's called Jesus. Yes, said the corporal and got a new charge ready for the next grave, I'll have to report him, I must, for the graves have got to be dug.

THE CAT WAS FROZEN IN THE SNOW

MEN were walking on the road at night. They were humming. Behind them there was a red spot in the night. It was a hideous red spot. For the spot was a village. And the village was burning. The men had set fire to it. For the men were soldiers. For it was war. And the snow shrieked under their nailed boots. Shrieked hideously, the snow. The people were standing round their houses. And the houses were burning. They had jammed pots and children and blankets under their arms. Cats screamed in the blood-stained snow. And it was so red with the fire. And it was silent. For the people were standing dumb round the crackling, sighing houses. And therefore the snow could not shriek. Some had wooden pictures with them. Small, in gold and silver and blue. There was a man to be seen on them with an oval face and a brown beard. The people were staring wildly into the eyes of this beautiful man. But the houses, they burned and burned and went on burning.

Near this village lay another village. There on this night they were standing in their windows. And sometimes the snow, the moon-bright snow, grew almost a little pink from over there. And the people looked at one another. The animals bumped against the stable walls. And the people perhaps nodded to themselves in the darkness.

Bald-headed men were standing at a table. Two hours ago one of them had drawn a line with a red pencil. On a map. On this map was a point. It was the village. And then one of them had telephoned. And then the soldiers had made the spot in the night: the bloodily burning village. With the freezing, screaming cats in the pink snow. And for the bald-headed men there was soft music again. A girl was singing something. And sometimes it thundered as well. A long way away.

Men were walking on the road at evening. They were humming. And they smelt the pear trees. It was not war. And the men were not soldiers. But then there was a blood-red spot in the sky. And one said: Look there, the sun. And then they walked on. But they were humming no longer. For under the blossoming pears pink snow shrieked. And they could never again escape the pink snow.

In a half village children play with charred wood. And then, suddenly there was a white piece of wood. It was a bone. And the children, they knocked with the bone against the stable wall. It sounded as though someone were beating a drum. Tock, said the bone, tock and tock and tock. It sounded as though someone were beating a drum. And they were delighted. It was so nice and white. The bone was the bone of a cat.

THE NIGHTINGALE SINGS

WE stand barefoot at night in our shirts and she sings. Herr Hinsch is ill, Herr Hinsch has a cough. He ruined his lungs in the winter, because the window was not tight. Herr Hinsch will no doubt die. Sometimes it rains. That is the lilac. It falls mauve from the branches and smells like young women. Only Herr Hinsch, he can smell it no longer. Herr Hinsch has a cough. The nightingale sings. And Herr Hinsch will no doubt die. We stand barefoot in our shirts and we listen to him. The whole house is full of his coughing. But the nightingale sings the whole world full. And Herr Hinsch will not rid his lungs of the winter. The lilac, it's falling mauve from the branches. The nightingale sings. Herr Hinsch has a summer-sweet death full of night and nightingale and mauve rain of lilac.

Timm had no such summer-death. Timm died the lonely icy winter-death. As I went to relieve Timm, there was his face all yellowish in the snow. It was yellow. It was not from the moon, because it was not there. But Timm was like clay in the night. As yellow as the clay in the wet-cold potholes of the suburb at home. We used to play there and make men of the clay. But I never thought that Timm could be made of clay, too.

When Timm went on guard, he would not take the steel helmet with him. I quite like feeling the night, he said. You must take your helmet with you, said the corporal, something can always happen and then I'm the stooge. Afterwards I'm the stooge. Then Timm looked at the corporal. And he saw through him, through to the end of the world. Then Timm made one of his world speeches:

We're stooges anyway, said Timm at the door, every man jack of us is a stooge already. We have schnaps and jazz and steel helmets and girls, houses and the Great Wall of China and lamps— we have all that. But we have it through fear. Against fear we have it. But for all that we're the stooges. We have ourselves photographed through fear and make children through fear and through fear we burrow into women, always into women, and we put wicks into oil through fear and make them burn. But still we're the stooges. We do all that through fear, against fear.

But none of it helps us at all. Just when we're forgetting our life in a silken petticoat or the moan of a nightingale, then fear catches us. Then, somewhere, it gives a cough. And no helmet can help us, when fear overtakes us. Then no house can help us, no woman, no schnaps and no helmet.

That was one of Timm's great speeches, one of the world speeches he used to make. He made them to the whole world and yet we were only seven men in the dug-out. And most of us slept when Timm made his speeches. Then he went on guard. World-orator Timm. And the others, they snored. His steel helmet lay in its place. And the corporal declared again: I'll be the stooge, I'll be the stooge later on, if anything happens. And then he slept.

When I relieved Timm, his face was all yellow in the snow. As yellow as the clay in the potholes of the suburb. And the snow was repulsively white.

I never thought that you could be made of clay, Timm, I said. Your great speeches are short, but they go to the end of the world. What you say then makes me forget the clay altogether. Your speeches are always terrific, Timm. They're real world speeches.

But Timm said nothing. His yellow face did not look good in the night-white snow. The snow was repulsively white. Timm's asleep, I thought. The man who talks so grandly about fear, he can even sleep here, with the Russians about in the forest. Timm was standing in the hole in the snow and had laid his yellow face on his gun. Get up, Timm, I said. Timm did not get up and his yellow face looked strange in the snow. Then I touched Timm's cheek with my boot. There was snow on the boot. It stayed on his cheek. The boot made a little hollow in the cheek. And the hollow, it stayed. Then I saw that Timm's hand lay round the gun. And the index finger was still bent.

For an hour I stood in the snow. For an hour I stood near Timm. Then I said to the dead Timm: You're right, Timm, nothing's any help to us. Neither women nor cross nor nightingale, Timm, and not even the falling lilac, Timm. For even Herr Hinsch, who can still hear the nightingale and still smell the lilac, he too must die. And the nightingale sings. And she sings only for herself. And Herr Hinsch, he dies entirely for himself. It's all one to the nightingale. The nightingale sings. (Is the nightingale too only made of clay? Just like you, Timm?)

THE THREE DARK MAGI

HE groped his way through the dark suburb. The houses stood, snapped off, against the sky. There was no moon and the pavement was startled by his belated tread. Then he found an old fence. He kicked it with his foot till a rotten lath heaved a sigh and broke off. The wood smelt over-ripe and sweet. Through the dark suburb he groped his way back. There were no stars.

As he opened the door (it cried as he did so, the door) the pale blue eyes of his wife looked towards him. They came from a tired face. Her breath hung white in the room, it was so cold. He bent his bony knee and broke the wood. The wood sighed. Then there was a sweet and over-ripe smell all round. He held a piece of the wood under his nose. Smells almost like cake, he laughed softly. Don't, said the eyes of his wife, don't laugh. He's asleep.

The man put the sweet over-ripe wood in the little tin stove. Then it glowed up and cast a handful of warm light through the room. The light fell bright on a tiny round face and paused for a moment. The face was only an hour old, but already it had everything that went with it: ears, nose, mouth and eyes. The eyes must be big, one could see that, although they were shut. But the mouth was open and soft breath came out of it. Nose and ears were red. He's alive, thought the mother. And the little face slept.

There are still some oat-flakes, said the man. Yes, answered the woman, good thing. It's cold. The man took some more of the sweet soft wood. Now she's got her baby and has to freeze, he thought. But he had no one he could hit in the face with his fists because of it. As he opened the door of the stove, another handful of light fell on the sleeping face. The woman said softly: Look, like a halo, do you see? Halo! he thought, and had no one he could hit in the face with his fists.

Then there were some people at the door. We saw the light, they said, from the window. We'd like to sit down for ten minutes. But we have a baby, the man said to them. They then said nothing more, but came on into the room, blowing mist out of their noses and lifting up their feet. We'll be very quiet, they whispered and lifted up their feet. Then the light fell on them.

There were three. In three old uniforms. One had a cardboard box, one a sack. And the third had no hands. Frostbite, he said, and held up the stumps. Then he turned his greatcoat-pocket towards the man. There was tobacco in it and thin paper. They rolled cigarettes. But the woman said: No, the child.

Then the four of them went out of the door and their cigarettes were four specks in the night. One had fat bandaged feet. He took a piece of wood out of his sack. A donkey, he said, it took me seven months to carve it. For the baby. He said that and gave it to the man. What's the matter with your feet? asked the man. Water, said the donkey-carver, from hunger. And the other, the third man? asked the man, as he felt the donkey in the darkness. The third man trembled in his uniform: Oh, nothing, he whispered, it's only nerves. One just had too much fear. Then they stubbed out their cigarettes and went in again.

They lifted up their feet and looked at the little sleeping face. The trembling one took two yellow sweets from his cardboard box and said: These are for your wife.

The woman opened wide her pale blue eyes as she saw the three dark men bowed over the child. She was frightened. But then the child pushed his legs against her breast and yelled so heartily that the three dark men lifted up their feet and crept to the door. Here they nodded again, then climbed out into the night. The man watched them go. Peculiar Wise Men, he said to his wife. Then he shut the door. Fine Wise Men they are, he grumbled, and looked for the oat-flakes. But he had no face for his fists.

But the baby yelled, said the woman, he yelled quite loud. So they went. Just look how lively he is, she said proudly. The face opened its mouth and yelled.

Is he crying? asked the man.

No, I think he's laughing, answered the woman.

Almost like cake, said the man and sniffed at the wood, like cake. Quite sweet.

Today *is* Christmas, too, said the woman.

Yes, Christmas, he growled and out of the stove a handful of light fell bright on the little sleeping face.

RADI

RADI was with me tonight. He was blond as ever and he laughed in his broad weak face. Even his eyes were as always: a little frightened and a little uncertain. He even had the few blond tufts of beard. Everything as it used to be.

But you're dead, Radi, I said.

Yes, he answered, please don't laugh.

Why should I laugh?

You always laughed at me, I know that. Because I had such a funny walk and on the way to school always used to talk about all sorts of girls whom I didn't even know. You always used to laugh at that. And because I was always a little frightened, I know that quite definitely.

Have you been dead long? I asked.

No, not at all, he said. But I fell in winter. They couldn't get me properly into the ground. Everything was frozen. Everything hard as rock.

Oh yes, you fell in Russia, didn't you?

Yes, right in the first winter. Don't laugh, will you, but it's not nice being dead in Russia. It's all so strange to me. The trees are so strange. So sad, you know. They're mostly alders. Where I'm lying, there are lots of sad alders. And sometimes the stones moan, too. Because they have to be Russian stones. And the forests scream at night. Because they have to be Russian forests. And the snow screams. Because it has to be Russian snow. Yes, everything's strange. Everything's so strange.

Radi sat on the side of my bed and was silent.

Perhaps you only hate it all so, because you have to be dead there, I said.

He looked at me: Do you think so? Oh no, man, it's all so frightfully strange. Everything. He looked at his knee. Everything is so strange. Even one's self.

One's self?

Yes, please don't laugh. That's it, actually. Just that one's

160

self is so frightfully strange to one. Please don't laugh, that's really why I came to you tonight. I just wanted to talk it over with you.

With me?

Yes, please don't laugh, just with you. You know me very well, don't you?

I always thought so.

Never mind. You know me very well. What I look like, I mean. Not what I am. I mean, the way I look, you'd recognize me, wouldn't you?

Yes, you're blond. You have a full face.

No, go on, say I have a weak face. I know I have. Well——

Yes, you have a weak face, a wide face that's always laughing.

Yes, yes. And my eyes.

Your eyes were always a little—a little sad and unusual——

You mustn't lie. I had very frightened and uncertain eyes, because I never knew whether you'd believe all the stories I used to tell about girls. And then? Was my face always smooth?

No, it wasn't. You always had a few blond tufts of beard on your chin. You thought people wouldn't see them. But we always saw them.

And laughed.

And laughed.

Radi sat on the edge of my bed and rubbed the palms of his hands on his knee. Yes, he whispered, that's what I was like. Exactly like that.

And then he suddenly looked at me with his frightened eyes.

Please do me a favour, will you? But please don't laugh, please. Come with me.

To Russia!

Yes, it's quite quick. Only for a moment. Because you still know me so well, please.

He seized my hand. He felt like snow. Quite cool. Quite loose. Quite light.

We were standing among some alders. Something bright was lying there.

Come, said Radi, there I lie. I saw a human skeleton, as I remembered it from school. A piece of brown-green metal lay

beside it. That's my steel helmet, said Radi, it's all rusted and
full of moss.

And then he pointed to the skeleton. Please don't laugh, he
said, but that's me. Can you understand that? You know me
well. Say it yourself, can I be this thing here? Do you think so?
Don't you find it frightfully strange? There's nothing familiar
about me. You can't recognize me any more. But it's me. It
must be me. But I can't understand it. It's so frightfully unfamiliar.
This has nothing more to do with all that I used to be. No, please
don't laugh, but it's all so frightfully strange to me, so incomprehensible, so far removed.

He sat down on the dark ground and looked sadly in front of
him. That has nothing more to do with the past, he said, nothing,
nothing at all.

Then with his fingertips he picked up a little of the dark soil
and smelt it. Strange, he whispered, quite strange. He held the
soil out to me. It was like snow. It was like the hand with which
he had gripped me earlier: Quite cool. Quite loose. Quite light.

Smell, he said.

I breathed in deeply.

Well?

Earth, I said.

And?

A little sour. A little bitter. Real earth.

But strange, surely? Quite strange? And so repulsive, too,
don't you think?

I breathed deeply of the soil. It smelt cool, loose and light.
A little sour. A little bitter.

It smells good, I said. Like earth.

Not repulsive! Not strange?

Radi looked at me with frightened eyes. It *does* smell disgusting, man.

I smelt.

No, all earth smells like that.

Do you think so?

Certainly.

And you don't find it disgusting?

No, it smells damn good, Radi. Just smell it properly.

He took a little between the tips of his fingers and smelt.

All earth smells like that? he asked.

Yes, all of it.

He breathed deeply. He put his nose right into the hand with the soil in it and breathed. Then he looked at me. You're right, he said. Perhaps it does smell quite good. But still strange, when I think that that's me, but still frightfully strange.

Radi sat and smelt and forgot me and smelt and smelt and smelt. And he said the word "strange" less and less. Ever more softly he said it. He smelt and smelt and smelt.

Then on tiptoe I went back home. It was half past five in the morning. Everywhere in the gardens earth looked through the snow. And with naked feet I stepped on the dark earth in the snow. It was cool. And loose. And light. And it smelt. I stood still and breathed deeply. Yes, it smelt. It smells good, Radi, I whispered. It smells really good. It smells like real earth. You can rest in peace.

ON THAT TUESDAY

THE week has one Tuesday.
    The year has half a hundred.
    The war has many Tuesdays.

On that Tuesday
in the school they were practising the capital letters. The
schoolmistress had glasses with thick lenses. They had no rims.
They were so thick that her eyes looked quite gentle.

Forty-two girls sat in front of the blackboard and wrote in
capital letters:
FREDERICK THE GREAT HAD A DRINKING MUG
OF TIN. BIG BERTHA SHOT AS FAR AS PARIS. IN
WAR ALL FATHERS ARE SOLDIERS.

Ulla touched her nose with the tip of her tongue. Then the
mistress nudged her. You've spelt "soldier" with a J, Ulla.
"Soldier" is spelt with D. D as in "ditch". How many times have
I told you. The mistress picked up a book and put a cross against
Ulla's name. You will write out the sentence ten times before
tomorrow, nice and clean, do you understand? Yes, said Ulla
and thought: Her and her glasses.

In the playground hooded crows ate the thrown-away bread.

On that Tuesday
Second Lieutenant Ehlers was summoned to the battalion
commander.

You must take off the red scarf, Herr Ehlers.

Sir?

Yes, Ehlers. That sort of thing doesn't go down with the
Second.

I'm going to 2 company?

Yes, and they don't like that sort of thing. You won't get
away with it there. 2 company are sticklers for dress. With that

164

red scarf the company'll just cut you dead. Captain Hesse never
wore such a thing.

Is Hesse wounded?

No, he's reported sick. Didn't feel well, he said. Since he's
been a captain, he's become a bit slack, has Hesse. Don't understand it. Always used to be so smart. Well, Ehlers, let's see what
you can do with the company. Hesse trained the men well. And
you'll take off that scarf, is that clear?

'Course, sir.

And see that the men are careful with their cigarettes. Any
decent sniper must have an itch in his trigger-finger when he
sees those little glow-worms flitting about. Last week we had five
shot in the head. So just watch out a bit, eh?

Very good, sir.

On the way to No. 2 Company Lieutenant Ehlers took off
the red scarf. He lit a cigarette. Company-commander Ehlers,
he said aloud.

There was a shot.

On that Tuesday
Herr Hansen said to Fräulein Severin:

We must send Hesse something again, too, Severin, my pet.
Something to smoke, something to chew. A little literature. A
pair of gloves or something. The boys have a damn bad winter
out there. I know what it's like, thank you very much.

Hölderlin perhaps, Herr Hansen?

Nonsense, little Severin, nonsense. No, much sooner something a bit more cheerful. Wilhelm Busch or something. Hesse
was always more for the light stuff. Likes laughing, you know
that. My God, little Severin, how that Hesse can laugh!

Yes, he certainly can, said Fräulein Severin.

On that Tuesday
they carried Captain Hesse into the Delousing Station on a
stretcher. On the door was a sign:

WHETHER GENERAL OR GRENADIER
YOUR HAIR STAYS HERE

He was shaved. The orderly had long thin fingers. Like spider's legs. They were rather red at the knuckles. They rubbed him down with something smelling of drugstores. Then the spider's legs felt for his pulse and wrote in a fat book: Temperature 106.9. Pulse 116. Unconscious. Typhus suspect. The orderly shut the fat book. Smolensk Isolation Hospital was written on it. And underneath: Fourteen hundred beds.

The bearers picked up the stretcher. On the stairs his head dangled out of the covers and swung to and fro with every step. Shaven and shorn. And he it was who had always laughed at the Russians. One bearer had a cold.

On that Tuesday
Frau Hesse rang her neighbour's bell. As the door opened, she waved a letter. He's been made captain, Captain and Company-commander, he writes. And they've over forty degrees of frost. The letter took nine days. "To Frau Hauptmann Hesse" he's written on it.

She held up the letter. But her neighbour didn't look at it. Forty degrees of frost, she said, the poor boys. Forty degrees of frost.

On that Tuesday
the Chief Medical Officer asked the Superintendent of the Smolensk Isolation Hospital: How many are there a day?

Half a dozen.

Dreadful, said the Chief Medical Officer.

Yes, dreadful, said the Superintendent.

They didn't look at one another as they spoke.

On that Tuesday.
they were doing *The Magic Flute*. Frau Hesse had painted her lips red.

On that Tuesday
Sister Elizabeth wrote to her parents: Without God one could

never endure it. But as the Assistant Superintendent approached, she stood up. His walk was bowed, as though he were carrying all Russia through the room.

Shall I give him a little more, asked the Sister.

No, said the Assistant Superintendent. He said it so softly, as though he were ashamed.

Then they carried Captain Hesse out. There was a tumbling noise outside. They always bump like that. Why can't they lay the dead down gently. Every time they let them bump like that on the ground. One said that. And his neighbour sang softly:

> Zicker-zacker upidee
> Snappy is the Infantree.

The Assistant Superintendent went from bed to bed. Every day. Day and night. All day long. Throughout the night. Bowed, he walked. He carried all Russia through the room. Outside two bearers stumbled away with an empty stretcher. Number 4, said one. He had a cold.

On that Tuesday
in the evening Ulla sat and drew in her exercise book in capital letters:

IN WAR ALL FATHERS ARE SOLDIERS.
IN WAR ALL FATHERS ARE SOLDIERS.

Ten times she wrote it. In capital letters. "Soldiers" with a D. Like ditch.

"And Nobody Knows Whither"

THE COFFEE IS INDEFINABLE

THEY were hanging on the chairs. They had been hung over the tables. Hung there by a terrible weariness. For this weariness there was no sleep. It was a world-weariness that expected nothing more. At best, perhaps a train. And in a waiting-room. And there they were hanging, hung there over chairs and tables. They were hanging in their clothes and in their skin, as though they were a nuisance to them, their clothes. And their skin. They were ghosts and had dressed themselves up in this skin and for a time were playing at being human. They were hanging on their skeletons like scarecrows on their posts. Hung there by life, to the scorn of their own brain and to the agony of their hearts. And every wind played with them. Played with them. They were hanging in life, hung there by a God with no face. By a God who was neither good nor evil. Who just was. And no more. And that was too much. And that was too little. And he had hung them there in life, so that they dangled for a while, thin-voiced bells in an invisible belfry, wind-inflated scarecrows. Abandoned to themselves and to the skin, of which they could not find the seam. Hung there over chairs, posts, tables, gallows and immeasurable depths. And no one heard their thin-voiced screaming. For the God had no face. Therefore he could have no ears, either, that was their greatest abandonment, the God without ears. God only let them breathe. Gruesome and grandiose. And they were breathing. Savagely, greedily, devouringly. But lonely, thin-voiced and lonely. For their screaming, their terrible screaming, did not even penetrate to the man beside them, sitting at the same table. Nor to the God without ears. Not even to the man beside them, sitting at the same table. At the very same table. Next to them. At the very selfsame table.

Four were sitting at the table and waiting for the train. They could not make each other out. Fog drifted between their white faces. A fog of night mist, coffee steam and cigarette smoke. The coffee steam stank and the cigarettes smelled sweet. The night mist was made of misery, perfume and the breath of old men.

And of girls, still growing. The night mist was cold and damp. Like the sweat of fear. Three men were sitting at the table. And the girl. Four people. The girl was looking into her cup. One man was writing on grey paper. He had very short fingers. The other was reading a book. The third was looking at the others. From one to the other. He had a cheerful face. The girl looked into her cup.

Then the one with the very short fingers got his fifth cup of coffee. Nauseating, this coffee, he said, and looked up briefly. The coffee's indefinable. A fantastic drink. And then he went on writing. But something suddenly occurred to him and he looked up again. You've let your coffee get cold, he said to the girl. Cold, it tastes even worse. Fantastic drink. If it's hot it's just tolerable. But indefinable. In-de-fin-able. It doesn't matter, said the girl to the one with the very short fingers. Then he stopped writing altogether. It was the way she had said it: It doesn't matter. He looked at her. I only want to take my pills with it, with the coffee, she said, embarrassed, and looked into her cup, it doesn't matter if it's cold. Have you a headache? he asked her. No, she said, again embarrassed, and looked into her cup. Looked into her cup for so long that the short-fingered man began to drum with his pencil. Then she looked at him. I must kill myself. I haven't a headache. I must kill myself. And she said it like: I'm taking the train at eleven: I must kill myself, she said. And looked into her cup.

Then the three men looked at her. The one with the book. And the one with the cheerful face. Splendid, he thought, a lunatic. A real lunatic. Well, you're a funny one, said the man with the very short fingers. Because she wants to kill herself? asked the one with the book and leaned interestedly over the table. No, but because she says it so casually. Just as one says departure or station, answered the other. Why, said the one with the book, she just says what she thinks. There's nothing funny about that. Actually, it's a very good thing. I think it's a very good thing. The girl looked embarrassed into her cup. A good thing? said the man with the very short fingers angrily and made an indignant fish-mouth, good, you think? Well, I don't know. What I think is—! Look here. Suppose I were to say straight out what I think. Eh? What? I was supposed to get five thousand loaves of bread here tonight. Only two hundred have come. That's minus four thousand and eight times one hundred. And now I must calculate. He made his fish-mouth and lifted his writing-pad and threw it back on the table. And do you know what I'm thinking now? The girl looked into her cup. The cheerful one gaped and grinned and was silent. And the one with the book said: Well? I'll tell you, my friend, I'll tell you. I'm thinking that tomorrow four thousand eight hundred families won't get their bread. Tomorrow morning four thousand eight hundred won't have any bread. Tomorrow four thousand eight hundred children will go hungry. And the fathers. And the mothers, too, of course. But they don't notice it. But the children, my good man, the four thousand eight hundred children. Tomorrow, now, they'll have no bread. You see, that's what I think, my friend, that's what I think and sit here and write here and drink this indefinable coffee. And all the time, that's what I'm thinking. What would you feel if I were to say that straight out, eh? Who could bear it, eh? There's not a soul would be able to bear it any longer, if one said everything one thought. He made his fish-mouth and made his forehead full of barbed wire. So full of wrinkles. Like barbed wire.

The girl looked into her coffee cup. She's drowning herself, thought the one with the book. And then it occurred to him that the cup was too small to drown in and he said: This coffee, scarcely drinkable. Then the one with the cheerful face hit the table a smack with the flat of his hand. She's mad; he said and at the same time, quite without his knowledge, his face grinned so cheerfully and he drank his coffee in greedy gulps. She's mad, he said right out of breath with drinking, she should be killed at once, because she's mad, I say. Well, listen, you're a little sweetheart, I must say! exclaimed the bread merchant. Makes a face like Whitsun and talks about killing. We'd better watch out with you, I think. Making a face like Whitsun and talking—! Then the one with the book smiled eagerly. Not at all, he said, not at all. That's schizophrenia, you understand? Typical schizophrenia. We've all got a bit of Jesus and a bit of Nero in us, you know. All of us. He made a grimace, pushed his chin and lower lip forward, screwed up his eyes and distended his nostrils. Nero, he said, in explanation. Then he made a soft, sentimental face, smoothed down his hair and made faithful dog's eyes, harmless

and rather dreary: Jesus, he declared. And added: You see, it's
in all of us. Typical schizophrenia. Now Jesus—now Nero. And
again he tried to make the two faces, very quickly one after the
other. It didn't work. Perhaps the coffee was too bad.

Who's Nero? asked the cheerful one, with a stupid face. Oh,
the name's unimportant. Nero was a man like you, and me, too.
Only that he wasn't punished for what he did. And he knew that.
So he did just about everything that a human being can do. If
he'd been a postman or a carpenter they'd have hanged him. But
as it happened he was emperor and did whatever entered his head.
Everything that enters a human head. That's the complete Nero.
And you think I'm that sort of Nero? asked the cheerful one.
Fifty-fifty, my friend. I'm sure you can be Jesus, too. But if you
want to kill this girl, then you're Nero, my friend, then you're
decidedly Nero. Do you understand?

As though on a word of command the three men lifted their
coffee cups and drank, laying their heads on the backs of their
necks and looking at the ceiling. But there was nothing to see up
there and they returned to earth. And the bread merchant said
for the seventeenth and eighteenth times: The coffee is indefinable.
The coffee is in-de-fin-able. The one with the Whitsun face, however, wiped his lips dry and burst out: You're mad, too. You're
all mad. What do I care about Nero. Or the other one. Nothing,
I tell you nothing, I say. I've come from the war and I want to go
home. D'you see? And at home I want to sit with my parents on
the balcony in the mornings and drink coffee. I've wanted that
all through the war. Sitting on the balcony in the mornings and
drinking coffee with my parents. D'you see. And now I'm on the
way. And then this lunatic comes along and casually says she
wants to kill herself. There's no one can stand it people saying
casually: I want to kill myself.

That's what the soldier said. And the bread merchant lifted
his eyes from the indefinability of his coffee and made a what-
did-I-tell-you face and said: That's just what I say, he said, that's
exactly what I keep saying. Just like the bread. Supposing I were
casually to blare it out, eh? Tomorrow four thousand eight
hundred children with no bread, eh? How would you feel then,
eh? Who in the world *can* stand it. There's no one can stand it
any longer now, gentlemen. And he looked at the man with the

book. And the cheerful one, who had come from the war, he looked at him too.

Then the latter stood up. With his little finger he flicked a few crumbs from the table: You're too materialistic for me, he said sadly. You come home from the war to drink coffee on the balcony. And you, you trade in bread. You calculate children and loaves of bread. My God, who'll guarantee that you won't mix them up. Who knows if you don't calculate with munitions as well. Thirty rounds a head. That's how it always was in the war: Thirty rounds a head. Well, and now it's loaves, my God, now it happens to be loaves. And he said sadly: Good night, you're just too materialistic for me, that's all, just too materialistic. Good night.

Then the bread merchant called after him: Have you ever been hungry, my good sir? Without my bread you couldn't even read your books, let me advise you of that, not without bread, my good sir! And without ammunition it's no go either, eh, it's no go without ammo either, my good sir! And meanwhile he looked at the soldier. And the soldier too shot at the bookman and bent forward to see where he hit. Like Nero, thought the book-owner and stared at him, just like Nero. And the soldier-Nero roared at him: Were you in the war at all, you? Were you ever in the war? Once get into the war, and the only thing you'll want afterwards is to sit on a balcony and drink coffee. You won't want anything else, my friend, I can tell you.

The book-owner looked at the two of them and tapped his book sadly against his lips. Then, as he stood, he drank his cup empty. And the two others drank, too. Indefinable, said the bread merchant, and shook himself. Like life, said the man with the book and bowed courteously towards him. And the bread merchant bowed courteously back. And they smiled politely above their quarrel. And each was a man of the world. And the bookman secretly felt himself the victor. And so he was ready to smile.

But then he ripped his mouth open for a frightful scream. But he didn't scream. The scream was so frightful that he couldn't get it out. It stuck, deep inside the bookman. Only his mouth gaped wide open, because the air went out of him. The book-owner stared at the fourth chair, where the girl had been sitting. The chair was empty. The girl was gone. Then the three men saw on the table a little glass phial. It was empty. And the girl was gone. And the cup, the cup was empty. And the girl was gone. The chair. And the glass phial. And the cup. Empty. Quite quietly, unobtrusively, emptied.

Was she hungry, d'you suppose? the bread merchant at last asked the others. She was mad, said the soldier cheerfully, she was mad, I keep telling you. Come, he said to the one with the book, sit down again. She was definitely mad. The book-owner sat down slowly and suggested: Perhaps she was lonely? I'm sure she was too lonely. Lonely, exploded the bread merchant indignantly, what d'you mean lonely? We were here. We were here the whole time. We? asked the bookman and looked into the empty cup. From the cup the girl looked back at him. But he could no longer recognize her.

Night mist drifted through the station, night mist of fog, misery and breath. And it was as thick as the indefinable coffee. And wet-cold. Like the sweat of fear. The man with the book shut his eyes. The coffee's disgusting, he heard the bread merchant say. Yes, yes, he nodded slowly, you're right there: Quite disgusting. Disgusting or not, said the soldier, we've got nothing else. Main thing is, it's hot. He rolled the glass phial across the table. It fell down. And was smashed. (And God? He didn't hear the ugly little noise: of it all, God heard nothing. For He had no ears. That was it. He had no ears.)

THE KITCHEN CLOCK

ALREADY from a distance they saw him coming towards them, for he looked odd. He had an old face, but from the way he walked one realized that he was only twenty. He sat down with his old face beside them on the bench. And then he showed them what he was carrying in his hand.

That was our kitchen clock, he said and looked at them all one after another, sitting on the bench in the sun. Yes, I found it. It was left over.

He held a round plate-white kitchen clock in front of him and stroked the blue-painted numbers with his finger.

It's of no particular value, he said apologetically, I know that, of course. And it's not particularly beautiful either. It's only like a plate—I mean the white enamel. But the blue numbers do look quite pretty, it seems to me. Of course, the hands are only tin. And they don't go now. No. It's broken inside, that's certain. But it still looks like it used to. Even if it doesn't go any more.

With his fingertip he made a careful circle round the edge of the plate-like clock. And he said softly: And it was left over.

The people sitting on the bench in the sun did not look at him. One man looked at his shoes and the woman looked into her pram. Then somebody said:

You've lost everything, have you?

Yes, yes, he said happily, just think, every single thing! Only this here, only this is left. And he lifted up the clock again, as though the others had not yet seen it.

But it won't go any more, said the woman.

No, no, it won't. It's broken, I know that. But otherwise it's just as it always was: white and blue. And again he showed them his clock. And the most wonderful thing, he went on excitedly, I haven't told you yet at all. The most wonderful thing is still to come: Just think, it stopped at half past two. Of all times at half past two, just think.

Then it must have been half past two when your house was hit, said the man and pushed his lower lip forward importantly.

I've often heard that. When the bombs drop, the clocks stop. It's because of the blast.

He looked at his clock with a superior shake of the head. No, my dear sir, no, there you're mistaken. The bombs have nothing to do with it. You mustn't keep talking about bombs. No. At half past two there was something quite different, only you don't know what. That's the joke, of course, that it stopped just at half past two. And not at a quarter past four or at seven. For at half past two I always used to come home. At night, I mean. Nearly always at half past two. That's just the joke.

He looked at the others, but they had taken their eyes off him. He did not find them. So he nodded at his clock: Naturally I was hungry then, you see? And I used to go straight to the kitchen. And then it was nearly always half past two. And then, then my mother would come. It didn't matter how quietly I opened the door, she always heard me. And while I was looking for something to eat in the dark kitchen, the light would suddenly go on. And then she'd be standing there in her woollen jacket and red shawl. And barefoot. Always barefoot. And our kitchen was tiled, at that. And she'd screw up her eyes because the light was so bright. Because of course she'd just been asleep. It was night, of course.

So late again, she'd say then. She never said more. Just: So late again. And then she'd hot up my supper and watch me eating. Rubbing her feet together all the time, because the tiles were so cold. She never put her shoes on at night. And she'd sit with me until I'd eaten my fill. And I would hear her putting the plates away again, when I'd already put the light out in my room. Every night was like that. And mostly at half past two. I felt it quite as a matter of course that she should make me a meal in the kitchen at half past two in the morning. I took it quite for granted. She always did it. And she never said more than: So late again. But she said it every time. And I thought it could never stop. It was so much a matter of course to me. All that. It had always been like that.

For a breathless second it was quite still on the bench. Then he said softly: And now? He looked at the others. But he did not find them. So he said to the clock, softly into its white-blue round face: Now, now I know that it was paradise. Real paradise.

It was quite still on the bench. Then the woman asked: And your family?

He smiled at her, embarrassed: Ah, you mean my parents? Yes, they're gone, too. Everything's gone. Everything, imagine it. Everything gone.

Then he lifted up the clock again and laughed. He laughed: Only this here. It's left over. And the most wonderful thing is that it stopped at exactly half past two. Exactly half past two.

Then he said nothing more. But his face was quite old. And the man sitting next to him looked at his shoes. But he didn't see his shoes. He kept thinking of the word "paradise".

PERHAPS SHE HAS A PINK VEST

The two men sat on the bridge parapet. Their trousers were thin and the parapet was icy. But one got used to it. And to its hardness, too. They sat there. It rained, it stopped raining, it rained. They sat there and took the parade. And because for a whole war they had seen only men, now they saw only girls.

One went past.

Got a pretty fine balcony. You could have tea on it, said Timm.

And if she runs around in the sun too long, the milk'll go sour, grinned the other.

Then came another one.

Prehistoric, registered the man beside Timm.

All full of cobwebs, said he.

Then came men. They got by without comment. Locksmiths' apprentices, clerks with white skins, elementary school-teachers with jovial faces and shabby trousers, fat men with fat legs, asthmatic men and tramwaymen with a sergeant's gait.

And then she came. She was quite different. One felt she must smell of peaches. Or of very clean skin. Surely she had also a quite special name: Evelyn—or something. Then she was past. They both looked after her.

Perhaps she has a pink vest, Timm said then.

Why, said the other.

Yes, answered Timm, that sort, their vests are usually pink.

Nuts, said the other, she can just as well have a blue one.

That's just what she can't, man, that's just what she can't. That sort have pink ones. I know that quite definitely, my lad. Timm got quite loud as he said that.

Then the one beside him said: You know one then, eh?

Timm said nothing. They sat there and the parapet was icy through their thin trousers. Then said Timm:

No, not me. But I once knew a man who had one with a pink vest. In the army. In Russia. In his wallet he always had a bit of pink cloth. But he let nobody see it. But one day it fell on the

180

ground. Then everyone saw it. And he said nothing. Only blushed. Like the piece of cloth. Quite pink. Then in the evening he told me he'd got it from his girl. As a talisman, you know. Of course, she's lots of pink vests, he said. And that's what it's from.

Timm stopped.

And then? asked the other.

Then Timm said quite softly: I took it away from him. And then I held it up. And we all laughed. For at least half an hour we laughed. And you can just imagine the sort of things they said.

And then? asked the man beside Timm.

Timm looked at his knee. He threw it away, he said.

And then Timm looked at the other: Yes, he said, he threw it away, and then he got it. On the next day he got it.

They both said nothing. Just sat there and said nothing. But then the other said: Tripe. And he said it again: Tripe, he said.

Yes, I know, said Timm. Of course it's tripe. That's obvious. I know that. And then he added: But it's funny, you know, it's funny all the same.

And Timm laughed. They both laughed. And Timm clenched his fist in his trouser-pocket. In doing so he crushed something. A small piece of pink material. There wasn't much pink in it now, for he'd had it in his pocket a long time. But it was still pink. He'd brought it along from Russia.

OUR LITTLE MOZART

FROM half past four in the morning till half past twelve at night. The district railway ran every three minutes. Each time a woman's voice shouted through the loudspeaker on the platform: Lehrter Strasse. Lehrter Strasse. It drifted over to us. From half past four in the morning till half past twelve at night. Eight hundred times: Lehrter Strasse. Lehrter Strasse.

Liebig stood at the window. Early in the morning. At midday. In the afternoons still. And through the endless evenings. Lehrter Strasse. Lehrter Strasse.

For seven months now he had been standing at the window and looking towards the woman. She must be over there somewhere. With quite pretty legs, perhaps. With breasts. And wavy hair. One could picture her. And other things, too. For hours Liebig looked across to where she sang. Through his brain went a rosary. At each bead Liebig prayed: Lehrter Strasse. Lehrter Strasse. From half past four in the morning till half past twelve at night. Early in the morning. At midday. And in the afternoons still. And through the endless evenings: Lehrter Strasse. Lehrter Strasse. Eight hundred times each day. And Liebig had been standing at the window now for seven months and looking towards the woman. For he could picture her. With quite pretty legs, perhaps. With knees. Breast. And with a lot of hair. Long, endlessly long like the endless evenings. Liebig looked towards her. Or was he looking towards Breslau? But Breslau was over a hundred miles away. Liebig came from Breslau. Was he looking towards Breslau in the evenings? Or was he worshipping this woman? Lehrter Strasse. Lehrter Strasse. Endless rosary. With quite pretty legs. Early in the morning. And with endless endless evening hair. And it went from the Lehrter Strasse to Breslau. Right into the dream. To Breslau. To Bres—Breslauer Strasse—Breslauer Strasse—All change—change—All out—all out—all—all—Bres —lau—

But Pauline sat bent on his stool and breathed on his finger-nails. Then he polished them on his trousers. He always did that.

For months now. And the nails were beautifully pink and shiny. Pauline was homosexual. He had been at the front as a medical orderly. He had made passes at the wounded. He told us he'd simply cooked pudding for them. Just pudding. Then for that he'd got two years penal servitude. He was called Paul. By us, of course, Pauline. Of course. And gradually he ceased to protest. When he came back from the trial, he was wailing: Me lovely savings! Me lovely savings! They'd'a bin such a help in me old age! Such a wonderful help! But then he forgot all that. He adjusted himself to the idea of penal servitude. He became stupid. And since then he had only polished his finger-nails. That was the only thing that he still did. And from then on, quite openly. And for months now. And perhaps for many more months, till there was a space free in the penal settlement. A plank-bed for Pauline. For so long Pauline would go on polishing. Outside, over there beyond the wall, the woman of the district railway sang her heroic song with eight hundred verses. Sang it from half past four in the morning till half past twelve at night. Sang, and had wavy hair and breasts. Sang into our cell the idiotic song, the song of the everyday grind, the everlasting song of humanity, the idiotic: Lehrter Strasse. Lehrter Strasse. One could picture her. The singsong woman. Perhaps she bit in the madness of kissing. Perhaps she groaned like an animal. (Perhaps she stammered Lehrter Strasse, when a man fumbled with her skirts?) Perhaps she stretched her swimming eyes wide open when one seduced her at night. Perhaps, too, she smelt like damp grass in the morning at four: so cold and so green and so terrific and so— ah, the woman sang eight hundred times each day: Lehrter Strasse. Lehrter Strasse. And nobody came and throttled her. Nobody thought of us. And nobody bit her in the throat, the trollop. But no, but never, for she went on singing, the woman of the district railway, singing her sentimental song of a homesick world, this silly, ineradicable song of the Lehrter Strasse. Enough.

But there were also clearheaded days. High days and holidays —Sundays simply. These were the Mondays. For on Mondays we were allowed to shave. These were the specially masculine days, the self-respecting, refreshing days. Once a week we were allowed to do it. That was on the Mondays. The soap was bad and the water was cold and the blades were pitifully blunt.

(You could ride to Breslau on one of those, cursed Liebig. He was always riding to Breslau. On the woman of the district railway, too.) So blunt the blades were. But they were Sundays, these Mondays. For on Mondays we were allowed, under supervision, to shave. Then our cell doors were open and outside sat Truttner with the clock on his lap. The clock was fat and loud and scratched. Truttner was a sergeant, dyspeptic, fifty-four, paterfamilias and a soldier in the First World War. And grim. His role in this life was grim. With his children he certainly wasn't grim. But with us. With us, indeed, very. That was odd. And when we were shaving on Mondays, Truttner sat in front of our cell with the clock in his hand and with his heels (they were hobnailed, of course), tapped out a Prussian march. And that made us cut ourselves. For he tapped with impatience. And because he grudged us our shave. For a fresh shave makes you cheerful. He grudged us that. He was dyspeptic. And sergeant in a prison. Where one was not cheerful. So he was annoyed when we shaved. And kept looking at his revoltingly loud clock. And tapping out his impatient marches. And what's more he had his pistol-holster open. He was a paterfamilias and had his holster open. That was very odd.

Naturally we had no mirror. With mirrors one could slit one's arteries open. They grudged us that. Such a harmless, secret death by bleeding we didn't deserve. So instead they'd nailed a piece of shiny tin on our locker. At a pinch one could see oneself in it. Not recognize. Only just see. And it was quite a good thing one didn't recognize oneself. One wouldn't have done so, anyway. The piece of shiny tin was nailed on our locker. For we had a little locker. Our four bowls were kept in it. The aluminium sort. Battered. Scratched. Reminiscent of pet dogs. How mean, was written on one, and: Seventeen months tomorrow. On the other was a calendar with lots of little crosses. And Elizabeth was written on it. Seven or eight times. In my bowl there was only: Everlasting soup. That was all. He was quite right. And in Pauline's bowl someone had scratched two hanging breasts. Always when Pauline had finished his soup, these gigantic hanging breasts grinned at him. Like the eyes of fate. Poor Pauline. He didn't care for that sort of thing, after all. But then he'd cooked pudding. This now was the punishment. Perhaps that was why he got so thin. Perhaps he was so sickened by the breasts.

The previous evening Mozart had thrown me his blue shirt. I shan't need it any more now, he said. Today was his trial. That morning they'd fetched him. I'm supposed to have stolen a radio, said Mozart. And now I stood in his blue shirt in front of our tin mirror and looked at myself. Pauline looked on. I was delighted with the shirt. For mine had gone at the seams when I'd been deloused. Now I had a shirt again. And the bright blue suited me rather well. At least that's what Pauline said. And I thought so, too. The blue suited me. Only I couldn't do up the collar. Mozart was a slim-built little chap. He had a neck like a schoolgirl. Mine was thicker. (The bit about schoolgirls, was what Pauline always said.) Leave it open, said Liebig from the window. Then you'll look like a Socialist.

But then you see the hairs on his chest so, said Pauline.

Exciting, answered Liebig, and went on staring towards the voice of the loudspeaker.

Mozart was really amazingly small and delicate. He had a neck like a schoolgirl. (Pauline always said.)

Then our Hungarian soup arrived. It was hot water with paprika pods. It burned in the stomach. So that one felt full. And that was worth a lot. But one was never off the can.

While we were eating Mozart came back from the trial. He'd had his trial. Four hours. He was somewhat embarrassed. Truttner unlocked the cell-door and let him in. But he didn't take the handcuffs off. We were surprised. Well, what did you get? we all three asked at once and laid our spoons on the table in suspense. Sore throat, said Mozart and looked somewhat embarrassed. We didn't understand him.

The sergeant had his holster open. He stood in the cell-door like a giant. Yet at most he was five foot six. Come on then, pack up your kit, Mozart. Mozart packed up his kit. A piece of soap. His comb. Half a towel. Two letters. That was all Mozart had. He was very embarrassed.

Just tell your pals all you've got on your account. It'll interest them. Mozart shrank. Truttner looked very mean as he said it. He certainly didn't look as mean as that at home. Mozart was embarrassed.

I wore sergeant's uniform—began Mozart very softly.

Although—prompted Truttner.

Although I was only a rifleman.

Go on, Mozart, what else?

I wore the Ritterkreuz——

Although, Mozart, although——

Although I was only allowed to wear the East Medal.

Go on, Mozart, keep it up.

I overstayed my leave——

Only a few days, Mozart, wasn't it, just a few days?

No, Sergeant.

But, Mozart, but?

Nine months, Sergeant.

And what's that called, Mozart? A.W.O.L.?

No.

Well, what then?

Desertion, Sergeant.

Right, Mozart, quite right. Well, and what else have you got to offer?

I took radios away.

Stole them, Mozart.

Stole them, Sergeant.

How many then, little Mozart, how many? Tell them. Your pals will be interested.

Seven.

And where, Mozart?

Broke in.

Seven times, Mozart?

No, Sergeant, eleven.

Eleven what, Mozart? Express yourself more clearly.

Broke in eleven times.

A complete sentence, Mozart, don't be so shy, speak in complete sentences. Well?

I broke into eleven houses.

That's fine, Mozart, that's correct. Otherwise there was nothing more, was there, Mozart, that was all?

No, Sergeant.

What, still more, Mozart, still more? What more then?

The old woman——

What, Mozart, what happened to her?

I pushed her over.

Pushed her, Mozart?

I kicked her.

Ah so. Well, and then? Just tell your pals. It'll interest them.
They're quite dumb with suspense. They're breathless already.
Come on, Mozart boy, then what happened to the old
granny?

She died. Mozart said it quite softly. Much more softly.
Almost only: di-ed. He was very embarrassed. Then he looked at
the sergeant, who straightened himself up. Have you your bits
and pieces?

Yes.

What did you say?

Yes, Sergeant.

Then stand to attention.

Mozart laid his hands on the seams of his trousers. The
sergeant did the same. Then he said:

I bring to your notice that I must make use of the firearm
if you attempt to escape. His pistol holster was already open.
Just as on Mondays at shaving time. Forward! he commanded.
Mozart wanted to shake hands. But he was altogether too embarrassed. In fact he had always been somewhat embarrassed. After
all he was only a small, delicate little chap. He had a neck like a
schoolgirl. Sometimes he'd sung in the evenings. When it was
dark. When it was light he was too embarrassed. He was a
barber. He had the hands of a child. He loved jazz music. For
hours on end he'd play jazz on his bowl with our spoons. Till we
called him Mozart.

He stood in the cell-door. He turned round again, although he
was very embarrassed. His schoolgirl-neck was quite red with
embarrassment.

Your shirt, I said.

My shirt? He smiled at us through the steam of our paprika
soup. But I've got a sore throat, he said. And then with his index
finger he made a half-circle along the collar of his uniform.
Above the larynx. From left to right. Then Truttner locked the
door.

When we put out buckets outside that evening, the sergeant
found our dinners in them. He could not understand it.

THE KANGAROO

MORNING. The guards were dozing. Their blankets were still
wet from the night. One was lying flat on the ground and with
his feet was beating out the measure:

> Now once there was a kangaroo
> Who shut her pouch and sewed it to,
>> With a nail-file and some cord
>> Because she was so bored
>> So very, very bored
>> Because she was so bored——

Keep quiet a minute, said the other. He suddenly stood
stock still.

> So very, very bored
> Because she was so——

Just keep quiet a minute.
What's up? The one on the ground turned towards him.
There's somebody coming.
Who?
Don't know. Can't see a thing. It just won't get light today.

> Now once there was a kangaroo
> Who shut her—well, can you see anything?

Yes, they're coming.
Where? Oh, women!—Who shut her pouch and sewed it
to——
I say, those are the two that were with the old man last night.
The ones that came from the town in the evening?
Yes, them.
Man alive! Don't think much of the old man's taste. The tall
one's a terrific hag, I can tell you.

I don't think so. She looks quite decent to me.

No, no, man. You know, so—so. No. Just look at those legs.
Perhaps he had the short one.

No. She just tagged along. He had the tall one.

Boy, those legs.

Why! They're not bad at all.

No, no, man. So—so—never!

Can't understand the old man.

What? He was drunk. What else? You can put him with
any old cow when he's drunk. Just look at those legs. Boy, is
that a hag! My God! The old man must have been pretty far gone
again. Hell, and from yesterday evening on.

Thanks, not for me.

Nor me either.

They wrapped themselves in their blankets again. The blankets
were still wet from the night. The man lying on the ground beat
time with his feet:

> Now once there was a kangaroo
> Who shut her pouch and sewed it to,
>   Who shut——
>   Who shut——

His feet were cold and he beat time with them:

>   Who shut——
>   Who shut——

Evening. The blankets were already wet. From the night.
And one beat time with his feet:

> Now once there was a kangaroo
> Who shut her——

I say!

Hm?

Quiet a minute.

Why?

They're coming.

They're coming? He stood up. The blankets fell to the ground.

Yes, they're coming. They're carrying him.

Yes, eight men.

I say!

Hm?

The old man's so small. Or is it because they're carrying him?

No, you know she cut his head off!

You think that's why he's so small?

Why else?

Will they bury him like that?

How?

Like that, without his head?

How else? You know she took it with her!

Boy, oh, boy. She was a one all right. The old man must have been pretty far gone.

Oh leave him be.

Good idea. It won't do him any good now, anyway.

No.

They wrapped themselves in the blankets again.

I say!

Yes?

Do you think that was a real girl?

Because of the head?

Well, yes.

No, no, man. A real girl? No.

And she took it away with her, too.

Man alive!

Did she do it just because of the town?

Why else?

Boy, oh, boy. His head, just like that!

No thank you.

Me too, fellah, me too.

And again he beat time with his feet:

> Now once there was a kangaroo
> Who shut her pouch and sewed it to,
>   And sewed it to
>   And sewed it to

As the two girls walked through the town, everyone shouted. The tall one carried a head. There were dark stains on her dress. She showed the head.

Judith! they all shouted.

She lifted her dress and made it into a pouch in front of her breast.

The head lay in it. She showed it.

Judith! they all shouted. Judith! Judith!

She carried the head in front of her in the dress. She looked like a kangaroo.

RATS DO SLEEP AT NIGHT

THE empty window in the lonely wall yawned blue-red, full
of early evening sun. Dust clouds shimmered between the steep-
stretched remains of chimneys. The ruined wilderness was
dozing. His eyes were shut. Suddenly it grew still darker. He
knew that someone had come and was now standing in front of
him, darkly, quietly. Now they've got me! he thought. But
when he blinked a little, he only saw two somewhat poorly clad
legs. They were standing in front of him, rather bandy, so that
he could see through between them. He risked a little blink up
the trouser-legs and saw an elderly man. Who had a knife and a
basket in his hand. And a little soil on his finger-tips.

This is where you sleep, eh? asked the man and looked down
at the tumble of hair. Jürgen blinked at the sun between the
man's legs and said: No, I don't sleep. I have to keep guard here.
The man nodded: I see, that's why you've got the big stick there
I suppose? Yes, replied Jürgen bravely, and held fast to the stick.

What are you guarding, then?

I can't tell you that. He held his hands tight round the stick.

Money, I'll bet, eh? The man set the basket down and wiped
the knife to and fro on the seat of his trousers.

No, not money at all, said Jürgen contemptuously. Something
quite different.

Well, what then?

I can't tell you. Just something different.

Well, don't then. And of course I won't tell you what I have
here in the basket. The man kicked the basket with his foot and
clicked the knife shut.

Pah, I can just imagine what's in the basket, observed Jürgen
disdainfully, rabbit food.

By jiminy, you're right! said the man, you're a smart lad.
How old are you, then?

Nine.

Aha, think of that, so you're nine. Then you certainly know
what three times nine are, eh?

Sure, said Jürgen, and to gain time he added: That's quite easy. And he looked through the man's legs. Three times nine, eh? he asked again, twenty-seven. I knew it at once.

Correct, said the man, and that's exactly the number of rabbits I've got.

Jürgen made a round mouth: Twenty-seven?

You can see them. Lots of them are still quite young. Would you like to?

But I can't. I have to keep guard, said Jürgen uncertainly.

All the time? asked the man, at night, too?

At night too. All the time. Always. Jürgen looked up the bandy legs. I've been here since Saturday, he whispered.

But don't you ever go home at all? You must eat, mustn't you?

Jürgen lifted up a stone. There was half a loaf lying there. And a tin box.

You smoke? asked the man, have you a pipe then?

Jürgen firmly clutched his stick and said timidly: I roll cigarettes. Don't like a pipe.

Pity. The man stooped towards his basket. You'd have been welcome to look at the rabbits. Specially the young ones. Perhaps you'd have chosen one for yourself. But you can't get away from here.

No, said Jürgen sadly, no, no.

The man picked up his basket and straightened up.

Well, if you *must* stay here—pity. And he turned round. Then Jürgen said quickly: If you won't give me away, it's because of the rats.

The bandy legs came back a pace: Because of the rats?

Yes, they eat dead bodies, you know. Of people. That's how they live.

Who says so?

Our teacher.

And now you're guarding the rats? asked the man.

No, not them! And then he said quite softly: My brother, he's lying under there. There. Jürgen pointed with his stick at the fallen-in walls. Our house got a bomb. All at once the light in the cellar went out. And he went, too. We shouted and shouted.

He was much smaller than me. Only four. He must be here still. He's so much smaller than me.

The man looked down on the tumble of hair. And then he said suddenly: Yes, but didn't your teacher tell you that rats sleep at night?

No, whispered Jürgen and all at once looked quite tired, he didn't say that.

Well, said the man, he's a fine teacher, if he doesn't even know that. Of course the rats sleep at night. You can safely go home at night. They always sleep nights. As soon as it gets dark.

With his stick Jürgen made little holes in the rubble.

Lots of little beds those are, he thought, all little beds.

Then the man said (and his bandy legs moved restlessly): Do you know what? I'll just go and feed my rabbits now, and as soon as it's dark I'll call for you. Perhaps I can bring one with me. A little one, or what do you think?

Jürgen made little holes in the rubble. Lots of little rabbits. White, grey, white-grey. I don't know, he said softly, and looked up the bandy legs, if they *really* sleep at night.

The man climbed over the remains of the wall out on to the street. Of course they do, he said from there, your teacher ought to pack it in, if he doesn't even know that.

Then Jürgen stood up and asked: Can I really have one? A white one perhaps?

I'll see what I can do, shouted the man, already walking away, but you'll have to wait for me here. Then I'll come home with you, see? I'll have to tell your father how to build a rabbit hutch. For you'd have to know how.

Yes, shouted Jürgen, I'll wait. I'll have to keep guard anyway, till it gets dark. I'll wait for certain. And he shouted: We've still got some boards at home. Boxboards, he shouted.

But the man was already out of earshot. With his bandy legs he was running towards the sun. It was already red with evening and Jürgen could see how it shone through his legs, they were so bandy. And the basket swung excitedly to and fro. There was rabbit food in it. Green rabbit food, a little grey from the rubble.

HE TOO HAD A LOT OF TROUBLE
WITH THE WARS

AT that time one had one's father when it grew dark. Even when one didn't see him any more in the violet dusk. But one heard him. When he coughed. And when he walked through the flat, coughing. And one could smell his tobacco. And then that sufficed. Then one could endure the violet evenings.

Later on, then, one had girls, who as yet had hardly any breasts. But all the same it was somehow pleasant to have them beside one in the violet dusk. On the jetty. And under the balcony at evening. Their hands were quite hot then, too. Then that sufficed. Then one could endure the violet darkness.

And in the Russian houses one sometimes had an old woman's face when the others were snoring and when the violet roar of the guns still kept one awake. Such an old woman's face, leathern-yellow as the cloth that was round it, that sufficed then, when it glowed like an oil-lamp across the snoring men from the other corner of the room. Only the metal of the slender rifles glimmered like reptile's skin: dumb and dangerous and shiny. And they made the dusk in the Russian houses uneasy. They made the soft evening violet so icy with their steel. But such a leathery old woman's face, shivered by gunfire, glows lifelong towards one out of the violet darkness. Sprinkled over with blood. Ripped sharply open by gunflash. Dark with nights of weeping. A woman's face. Behind the curtains of suburbs one sometimes sees it so pale. In the cities so often. In the evenings.

Those evenings are violet in the streets. In the narrower streets of the city, at least. In our city, at least. There, where the little people live and the streets are quite narrow. The ones with the wonderful longings. The clerks with the violet ink-spots on their fingers and sleeves. And sometimes with jaundice. The paper-hangers with the smell of oil in their skin. And the sewer-workers, who still cough from the gas of the previous war. Or something. The bricklayers and postmen, with the good and somewhat bandy-legged gait of people who walk a lot. The tramway sweepers with the brushed-up pride of their uniforms. And in among them sometimes a café violinist and a socialist poet. Cigarette-grey, long-haired, with wasted faces. Quite different. They live in the narrower streets of the city, where the violet evenings are.

Violet and quite soft in the evenings grow the corners of stone, the mausoleum-cool mouths of the gateways, the square-set tenement houses, the barracks now grey that at one time were certainly brighter, the woodsheds, still standing aslant. And the lamp-posts, so soldierly-smart, even they stand drowsily lost in the violet haze of the evening. And then the tissue-paper moths and midges and the other strawlike dusty-winged insects of the night rattle against the yellow glimmer of the lamps.

A bowl is rinsed out under the tap. There had been currants in it. No fat, for the bowl is quickly clean. One can hear it. It's put in the cupboard. The cupboard creaks. It is shut. It must be old, for it creaks. Then the water that's been poured over the petunias dribbles from four balconies. From above it dribbles on to the street. Sometimes a petal comes with it. Part withered. From left to right—from left to right. Then it's down. Tomorrow morning it will be trampled on. Perhaps even tonight. And then a woman says: Will you be quiet now! And in protest, a child croaks like a hen half asleep. Half aloud. And then one hears an aluminium vessel set down on the floor. Under the bed very possibly. Very possibly the chamber pot. Then a door shuts, asthmatically. The child cries again, twice. But then a very beautiful steamer (it's bound to be very beautiful!) hoots from the harbour. And in the pub at Steenkamp, they're bawling out for the fourteenth time this evening:

> You-u-u—my qui-et val-ley
> Whe-e-e-re—I loved to dal-ly

And with it all the evening grows ever more violet.

It is so violet now that one can no longer see the smoke that comes from Herr Lorenz's pipe. Herr Lorenz is standing in front of the door now. He is really only sort of touched in and at the same time somewhat smudged in this evening, violet. That's because of his violet-blue uniform. For he's in service with the street-cleaning department, where they wear them. Actually, in uniform there's not much of Herr Lorenz left. He's completely dissolved in it. It has swallowed him up with its smug functionary's violet. With that smug state violet. And the brass buttons hang like ten-pfennig pieces one under the other in the doorway. That's the complete Herr Lorenz. Above it there floats a bright yellow cheese. That is Herr Lorenz's head. And sometimes there's a reddish dot in it. That is Herr Lorenz's pipe. But only when he draws in is the reddish dot there. At other times the bright yellow cheese is alone in the doorway. And under it the brass buttons float like ten-pfennig pieces. Six. Three on each side. That is Herr Lorenz from the street-cleaning department at evening in the violet doorway.

And beside him something else. Small and wizened and grey. With a flour-pale disc above it. That is Helene. She has difficulty in breathing. Helene is Herr Lorenz's sister. Every three years she comes into the city to see if her brother is still alive. And always he's still with the street-cleaning department. Now they're both standing there in the violet mouth of the doorway. He in uniform. She breathing heavily. They have just been looking up at the sky, to see if Helene can still get home dry. Like farthings, said Herr Lorenz, like so many farthings. He meant the stars. And then he said suddenly: No, no, you mustn't say that. It's not right. Our roadways here are not bad. You mustn't say that. I've been sweeping now for thirty-seven years. But they're not bad. I know almost every stone here. They lie very well. Let them be.

But it's tiring, I mean.

Habit, Helene, sheer habit.

I don't mean that exactly, you see, I mean figuratively. Symbolically, do you understand?

Ah, symbolically, you mean, symbolically?

Yes, metaphorically, you understand?

Ah, I know what you mean. Now I know, metaphorically. Symbolically. Symbolically the roadways are bad, is what you want to say? Ah.

Yes, you see, out there at home you walk on the earth. So you always know where you are. And what you've got, too. But here with you it's all smooth. And when you've been walking for a while, you get tired. Then you don't see the slippery bits any

more. Suddenly, you're laid flat. And where can you lie in this
town, Hermann, I ask you, where can you lie down here?

Don't say that, Helene, no, don't say that. Our roadways are
always clean. I've been sweeping for thirty-seven years. I know
every stone. When I've finished my round, it's as though they'd
been licked, my good woman. Licked—clean!

I know, Hermann, but——

They haven't kept me thirty-seven years in the public service
for nothing. We've all been in that long. And not for nothing,
Helene, believe me. When I've finished my round, then it's as
though they'd been licked, my good woman. Licked—clean!

I know that, Hermann. I only mean it indirectly, symbolically,
you understand?

Symbolically, if you like. But my round is clean, when I've
finished. But if you mean it symbolically, then you may be right.
But out there with you, it's not all that clean either, Helene, don't
forget that. All sorts of things happen in the country, too, sometimes, my good woman.

I know that, Hermann, I know that. But here in the city——

Naturally, here in the city——

For a long time the two of them stand in the doorway. The
evening grows more violet. The evening slowly becomes night.
Now and then loving couples float past. The whole city is violet.
Only the windows are sometimes yellow or green. Sometimes
even red. But otherwise everything is quite violet. And from the
loving couples one hears perhaps only a word. Sometimes nothing
at all. The violet has swallowed them completely. The violet has
swallowed up everything.

Then Herr Lorenz smacks himself on the forehead. These
midges, he says, as soon as you stop smoking!

I think I'll be going, says his sister, or it'll be too late.

Yes, says Herr Lorenz, and don't think so much, d'you hear?
He'll come back all right. You often hear of it, that someone
who's missing suddenly comes back. When the war's long since
over, you still hear of it. You hear it quite often.

Oh, Hermann——!

No, no, Helene, you mustn't let it get you down. A Lorenz
never lets things get her down, Helene. If only because of the
children. After all, they need you. You mustn't weaken. Just
wait, all of a sudden he'll be back again.

Ah, Hermann——

Stick it out, Helene, stick it out. Watch out, you'll see, all of a sudden he'll come back. Everything evens itself out, Helene. A war like that makes a lot of trouble. But it all evens itself out again. I've had my trouble with the wars, too, I can tell you. A fair amount of it. But it all evens itself out again, Helene I tell you, it all evens itself out. I've had a mountain of trouble with the wars. First with that one. And then with this. You just listen to me. Sweeping a double round for all those years. They were all out there too, from the cleaning department. Except for the ones that weren't fit. And the ones that stayed behind, they had a mountain of trouble, I can tell you. All those years a double round. And the food. And the brooms got so bad. And the streets were so messy. When the lads came from the barracks and went to the station, there was three days' sweeping. How do you think the streets looked from the barracks to the station? I can tell you. But it all evens itself out again. Watch out, Helene, he'll be back yet, I tell you, he'll be back again yet. Slowly it all evens itself out. It was the same with us, too. The trouble we had. And now the lads are coming back. Now that it's over. And now they gather up every mortal thing. Not only the soldiers. Everyone. Now there's hardly anything left lying in the street. Nowadays no one throws anything away, I tell you. Nowadays they pick everything up. And how they used to muck up the streets. From the barracks to the station. To music. Dear, oh dear! We had a job after that, I can tell you. These wretched wars.

Do you think so? asked Helene.

What? said Herr Lorenz.

That he can still come back?

But of course, Helene, but of course. I tell you, it all evens itself out. Think of the streets. How they were mucked up. From the barracks right down to the station—filthy. Every time a wave went to the front, then we had a job, too. But now it's all over, now they look as though they'd been licked. And it isn't only the soldiers, Helene. It's everyone. Everyone, Helene.

That'd be something.

What d'you say?

If he comes back——

But of course. It all evens itself out, Helene. You watch out. It'll all come right again.

That'd be something. Oh yes, that'd be something.

Herr Lorenz's sister says it several times more. Again and again: That'd be something. Then suddenly there's a wooden knocking.

Oh, it's you, Hermann.

Yes, it's out.

He sticks the pipe in his pocket.

Yes, he says.

Well, good night, Hermann.

Good night, Helene, my love to the children.

Yes, Hermann.

Come back again soon.

Yes, Hermann.

Or write once in a while.

Yes, Hermann.

You'll see, it'll all even itself out. Just watch out.

No one answers any more. She looks round again. Only his brass buttons are there. Nothing else. Like farthings, she thinks. Then suddenly the farthings are gone.

Herr Lorenz shuts his window. Just like farthings, he thinks. Herr Lorenz means the stars. And then he soon falls asleep. His uniform hangs on a chair. It is bluish. Almost more of a violet. The sort they wear in the street-cleaning department. Herr Lorenz had had it for thirty-seven years. And two wars.

Outside an elderly woman walks through the suburb. That'd be something, she says now and then. But she cannot be seen. The night is too violet. It swallows everything. And the elderly woman wears black. But now and then she still says: That'd be something. That'd be something.

In a foreign country there is a village. It has a field. In one place the earth is a little higher than elsewhere. Roughly six feet long and eighteen inches high. But Herr Lorenz's sister does not know that country. Nor the village. Nor the field. That is well.

IN MAY, IN MAY CRIED THE CUCKOO

MAD are the March mornings by the river, one lies still in a half sleep, about four or so, and the ship-monsters blow their vital saurian groan restlessly over the city, into the icy-pink early mist, into the sun-breathed silver stream of the living river, and in the last dream before day, then one dreams no more of bright-legged sleep-warm women, around four or so, in the pink early mist, in the blowing of steamers, in their big-muzzled Oo-roar, by the river at morning, then one dreams quite different dreams, not those of black bread and coffee and cold stewed meat, not those of stammering, scampering women, no, then one dreams the quite different dreams, the foreboding, early, the last, the almighty, the uninterpretable dreams, they are the dreams one dreams on the mad March mornings by the river, early, around four or so. . . .

Mad are the November nights in the lonely mouse-grey cities, when the locomotives cry over from the blue-black suburban distances, fearful, hysterical, bold and adventurous, crying into the first sleep scarcely begun, the cry of locomotives, long, longing, elusive, so that one draws the covers still higher and presses yet closer to the magical, passionate animal of the night, that's called Evelyn or Hilda, that in such nights, full of November and the cry of locomotives, loses its speech in pleasure and pain, becomes animal, dream-heavy, quivering, insatiable beast of November, locomotive beast, for mad, oh so mad are the nights in November.

Those are the March morning cries, the saurian cries of the ships in the river, those are the November night cries of loco-motives over silvery tracks through fear-blue forests—but one knows too, one knows, too, the clarinet's cry on September evenings from the bars stinking of schnaps and of perfume, and the April cries of the cats, shuddering, sensual, and the July cries of girls of sixteen, bent backwards over the railings of some bridge till their eyes fill with tears, lustful and frightened, and one knows the lonely icy January cries of young men, the cries of genius over dramas destroyed and flower-sonnets ruined.

All these world-cries, these dark-nightly, night-befogged,

blue-stained, ink-coloured, aster-blossoming, bloody cries, one knows them, one remembers them, one endures them again and again, and year after year, day after day, night by night.

But the cuckoo, the cuckoo in May, who among us can endure in the sultry May nights, on the May afternoons its maddening, lazy, excited cry? Who of us has ever grown used to May with its cuckoo, what woman, what man? Year after year again, night by night again, he drives women, the greedily breathing, and men, the benumbed, he drives them wild, the cuckoo, the cuckoo in May, this May cuckoo. In May the locomotives cry too, and ships and cats and women and clarinets—they cry at you, when you're alone in the street, but then, when it grows dark, then the cuckoo assaults you. The whistle of railways, the droning of steamers, the yowling of cats, the quaver of clarinets and the sobbing of women—but the cuckoo, the cuckoo cries like a heart through the May night, like a throbbing, living heart, and when, unexpected, the cuckoo's scream assails you in the night, in the May night, then no steamer can help you and no locomotive, no fussing of women or cats, and no clarinet. The cuckoo drives you insane. The cuckoo laughs at you, when you flee. Where to? laughs the cuckoo, where to, then, in May? And you stand there, made mad by the cuckoo, with all your earthly desires, alone, with nowhere to go, so alone, and then you hate May, hate it in passion and love and despair, hate it with all your loneliness, hate this cuckoo in May, this. . . .

And then we run with our cuckoo destiny through the dewy nights, ah, we cannot escape our cuckoo lot, the fate to which we are fated. Cry, cuckoo, cry your loneliness into the spring of May, cry, cuckoo, brotherly bird, turned out, rejected, I know, brother cuckoo, all your crying is crying for the mother who abandoned you to the May nights, rejected you as a stranger among strangers, cry, cuckoo, cry out your heart to the stars, brother stranger, motherless, cry. . . . Cry, bird of loneliness, make fools of the poets, they lack your mad syllables, and their lonely distress becomes drivel, and only when they're dumb do they do their best, bird of loneliness, when mothercry hunts us through sleepless May nights, then we do our most heroic deed. The unspeakable loneliness, this icy, male loneliness, we live then, we live without your mad sounds, brother bird, for the last, the ultimate cannot be put into words.

They should go, the heroic, dumb, solitary poets, and learn how a shoe is made, a fish caught, and a roof thatched, for all they deliver is drivel, agonized, bloody, despairing, against the May nights, the cry of the cuckoo, against the true sounds of the world. For who among us, who then, oh, who knows a rhyme for the rattle of lungs shot to pieces, a rhyme for the scream at the gallows, who knows the metre, the rhythm, for rape, who knows a metre for the bark of machine-guns, a sound for the new-smothered scream of a dead horse's eye, in which no further heaven is mirrored, not even the blazing of villages, what press has a sign for the rust-red of freight cars, this world-in-flames red, this dried-up blood-encrusted red on white human skin? Go home, poets, go into the forests, catch fish, chop wood and do your most heroic deed: Be silent! Let the cuckoo cry of your lonely hearts be silent, for there's no rhyme and no metre for it, and no drama, no ode and no psychological novel can encompass the cry of the cuckoo, and no dictionary and no press has syllables or signs for your wordless world-rage, for your exquisite pain, for the agony of your love.

For we have fallen asleep to the crackling of houses blown open (ah, poets, for the sighing of houses in death every syllable fails you!) fallen asleep to the grind of grenades (what press has a sign for this screaming of metal?) and we fall asleep to the groans of the punished and of women taken in rape (who knows a rhyme for it, who knows the rhythm?)—but we have been shocked in the May nights by the dumb agony of our strangers' hearts here in this world of spring, for only the cuckoo, only the cuckoo knows a sound for all its lonely, motherless misery. And to us there remains the one heroic deed, the deed of adventure: Our solitary silence. Since for the grandiose roar of this world and for its hellish stillness the paltriest words are lacking. All we can do is: to add up, collect the sum, count it, note it down.

Yet we must have this foolhardy, senseless courage for a book! We must make a note of our misery, perhaps with trembling hands, we must put it down before us in stone, ink or notes, in unbelievable colours, in unique perspective, added up, counted and piled, and then there's a book of two hundred pages. But there'll be nothing more in it than a few comments, observations, notes, sparsely illustrated, never explained, for the two hundred printed pages are only a commentary on the twenty thousand invisible pages, on the Sisyphus pages which make up our life, for which we know no words, no grammar and no punctuation. But on these twenty thousand invisible pages of our book stands the grotesque ode, the ridiculous epic, the most prosaic and bewitched of all novels: Our crazy, spherical world, our quivering heart, our life! That is the book of our mad, bold, fearful loneliness on night-dead streets.

But those who go through the stony city at night in the lighted, yellow-red, tinny trams, they, they must be happy. For they are going somewhere, they know the exact name of their destination, they have said it with the lazy lips of people to whom nothing more can happen, without looking up, they know where their stop is (it's not far for any of them) and they know that the tram will take them there. After all, they have paid the State for it, some with taxes, some with an amputated leg, and with twenty pfennigs ticket money. (War-wounded half price. A one-legged man travels by tram 7862 times in life at half price. He saves 786 marks and 20 pfennigs. His leg, it has long since rotted away near Smolensk, was worth 786 marks and 20 pfennigs. No matter.) But those in the tram are happy. They must be. They are neither hungry nor homesick. How can they be hungry or homesick? Their destination is certain and they all have leather bags, cardboard boxes or baskets with them. Some are even reading. Faust, film magazines or their tickets, you can't tell from their faces. They are good actors. They sit there with their stiff, suddenly aged children's faces and play at being grown-up. And the nine-year-olds believe them. But best of all they'd like to make little balls of their tickets and throw them at one another, secretly. They are quite happy, for in the baskets and bags and the books, which the people have with them at night in the tram, therein are the prescriptions against hunger and homesickness (even if it's a butt end on which one chews one's fill—or a ticket for flight—). Those who have baskets and books with them, those in the trams at night, they must indeed be happy, for they are safe between the people on either side, who have spectacles, coughs or purple noses, and with the conductor, who wears an official uniform, has dirty finger-nails and a gold wedding ring, which reconcile, one to the finger-nails, for only a bachelor's nails are unpleasant when dirty. A married tram conductor has perhaps a little garden, a window-box or makes sailing-ships for his five children (no, he builds them for himself, for his secret journeys!). Those who are safely with such a conductor, at night in the discreetly lit tram, for the lamps are not too bright and not too dim, they must be comforted and happy—no cuckoo cry bursts from their cheap, thrifty, bitter mouths and no cuckoo cry from outside pierces through the thick glassy windows. They are undismayed and how safe, oh, how infinitely safe they are under the respectable, blinkered lamps of the tramcar, under the so ordinary stars of their everyday life, this dismal light that the Fatherland bestows on its children in offices, stations, public conveniences (greenshaded, cobwebby) and in trams. And the aged, absurd, sullen children in the trams at night, under the officially prescribed type of lamp, they must be happy, for fear (this May fear, the cuckoo fear), fear they cannot have: they have light. They do not know the cuckoo. They are together, if anything happens (a murder, a collision, a storm). And they know where they're going. And in the yellow-red tinny trams under the lamps with conductor and neighbour (even if he does belch of herring) in the middle of the dark, stony evening city, they are safe.

Never will the world burst in on top of them, as on him who stands alone in the street: With no lamp, no destination, no one beside him, hungry, with no basket, no book, full of the cuckoo's cry, full of fear. Those who stand so naked and poor in the street, when, full of cigarette smoke, the trams clang past (this clanging alone chases homesickness and fear back into the gloomy gate-ways!) with their comforting so ordinary lamps inside and the comforted faces beneath them preserved for ten thousand every-day days—those who are still standing there, when the tram, already far off, screams and howls round a rusty curve, they—they belong to the street. The street is their heaven, their pious pilgrimage, their mad dance, their hell, their bed (with park-benches and the arches of bridges), their mother and their girl. This grey-hard street is their dusty silent reliable pal, stubborn, loyal and steadfast. This rain-wet sunblazing star-studded moon-

bright wind-inspired street is their curse and their evening prayer
(is their evening prayer when a woman has a spare glass of milk—
is their curse, when the next town, the next town fails to arrive
before nightfall). This street is their despair and their lust for
adventure. And when you pass them, then they look at you like
princes, these patched-up kings by the grace of rags, and with
tight bitter mouths they tell their whole great hard proud
cloddish wealth:

The street belongs to us. The stars above, the sunwarmed
stones beneath us. The singsong wind and the earth-scented rain.
The street belongs to us. We have lost our heart, our innocence,
our mother, our house and the war—but the street, our street,
we shall never lose. It belongs to us. Its night under the Great
Bear. Its day under the yellow sun. Its singing, tingling rain: All
this: This smell of sun, rain and wind, this damp-grassy, wet-
earthy, girl-flowery smell, which smells so good, as does nothing
else in the world: This street belongs to us. With its enamelled
midwife's signs and privet-hedged graveyards to right and left,
with the forgotten mist-world of yesterday lying behind us, with
the unforeseen mist-world of tomorrow there before us. There we
stand, abandoned to May, to the cuckoo, with tears bitten back,
heroically sentimental, deceived by a little romance, lonely,
masculine, mother-yearning, arrogant, lost. Lost between village
and village. Solitary in the million-windowed city. Cry, bird of
loneliness, cry for help, cry for us and with us, for the last syllables,
the rhyme and the metre are lacking for all our distress.

But sometimes, bird of loneliness, sometimes, seldom, oddly
and seldom, when the yellow-glowing tram has mercilessly flung
the street back into its black abandonment; then sometimes,
seldom, oddly and seldom, then sometimes in some city (oh so
seldom) there is still a window left open. A bright warm seductive
square in the cold, stony colossus, in the terrible blackness of
night. A window.

And then everything happens quite quickly. Quite matter of
factly. One merely notes in one's head: the window, the woman,
and the May night. That's all, desperate, wordless, banal. One
must toss it down like a schnaps, hastily, bitter, sharp and stunning. Against it, everything's drivel, everything. For this is life:
The window, the woman and the May night. A dirty banknote

on the table, chocolate or a piece of jewellery. Then one notes:
Legs and knees and thighs and breasts and blood. Toss the schnaps
back. And tomorrow the cuckoo will cry again. Everything else
is emotional drivel. For this is the life, for which there's no word:
hot, hectic confusion. Swallow the schnaps. It burns and inflames
you. On the table is the money. All else is drivel, for tomorrow,
soon tomorrow the cuckoo will cry again. This evening only this
short banal note: The window, the woman. That suffices. All
else is—at three in the morning, the cuckoo will begin again.
When it's greying. But for the moment this evening a window is
there. And a woman. And a woman.

On the ground floor a window is open. Still open to the night.
The cuckoo cries, green as an empty bottle of gin, into the silky
jasmine night of the suburban streets. A window is still open.
A man is standing in the green-crying cuckoo night, a jasmine-
stunned man hungry and homesick for an open window. The
window is open. (Oh so seldom!) A woman leans out. Pale.
Blonde. Long-legged perhaps. The man thinks: long-legged
perhaps, that's her type. And she talks like all women who stand
at the windows at evening. So animal-warm and softly. As
unashamedly lazy and excited as the cuckoo. As heavy-sweet as
the jasmine. As dark as the city. As mad as May. And her speech
is so professionally of the night. As minor-keyed green as a bottle
of gin that's been drunk. So undisguisedly flowery. And the man
by the window creaks unloved and lonely, like the dried-up
leather of his boot:

So you won't?
I've just told you——
So you won't?

——

And if I give you the bread?

——

Not without the bread, but if I do give you the bread, then?
I just told you, boy——
So it's yes?
Yes.
So it's yes. Hm. Well then!
I just told you, boy, if the children hear us, they'll wake up.
And then they'll be hungry. And then if I've no bread for them,

they won't go to sleep again. Then they'll cry all night. Do understand.

I'll give you the bread. Open the door. I'll give it you. Here it is. Open the door.

I'm coming.

The woman opens the door, then the man shuts it behind him. He has a loaf under his arm. The woman shuts the window. The man sees a picture on the wall. It's of two naked children with flowers. The picture has a broad golden frame and is brightly coloured. Especially the flowers. But the children are much too fat. 'Amor and Psyche', the picture is called. The woman shuts the window. Then the curtain. The man lays the bread on the table. The woman comes to the table and takes the bread. Over the table hangs the lamp. The man looks at the woman and shoves out his lower lip, as though he were tasting something. Thirty-four, he thinks then. The woman goes with the bread to the cupboard. What a face, she thinks, what a face he's got. Then she comes back from the cupboard to the table again. Yes, she says. They both look at the table. The man starts to flick breadcrumbs from the table with his finger. Yes, he says. The man looks her legs up and down. One can see her legs almost complete. The woman is wearing a thin transparent bright-blue petticoat. One can see her legs almost complete. Then there are no more bread-crumbs on the table. May I take off my jacket? says the man. It looks silly.

Yes, the colour, you mean?

It's dyed.

Oh, dyed! Like a beer-bottle.

Beer-bottle?

Yes, so green.

Oh yes, I see. So green. I'll hang it in here.

Just like a beer-bottle.

Well, but your dress is—

What then?

Well, sky-blue.

This is not my dress.

Oh!

But nice, eh?

Yes——

Shall I keep it on?

Yes yes, of course.

The woman still stands at the table. She doesn't know why the man is still sitting. But the man is tired. Yes, says the woman and looks down at herself. Then the man looks at her. He looks down her, too. I say—says the man and looks at the lamp. But of course, she says, and puts out the light. In the darkness the man still sits quietly on his chair. She passes close by him. He feels a warm breath of air as she passes him. Close by him she passes. He can smell her. He is tired. Then from over there (from far, far away, thinks the man) she says: Come now. Of course, he says and acts as though he had been waiting for this. He knocks against the table: Oh, the table. Here I am, she says in the darkness. Aha. He hears her breath quite close beside him. Cautiously he stretches out his hand. They hear each other breathing. Then his hand touches something. Oh, he says, there you are. It's her hand. I've found your hand in the dark, he laughs. I held it out to you, she says softly. Then she bites his finger. She pulls him down. He sits. They both laugh. She hears that he is breathing quite quickly. At the most he is twenty, she thinks, he's afraid. You old beer-bottle, she says. She takes his hand and puts it on her hot night-cool skin. He feels that she has taken the bright-blue thing off. He feels her breast. He says arrogantly into the darkness (but he is quite out of breath): You milk-bottle you. You're a milk-bottle, d'you know that? No, she says, I never knew that before. They both laugh. He is much too young, she thinks. She's just like them all, he thinks. He is frightened of her naked skin. He keeps his hands quite still. Such a child, she thinks. They're all the same, he thinks, yes, they're all the same, all of them. He doesn't know what he should do with his hands on her breast. You're cold, I think, he says, I think you're cold, eh? In the middle of May, she laughs, in the middle of May? Well yes, he says, still at night. But in May, she says, we're in the middle of May. One can even hear the cuckoo, keep quiet a moment, d'you hear, one can even hear the cuckoo, listen, don't breathe so loud, listen, d'you hear, the cuckoo. All the time. One two three four five—well?—there!—six seven eight—d'you hear? There again—nine ten eleven—listen: cuckoo cuckoo cuckoo cuckoo—beer-bottle you, old beer-bottle, says the woman tenderly. She is contemptuous and maternal and tender. For the man is asleep——

It is dawning. Already it's growing grey outside the curtains. It will soon be four o'clock. And the cuckoo is already there

again. The woman lies awake. Someone is already walking about
upstairs. A bread-machine bumps three—four—five times. A
water-pipe. Then the landing, the door, the stairs: steps. At half
past five the man from upstairs must be at the wharf. It must be
four-thirty. Outside, a bicycle. Bright-grey, really almost pink.
Bright-grey seeps slowly through the curtains from the window
across the table, the back of a chair, a bit of ceiling, the gold
frame, Psyche, and a hand that makes a fist. Even at half past four
in the morning in the bright-grey before daylight a man in his
sleep clenches his fist. Bright-grey seeps from the window through
the curtain on to a face, a piece of forehead, an ear. The woman
is awake. Perhaps a long time already. She does not move. But
the sleeping man with the fist has a heavy head. It fell on her
breast yesterday evening. Half past four it is now. And the man
is still lying as he lay last night. A tall, bony young man with a
heavy head. As the woman goes cautiously to push his head
away from her, she touches his face. It is wet. What a face he has,
thinks the bright-grey woman in the morning before daylight,
with a man lying on her, who has slept the whole night, with a
fist, and now his face is wet. And what a face it is now in the
bright-grey. A wet, long, poor, mild face. A soft face, lonely
grey, bad and good. A face. The woman pulls her shoulder
slowly away from under the head, till it falls on the pillow. Then
she sees the mouth. The mouth looks at her. What a mouth.
And the mouth looks at her. Looks at her, till her eyes dissolve.

It's the usual thing, says the mouth, it's nothing out of the
ordinary, it's only the usual thing. You've no need to smile,
superior, so contemptuously maternal, stop it, I say, stop it, you,
or—you, I tell you, I've learnt everything, stop it. I know I
should have fallen on you last night, bitten your white shoulders
and the soft flesh high above your knees, I should have torn it
out of you till you lay flat in the corner, and then, in pain, you'd
still have moaned: More, darling, more. That's how you thought
of it. Oh, he's still young, you thought in your window last
night, he's not so worn out as the cowardly old fathers of families
who for a quarter of an hour here in the evenings play the Don
Juan. Oh, you thought, there goes a young stripling, he'll throw
you around, you'll get no peace from him. Then I came in. You
smelt of animal, but I was tired, you see, I only wanted to put my

legs up for an hour. You could have kept your petticoat on. The night is over. You grin because you're ashamed. You despise me. You probably think I'm not even a man. Of course you think that, for now you're being all maternal. You think I'm still a boy. You're pitying me, contemptuous maternal pity, because I didn't fall on you. But I am a man, do you hear, I've long been a man. I was only tired last night, or I'd have shown you all right, I can tell you, for I've long been a man, says the mouth, do you hear, long since. For I've drunk vodka, my love, and I've yelled shit, you know, I've had a gun and yelled shit and I've shot and stood alone on guard and the Company Commander's called me by my first name and Sergeant Brand always swapped cigarettes with me, because he wanted artificial honey so much and then I had his cigarettes in addition, if you think I'm still only a boy! Already, on the evening before we started for Russia, I went with a woman, long ago, my love, with a woman and for more than an hour and she was hoarse and dear and a proper woman, that was, a grown-up, my love, she didn't go all maternal with me, she stuck my money away and said: Well, when do you go, darling, going to Russia? Want another go with a German woman, eh, darling? Darling she called me and unbuttoned the collar of my uniform. But then she twisted the fringe of the tablecloth round her fingers the whole time and looked at the wall. Now and again she said darling, but afterwards she stood up at once and washed herself and then at the door downstairs she said 'Bye. That was all. Next door they were singing Rosamunde and from the other windows everywhere they were hanging out and they all said darling. They all said darling. That was the farewell to Germany. But the worst came next morning at the station.

The woman shut her eyes. For the mouth, it was growing. For the mouth was growing big and brutal and big.

It was the usual thing, said the giant mouth, it was nothing out of the ordinary. It was only the usual thing. A lead morning. A lead railway. And lead soldiers. We were the soldiers. It was nothing out of the ordinary. Just the usual thing. A station. A freight train. And faces. That was all.

Then when we climbed into the freight train, they stank of cattle, the trucks, the blood-red trucks, then our fathers grew loud and jovial with their lead faces and desperately they waved their hats. And with brightly coloured handkerchieves our mothers wiped away their measureless sorrow: And don't lose your new socks, Karlheinz. And sweethearts were there, their mouths still sore from the farewell and their breasts and their—everything hurt, and their heart and their lips still burned and the burn of the farewell night was not yet, oh far from it, extinguished in lead. But we sang so wonderfully out into God's wide world and grinned and bawled till our mothers' hearts froze. And then the station grew smaller—*der wollte keine Knechte*—then the mothers grew smaller—*Säbel, Schwert und Spiess*—the mothers and sweethearts grew smaller and smaller and father's hat—*dass er bestände bis aufs Blut*—father's hat went on still waving: Make a job of it, Karlheinz—*bis in der Tod*—make a job of it, my boy—*die Feeeheeede*. And our Company Commander sat at the front of the truck and wrote in his report book: Departed 0623. In the kitchen car the recruits, with manly faces, peeled potatoes. In an office in the Bismarkstrasse that morning Herr Dr. Sommer, Notary and Barrister-at-law said: My fountain-pen is broken. It's high time the war was over. Outside the city a locomotive cheered. But in the trucks, in the dark trucks, one still had the smell of the burning sweethearts to oneself, all to oneself in the dark, but in the light of the oil-lamp none of us risked a tear. Not one of us. We sang the comfortless men's song of Madagascar and the blood-red trucks stank of cattle, for we had human beings on board. Ahoy, comrades, and nobody risked a tear, ahoy, little lady, daily one went overboard and in the craters, there the warm-red raspberry lemonade went bad, the unique lemonade, for which there is no substitute and for which no one can pay, no, no one. And when fear made us swallow the slime and threw us into the ripped-up lap of Mother Earth, then we cursed to heaven; to the deaf dumb heaven: And lead us not into desertion and forgive us our machine-guns, forgive us, but nobody, nobody was there to forgive us, there was no one there. And what came after, for that there is no expression, against it all else is drivel, for who knows a metre for the tinny bleating of machine-guns and who knows a rhyme for the scream of an eighteen-year-old man whimpering between the lines with his entrails in his hands, who then, ah no one ! ! !

As we left the station on that leaden morning and the waving mothers grew tiny and tinier, then we sang magnificently, for the war came just right for us. And then it came. Then it was there. And against it all else was drivel. No one word could withstand it, the roaring, poisoning, strength-swelling beast, no word. What's the significance of *la guerre* or *der Krieg* or the war? Pitiful drivel, against the animal roar of its glowing mouths, the mouths of the guns. And treason, against the glowing mouths of heroes betrayed. To the metal, to the phosphorus, to hunger and ice-storms and desert sand, pitifully betrayed. And now we're saying again *la guerre und der Krieg* and the war and no shuddering attacks us, no scream and no horror. Today we simply repeat: *C'était la guerre*—that was the war. We no longer say more today, for the words are lacking to reflect for one second even one second of it and we simply repeat: Oh yes, that was it. For all else is mere drivel, for there's no word and no rhyme and no metre for it and no ode and no drama and no psychological novel that can bear it, that does not burst with its roar of vermilion. And as we weighed anchor, and the quayside crunched with joy, as we steered away to the land, to the dark land of war, we sang bravely, we men, oh so ready we were and so we sang, we in the cattle-trucks. And on the marching musical stations they cheered us on into the dark, dark land of war. And then it came. Then it was there. And then, before we'd understood, it was over. In between lies our life. And that's ten thousand years. And now it's over and from the rotting planks of the lost ships we are spewed out at night, secretly, contemptibly, on to the coast of the land of peace, the incomprehensible land. And no one, no one can still recognize us, twenty-year-old old men, so has the roaring ravaged us. Is there anyone who still knows us? Where are they, those who still know us now? Where are they? The fathers hide themselves deep in their faces and the mothers, the seven thousand five hundred and forty-eight times murdered mothers, stifle in their helplessness before the torment of our estranged hearts. And the sweethearts, the terrified sweethearts sniff the smell of catastrophe breaking from our skins like the sweat of fear, at night, in their arms, and they smell the lonely metal taste in our desperate kisses and numbly they breathe the blood-fumes of slain brothers, sweet as marzipan, out of our hair and they do not understand our bitter tenderness. For in them we violate all our misery, for we murder them every night, until one delivers us. One. Delivers. But nobody knows us.

And now we're under way between the villages. The squeaking of a pump is a scrap of home. And a hoarse watchdog. And a wench, who says good day. And the smell of raspberry juice from a house. (Our Company Commander suddenly had his face full of raspberry juice. It came out of his mouth. And he was so surprised by it, that his eyes were like fish eyes: immeasurably astonished and silly. Our Company Commander was very surprised by death. He could not understand it at all.) But the scent of raspberry juice in the villages, for us that's already a scrap of home. And the wench with the red arms. And the hoarse dog. A scrap, a priceless, irreplaceable scrap.

And now we're in the cities. Ugly, greedy, lost. And windows are there for us seldom, oddly and seldom. But they are still, at night in the darkness, with sleep-warm women, a unique, heavenly scrap for us, oh so seldom. And we're on the way to the unbuilt new city, in which all the windows belong to us, and all the women, and everything and everything and everything: We're on the way to our city, to the new city, and our hearts cry like locomotives at night with desire and with homesickness— like locomotives. And all the locomotives are going to the new city. And the new city, that is the city in which the wise men, the teachers and ministers, do not lie, in which the poets are not seduced by anything other than the understanding of their hearts, that is the city in which the mothers do not die and the girls have no syphilis, the city in which there are no workshops for artificial limbs and wheelchairs, that is the city where rain is called rain and the sun the sun, the city in which there are no cellars where at night pale-faced children are devoured by rats, and in which there are no attics where the fathers hang themselves, that is the city in which the youngsters are not blind and not one-armed and in which there are no generals, it is the new, the wonderful city, in which everyone listens and sees and in which everyone understands: *mon coeur, der Tag, die Nacht, das Herz,* the night, your heart, the day.

And to the new city, the city of all cities, we are on the way, full of hunger, through our lonely May cuckoo nights, and if we wake up in the morning and know, oh how terribly we shall

know it, that the new city can never be, that the new city cannot
possibly be, then we shall again be ten thousand years older and
our morning will be cold and bitter, lonely, oh lonely, and only
the yearning locomotives, they will remain, still sobbing their faraway homesick-cry into our tortured sleep, greedy, gruesome,
great and excited. In pain they still cry at night on their cold and
lonely tracks. But never again will they go to Russia, no, never
again will they go to Russia, for no locomotive will go to Russia
no locomotive will go to Russia no locomotive will go to Russia
to Russia no for no locomotive will go to go to for no locomo
no locomo no locomo no——

In the harbour, up from the harbour, there comes the ooooh
of an early ship. A launch is already screaming excitedly. And a
car. Next door a man sings as he washes: Gonna take a sentimental journey. In the other room a child's already asking: Why
does the steamer say oooh, why is the launch screaming, why the
car, why is the man singing next door, and about what about
which asks the child?

The man who came with the bread last night, the one with
the beer-bottle jacket, the green-dyed one, who had a fist and a
wet face in the night, this man opens his eyes. The woman looks
away from his mouth. And the mouth is so small and so poor and
so full of bitter courage. They look at each other, one beast at
the other, one God at the other, one world at the other world.
(And for that there is no word.) Grandly, kindly, strange, endlessly, and warm and in amazement they look at one another, from
the beginning of time loving and hating and indissolubly lost in
each other.

The end is then like all other ends in real life: banal, wordless,
overwhelming. The door is there. He is standing outside but will
not yet risk the first step. (For the first step means: lost all over
again.) She is still standing inside and cannot yet slam the door.
(For every slammed door means: lost all over again.) But then
suddenly he is several paces away. And it's good that he said
nothing more. For what, what could she answer? And then into
the early haze (that comes up from the harbour and smells of
fish and of tar), into the early haze he has vanished. And it's so
good that he didn't even turn round again. It's so good. For what
could she have done? Wave? Perhaps wave?

ALONG THE LONG LONG ROAD

LEFT right left right left right left right left right come on, Fischer! left right left right forward, Fischer! snappy Fischer! left right breathe, Fischer! come on, Fischer, keep it going, zicker zacker left right left snappy is the infantree zicker zacker upidee snappy is the infantree the infantree the infantree——

I'm on my way. Twice already I've been down. I want the tram. I must catch it. Twice already I've been down. I'm hungry. But I must catch it. Must. I must get to the tram. Twice already I've been left right left I had a good job and I left but I must catch it left right zicker zacker zacker left right upidee is the infantree the infantree infantree fantree fantree——

At Voronezh they buried 57. 57, they had no notion, neither before nor afterwards. Beforehand they were still singing. Zicker zacker upidee. And one of them wrote home: . . . then we'll buy ourselves a gramophone. But then four thousand yards further on the others pressed a button on a word of command. Then it rumbled like an old lorry carrying empty drums over cobblestones: Cannon-music. Then they buried 57 at Voronezh. Beforehand they were still singing. Afterwards they had nothing more to say. Nine motor mechanics, two gardeners, five officials, six salesmen, one barber, seventeen peasants, two teachers, one clergyman, six labourers, one musician, seven schoolboys. Seven schoolboys. These they buried near Voronezh. They had no notion. Fifty-seven.

And me they forgot. I wasn't quite dead yet. Upidee. I was still a little bit alive. But the others, they buried them at Voronezh. 57. 57. Stick a naught on. 570. Another naught and another naught. 57000. And another and another and another. 57000000. These they buried at Voronezh. They had no notion. They didn't want it. They hadn't wanted that at all. And beforehand they were still singing. Upidee. Afterwards they had nothing more to say. And the one didn't buy the gramophone. They buried him at Voronezh and the other 56, too. 57 bods. Only me. Me, I wasn't quite dead yet. I must get to the tram. The street's grey.

But the tram's yellow. Such a beautiful yellow. And I must catch it. Only that the street's so grey. So grey and so grey. Twice already I've been zicker zacker get on, Fischer! left right left right left right been down left right come on, Fischer! zicker zacker upidee snappy is the infantree snappy, Fischer! come on, Fischer! left right left right if only hunger miserable hunger always this miserable left right left right left right left right left right——

If only there were no nights. If only there were no nights. Every sound is a beast. Every shadow is a black man. You're never rid of fear of the black men. On the pillow the guns rumble all night: your pulse. You should never have left me alone, mother. Now we shan't find each other again. Never again. You should never have done that. You knew the nights. You knew about the nights. But you screamed me out of yourself. Screamed me right out of yourself and into this world with the nights. And since then every sound is a beast in the night. And in the blue dark corners the black men are waiting. Mother! Mother! in every corner the black men stand. And every sound is a beast. Every sound is a beast. And the pillow's so hot. The whole night long the guns are growling on it. And then they buried 57 at Voronezh. And the clock shuffles like an old woman in carpet slippers away away away: It shuffles and shuffles and shuffles and nobody nobody stops it. And the walls come nearer and nearer. And the ceiling comes lower and lower. And the floor the floor it sways with the world's wave. Mother! Mother! why have you left me alone, why? Sways with the wave. Sways with the world. 57. Crump. And I want the tram. The guns rumbled. The ground sways. Crump. 57. And I'm still a little bit alive. And I want the tram. It's yellow in the grey street. Wonderfully yellow in the grey. But I shan't make it, I know. Twice already I've been down. For I'm hungry. And that's why the earth sways. Sways so wonderfully yellow with the world's wave. Sways with the hungerworld. Sways so world-hungry and tram-yellow.

Just now someone said to me: Good day, Herr Fischer. Am I Herr Fischer? Can I be Herr Fischer, simply *Herr* Fischer again? I used to be Second *Lieutenant* Fischer. Then can I be *Herr* Fischer again? Am I Herr Fischer? Good day, he said. But *he* doesn't know that I used to be Second Lieutenant Fischer. He wished me good day—for Second Lieutenant Fischer there are no more good days. He didn't know that.

And Herr Fischer walks along the road. Along the long road. Which is grey. He wants the tram. Which is yellow. So wonderfully yellow. Left right, Herr Fischer. Left right left right. Herr Fischer is hungry. He's no longer in step. All the same he must catch the tram, for the tram is so wonderfully yellow in the grey. Twice already Herr Fischer has been down. But Second Lieutenant Fischer orders: Left right left right get on, Herr Fischer! Come on, Herr Fischer! Snappy, Herr Fischer, orders Second Lieutenant Fischer. And Herr Fischer marches along the grey road, along the grey grey long road. Dustbin Avenue. Ashcan Lane. Gutter Embankment. The Champs-Ruinés. Mud-rubble-toil-and-trouble Broadway. Devastation Parade. And Second Lieutenant Fischer commands. Left right left right. And Herr Fischer Herr Fischer marches, left right left right left right left bereft bereft bereft——

The little girl has legs like fingers they're so thin. Like fingers in winter. So thin and so red and so blue and so thin. Left right left right go the legs. The little girl keeps saying and Herr Fischer's marching nearby she keeps saying: Dear Lord, give me soup. Dear Lord, give me soup. Only a little spoonful. Just a little spoonful. Just a little spoonful. What hair the mother has, it's already dead. Long since dead. The mother says: The dear Lord can't give you any soup, he just can't. Why can't the dear Lord give me any soup? He hasn't a spoon. He hasn't got one. The little girl walks on her fingerlegs, her thin blue winterlegs, beside the mother. Herr Fischer walks alongside. The mother's hair is already dead. It looks quite strange round her head. And the little girl dances round about round the mother round about round Herr Fischer round round about: He hasn't got a spoon. He hasn't got a spoon. He hasn't got oh no he's not he hasn't got a spoon. Thus the little girl dances round about. And Herr Fischer marches along behind. Sways alongside on the world's wave. Sways with the world's wave. But Second Lieutenant Fischer orders: Left right chances slight, snappy, Herr Fischer, left right and the little girl sings with it: He hasn't got a spoon— He hasn't got a spoon. And twice already Herr Fischer's been down. Down with hunger. He's got no spoon. And the other

commands: Upidee upidee the infantree the infantree the
infantree——

57 they buried at Voronezh. I am Second Lieutenant Fischer.
They forgot me. I wasn't yet quite dead. I've been down twice.
Now I'm Herr Fischer. I'm 25 years old. 25 times 57. And they
buried those at Voronezh. Only me, me, I'm still going along.
I've still got to get that tram. Hungry, that's what I am! But the
dear Lord has no spoon. He hasn't got a spoon. I'm 25 times 57.
My father betrayed me and my mother thrust me out of herself.
She screamed me alone. So terribly alone. So alone. Now I'm
walking along the long road. And it sways with the world's
wave. But there's always someone playing the piano. There's
always someone playing the piano. When my father saw my
mother—someone played the piano. When it was my birthday—
someone played the piano. At the Heroes' Memorial Ceremony
at school—someone played the piano. Then when we were
allowed to become heroes ourselves, when the war came—
someone played the piano. In hospital—someone also played the
piano. When the war was over—someone was still playing the
piano. Someone's always playing. Someone's always playing
the piano. All along the long road.

The engine's whistling. Timm says it's crying. If you look up,
the stars tremble. Again and again the engine whistles. But Timm
says it cries. It keeps on. The whole night. The whole long night
through now. It's crying, it hurts you in the stomach when it
cries like that, says Timm. It cries like kids, he says. We have a
truck with timber. It smells of forest. Our truck has no roof.
The stars tremble when you look up. There she toots again. Do
you hear? says Timm, it's crying again. I can't understand why
the engine cries. Timm says that. Like kids, he says. Timm says I
shouldn't have shoved the old man off the truck. I didn't shove
the old man off the truck. You shouldn't have done it, says Timm.
I didn't do it. It's crying, d'you hear how it's crying, says Timm,
you shouldn't have done it. I didn't shove the old man off the
truck. It's not crying. It's whistling. Engines whistle. It's crying,
says Timm. He fell off the truck by himself. Quite by himself,
the old man. He was snoozing, Timm, snoozing, that's what he
was, I tell you. Then he fell off the truck by himself. You
shouldn't have done it. It's crying. The whole night through now.

Timm says you shouldn't shove old men off trucks. I didn't do it. He was snoozing. You shouldn't have done it, says Timm. Timm says that in Russia he once kicked an old man's backside. Because he was so slow. And he always took so little at a time. They were carting ammo. So Timm kicked the old man's backside. Then the old man turned round. Quite slowly, Timm says, and he looked at him very sadly. That was all. But he had a face like his father. Exactly like his father. That's what Timm says. The engine's whistling. Sometimes it sounds as though it's screaming. Timm even thinks it's crying. Perhaps Timm's right. But I didn't shove the old man off the truck. He was snoozing. So he fell off by himself. The rails jolt a good bit, of course. When you look up, the stars tremble. The truck sways with the world's wave. It whistles. It screams. Screams, so that the stars tremble. With the world's wave.

But I'm still going. Left right left. On the way to the tram. Twice already I've been down. The ground sways with the world's wave. Because of hunger. But I'm going along. I've already been going along so long so long. Along the long road. The road.

The little boy holds up his hands. I've come for the nails.

The smith counts the nails. Three men? he asks. Daddy says for three men.

The nails drop into his hands. The smith has fat broad fingers. The little boy's are quite thin, they bend under the big nails.

Is the one who says he's God's son one of them?

The little boy nods.

Does he still say he's God's son?

The little boy nods. The smith picks up the nails again. Then he drops them back into the hands. The little hands bend under them. Then the smith says: Oh well.

The little boy walks away. The nails are lovely and bright. The little boy runs. Then the nails make a noise. The smith takes his hammer. Oh well, says the smith. Then behind him the little boy hears: Ping Pang Ping Pang. He's hammering again, thinks the little boy. He's making nails, lots of shiny nails.

57 they buried at Voronezh. I'm left over. But I'm hungry. My kingdom is of this of this world. And the smith made the

nails in vain, upidee, nails in vain, the infantree, in vain the lovely shiny nails. For they buried 57 at Voronezh. Ping pang goes the smith. Ping pang at Voronezh. Ping pang. 57 times ping pang. Ping pang goes the smith. Ping pang goes the infantree. Ping pang go the guns. And the piano keeps on playing ping pang ping pang ping pang——

Every night 57 come to Germany. 9 motor mechanics, 2 gardeners, 5 officials, 6 salesmen, 1 barber, 17 peasants, 2 teachers, 1 clergyman, 6 labourers, 1 musician, 6 schoolboys. Every night 57 come to my bed, every night 57 ask: Where is your Company? At Voronezh, I say then. Buried, I say then. Buried at Voronezh. 57 ask man by man: Why? And 57 times I am dumb.

57 go by night to their father. 57 and Second Lieutenant Fischer. Second Lieutenant Fischer, that's me. 57 ask their father at night: Why, father? And the father is 57 times dumb. And he shivers in his nightshirt. But he comes, too.

57 go by night to the mayor. 57 and the father and I. By night 57 ask the mayor: Why, mayor? And the mayor is 57 times dumb. And he shivers in his nightshirt. But he comes, too.

57 go by night to the clergyman. 57 and the father and the mayor and I. By night 57 ask the clergyman: Why, clergyman? And the clergyman is 57 times dumb. And he shivers in his nightshirt. But he comes, too.

57 go by night to the schoolmaster. 57 and the father and the mayor and the clergyman and I. By night 57 ask the schoolmaster: Why, schoolmaster? And the schoolmaster is 57 times dumb. And he shivers in his nightshirt. But he comes, too.

57 go by night to the general. 57 and the father and the mayor and the clergyman and the schoolmaster and I. By night 57 ask the general: Why, general? And the general—the general doesn't even turn round. So the father kills him. And the clergyman? The clergyman stays dumb.

57 go by night to the minister. 57 and the father and the mayor and the clergyman and the schoolmaster and I. By night 57 ask the minister: Why, minister? That scares the minister out of his wits. For he has hidden himself so beautifully behind the champagne basket, behind the champagne. And then he lifts his glass and gives a toast to North and South and West and East. And then he says: Germany, my friends, Germany! That's why! Then the 57 look round. Dumbly. So long and so dumbly. And they look

to North and South and West and East. And then they ask softly:
Germany? Is that why? Then the 57 turn away. And never
again look back. 57 lay themselves down again in the grave at
Voronezh. They have old, poor faces. Like women. Like mothers.
And through eternity they say: Is that why? Is that why? Is
that why?

57 they buried at Voronezh. I'm left over. I am Second
Lieutenant Fischer. I am 25. I still want the tram. I want to catch
it. I've been going so long so long. Only I'm hungry. But I
must. 57 ask: Why? And I'm left over. And I've been going so
long now along the long, long road.

Going along. A man. Herr Fischer. That's me. The subaltern
stands over there and gives orders: Left right left right left right
left right zicker zacker upidee left right left left right left right
the infantree the infantree ping pang ping pang left right ping
pang left right ping pang ping pang long road long road ping
pang on along round and round why why why why ping pang
ping pang at Voronezh that's why at Voronezh that's why ping
ping along the long long road. A human being. 25. Me. The road.
The long long. Me. House house house wall wall dairy front-
garden cow-smell front door.

Dentist
Saturdays by appointment only

Wall wall wall

Hilda Bauer is daft

Second Lieutenant Fischer is dumb. 57 ask: why? Wall wall door
window glass glass glass lamp old woman red red eyes fried
potato smell house house piano lesson ping pang the whole street
long the nails are so shiny the guns are so long ping pang the
whole street long child child dog ball car paving stone paving
stone cobblestone-heads heads ping pang stone stone grey grey
violet petrol patch grey grey along the long long road stone stone
grey blue dull dull so grey wall wall green enamel

Treatment for defective sight
Optician Streit
2nd storey on the right

Wall wall wall stone dog dog lifts leg tree soul dogs dream car
hoots dog roots pavement red dog dead dog dead dog dead

wall wall wall along the long road window wall window window
window lamps people light men more men more men shiny
faces like rails so shiny so wonderfully shiny——

A hundred years ago they were playing skat. A hundred years
ago they played it. And now now they're playing still. And in
a hundred years they'll still be playing. Still playing skat. The
three men. With shiny honest faces.

Pass.

Karl, put it up.

I pass, too.

Aha then—you're passing the buck to me, gentlemen.

You could have passed too, then we'd have had a fine
goulash.

Come on then. Come on then. What's it to be?

Spades are shovels. Whose lead?

Always the one who asks.

Mother only lets you ask once. Another trump!

Hey, Karl, haven't you any more spades?

Not this time.

Well, then where do we go for honey, eh? Every man has a
heart.

Trump! Now come on, Karl, get the big one off your
chest. 28.

And another trump!

A hundred years ago they were playing. Playing skat. And
in a hundred years they'll still be playing. Still playing skat with
shiny honest faces. And when they make their fists thunder on
the table, then it thunders. Like guns. Like 57 guns.

But one window further on sits a mother. She has three
pictures in front of her. Three men in uniform. On the left
stands her husband. On the right stands her son. And in the
middle stands the general. Her husband's general and her son's.
And when the mother goes to bed at night, she places the pictures
so that she can see them, when she's lying down. The son. And
the husband. And in the middle the general. And then she reads
the letters the general wrote. 1917. For Germany—is in one.
1940. For Germany—in the other. More the mother does not read.
Her eyes are quite red. So red.

But I'm left over. Upidee. For Germany. I'm still going

along. To the tram. Twice already I've been down. Because of hunger. Upidee. But I must get there. Lieutenant's orders. I'm already on my way. On the way a long, long time.

There's a man standing in a dark corner. Men are always standing in the dark corners. Always there are dark men in the corners. There's one standing there and holding a box and a hat. Pyramidon! barks the man. Pyramidon! 20 tablets are enough. The man's grinning, for business is good. Business is so good. 57 women, red-eyed women, they're buying Pyramidon. Stick a naught on 570. Another and another. 57000. And another and another and another. 57000000. Business is good. The man barks: Pyramidon! He's grinning, trade's flourishing: 57 women, red-eyed women, they're buying Pyramidon. The box is nearly empty. And the hat is nearly full. And the man's grinning. He may well grin. He has no eyes. He is happy: He has no eyes. He doesn't see the women. Doesn't see the 57 women. The 57 red-eyed women.

Only I'm left over. But I'm already on my way. And the road is long. So terribly long. But I want to get to the tram. I'm already on my way. On the way a long, long time.

In a room sits a man. The man is writing with ink on white paper. And he says out into the room:

> On the soil-brown fallow field
> Bright green grasses blew
> And a pale blue flower
> Wet with morning dew.

He writes it on the white paper. He reads it out into the empty room. He crosses it out again with ink. Out into the room he says:

> On the soil-brown fallow field
> Bright green grasses blew
> And a pale blue flower
> All hatred did subdue.

The man writes it down. He reads it out into the empty room. He crosses it out again. Then out into the room he says:

On the soil-brown fallow field
Bright green grasses blew
And a pale blue flower—
And a pale blue flower—
And a pale blue flower—

The man stands up. He walks round the table. Round and round the table. He stands still:

On the soil-brown fallow field
Bright green grasses blew

The man walks round and round the table.

57 they buried at Voronezh. But the earth was grey. And like stone. And no bright green grass blows there. Snow was there. And it was like glass. And without a blue flower. A million times snow. And no blue flower. But the man in the room doesn't know that. He never knows it. He always sees the blue flower. Blue flowers everywhere. And yet they buried 57 at Voronezh. Under glassy snow. In the grey grizzly sand. Without green. And without blue. The sand was icy and grey. And the snow was like glass. And snow subdues no hatred. For they buried 57 at Voronezh. Buried 57. Buried at Voronezh.

That's nothing, that's nothing at all! says the lance-corporal with the crutch. He lays the crutch across his toes and takes aim. He screws up one eye and takes aim with the crutch across his toes. That's nothing, he says. We got 86 Ivans in one night. 86 Ivans. With one machine-gun, my friend, with one single machine-gun in one night. Next morning we counted them. On top of each other, they were lying. 86 Ivans. Some of them still had their mouths open. A lot of them even their eyes. Yes, a lot still had their eyes open. In one night, my friend. The lance-corporal aims with his crutch at the old woman sitting on the bench opposite. He aims at the old woman and he hits 86 women. But they live in Russia. About that he knows nothing. It's a good thing he doesn't know it. Else what should he do? Now, when it's getting dark?

Only I know. I am Second Lieutenant Fischer. 57 they buried at Voronezh. But I wasn't yet quite dead. I'm still going along.

Twice already I've been down. With hunger. For the dear Lord
has no spoon. But at all costs I want to get to the tram. If only
the road weren't so full of mothers. 57 they buried at Voronezh.
And next morning the lance-corporal counted 86 Ivans. And with
his crutch he shoots 86 mothers dead. But he doesn't know it,
and that's a good thing. Else where should he go? For the dear
Lord has no spoon. It's good if poets make the blue flowers bloom.
It's good if someone's always playing the piano. It's good if they
play skat. They're always playing skat. Else where should they
go, the old woman with the three pictures by her bed, the lance-
corporal with the crutches and the 86 dead Ivans, the mother
with the little girl who wants soup and Timm, who kicked the
old man? Else where should they go?

But I must go along the long, long road. Wall wall door lamp
wall wall window wall wall and coloured paper, coloured printed
paper.

Are you insured?
Give yourself and your family
A Christmas treat
With a subscription to the
URANIA LIFE INSURANCE

57 didn't insure their lives properly. Nor the 86 dead Ivans,
either. And they didn't give their families any Christmas treat.
Red eyes were what they gave their families. Nothing more, red
eyes. Why weren't they, they in the Urania Life Insurance, too?
And now I've got the red eyes to contend with: Everywhere the
red, red-wept, red-sobbed eyes. Mothers' eyes, women's eyes.
Everywhere the red, red-wept eyes. Why didn't the 57 have
themselves insured? No, they didn't give their families any Christmas treat. Red eyes. Just red eyes. And yet there it is on a thousand
coloured posters: Urania Life Insurance Urania Life Insurance—

Evelyn stands in the sun and sings. The sun is with Evelyn.
One can see her legs and everything through her dress. And
Evelyn is singing. Through the nose a bit she sings and she sings a
little hoarse. She was standing too long in the rain tonight. And
she sings, so that I get hot when I close my eyes. And when I
open them, then I see right up her legs and everything. And
Evelyn sings, so that my eyes mist over. She sings the sweet ruin

of the world. The night she sings and schnaps, dangerous, clawing schnaps full of wounded world groaning. The end sings Evelyn, the world's end, sweet and between naked narrow girls' legs: holy heavenly hot world's ruin. Ah, Evelyn sings like wet grass, so heavy with smell and sensual and so green. As dark green, as green as empty beer-bottles beside the benches, on which Evelyn's knees, moonpale, look out of her dress at night, so that I get hot.

Sing, Evelyn, sing me dead. Sing the sweet ruin of the world, sing a clawing schnaps, sing a grass-green ecstasy. And Evelyn presses my grass-cold hand between her moon-pale knees so that I get hot.

And Evelyn sings. Come sweet May and make, sings Evelyn and holds my grass-cold hand with her knees. Come sweet May and make the graves green again. That's what Evelyn sings. Come sweet May and make the battlefields beer-bottle green and make the rubble, the gigantic rubblefield, green as my song, as my schnaps-sweet song of ruin. And Evelyn sings on the bench a hoarse hectic song, so that I get cold. Come sweet May and make their eyes shine again, sings Evelyn and holds my hand with her knees. Sing, Evelyn, sing me back under the beer-bottle green grass, where I was sand and was clay and was country. Sing, Evelyn, sing and sing me away over the rubblefields and over the battlefields and over the mass grave into your sweet hot womanly-secret moon-ecstasy. Sing, Evelyn, sing, when the thousand companies march through the nights, then sing, when the thousand cannon plough and dung the fields with blood. Sing, Evelyn, sing, when the walls lose their clocks and pictures, then sing me into schnaps-green ecstasy and into your sweet world's ruin. Sing, Evelyn, sing me right into your woman's being, into your secret, nightly woman's longing, that's so sweet, that I get hot, hot again with life. Come sweet May and make the grass green again, so beer-bottle green, so Evelyn-green. Sing Evelyn!

But the girl, she doesn't sing. The girl, she counts, for the girl has a round belly. Her belly is rather too round. And now she has to stand all night at the station, because one of the 57 wasn't insured. And now she counts the cars all night. An engine has 18 wheels. A passenger carriage 8. A freight car 4.

The girl with the round belly counts the trucks and the wheels—
the wheels the wheels the wheels—78, she says once, that's not at
all bad. 62, she says then, that mightn't be enough. 110, she says,
that'll do. Then she lets herself fall and falls in front of the train.
The train has an engine, 6 passenger-carriages and 5 freight
cars. That's 86 wheels. That's enough. The girl with the round
belly isn't there any more, when the train with its 86 wheels has
gone. She simply isn't there any more. Not one bit. Not one
single little bit of her is there any more. She has no blue flower
and nobody played the piano for her and nobody played skat
with her. And the dear Lord had no spoon for her. But the train
had lots of lovely wheels. Where else should she go? What else
should she do? For the dear Lord hadn't even got a spoon. And
now there's nothing left of her, nothing at all left over.

Only me. I'm still on my way. Still, still on my way. Already
a long time, so long already so long already on my way. The road
is long. I cannot get along the road and the hunger. They are
both so long.

Now and then they cry out. To the left on the football field.
To the right in the big house. Sometimes they cry out there. And
the road runs through the middle. I'm walking on the road. I am
Second Lieutenant Fischer. I'm 25. I'm hungry. I've come all
the way from Voronezh. I've been going such a long time. Left
is the football field. And right the big house. They're sitting there
inside. 1000. 2000. 3000. And no one says a word. In front they're
making music. And some are singing. And the 3000 don't say a
word. They are washed clean. They've tidied their hair and put
on clean shirts. So they sit there in the big house and let themselves be shattered. Or edified. Or entertained. You can't tell the
difference. They sit and let their clean-washed selves be shattered.
But they don't know that I'm hungry. They don't know that.
And that I'm standing here by the wall—I, the one from
Voronezh, who's on his way on the long road with the long
hunger, so long already on his way—that I'm standing here by
the wall, because for hunger for hunger, I can't go on. But they
can't know that. The wall, the thick stupid wall is in between.
And I'm standing in front of it with wobbly knees—and behind it
they're in clean linen and let themselves be shattered Sunday after
Sunday. For ten marks they have their souls churned up and their

stomachs turned over and their nerves stunned. Ten marks, that's such a frightful lot of money. For my belly that's a frightful lot of money. But for that the word PASSION is written on the tickets they get for ten marks. ST. MATTHEW PASSION. But then when the great choir screams BARABBAS, screams blood-thirstily bleedingly BARABBAS, then they don't fall from their pews, the thousands in clean shirts. No and they don't weep either and don't pray either and one hardly sees their faces, hardly sees their souls at all really, when the great choir screams BARABBAS. On the tickets it says for ten marks ST. MATTHEW PASSION. At the Passion one can sit right in front, where the Passion's suffered at full strength, or rather further back, where one's suffering is a little more subdued. But it's all the same. Their faces give nothing away when the great choir screams BARABBAS. They have themselves well under control at the Passion. No coiffure becomes dishevelled with misery or torment. No, misery and torment, they're only sung and fiddled there in front, turned into music for ten marks. And the BARABBAS-screamers, they're only play-acting, after all they're paid to scream. And the great choir screams BARA-BBAS. MOTHER! screams Second Lieutenant Fischer on the endless road. BARABBAS! screams the great choir of clean-washed people. HUNGER! yelps the belly of Second Lieutenant Fischer. I am Second Lieutenant Fischer. GOAL! scream the thousands on the football field. BARABBAS! they scream to the left of the road. GOAL! they scream to the right of the road. VORONEZH! I scream in the middle. But the thousands scream against each other. BARABBAS! they scream on the right. GOAL! they scream on the left. PASSION they're playing on the right. FOOTBALL they're playing on the left. I'm standing between. I. Second Lieutenant Fischer. 25 years young. 57 million years old. Voronezh-years. Mother-years. 57 million road-years old. Voronezh-years. And to the right they scream BARABBAS. And to the left they scream GOAL. And in between stand I motherless, alone. On the swaying world's wave motherless alone. I am 25. I know the 57 they buried at Voronezh, the 57 who knew nothing, who wanted nothing, I know them day and night. And I know the 86 Ivans who were lying in the morning with open eyes and mouths in front of the machine-guns. I know the little girl who has no soup, and I know the lance-corporal with the crutches. BARABBAS they scream for ten marks in the ears of the clean-washed on the right. But I know the old woman with the three pictures by her bed and the girl with the round belly who jumped under the train. GOAL! they scream on the left, a thousand times GOAL! But I know Timm, who can't sleep because he kicked the old man and I know the 57 red-eyed women who buy Pyramidon from the blind man. PYRAMIDON it says for 2 marks on the little box. PASSION it says on the tickets to the right of the street, for ten marks PASSION. CUPTIE it says on the blue, the flower-blue tickets for 4 marks to the left of the street. BARABBAS! they scream on the right. GOAL! they scream on the left. And the blind man keeps on yelping: PYRAMIDON! Between stand I, quite alone, without mother alone, on the wave, the swaying world's wave alone. With my yelping hunger! And I know the 57 of Voronezh. I am Second Lieutenant Fischer. I am 25. The others scream GOAL and BARABBAS in the great choir. Only I am left over. So terribly left over. But it's good that the clean-washed don't know the 57 from Voronezh. Else how could they endure it at the Passion and the Cuptie. Only I'm still on my way. Right from Voronezh. With hunger already long long on my way. For I was left over. The others they buried at Voronezh. 57. Only me did they forget. Why did they have to forget me? Now I have only the wall. It supports me. I must go along it. GOAL! they scream after me. BARABBAS! they scream after me. Along the long long road. And I can't go on any longer. I can't possibly go on any longer. And I have only the wall now, for my mother's not there. Only the 57 are there. The 57 million red-eyed mothers, they run after me so frightfully. Along the road. But Second Lieutenant Fischer orders: Left right left right left right left right zicker zacker BARABBAS the blue flower is so wet with tears and blood zicker zacker upidee buried is the infantree under the football field under the football field.

I'm long since all in, but the old organ-grinder plays such snappy music. Rejoice in life, he sings along the street. Rejoice, you of Voronezh, upidee, enjoy each day as long you may the flowers of blue are blooming enjoy your life as long you may the barrel-organ's playing——

The old man sings like a coffin. So softly. Rejoice! he sings, as long as you may, he sings, so softly, so like a grave, so wormy, so earthy, so like Voronezh, he sings, enjoy each day as long you may the lamp of swindle's glowing! As long as swaddling-clothes are blowing!

I am Second Lieutenant Fischer! I scream. I was left over. I've been going a long time along the long road. And they buried 57 near Voronezh. I know them.

Rejoice, says the organ-grinder.

I am 25, I scream.

Rejoice, sings the organ-grinder.

I am hungry, I scream.

Rejoice, he sings and the coloured jumping jacks jump about on his organ. The organ-grinder has lovely coloured jumping jacks. Lots of lovely jumpy men. The organ-grinder has a boxer. The boxer swings his stupid fat fists and shouts: I'm boxing! And he moves in manner masterly. The organ-grinder has a fat man. With a stupid fat sack full of gold. I rule, shouts the fat man and moves in manner masterly. The organ-grinder has a general. With a stupid fat uniform. I command, he keeps on shouting. I command! And he moves in manner masterly. And the organ-grinder has a Dr. Faustus with a white white smock and black spectacles. And he doesn't shout and doesn't scream. But he moves in manner frightful oh so frightfully.

Rejoice, sings the organ-grinder and his jumping jacks are jumping. Jumping frightfully. Pretty jumping jacks you've got, organ-grinder, I say. Rejoice, sings the organ-grinder. But what's the spectacled man doing, the spectacled man in the white smock? I ask. He doesn't shout, he doesn't box, he doesn't rule, and he doesn't command. What does the man in the white smock do, he moves, he moves so frightfully! Rejoice, sings the organ-grinder, he thinks, sings the organ-grinder, he thinks and seeks and finds. What does he find, then, the spectacled man, for he moves so frightfully. Rejoice, sings the organ-grinder, he invents a powder, a green powder, a hope-green powder. What can one do with the green powder, organ-grinder, for he moves so frightful frightfully. Rejoice, sings the organ-grinder, with the hope-green powder, with one teaspoonful one can kill 100 million people, if one puffs, if one puffs hopefully. And the

spectacled man invents and invents. Enjoy each day as long you
may, sings the organ-grinder. He invents! I scream. Enjoy each
day as long you may, sings the organ-grinder, enjoy each day
as long you may.

I am Second Lieutenant Fischer. I am 25. I have taken the man
in the white smock away from the organ-grinder. Enjoy each day
as long you may. I've ripped off the head of the man, the spectacled man in the white smock! Enjoy each day as long you
may. I've twisted the arms off the white smock spectacled
man, the green-powder man. Enjoy each day as long you may,
I've broken the hope-green inventor man right through the
middle. I've broken him right through the middle middle. Now
he can mix no more powder, now he can invent no more powder.
I've broken him right through the middle middle.

Why have you smashed my lovely jumping jack, shouts the
organ-grinder, he was so clever, he was so wise, he was so faustus
clever and wise and inventive. Why have you smashed the
spectacled man, why? the organ-grinder asks me.

I'm 25, I scream. I'm still on my way, I scream. I'm afraid,
I scream. That's why I've smashed your white-smocked man.
We live in huts of wood and hope, I scream, but we live. And in
front of our huts there still grow roots and rhubarb. In front of
our huts there grow tomatoes and tobacco. We are afraid! I
scream. We want to live! I scream. In huts of wood and hope!
For the tomatoes and tobacco, they do still grow! They do still
grow. I'm 25, I scream, that's why I've killed the spectacled man
in the white smock. That's why I've smashed your powder-man.
That's why that's why that's why——

Rejoice, sings the organ-grinder enjoy each day as long you
may as long you may as long you may rejoice, sings the organ-
grinder and takes out of his awful big box a new jumpy jack with
spectacles and with a white smock and with a teaspoon yes a teaspoon full of hope-green powder. Rejoice, sings the organ-
grinder, enjoy each day as long you may I still have many many
white men so awful awfully many. But they move so frightful
frightfully, I scream, and I am 25 and I'm afraid and I live in a hut
of wood and hope. And tomatoes and tobacco, they do still grow.

Enjoy each day as long you may, sings the organ-grinder.

But he does move so frightfully, I scream.

No, he doesn't move, he is made he is only made to move.

And who then makes him move, who who then makes him move?

I, then says the organ-grinder so frightfully, I!

I'm afraid, I scream and clench my fist and hit the organ-grinder's face, the frightful organ-grinder's face. No, I don't hit him for I cannot find the face the frightful face. The face is so high on his neck. I cannot reach it with my fist. And the organ-grinder he laughs so frightful frightfully. Yet I cannot find it I cannot find it. Because the face is so far away and laughs so laughs so frightfully. It laughs so frightfully!

Along the road runs a man. He's afraid. His mother has left him alone. Now they're screaming after him so frightfully. Why? scream 57 from Voronezh. Why? Germany, screams the minister. Barabbas, screams the choir. Pyramidon, shouts the blind man. And the others scream: Goal. Scream 57 times Goal. And the smockman, the white spectacled smockman, moves so frightfully. And invents and invents and invents. And the little girl has no spoon. But the white man with the spectacles has one. It's just enough for 100 million. Rejoice, sings the organ-grinder.

A man runs along the road. Along the long long road. He's afraid. He runs with his fear through the world. Through the swaying world's wave. That man am I. I am 25. And I am on my way. I've been long on my way and I'm still on my way. I want the tram. I must catch the tram, for they are all after me. After me terribly.

A man runs along the road with his fear. That man am I. A man runs away from the screaming. That man am I. A man believes in tomatoes and tobacco. That man am I. A man jumps on to the tram, the kind yellow tram-car. That man am I.

I'm travelling in the tram, the kind yellow tram. Where are we going? I ask the others. To the football field? To the St. Matthew Passion? To the huts of wood and hope with tomatoes and tobacco? Where are we going? I ask the others. But no one says a word. But there sits a woman, who has three pictures in her lap. And next to her sit three men playing skat. And there too sits the man with crutches and the little girl with no soup and the girl with the round belly. And there's a man making poems. And one playing the piano. And 57 march along beside the tram.

Zicker zacker upsidee snappy was the infantree near Voronezh hi upidee. At the head marches Second Lieutenant Fischer. I am Second Lieutenant Fischer. And my mother's marching behind me. Marching 57 million times after me. Where are we going then, I ask the conductor. Then he gives me a hope-green ticket. St. Matthew—Pyramidon it says on it. We all have to pay, he says and holds out his hand. And I give him 57 men. But where are we going then? I ask the others. We must know where. Then Timm says: we don't know that either. There's not a sucker knows that. And they all nod their heads and rumble: Not a sucker knows. But we go on. Jingle-jangle, goes the bell of the tram and nobody knows where to. But everyone goes along. And the conductor makes an inscrutable face. He is an age-old conductor with ten thousand wrinkles. One cannot tell whether he is an evil or a good conductor. But everybody pays him. And everyone comes along. And nobody knows: is he good or evil. And nobody knows where to. Jingle-jangle, goes the bell of the tram. And nobody knows where to. And everyone comes along. And nobody knows—and nobody knows—and nobody knows.

POSTHUMOUS STORIES

These stories are arranged chronologically according to the date at which they were written. The story "Thithyphuth" belongs to Borchert's early prose pieces. The inspiring exhortation "There's only one thing to do" is the author's last work. He wrote it—as a legacy to Europe and humanity— shortly before his death in Basle.

THE WRITER

THE writer must put a name to the house which everyone is helping to build. To the different rooms, as well. He must call the sick-room "The Sad Room", the attic "The Windy Room" and the cellar "The Gloomy Room". He may not call the cellar "The Beautiful Room".

If no one gives him a pencil, he is in an agony of despair. He has to try scratching on the wall with the handle of a spoon. Just as in prison: This is a hateful hole. If in his misery he does not do that, then he is not a genuine writer. He should be sent to join the roadsweepers.

When in other houses one reads his letters, one must know: Aha. Yes. So that's what they're like in that house. It is no matter whether he writes big or small. But he must write legibly. In the house he should live in the attic. Thence the views are at their most fantastic. Fantastic, that means lovely and horrible. It is lonely up there. And it is coldest there, and hottest.

When Wilhelm Schroeder, the stonemason, visits the writer in the attic, he may well grow dizzy. The writer must give him no consideration. Herr Schroeder must get used to the height. It will do him good.

At night the writer may look at the stars. But woe to him if he does not feel that his house is in danger. Then he must blow the trumpet till his lungs burst!

THITHYPHUTH
OR MY UNCLE'S WAITER

IT wasn't that my uncle was a publican. But he knew a waiter. This waiter so thoroughly persecuted my uncle with his loyalty and his adoration that we always said: That's his waiter. Or: Aha, his waiter.

I was there when they got to know one another, my uncle and the waiter. At the time I was just big enough to put my nose on the table. I was only allowed to do so, however, when it was clean. And, naturally, it could not always be clean. Nor was my mother much older. A little older, of course, but we were both still so young that we were quite terribly ashamed, when my uncle and the waiter got to know each other. Yes, my mother and I, we were there.

My uncle was too, of course, as indeed was the waiter, for they were to make each other's acquaintance and they were the protagonists. My mother and I were there only as supernumeraries, and afterwards we bitterly regretted that we had been there at all, for we were really very ashamed when the acquaintanceship of the pair of them started. It actually came to all sorts of alarming scenes with curses, complaints, laughter and crying. And there had nearly been even a fight. The fact that my uncle had an impediment in his speech was what almost occasioned the fight. But in the end the fight was prevented by the fact that he had only one leg.

Well, we were sitting, we three, my uncle, my mother and I, on the afternoon of a sunny summer's day in a big, gay, magnificent beer-garden. Around us there sat some two to three hundred other people, who were all sweating, too. Dogs sat under the shady tables and bees sat on the plates of cakes. Or circled round the children's lemonade glasses. It was so warm and so full, that the waiters' faces all looked deeply offended as though everything was happening out of devilment. At last one came to our table.

As I was just saying, my uncle had an impediment in his speech. Nothing serious, but nevertheless clear enough. He could not pronounce an "s". Nor a "z". He simply could not manage it. Whenever in any word a hard "s" sound cropped up, he would turn it into a soft, moist, watery "th". At the same time pushing his lips far forward, so that his mouth bore a distant resemblance to a hen's behind.

Well, the waiter stood by our table and whisked our predecessors' cake-crumbs off the cloth with his handkerchief. (Only many years later did I discover that it was not his handkerchief but must have been a kind of napkin.) Anyway he whisked with it and asked shortwinded and nervously:

"Yeth thir? Your order, pleathe!"

My uncle, who had no time for non-alcoholic drinks, said in his usual way:

"Let'th thee: two thtrong beerth and for the boy theltther or lemonthoda. Or what elthe have you got?"

The waiter was very pale. Yet it was midsummer and he was a waiter outside in a beer-garden. But perhaps he was overworked. And suddenly I noticed that beneath his shiny brown skin my uncle also grew pale. In fact as the waiter, for safety's sake, repeated the order:

"Yeth thir. Two thtrong beerth. One thoda. Thertainly thir."

My uncle looked at my mother with raised eyebrows, as though he wanted something urgently from her. But he only wished to assure himself that he was still of this world. Then he said in a voice reminiscent of the distant thunder of guns:

"Jutht a thecond, are you crathy? You thee fit to make fun of my lithp? Eh?"

The waiter stood there and then he began to tremble. His hands trembled. His eyelids. His knees. But above all his voice trembled. It trembled with pain and rage and utter bewilderment as he tried hard to thunder back in reply:

"It'th dithgratheful of you, to amuthe yourthelf at my ecthpenthe, motht tactleth, if you pleathe, thir."

Now he was trembling all over. The tails of his coat. The brilliantined strands of his hair. The tip of his nose and his thin lower lip.

My uncle did not tremble. I looked at him very carefully: Not a tremor. I admired my uncle. But when the waiter called him disgraceful, then at least my uncle stood up. That is to say, he did not really stand up at all. With his one leg that would have been far too cumbersome and inconvenient for him. He remained sitting and yet nevertheless stood up. Spiritually he stood up. And that completely sufficed. The waiter felt this spiritual "standing up" of my uncle's as an attack and recoiled two short, trembling, uncertain steps. Hostile, they stood facing each other. Although my uncle was sitting. If he had really stood up, the waiter would very probably have sat down. My uncle could actually afford to remain seated, for, seated, he was just as tall as the waiter and their heads were on the same level.

So there they stood and looked at each other. Both with tongues that were too short, both with the same impediment. But each with a completely different lot in life.

Small, embittered, overworked, crushed, careless, colourless, timid, oppressed: the waiter. The little waiter. A proper waiter: Peevish, professionally polite, with no smell, with no face, numbered, over-washed and yet slightly grubby. A little waiter. Nicotine-stained, servile, sterile, smooth, well-combed, blue-shaven, jaundiced with trousers empty at the back and fat pockets at the sides, crooked heels and chronically sweaty collar—the little waiter.

And my uncle? Ah, my uncle! Broad, brown, booming, bass-throated, loud, laughing, lively, rich, regal, serene, certain, sound, satisfied—my uncle!

The little waiter and my big uncle. Different as a carthorse and a zeppelin. But both short-tongued. Both with the same failing. Both with a moist watery soft "th". But the waiter, ostracized, crushed by his short-tongued fate, sulky, abashed, disappointed, lonely, snappy.

And tiny, grown quite tiny. Ridiculed a thousand times a day, at every table smiled at, laughed at, pitied, grinned at, shouted at. A thousand times a day at every table in the beer-garden creeping another inch into himself, bowed, crumpled. A thousand times a day with every order at every table, with every "If you pleathe, thir" getting smaller, ever smaller. His tongue, gigantic misshapen fleshy clout, his much too short tongue, shapeless Cyclopean mass of flesh, clumsy, inept red lump of muscle, this tongue had reduced him to a pygmy: tiny, tiny waiter.

And my uncle! With too short a tongue, but as though he had no such thing. My uncle, himself laughing loudest when laughed at. My uncle, one-legged, colossal, lisp-tongued. But Apollo in every inch of his body and every atom of his soul. Car driver, woman driver, man driver, racing driver. My uncle, drinker, singer, superman, seducer, wit, Rabelaisian, short-tongued, bubbling, sparkling, spitting worshipper of women and brandy. My uncle, carousing conqueror, wooden-leg creaking, broad-grinning, with far too short a tongue, but—as though he had no such thing!

So they stood, facing each other, the one, murderous, mortally hurt, the other, brimful of laughter on the point of eruption. Around them six to seven hundred eyes and ears, strollers, coffee-drinkers, cake-addicts, enjoying the scene far more than their lemonade, lager or layer-cake. Oh, and right in the middle, my mother and I. Red-faced, ashamed, shrivelling into our clothes. And our sufferings had only begun.

"Find the landlord at onth, you intholent thparrow, you. I'll teach you to inthult your cuthtomerth."

My uncle was now purposely speaking so loud that the six to seven hundred ears should not miss a word. The beer stimulated him agreeably. He grinned with joy all over his great good-humoured, broad, brown face. Bright salty pearls came out of his forehead and trundled down over his massive cheekbones. But the waiter took everything about him for wickedness, vulgarity, insult and provocation. He stood there with wrinkled hollow gently fluttering cheeks and did not move from the spot.

"Ith there thand in your earholeth? Thend me the both, you beerthodden ath, you. At onthe or have you the breethe up, you miththapen dwarf?"

Then the tiny, tiny pygmy, the tiny lisping-tongued waiter, took heart, grandly, courageously, startling us all, and himself. He stepped close up to the table, whisked over our plates with his handkerchief and bent himself double in the formal waiter's bow. In a small, manly and decisively soft voice, with overwhelming, quivering courtesy, he said: "If you pleathe, thir!" and sat himself down, small, brave and cold-blooded, on the empty fourth chair at our table. Cold-blooded, of course, only in appearance. For in his gallant little waiter's heart there flickered the rebellious flame of the despised, scared, misshapen hireling. He had not even the courage to look at my uncle. He just sat himself down so positively and neatly, and I believe that at most an eighth of his seat touched the chair. (If indeed he possessed more than an eighth—out of sheer diffidence.) He sat, looked straight in front of him at the coffee-spotted grey-white cloth, pulled out his fat wallet and laid it, admittedly in quite a manly way, on the table. He risked a short half second's glance upwards to see whether he had indeed gone too far by bumping out his wallet, then, as he saw that the mountain, my uncle in fact, remained motionless, he opened his wallet and took out a piece of pasty, tightly folded paper, whose creases betrayed the typical yellow of an oft-used document. He flapped it importantly open, denied himself all expression of insult or dispute and put his short, worn-out finger positively on a certain place on the piece of paper. Meanwhile he said quietly, a trace hoarsely and with long pauses for breath:

"If you pleathe thir. If you will look at thith. Be tho kind ath to thee for yourthelf. My path. Been in Parith. Barthelona. Othnabrück. If you pleathe. All to be theen in my pathport. And here: thpetial dithtinguithing marth: Thcar on left knee. (From playing football.) And here, and here? What ith there here? Here, if you pleathe thir: Thpeech impediment thinthe birth. If you pleathe thir. You may thee for yourthelf!"

Life had been so much of a cruel stepmother to him that now he lacked the courage to savour his triumph and look at my uncle in challenge. No, silent and small, he looked straight in front of him at his outstretched finger and the proven congenital defect and patiently awaited the bass voice of my uncle.

It was a long time before it came. And when it did come, what he said was so unexpected that I started to hiccough with fright. With the square heavy hands of a man of action my uncle seized the small wavering paws of the waiter and with vital, furious good temper and animal-warm softness, the primary characteristics of all giants, he said: "Poor little rathcal! Have they been after you and baiting you ever thinthe you were born?"

The waiter sobbed. Then he nodded. Nodded six or seven times. Delivered. Contented. Proud. Safe. He could not speak. He understood nothing. Understanding and speech were stifled by two fat tears. Nor could he see, for the two fat tears pushed themselves in front of his pupils like two opaque all-expiating curtains. He understood nothing. But his heart welcomed this wave of sympathy like a desert that for a thousand years has waited for an ocean. Till his life's end he could have let himself be so inundated! Till his death he would have liked to hide his little hands in my uncle's giant paws! Till all eternity he could have listened to it, this: "Poor little rathcal!"

But for my uncle it had all gone on too long already. He was a driver. Even when sitting in a beer-garden. He let his voice boom away across the garden like a salvo of artillery and thundered at some terrified waiter:

"You, Herr Ober! Eight thtrong beerth! At onthe, I thay! What'th that? Not your table? Will you bring me eight throng beerth thith minute or will you not, eh?"

The strange waiter looked at my uncle, intimidated and nonplussed. Then at his colleague. He would have liked to read in his eyes (by means of a wink or something) what it all meant. But the little waiter hardly recognized his colleague, so far away was he from everything that meant waiter, cake-plate, coffee-cup and colleague, far, far away.

Then there were eight beers standing on the table. Four of the glasses the strange waiter had to take back immediately, they were empty before he had breathed once. "Fill that lot up again!" commanded my uncle and rummaged in the inside pocket of his coat. Then he whistled a parabola through the air and now in his turn laid his fat wallet beside that of his new friend. At last he fumbled out a wrinkled card and put his second finger, which had the measure of a child's arm, on a certain part of it.

"You thee, you thilly ath, here it ith: Leg amputated and thot in the lower jaw. War wound." And as he said it, with his other hand he pointed to a scar concealed beneath his chin.

"The cadth thimply thot a piethe off the tip of my tongue. In Franthe it wath."

The waiter nodded.

"Thtill croth?" asked my uncle.

The waiter shook his head quickly to and fro, as though to ward off something quite impossible.

"I only thought at firtht you wanted to take a rithe out of me." Shattered by this mistake in his knowledge of human nature, he shook his head again and again from left to right and back again.

And now all of a sudden it seemed as though he had thereby

shaken off all the tragedy of his lot. The two tears, which were now running into the hollows of his face, took all the agony of his previously despised existence with them. This new epoch in his life, which he entered clutching my uncle's huge paw, began with a little hiccoughed giggle, a tiny laugh, timid, shy, but unmistakably accompanied by the smell of beer.

And my uncle, this uncle who on one leg, with his tongue shot to pieces and with a bear-like bass-voiced humour, laughed his way through life, this uncle of mine was now so incredibly happy, that at last at last he could laugh. He had already blushed bronze, so that I was afraid he would burst any minute. And his tremendous laugh broke out, exploded, rattled, shouted, gonged, gurgled —laughed, as though he were some gigantic saurian from which these prehistoric sounds belched out. The first little newly tested human laugh of the waiter, of the new little waiter-human, was by contrast the thin coughing of a baby goat with a cold. Fearfully I clutched my mother's hand. Not that I would have been afraid of my uncle, but I had a deep animal instinctive fear of the eight strong beers bubbling inside him. My mother's hand was ice-cold. All the blood had deserted her body to make her face a glaring poster-like symbol of modesty and bourgeois propriety. No Vierlande tomato could have shone out a redder red. My mother blazed. Poppies were pale compared with her. I slipped down from my chair, under the table. Seven hundred eyes were round and gigantic all round us. Oh, how ashamed we were, my mother and I.

The little waiter, who, under my uncle's hot alcoholic breath had become a new man, seemed to want to begin the first part of his new life immediately with a complete cough-laugh-and-a-goat's-bleat. He maa-ed, baa-ed, clucked and snickered like a whole flock of lambs at once. And as the two men now flung four additional beers across their short tongues, the lambs, the rosy thin-voiced, soft, shy little waiter-lambs turned into powerful, wooden-bleating, age-old, white-bearded tinny-rattling babble-baa-ing bucks.

This transformation from the tiny spiteful barren pinched sourpuss into the continually, everlastingly bleating thigh-slapping rip-roaring tinnily baa-ing he-goat-man was, even to my uncle, rather extraordinary. His laughter gurgled slowly away like a waterfall drying up. With his sleeve he wiped the tears from his broad brown face and gaped with beer-bright blank-astonished eyes at the white-coated dwarf waiter, heaving with gusts of laughter. Around us grinned seven hundred faces. Fourteen hundred eyes could not believe what they saw. Seven hundred midriffs ached. Those sitting furthest away stood up excitedly so that nothing should escape them. It was as though the waiter had made up his mind to continue his life as a gigantic mischievous baa-ing buck. Latterly, after he had, as though wound up, been submerged for some minutes in his own laughter, latterly he attempted successfully, between the salvoes of laughter, which sparkled from his round mouth like tinny machine-gun fire, to utter short shrill screams. He succeeded in saving up so much breath, between gusts of laughter, that he was now able to neigh these screams into the air.

"Thithyphuth!" he screamed and slapped himself on the forward. "Thithyphuth! Thiiithyyyphuuuth!" With both hands he held firmly to the top of the table and neighed: "Thithyphuth!" When he had neighed nearly two dozen times, full-throatedly neighed this "Thithyphuth", the Thithyphuthing became too much for my uncle. In a single grip he crumpled the starched shirt of the ceaselessly neighing waiter, banged his other fist on the table so that twelve empty glasses started to jump, and thundered at him: "Thtop! Thtop it, I thay! What *ith* all thith thtupid thilly Thithyphuth? Thtop it now, do you underthtand?"

At the same moment, this grip and my uncle's thundered bass turned the Thithyphuth screaming he-goat back into the tiny lisping miserable waiter.

He stood up. He stood up, as though it had been the greatest mistake of his life ever to have sat down. He passed the napkin across his face and swept away tears, sweat, beer and laughter as though they were something execrable and outrageous. He was so drunk however that it all seemed to him like a dream, the unpleasantness at the beginning, the pity and friendship of my uncle. He did not know: Have I jutht been thcreaming Thithyphuth? Or not? Have I· thunk thickth beerth, I, waiter in thith beer-garden, all among the cuthtomerth? I? He was uncertain. And to cover all eventualities he made a little cut-off bow and whispered: "Ecthcuthe me!" And then he bowed again: "Ecthcuthe me.

ı etn, ecthcuthe the Thithyphuth thcreaming, if you pleathe, thir. The gentleman will ecthcuthe me, if I wath too loud, but the beer, you know yourthelf, thir, if one hath eaten nothing, on an empty thtomach. If you pleathe, thir, pleathe. Thithyphuth wath actually my nickname. Yeth, when I wath at thcool. The whole clath called me that. You know, of courthe, Thithyphuth, he wath the man in hell, the old thtory, you know, the man in Hadeth, the poor thinner, who wath thuppothed to, eh, *had* to puth a big rock up a huge mountain, yeth, that wath Thithyphuth, you know, of courthe. I alwayth had to thay it at thcool, alwayth thith Thithyphuth. And then they all burtht with laughter, ath you can well imagine, thir. Then they all laughed, you know, becauthe I have thith too thort tongue. And tho it happened, that later on I wath called Thithyphuth everywhere and teathed, you thee. And the beer, if you'll ecthcuthe me, recalled it to my memory, tho that I thcreamed, you underthtand. Ecthcuthe me, if you pleathe, thir, ecthcuthe me if I have annoyed you, if you pleathe, thir."

He was silent. His napkin meanwhile had wandered countless times from one hand to the other. Then he looked at my uncle.

Now it was he who sat quietly at the table and stared straight in front of him at the cloth. He did not dare to look at the waiter. My bear-like, bull-like gigantic uncle did not dare to glance up and respond to the look of this tiny embarrassed waiter. And the two fat tears, they were now sitting in his eyes. But no one saw that except me. And I only saw it because I was so small that I could look up into his face from below. He pushed a substantial banknote towards the quietly waiting waiter, waved him impatiently away when he wanted to give it back, and stood up, without looking at anyone.

Timidly the waiter brought out another sentence: "I would have liked to pay for the beer, if you pleathe, thir."

Meanwhile he had already put the note in his pocket as though he expected no answer and no objection. Nor had anyone heard the sentence and his generosity fell noiselessly on to the hard gravel of the beer-garden, later to be indifferently trampled underfoot. My uncle grasped his stick. We stood up, my mother supporting my uncle, and we walked slowly towards the street.

None of the three of us looked at the waiter. Neither my mother nor I because we were ashamed. Nor my uncle, because he had the two tears sitting in his eyes. Perhaps he was also ashamed, this uncle. Slowly we approached the way out, my uncle's stick grated horribly on the garden gravel and for the moment that was the only noise, for the three to four hundred faces at the tables were concentrated, dumb and saucer-eyed, on our departure.

And suddenly I was sorry for the waiter. As we went to turn the corner at the exit from the garden, I quickly looked round at him again. He was still standing at our table. His white napkin hung down to the ground. He seemed to me to have become much, much smaller. He was standing there, so tiny, and I suddenly loved him, as I saw him looking after us, so neglected, so small, so grey, so empty, so hopeless, so poor, so cold and so boundlessly alone! Ah, how tiny! I felt so infinitely sorry for him, that I tapped my uncle's hand excitedly and said softly: "I think he's crying now."

My uncle stopped dead. He looked at me and I could see the two fat tears in his eyes quite clearly. Again I said, without really knowing exactly why I did it: "Oh, he's crying. Just look, he's crying."

Then my uncle let go of my mother's arm, hobbled rapidly and heavily two paces back, brandished his stick like a sword, stabbed it into the heavens and roared with all the magnificent strength of his mighty body and throat:

"Thithyphuth! Thithyphuth! D'you hear? Auf Wieder-thehen, old Thithyphuth! Till nectht Thunday, thilly rathcal! Wiederthehen!"

The two fat tears were crushed to nought by the wrinkles which now appeared on his kind brown face. They were laughter-wrinkles and his whole face was full of them. Once more he swept the heavens with his stick, as though to rake down the sun and once more his giant laugh thundered across the tables of the beer-garden: "Thithyphuth! Thithyphuth!"

And Thithyphuth, the poor little grey waiter, woke up out of his death, lifted his serviette and waved it up and down like a window-cleaner gone mad. With his waving he wiped the whole grey world, every beer-garden in the world, every waiter and every speech impediment in the world, finally and forever out of his life. And he screamed back shrilly and overjoyed, standing on his toes and without interrupting his window-cleaning.

"I underthtand! If you pleathe, thir! On Thunday! Yeth, Wiederthehen! On Thunday, if you pleathe, thir!"

Then we turned the corner. My uncle gripped my mother's arm again and said softly: "I know it mutht have been dithgutht-ing for you. But what elthe could I do, tell me. Thuch a thilly ath. Running around all hith life with a foul impediment like that in hith thpeech. Poor rathcal!"

FROM THE OTHER SIDE
TO THE OTHER SIDE

SHIVERING Charlotte! I say, just take a look at that one there! There, the little one with the cropped hair. He's come from the other side, I'll bet. He's still acting so new. They all go on like that.

Whatever's he looking for on the trees, I'd like to know.

Perhaps a branch to hang himself on.

Well, then, let him be.

The two roadmen, who were busy filling the grooves between the freshly laid paving-stones with tar, picked up their long-necked cans again and let a well-aimed square pattern of hot black gravy trickle on to the street.

By "the other side" they meant the jail, whose fat red wall bounded the prison yard on the far side of the street. On the wall, above which, in unfeeling authority, towered several comfortless flat-roofed buildings with endless rows of barred windows, lay nails and bits of glass. At least, that's what was said. No one as yet had tried it out.

The man who had come from the "other side" was small, thin, tired and cropped. With his left elbow he clamped against his ribs a cardboard box tied together with bootlaces. In big green letters on its lid could be read that Persil would always be Persil. No one could take exception to that. Persil had been Persil seven years ago and Persil no doubt would still be Persil seven years hence. Only Erwin Knoke, book-keeper, had in the meantime become Convict No. 1563. But Persil had remained Persil. The whole seven years.

The man with the cropped head stood and stared at the trees. Stiffly. Stubbornly. Sometimes he made a nervous, evasive movement. Whereby one realized that he was still new. And unaccustomed. He was afraid of knocking against the people hurrying past, or of getting in their way. They might possibly hit him on the back of the head with a key-ring or make him do knees-bends. With every knees-bend a kick in the backside. Gratis, at that. He just didn't remember that decent civilians thoroughly detest that sort of thing, for, after all, he was quite new again and unaccustomed. They would more probably say, if one knocked against them: Pardon. 'Scuse me. But knees-bends? For that one has to be wearing uniform. Yes, and that's just what the man with the cropped head, who came from the other side, had forgotten. He was still too new.

He was disappointed. If he had had tears, he would have filled his pale grey eyes with them. He would have liked to weep a little, quietly. But one had completely lost the habit. One had laughed, mostly. It's easier to bear. Weeping only makes one still weaker. He was disappointed and stared at the trees. Stubbornly. Stiffly. It was the trees, in fact, that so immeasurably disappointed him. Now he stared stubbornly at them and in doing so grew quite poor. The trees, which for seven long years had been his trees, his living, all-promising trees, these trees he had lost in this moment, the moment of his release from the other side. He stared at them. No, they were not the same ones. Not his trees.

It wasn't that he'd been so great a friend of nature or even a forester or a gardener that he made so much of the trees. He was a book-keeper and had no idea about trees. The big city was his home and there lamp-posts were more frequent than trees. For him trees were either forest or fruit trees. That they also have names, he knew only vaguely. That these trees here were limes would probably have astonished him a lot. Trees meant either forest or fruit trees. Or perhaps avenue. Oh, sometimes trees could mean "avenue".

When in the late afternoon the sun threw the pattern of the barred window on the inner wall of his cell and the light between the four walls grew tired and tender, he had stood on his stool under the window and waited for the evening twilight. Then swinging his arms and with great solemn strides he had walked up the avenue. Where to? Away, afar, beyond. Far, far away. Every evening he had left his cell and walked up his avenue with its lovely, lovely living trees, that were so alive and so green. Every evening. Two thousand five hundred times in seven years. Far, far, away. Away. Away. Dear, kind avenue. At its end, shortly before the palace (for a palace stood at the end of the avenue, dead certain. Palaces always did) his wife waved, and

his two children. They had a basket of potato-cakes with them.
And they shouted: Oh, how we've waited! Where have you been
all this time? Will you have a potato-cake?

And his wife had secretly poked him in the ribs with her arm
and whispered: But that was far too long, Erwin! Now he was
staring at the trees in unfathomable sadness and they disappointed
him immeasurably. They belonged to a perfectly ordinary hideous
grey noisy street in which were passing perfectly ordinary people
and perfectly ordinary trams and cars. People like: Postmen,
schoolteachers, plumbers, grocers, clerks, hairdressers, musicians,
and lawyers. And milk-vans, smelling of cheese, fire-engines,
taxis, laundry-vans. The street was heartless and noisy and the
trees were dusty and grey. Children picked at their bark and dogs
nonchalantly lifted their legs against their grey trunks.

The man with the cropped head walked slowly on. Once
again he looked back at the trees. He did not understand. It was
all too grey, too naked, too inexorable. But he did not weep,
when suddenly he was so poor. He laughed. In embarrassment.
But he laughed. They had grown so used to it over there. He
laughed and stared at the lying, stupid, dirty trees and laughed.
And then suddenly he laughed still louder and no longer so
embarrassed, when it occurred to him that he no longer had any
need of the avenue. What did he want an avenue with lovely
green trees for now? For nothing. The hideous street could go
where it liked! God knows he didn't need an avenue any more.
No! God knows he didn't. He'd just swing himself on to the
tram and in an hour at the latest he'd be eating potato-cakes. Ten,
or even twelve. And sitting beside his wife. Did he still need
avenues? He laughed scornfully at the poor poverty-stricken
trees, quickly gave them a last wry look and turned about. Let
them lie, as long as they like. I'm going home.

As he came past the two roadmen, they were having their
lunch. It smelt strongly of tar, margarine and sweet coffee. But
in the main of tar. The two tar-spreaders had been watching him
the whole time, grinning. He'd brought a fine lot of bats in his
belfry from the other side, that was clear to them at once. They
looked towards him expectantly, as though he was bound to offer
them something more. They expected something more from him.
As the man with the cropped hair felt himself looked at so chal-

lengingly, he greeted them and four times one after another, out of sheer love for his new life, he said: Good appetite! Good appetite! Good appetite! Good appetite!

With the inquisitive sympathy that one accords the crazy, the two tarmen chewed back a friendly unintelligible greeting. It was all they could do to stifle their laughter. They swallowed and grinned. For two pins one of them would have burst out. But the precious piece of Bologna sausage on his margarine occurred to him just in time. He left it there.

As the man with the cropped head wanted to walk on, the smell of tar (that sweet, unforgettable perfume of childhood, city, dirty fingers and streets) obtrusively and powerfully ascended his nose. It overwhelmed him so unexpectedly, that he stood stock still and breathed deeply. Tar smell. Intoxicating perfume full of memory! Holy heavenly smell of tar!

He thought of his two boys at home and he thought of the tar. And he thought of the splendid things one could make out of tar half-dried. Animals, men, balls. Balls, chiefly, of course, balls. In his day they had nearly always made balls out of tar, which they carved from the grooves of the newly paved street when the workers had knocked off. He thought how fine it would be and what a surprise if he brought such a present home to his two children. And he summoned bold, unsuspected courage. He fumbled up to the two astounded tarmen and begged, softly and smiling helplessly, for permission to take a bit, just a tiny little bit of cold tar, away with him. He smiled, uncertainly and yet bravely, although in every nerve he was ready to run away. They could not speak, otherwise they would have had to spit out their sweet coffee without further ado. So the tarmen nodded word-lessly and generously, and with sheer grinning and astonishment their faces had become quite serious and childish.

Foolish and dumbfounded they gaped after the complete madman, who floated blissful and wavering across the road, the Persil box with its philosophical inscription in his left hand and he busily kneading the tar in his right.

And the man with the cropped hair forgot the world of barred windows, of key-rings and of knees-bends and of the untrue, untruthful avenues. He was rolling home on a gigantic ball of tar. Towards potato-cakes, towards his wife. Rolling, running, racing! And he forgot the world with its evil seven years. And once, as though drunk, he gave a quiet little cheer. Out of pure delight in the world!

Then suddenly the brakes of a laundry-van screamed sharply and hideously. Eight giant rubber wheels whined and screeched, skidding over the paving. And a woman screamed and a child. And from all sides people came running towards the van.

There! He's copped it this time! cried one of the tarmen. Ts, poor blighter, what bad luck, muttered the other, poured the rest of his sweet coffee down his throat and pushed along behind his colleague in the direction of the laundry-van.

The van stood diagonally across the street. The tram stopped. Five or six cars stopped, a team of horses, some twenty of the inevitable cyclists. People who had just been acting so frightfully hurried and pressed for time and busy, suddenly had vast quantities of time to look their fill at a man and a Persil box squashed flat. The tiny squashed-flat piece of tar, the magnificent ball of a moment since, no one noticed. No one could have done anything with it, anyway. Instead, they all saw the blood that trickled over the paving, peaceful and poppy-coloured, from the squashed-flat man.

The driver of the murderous laundry-van, which perhaps had a load of Persil-washed laundry on board, bent sweating (and more for propriety's sake than genuinely worried) over his victim. Then sullenly, he mumbled: No, he's gone, he's on the other side now. He's on the other side.

Shivering Charlotte! There's a change come over *him*! Boy, what a thing! said one tarman and piously chewed the last shreds of his Bologna sausage into little bits.

Oh, how original! shrilled a young woman at her bespectacled escort and asked him if he'd heard that.

What do you mean shivering Charlotte? asked the young policeman with excessive good humour and looked up laughing sunnily from his note-book. Above all they were to realize that despite his youth he had the situation well in hand.

Oh, nothing in particular, smirked the sausage-eating tar-spreader, it was the name of my first wife.

Widower? asked the policeman, interested.

No, divorced, volunteered the other.

He must have been a foreigner, said an elderly lady. And everyone looked again at the human remains in their middle. They had almost forgotten him.

No, the driver shook his head, there's nothing we can do about it. He's on the other side. Completely.

When in the late afternoon the two roadmen went home with empty coffee-flasks, it occurred to one of them in the tram:

I say, he'd have been pretty annoyed, that little fellow, if he'd been able to. Just when he'd got out from the other side. What a guy!

(But the tarman was mistaken. Erwin Knoke, now neither book-keeper nor Number 1563, but quite simply Erwin Knoke, strolled in search of adventure with an enormous blow-pipe and a countless number of tar-balls through the eternal hunting grounds of Winnetou. And he shot and killed with his self-kneaded tar-balls everything he wanted. He had always read his Red Indian books, and the eternal hunting grounds, for lack of any other conception of eternity, still haunted secretly about inside him. That had been his one modest little vice.)

THE BREAD

SUDDENLY she woke up. It was half past two. She considered why she had woken up. Oh yes! In the kitchen someone had knocked against a chair. She listened to the kitchen. It was quiet. It was too quiet and as she moved her hand across the bed beside her, she found it empty. That was what had made it so particularly quiet: she missed his breathing. She got up and groped her way through the dark flat to the kitchen. In the kitchen they met. The time was half past two. She saw something white standing on the kitchen cupboard. She put the light on. They stood facing one another in their night-shirts. At night. At half past two. In the kitchen.

On the kitchen table lay the bread-plate. She saw that he had cut himself some bread. The knife was still lying beside the plate. And on the cloth there were bread-crumbs. When they went to bed at night, she always made the table-cloth clean. Every night. But now there were crumbs on the cloth. And the knife was lying there. She felt how the cold of the tiles crept slowly up her. And she looked away from the plate.

"I thought there was something here," he said and looked round the kitchen.

"I heard something, too," she answered and thought that at night, in his night-shirt, he really looked quite old. As old as he was. Sixty-three. During the day he sometimes looked younger. She looks quite old, he thought, in her night-dress she really looks pretty old. But perhaps it's because of her hair. With women at night it's always because of their hair. All at once it makes them so old.

"You should have put on your shoes. Barefoot like that on the cold tiles! You'll catch cold."

She didn't look at him, because she couldn't bear him to lie. To lie when they had been married thirty-nine years.

"I thought there was something here," he said once more and again looked so senselessly from one corner to the other, "I heard something in here. So I thought there'd be something here."

"I heard something, too. But it must have been nothing."

255

She took the plate off the table and flicked the crumbs from the table-cloth.

"No, it must have been nothing," he echoed uncertainly.

She came to his help: "Come on. It must have been outside. Come to bed. You'll catch cold. On the cold tiles."

He looked at the window. "Yes, it'll have been outside. I thought it was in here."

She raised her hand to the switch. I must now put the light out, or I shall have to look at the plate, she thought. I dare not look at the plate. "Come on," she said and put out the light, "it must have been outside. The gutter always bangs against the wall when there's a wind. I'm sure it was the gutter. It always rattles when there's a wind."

They both groped their way along the dark corridor to the bedroom. Their naked feet slapped on the floor.

"It is windy," he said, "it's been windy all night."

As they lay in bed, she said: "Yes it's been windy all night. It must have been the gutter."

"Yes. I thought it was in the kitchen. It must have been the gutter." He said it as though he were already half asleep. But she noticed how false his voice sounded when he lied.

"It's cold," she said and yawned softly, "I'll creep under the covers. Good night."

" 'Night," he replied and added: "Yes, it really is pretty cold."

Then it was quiet. Many minutes later she heard him softly and cautiously chewing. She breathed deeply and evenly so that he should not notice that she was still awake. But his chewing was so regular that it slowly sent her to sleep.

When he came home the next evening, she put four slices of bread in front of him. At other times he had only been able to eat three.

"You can safely eat four," she said and moved away from the lamp. "I can't digest this bread properly. Just you eat another one. I don't digest it very well."

She saw how he bent deep over the plate. He didn't look up. At that moment she was sorry for him.

"You can't eat only two slices," he said to his plate.

"Yes, I can. I don't digest this bread properly in the evening. Just eat. Eat it."

Only a while later did she sit down at the table under the lamp.

GOD'S EYE

GOD's eye lay round and red-rimmed in the middle of a white soup-plate. The soup-plate lay on our kitchen table. The blood-flecked intestines and milk-pale skeleton of a fairly large fish made the kitchen table look like a battlefield. The eye on the white plate belonged to a cod. It lay in great white fleshy pieces in our saucepan and let itself be cooked. The eye was all alone. It was God's eye.

You mustn't keep slithering that eye all over the plate with the fork, said my mother.

I made the smooth globular eye whiz round the curves of the soup-plate and asked: Why not? He won't notice it now. He's cooking.

Eyes are not meant to be played with. God made that eye exactly like yours, said my mother.

As I suddenly stopped the whizzing circuits of the cod's eye, I asked: Is it supposed to be God's?

Of course, answered my mother, the eye belongs to God.

Not to the cod, I bored further.

To the cod as well. But chiefly to God.

As I looked up from the plate, I noticed that my mother was crying. On that day, when we had cod, my grandfather had died. My mother was crying, and went out. Then I pulled the plate with the lonely eye in the middle, with the red-rimmed eye that was supposed to belong to God, quite close to me. I put my mouth quite close over the plate.

You are God's eye? I whispered, then you can tell me why today all of a sudden Grandfather's dead. Tell me, you!

The eye said nothing.

You don't even know, I whispered triumphantly, and you pretend to be God's eye, and don't even know why Grand-father's dead. Won't he come back again either, Grandfather, I asked close over the plate, don't you know if he'll come back again, you, tell me that. You must know that. Will he never come back again?

Tell me. Are we ever going to see him again? We can meet him again somewhere, can't we? You, tell me, shall we meet him again? You, tell me, you're from God, tell me!

The eye said nothing.

I pushed the plate furiously away from me. The eye slithered high over the rim and fell on to the floor. There it lay. Intently I looked at it. The eye was lying on the ground. But it said nothing. I looked at it again. No, nothing. I stood up. I stood up slowly, so as to give God time Very slowly I walked to the kitchen door. I seized the door-handle. I pressed it slowly down. With my back to the eye I still waited a long long moment at the kitchen door. There was no answer. God said nothing. Then, without looking round at the eye, I went loudly through the door.

THIS IS OUR MANIFESTO

HELMETS off helmets off:
  We've lost!

The companies are scattered. The companies, battalions, armies. The great armies. Only the hosts of the dead, they still stand. Stand like measureless forests: dark, purple-coloured, full of voices. But the guns lie like frozen dinosaurs with rigid limbs. Purple with steel and ambushed fury. And the helmets, they are rusting. Take your rusty helmets off: we've lost.

In our mess kits thin children now fetch milk. Thin milk. The children are purple with frost. And the milk is purple with poverty.

Never again shall we fall in to a whistle and say "Yessir" to a bellow. Guns and sergeants bellow no more. We shall weep, spit and sing as we will. But the song of the roaring tanks and the song of the edelweiss we shall sing no more, for the tanks and the sergeants rage no more, and the edelweiss has rotted away to the sing-song of blood. And no general calls us "Thou" before the battle. Before the terrible battle.

We shall never again have sand in our teeth with fear. (No sand of the steppes, no Ukrainian sand and none from Cyrenaica or Normandy—nor the bitter angry sand of our homeland!) And never again the hot mad feeling in brain and belly before the battle.

Never again shall we be so happy, to feel another beside us. Warm and there and breathing and belching and humming—at night on the advance. Never again shall we be as happy as gipsies about a loaf of bread and five grams of tobacco and two armfuls of hay. We shall never march together again, for from now on all march alone. That is good. That is hard. No longer to have the stubborn grumbling other man beside you—at night, at night on the advance. Who hears everything too. Who never says anything. Who stomachs everything.

And if at night a man must weep, he can do so again. For he need no longer sing—with fear.

Now jazz is our song. Excited, hectic jazz is our music. And the hot mad frantic song, through which the drums race, catlike, scratching. And sometimes still the old sentimental soldiers' bawl, with which anguish was outscreamed and with which mothers were denied. Terrible male chorus from bearded lips, sung into the lonely twilight of dug-out and freight train, over-pitched by the mouth-organ's tinny tremolo:

Virile song of men—did no one hear the children bawling away their fear of the purple maw of the guns?

Heroic song of men—did no one hear the hearts sobbing when they sang upidee, the grimy, the crusty, the bearded, the lousy?

Song of men, soldiers' bawling, sentimental and high-spirited, virile and deepthroated, valiantly bawled by the youngsters, too: Does none hear the cry for mother? The last cry of man, the adventurer? The terrible cry: Upidee?

Our upidee and our music are a dance over the abyss that yawns at us. And that music is jazz. For our hearts and our heads have the same hot-cold rhythm: excited, crazy and hectic, unrestrained.

And our girls, they have the same hot beat in their hands and their hips. And their laughter is hoarse and brittle and hard as a clarinet. And their hair, it crackles like phosphorus. It burns. And their heart has a syncopated beat, savage and sad. Senti-mental. Our girls are like that: like jazz. And the nights are like that, the girl-jangling nights, like jazz: hot and hectic. Excited.

Who will write us new laws of harmony? We have no further use for well-tempered clavichords. We ourselves are too much dissonance.

Who will cry a purple cry for us? Who a purple deliverance? We have no further use for still life. Our life is loud.

We have no further use for a poet's good grammar. We lack patience for good grammar. We need those with the hot hoarse-sobbed emotion. Who call a tree tree and a woman woman and say yes and say no: loud and clear and triply and without sub-junctives.

For semi-colons we have no time and harmonies make us soft and still life overwhelms us: for at night our skies are purple. And purple leaves no time for grammar, purple is shrill and unremitting and frantic. Over the chimneys, over the roofs: the world: purple. Over our sprawled bodies the shadowy hollows: the blue-snowed eye sockets of the dead in the ice-storm, the violet-raging gullets of the cold guns—and the purple skin of our girls at the neck and a little below the breast. Purple at night the groans of the starving and the stammer of those who kiss. And the city stands so purple by the night-purple river.

And the night is full of death: our night. For our sleep is full of battle. Our night in its dream-death is laden of the noise of battle. And those who stay with us at night, the purple girls, they know that and in the morning they are pale with our night's anguish. And our morning is full of solitude. And then in the morning our solitude is like glass. Brittle and cool. And quite clear. It is the solitude of man. For we lost our mothers in the raging gunfire. Our cats and cows and the lice and the worms, they alone can endure the great icy solitude. Perhaps they are not so close together as we. Perhaps they are more with the world. With this measureless world. In which our heart almost freezes to death.

Why is our heart racing? From the flight. For only yesterday we escaped in desperate flight from the battle and from the gun-gullets. From the fearful flight from one shell hole to another—those motherly hollows—from that our heart still races—and still from fear. Listen within to the tumult in your depths. Do you shrink? Do you hear the chaos chorale of Mozart melodies and Herms Niel cantatas? Do you still hear Hölderlin? Do you recognize him, drunk with blood, in fancy dress and arm in arm with Baldur von Schirach? Do you hear the infantryman's song? Do you hear the jazz and the Luther hymns?

Then try to live above your purple depths. For the morning that rises behind the grass dykes and the tarred roofs comes only out of yourself. And behind everything? Behind all that you call God, stream and star, night, mirror or cosmos and Hilda or Evelyn—behind everything you yourself are always standing. Icily alone. Pitiable. Great. Your laughter. Your grief. Your question. Your answer. Behind everything, in uniform, naked or costumed I know not how, tottering in shadow, in strange dimensions, now almost timid, now of unsuspected grandeur: yourself. Your love. Your fear. Your hope.

And when our heart, that pitiful proud muscle, can no longer endure itself—and when our heart grows too soft for us in those sentimentalities to which we are all abandoned, then we wax vulgarly loud. Old sow, we say then to her we love most. And when Jesus or the Meek One, who always pursues us in our dreams, says in the night: You, be kind!—then with an insolent lack of respect for our confession, we ask: Kind, Lord Jesus, why? We slept in God just as well with the dead Ivans in front of our trench. And in the dream we riddle everything with our machine-guns: the Ivans. The earth, Jesus.

No, our vocabulary is not nice. But it's fat. And it stinks. Bitter as T.N.T. Sour as the sand of the steppes. Sharp as dung. And loud as the noise of battle.

And we brag insolently away over our sensitive German Rilke heart. Over Rilke, our strange lost brother, who speaks our heart and unexpectedly moves us to tears: But we will conjure no oceans of tears—for then we must all drown. We will be coarse and common, grow tobacco and tomatoes, be noisily afraid right into our purple beds—right into our purple women. For we love the loud, noisy assertion, the one that is not of Rilke, which rescues us from the battle-dreams and from the purple depths of the night, of the blood-drenched fields, of the passion-ate, bloody women.

For the war has not made us hard, do not, above all, believe that, and not rough and not superficial. For we bear many world-heavy waxen dead on our thin shoulders. And never did our tears sit so loosely upon us as after those battles. And therefore we love the blustering loud purple merry-go-round, the jazz hurdy-gurdy that blares away over our abysses, thudding, clownish, purple, gay and silly—perhaps. And our Rilke heart—before the clown crows, we have denied it thrice. And our mothers weep bitterly. But they, they do not turn away. Not the mothers!

And we will promise the mothers:

Mothers, it is not for this that the dead are dead: not for the marble war memorial, that the best local stonemason builds in the market place—set round with the green of living grass and with benches for widows and cripples. No, not for that. No, it is not for this that the dead are dead: so that the survivors may live on in their parlours and ever and again fill new and the same

parlours with photos of recruits and portraits of Hindenburg.
No, not for that.

And not for this, no, not for this did the dead let their blood
in the snow, in the wet-cold snow their living mother-blood.
So that the same schoolmasters who once so gallantly prepared
the fathers for war may now make monkeys of the children.
(Between Langemark and Stalingrad lay only one mathematics
lesson.) No, mothers, not for this did you die in each war ten
thousand deaths!

This we admit: our moral philosophy has nothing more to do
with beds, breasts, parsons or petticoats—we can do no more
than be good. But who will measure it, this "good"? Our
philosophy is the truth. And the truth is new and hard as death.
Yet also as gentle, as surprising and as just. Both are naked.

Tell your pal the truth, rob him in hunger but then tell him.
And never tell your children stories about a holy war: tell the
truth, tell it red as it is: full of blood and gunflash and screaming.
Fool your girl at night, but in the morning, in the morning then
tell her the truth: Say that you're going, and for ever. Be kind
as death. Nitchevo. Kaputt. For ever. Parti, perdu and never-
more.

For we are no-men. But we do not say No in despair. Our
No is a protest. And there is no peace for us in kisses, for us
Nihilists. For into the nothingness we must again build a Yes.
Houses we must build in the free air of our No, over the abysses,
the craters and the slit-trenches and over the open mouths of the
dead: build houses into the clean-swept air of the Nihilists, houses
of wood and brain and houses of stone and thought.

For we love this gigantic desert called Germany. This
Germany we love now. And now most of all. And for Germany
we will not die. For Germany we will live. Over the purple
depths. This acrid, bitter, brutal life. We'll take it on ourselves
for this desert. For Germany. We will love this Germany as the
Christians their Christ: For her sorrow.

We will love the mothers who had to fill bombs—for their
sons. We must love them for that sorrow.

And the sweethearts who now push their heroes in wheelchairs, with no sparkling uniform—for their sorrow.

And the heroes, the Hölderlin heroes, for whom no day was

too bright and no battle bad enough—we will love them for their shattered pride, for their dyed, secret, night-watchman's existence.

And the girl whom a company debauched in the park at night and who still says shit and must now make a pilgrimage from hospital to hospital—for her sorrow.

And the soldier who will now never again learn to laugh.

And him, who still tells his grandsons the story of the thirty-one corpses at night in front of his machine-gun or Grandad's——

All those who are afraid and in sorrow and in humility: we will love them in all their misery. We will love them as the Christians their Christ: For their sorrow. For they are Germany. And we ourselves are this Germany, too. And we must build this Germany again in nothingness, over abysses: Out of our misery, with our love. For we love this Germany. As we love the cities for their rubble, so we will love the hearts for the ashes of their sorrow. For their burned pride, for their calcined hero's garb, for their seared faith, for their shattered trust, for their ruined love. Above all we must love the mothers, be they eighteen or eighty-six—for the mothers must give us the strength for this Germany in the rubble.

Our manifesto is love. We will love the stones in the cities, our stones which the sun still warms, warms again after the battle——

And we will love the great sighing wind again, our wind, that still sings in the forests. And that sings also in the fallen beams.

And the yellow-warm windows with Rilke poems behind them——

And the rat-riddled cellars with purple-starving children inside them——

And the huts of cardboard and wood, in which people still eat, our people, and still sleep. And sometimes still sing. And sometimes and sometimes still laugh——

For that is Germany. And her we will love, we of the rusty helmet and the lost heart here on earth.

Yes, yes: on this lunatic earth we will love again, love, ever and again.

STORIES FROM A PRIMER

EVERYBODY has a sewing machine, a radio, a refrigerator, and a telephone. What shall we make now? asked the factory owner.
Bombs, said the inventor.
War, said the general.
Well, if there's nothing else for it! said the factory owner.

The man in the white smock was writing numbers on a piece of paper.
He made little delicate letters to go with them.
Then he took off the white smock and for an hour tended the flowers in the window-box. When he saw that one flower had withered away, he grew very sad and wept.
And on the paper stood the numbers. With half a gramme, according to these, one could kill a thousand people in two hours.
The sun shone on the flowers.
And on the paper.

Two men were talking.
Your estimate?
With tiles?
Of course, with green tiles.
Forty thousand.
Forty thousand? Right. You know, my dear fellow, if I hadn't gone over in time from chocolate to T.N.T., I wouldn't have been able to give you this forty thousand.
Nor I you a bathroom.
With green tiles.
With green tiles.
The two men parted.
They were a factory owner and a building contractor.
It was war.

Skittle-alley. Two men were talking.
Hallo, schoolmaster, dark suit? In mourning?

Not a bit of it. Had a ceremony. Boys off to the front. Made
a little speech. Recalled Sparta. Quoted Clausewitz. Gave 'em
a few ideas:
Honour, Fatherland. Had some Hölderlin read. Touched on
Langemark. Gripping ceremony, quite gripping. The boys sang:
God, who made the iron grow. Eyes lit up. Gripping. Quite gripping.
My God, schoolmaster, stop! It's horrible, horrible.
The schoolmaster gazed thunderstruck at the other. As he told
his story he had been making lots of little crosses on a piece of
paper. Lots of little crosses. He stood up and laughed. Took a
new wood and played it down the alley. There was a soft
rumbling sound. Then the skittles at the end crashed over. They
looked like little men.

Two men were talking.
Well, how's it going?
Pretty badly.
How many have you left?
If all goes well, four thousand.
How many can you give me?
Eight hundred at the outside.
There'll be no change out of that.
Well, then, a thousand.
Thanks.
The two men parted.
They were talking about people.
They were generals.
It was war.

Two men were talking.
Volunteer?
'Course.
How old?
Eighteen. And you?
Me too.
The two men parted.
They were two soldiers.
Then one fell down. He was dead.
It was war.

When the war was over, the soldier came home. But he had no bread.

Then he saw a man who had. He killed him.

You mustn't kill people, you know, said the judge.

Why not, asked the soldier.

When the peace conference was over, the ministers walked through the city. They came to a shooting-gallery.

Would the gentleman like a shot? shouted the girls with red lips. Then all the ministers took a rifle and shot at little cardboard men. In the middle of the shooting an old woman came and took their rifles away. When one of the ministers wanted his back, she boxed his ears.

It was a mother.

There were once two human beings. When they were two years old they hit each other with their hands.

When they were twelve, they hit each other with sticks and threw stones.

When they were twenty-two, they shot at each other with rifles.

When they were forty-two, they threw bombs at each other.

When they were sixty-two, they used bacteria.

When they were eighty-two, they died. They were buried beside each other.

When, a hundred years later, a worm ate its way through their two graves, it never noticed that two different people had been buried there. It was the same soil. All the same soil.

When in the year 5000 a mole peeped out of the earth he was comforted to observe:

the trees are still trees.

The crows still caw.

And the dogs still lift their legs.

The fish and the stars,

the moss and the sea

and the midges;

all have remained the same.

And sometimes—

sometimes you meet a man.

THERE'S ONLY ONE THING

You. Man at the machine and man in the workshop. If tomorrow they tell you you are to make no more water-pipes and saucepans —but to make steel helmets and machine-guns, then there's only one thing to do:
Say NO!

You. Girls at the counter and girls in the office. If tomorrow they tell you you are to fill shells and assemble telescopic sights for snipers' rifles, then there's only one thing to do:
Say NO!

You. Factory owner. If tomorrow they tell you you are to make T.N.T. instead of face-powder and cocoa, then there's only one thing to do:
Say NO!

You. Research worker in the laboratory. If tomorrow they tell you you are to invent a new death for the old life, then there's only one thing to do:
Say NO!

You. Poet in your room. If tomorrow they tell you you are to sing no love-songs, but songs of hate, then there's only one thing to do:
Say NO!

You. Doctor at the sick-bed. If tomorrow they tell you you are to write men fit for military service, then there's only one thing to do:
Say NO!

You. Priest in the pulpit. If tomorrow they tell you you are to bless murder and declare war holy, then there's only one thing to do:
Say NO!

You. Captain of the steamer. If tomorrow they tell you you are to carry no more wheat—but to take guns and tanks, then there's only one thing to do:
Say NO!

You. Pilot on the aerodrome. If tomorrow they tell you you are to carry bombs and phosphorus over the cities, then there's only one thing to do:

Say NO!

You. Tailor on your table. If tomorrow they tell you you are to cut uniforms, then there's only one thing to do:

Say NO!

You. Judge in your robes. If tomorrow they tell you you are to go to court martial, then there's only one thing to do:

Say NO!

You. Man at the station. If tomorrow they tell you you are to give the departure signal for the munitions train and the troop-train, then there's only one thing to do:

Say NO!

You. Man of the village and man of the town. If tomorrow they come and give you your call-up papers, then there's only one thing to do:

Say NO!

You. Mother in Normandy and mother in the Ukraine, you, mother in Frisco and London, you, on the Hwangho and on the Mississippi, you, mother in Naples and Hamburg and Cairo and Oslo—mothers in all parts of the earth, mothers of the world, if tomorrow they tell you you are to bear children, nursing sisters for military hospitals and new soldiers for new battles, then there's only one thing to do:

Say NO!

For if you do not say NO, if YOU do not say no, mothers, then: then:

In the bustling, steam-hazy harbour towns the big ships will fall groaningly silent and like titanic mammoth cadavers sway sluggish as water-corpses against the dead deserted quay walls, the once so shimmering rumbling body overgrown with seaweed and barnacles, smelling of graveyards and rotten fish, decaying, diseased, dead——

the trams will lie like senseless shineless glass-eyed cages crazily battered and peeled off beside the twisted steel skeletons of wires and track, under the perforated roofs of decaying sheds, in lost crater-torn streets——

a slime-grey thick pulpy leaden stillness will roll up, devouring, growing, will swell in schools and universities and theatres, on the recreation grounds and children's playgrounds, gruesome and greedy, irresistible——

the sunny juicy vine will rot on its decaying slopes, rice will dry in the withered earth, potatoes will freeze on the unploughed land and cows will stick their death-stiff legs into the air like overturned milk-stools——

in the institutes the brilliant inventions of great doctors will go sour, rot, moulder in mildew——

in kitchen, larder and cellar, in cold storage and granary the last sacks of flour, the last bottles of strawberry, pumpkin and cherry juice will go bad—bread will go green under capsized tables and on splintered plates and the spread butter will stink like soft soap, in the fields beside rusted ploughs the corn will be flattened like a beaten army and the smoking chimneys, the forges and flues of the pounding factories, covered over with the everliving grass, will crumble away—crumble—crumble

then the last human creature, with mangled entrails and infected lungs, will wander around unanswered and lonely under the poisonous, glowing sun and wavering constellations, lonely among the immense mass graves and the cold idols of the gigantic concrete-blocked devastated cities, the last human creature, withered, mad, cursing, accusing—and his terrible accusation: WHY? will die away unheard on the steppes, drift through the splitting ruins, seep away in the rubble of churches, lap against the great concrete shelters, fall into pools of blood, unheard, unanswered, the last animal scream of the last human animal——

all this will happen tomorrow, tomorrow perhaps, perhaps even tonight, perhaps tonight, if——if——

you do not say NO.